The Time-Lost Girl

HEATHER RIFFLE

ISBN: 978-1-692-09645-8

To my empath… Love.

ACKNOWLEDGMENTS

Thank you to everyone who has read, commented on, or helped edit this book. It wouldn't be here without you and your enthusiasm.

1

Two weeks — almost — since the attack. And there I stood. Alone.

Finally.

Not that I didn't appreciate the company *after*... But it is so much easier to just *be* when I'm on my own.

I stood at the threshold to the porch, and soft fur brushed against my leg.

Not completely alone, I thought, as I watched the dog pad across the porch.

I took a deep breath, releasing the tension from my shoulders, and looked out over the expanse of the backyard. Acres of tall grass waved in the breeze. The old barn leaned at a dangerous angle.

It might not make it through another storm.

Then the wind picked up, and the smell of honeysuckle tickled my nose, coaxing a memory. I closed my eyes and let the warm scent wash over me.

I couldn't have been more than eight years old, when Aunt Bethany taught me how to extract the honey from the flower.

I sighed and blinked away tears. *And now I have to appreciate it without her.*

I let the screen door slam behind me and drifted down the steps.

My attention flickered to the square patch of earth surrounded by white picket fence. Despite the spring air, I hugged myself, as a cold feeling seeped into me and chased the good memory away. The wind caught the creaking gate and, each time it blew open, I caught a glimpse of the garden behind it.

Nature had wiped away any evidence of the events that had occurred there. The grass appeared untouched, but my mind created its own image of the violence.

My mother's voice rang through my head. *I'm just glad you weren't home…*

I wasn't *home. Maybe if I had been…*

Tears prickled at my eyes again. Before they could fall, I squared my shoulders, walked to the gate, and latched it.

Turning, I nearly stumbled over my dog, who had settled silently behind me. "Sheesh, Lobo."

I started to pat his head, when he perked one ear up and looked toward the trees. Scratching him behind his ear, I took a deep breath and cast a glance toward the soon-to-be flourishing garden.

I hesitated as I turned away. *Aunt Bethany would never spend such a pretty day indoors.*

It took me a few minutes to dig out my old sneakers and a pair of worn gloves. As I headed back out to the garden, I hummed a little tune to which I had forgotten the words and, preoccupied with remembering it, walked through the gate. When I realized the gate was open, I stopped reminiscing and rolled my eyes.

Oh, come on. *Cheap piece of…* I stooped to examine the latch but could find nothing wrong with it. I frowned. *Huh.* Tossing my gloves and trowel down, I pulled the gate closed and jiggled it. Nothing. I barely got it to rattle, let alone unfasten. *It must not have closed all the way.* With my hand still on the white picket, I glanced around for Lobo and caught sight of him at the edge of the yard.

He paced, sniffing at the ground. When he paused and gave a whine, I called for him. He scurried to me without his earlier excitement and sat by the gate.

I moved to his side. "What is it, boy? Huh?" Glancing at the trees, I crouched down and rubbed him behind the ears.

He whimpered and lowered his head to his paws. At a loss, I stood and frowned toward the forest, before forcing myself to shake off my misgivings and confront the garden.

The task ahead was daunting, but I didn't let that stop me. Moving to the opposite end, I began my work.

I had been pulling weeds for about fifteen minutes and had a nice-sized pile, when I heard the crunch of tires on the driveway. Shielding my eyes from the sun, I looked up to see the familiar County Sheriff's emblem emblazoned on the side of the vehicle. I tossed my gloves down to mark my place and dusted off my knees, before going to meet the man climbing from the car.

He nodded at me, as I approached. "Hi there, Miss Haylee."

Glancing over the garden, he added, "Are you sure you're up for that?"

"Hello, Sheriff." I looked back at the plot, blinking as tears threatened to form. Straightening my back, I opened my mouth in an effort to reply to his question, but my resolve wavered. I didn't want to get into my conflicting emotions over the garden. It had been a sanctuary to my aunt, and we'd spent a lot of time there, especially since my parents moved out West. I wasn't about to let what happened in there ruin that. Instead, I nodded and said, "It's… difficult. But I'm okay."

"Well, I'm glad to hear it." He paused, shifting his weight to one leg. "You can call me Jimmy, Miss Haylee. Everybody does. No need to be formal." He squinted past me, emphasizing the wrinkles around his eyes. "You have any trouble here since the funeral?"

I frowned, following his line of sight, and found Lobo staring off into the forest as well. "What kind of trouble would I have, Sher – Jimmy?" I shook my head at the strange feeling of calling an authority figure by his first name. I didn't think I could ever get used to calling my high school teachers by theirs, even if I'd graduated five years instead of nearly five weeks ago.

"There've been reports of coyotes in the area. I thought I'd check in here, see if there were any signs. What's that dog after?" he asked.

"I don't know. Now that I think about it, it's weird he didn't bark when you pulled up. Probably a deer." I shrugged, more interested in the sheriff's news, and turned back toward him. "Is that what they're saying killed Aunt Bethany? Coyotes?" I tried to keep the skepticism out of my voice.

He met my eyes again. "I reckon so, from the look of things. We don't see any other explanation for it. Not many wolves in the county anymore, and it's been fifteen years since the last mountain lion was spotted. So, stands to reason." His face was grim, causing him to look older than his fifty odd years. "So, you ain't seen nothin'?"

I stared at the gravel under our feet and kicked at one of the larger rocks. "No, I haven't seen anything. Not that I'd know what to look for, I guess." I still wasn't convinced. My mind flashed on the newspaper's description of the body. "I didn't think coyotes would… do that. I mean, are they really *that* dangerous? And wouldn't they just ea-eat her, not leave her all c-clawed up like that?" I asked, looking up at him again.

"Well, it ain't normal. They tend to stay away from people. But they could be rabid, so it's best to be careful." He glanced back toward my dog. "Is he always here like this?"

"Lobo? He's stuck close by ever since… what happened. Usually, he roams. I think he misses her." I shoved a stray strand behind my ear and looked away.

"Well, Miss Bethany'll be missed by near everybody. If you don't mind my sayin', you look just like her. And your daddy. It was good that he could come in for the funeral. Good you didn't have to take that on all on your own. He gone back to California already?"

I fidgeted a little, as I replied, "Yeah. They caught an early flight. This morning. They had to get back to work."

He must have noticed my discomfort. "I'm kinda surprised he didn't take you with him, is all."

I opened my mouth to speak.

But the sheriff raised his hand. "I know, legally you can live on your own. But that don't mean you should."

And there it was. The real reason for his visit. He made it sound as if emancipation had been *my* idea. As if I was some rebellious teen and not the daughter of a career-driven mother who decided her child wasn't as ambitious as she should be. If I had been a boy, people wouldn't take issue with me living alone. But I was a freckle-faced, teenaged girl with her father's dimples. I struggled not to show my irritation.

"I'll be fine, Sheriff. My dad wouldn't have left otherwise. They know I can handle myself. Besides, *this* is my home, and when I turn eighteen in two months, it'll be official. It was in – in Aunt Bethany's will." I couldn't meet his eyes with tears in mine, so I looked at my feet instead.

He sighed. "Well, like I said, it's legal, so there ain't nothin' I can do about it. Just remember the Logans live on the other side of those trees." He indicated behind me and glanced up at the sky. "We've got a storm comin' in, so don't be afraid to call your neighbors if you need somethin', okay?"

I nodded and gave a weak smile. "Thank you. I will. You don't need to worry, Sheriff. Lobo's here with me, and I always have my cell nearby."

"All right. Well, I'll be movin' on now. I just wanted to check in on you and, again, I'm real sorry for you loss." He tilted his head and began to move toward his car. "We'll let you know if we learn anything else, Miss Haylee."

"Thanks, Sheriff." I gave a small wave.

He chuckled at my failure to use his given name, shaking his head as he climbed back into his car.

As the sheriff drove out of sight, I relaxed, pausing to let the encounter sink in. However, as I stood there, I became aware of the stillness around me. A feeling of total isolation overcame me. I felt completely cut off from the world. My nearest neighbors seemed light years away, and I could no longer hear the Sheriff's car engine beyond the trees. It was as if the world had ended, and my little clearing was all that was left. An island in a sea of nothing. If I were to step outside the tree line, where would I go? The thought held me frozen. And for a moment, I could barely breathe. Until a breeze sent a shiver through me, clearing my thoughts. Then it was as if not only I, but the entire world, could breathe again, and everything was as it had been. Had the birds stopped chirping? It had been so quiet. I turned to find Lobo standing behind me. He gave a whine before nudging my hand with his nose.

"It's okay, boy. I'm just being silly." I shook my head, trailing my hand down his back, but my mind was still distracted. Though I wasn't sure whether the explanation satisfied him, he settled back down by the garden gate. Taking brief note of the clouds that had moved overhead, I got back to work.

As my aunt had taught me, I now used the garden as a kind of meditation. The methodical movements, combined with the light breeze and the sounds of nature, succeeded in calming my nerves, and I soon lost track of time.

The growl of my stomach brought me back to reality. My mouth was dry, and my skin was pink.

Ugh, I should've put on sunblock. That's gonna smart tomorrow. I wiped my forehead with my arm before the sweat could drip into my eyes and looked up to see the sky had darkened. My back cramped up as I stood, so I did a few little stretches.

A low rumble caught my attention.

That doesn't sound like thunder.

I looked up to see Lobo was no longer guarding the gate. He stood alert between it and the spot in the trees.

Is he growling? I made my way over to him and rested my hand on his head. *What's he looking at? The path?* "What's wrong, ol' boy?"

He whined and settled onto his haunches, continuing his sentry.

I stood next to him for a moment. *What's out there that's got him so worked up?*

I'd walked the path many times. It led into the woods, circled back in on itself, and returned to its point of origin. There was nothing extraordinary about it. However, now it called to me, like a siren drawing me in. My heart thumped, as dread filled me, but I couldn't stop myself from stepping toward the trail.

The first drop of rain hit my face. I blinked, and the strange feeling was gone. Thunder rumbled in the distance.

I shook my head and looked down at my ever-vigilant dog. "Silly. Just a deer. Better go to your house. You don't want to get wet."

More drops fell as I turned toward the porch.

I looked back to see Lobo still at his station in spite of the steadily increasing shower.

* * *

I bolted up from my pillow.

Sweat dampened my clothes. My heart pounded in my ears. I struggled to catch my breath.

Something's wrong.

I glanced around my room, completely dark except for the nightlight I always used and the bright red glare of my clock. *3:02.*

I closed my eyes and took a deep breath. *Everything's fine. You're okay.* When I opened them again, I felt calmer. *I must have been dreaming…*

Though I wanted to pull the blankets over my head, I forced myself to throw them off. The floor was cold on my bare feet, so I dug out a pair of mismatched socks, and pulled them on as I stumbled to the window.

The rain had diminished to a heavy drizzle, and the wind had quieted down. I could make out the shape of Lobo in the dark. Either he had vacated the spot during the storm and returned, or he had never left.

"I've gotta check on him."

As I pulled on my rumpled jeans, I became vaguely aware of a pain at the back of my head. I rolled my eyes. *Ugh. I fell asleep with my hair clipped up. Again.* The plastic clip had dug into my head a bit, but I ignored it.

The air outside was cold. I hugged myself, as I hurried over to Lobo. He was soaked and shivering.

"Oooh, Lobo. You didn't stay here through the entire storm!? Come on. Let's get you warmed up." I grabbed his collar and prepared to drag him into the house, but movement caught my eye.

Lobo tensed, rose onto all four feet, and barked. We both stared toward the path in the woods. In a second, he pulled from my grasp and ran into the trees.

"Lobo!"

When he didn't stop, I suppressed my mounting fear and ran after him.

Thunder boomed overhead, and rain came pouring down. Even through the canopy, I was drenched in seconds. I lost track of Lobo. By the time I reached the loop in the path, water streamed into my eyes. I stopped, swiping at them, and called for him again.

"Lobo! Come here, boy!" My chest tightened. *Where* is *he?!* "Lobo!" I strained to see or hear anything other than rain.

Then I heard barking, and Lobo leapt from the underbrush only to head toward the other side of the loop. I didn't see what he was chasing.

I grabbed for his collar. Just as my fingers wrapped around the material, lightning flashed.

I froze.

Was that… a man? A man in the path? The tightness spread to my throat. I tried to swallow it down. *Just breathe. Breathe.* I was willing to reject the possibility and dismiss the vibrations coursing through Lobo's body, until his growling became audible over the storm.

Thunder boomed, releasing a torrent. I rubbed more water out of my eyes. The sky lit up again, and the path was clear. But I was certain I saw movement to my right. With Lobo alongside me, I inched my way toward home.

When the rain suddenly stopped, the unnatural silence had me rooted to the spot. It was a much more intense version of the feeling I'd had after the sheriff's visit. Eyes were on me, and I couldn't shake the feeling. Unlike before, I felt alone and *watched.*

This is it. Why you're afraid of the dark. Why you still sleep with a light on.

I could feel a presence. Could almost feel breath on my neck. I turned as I sidestepped toward escape.

Standing before me was a figure I could not quite make out. He had the shape of a man. A very large man. Tall and wide. I was staring into what must be his chest and trailed my eyes up and up, unable to stop myself. Lobo's growl grew into a snarl. Though I could not see them, I *knew* hands reached for me. And still, I could not move.

Lightning splintered the night once more, revealing a colorless face, a leering mouth full of sharp teeth, and silver eyes. Eyes that, much like those of an animal, reflected the light back at me.

My mind couldn't reconcile the opposing features. I screamed and covered my face with my arms.

Just as its hands brushed against me, Lobo leaped, and it only succeeded in raking its talon-like claws down my arms. Lobo seized it by the throat, and it yowled in pain. It then grabbed Lobo, sinking its claws into each of his sides. Lobo whimpered but didn't let go. Whatever this creature was, it was strong. It thrust Lobo against a tree with enough force to withdraw a yelp. He managed to take a huge chunk of the thing's neck with him. It recovered much faster than Lobo, but still stumbled and swayed as it staunched the flow of blood. It advanced toward me, and Lobo interceded a second time.

I snapped out of my stupor. And ran. I hated to leave Lobo. He was giving me the chance I needed to get somewhere safe. I hadn't even noticed the rain pick up again. It ran into my eyes and made the path almost impossible to traverse.

I couldn't see anything beyond the opening to the clearing. It was as if a black curtain existed between the forest and my home. Between me and safety.

Where's the house? I slowed for a moment. *I know it's there. Straight ahead. It's gotta be! Just keep going!* I propelled myself forward.

As I cleared the trees, a light bloomed around me. It blinded me, and I was half convinced I had been struck by lightning. Then, my body hit something solid, and I fell into darkness.

2

I was weightless, floating in darkness. There was no sound, no smell. Only me.

Then there *was* something. Muffled voices – a man and a woman, from the sound of it – and a pinprick of light slowly began to spread to a soft glow.

My eyelids fluttered open, and I could make out a dimly lit room, but even that small amount of light hurt my eyes and made my head ache. Raising my hand to my face, I saw the clean, white bandages on my arms.

And I remembered.

Lobo! I sat up too quickly, fighting off a wave of dizziness. When I realized I was wearing nothing but underwear beneath the rough blanket, I clasped it to me. Wide awake, I looked around the room. It was large with big dingy windows, the kind I've seen in warehouses or old school buildings. The light in the room filtered through these windows, so I knew it was daytime. The room was filled wall-to-wall with cots, like the one on which I was now sitting. On the cot next to me, I found my folded clothes. Sleeping figures occupied several of the others. I could still hear the voices from outside the room, just on the other side of the door. I dressed under the blanket and slipped into my shoes, before moving to hear more clearly.

"You say she is not one of them," a female voice said.

"Right, but – "

"Well, then there is no reason why she cannot remain here with us," the woman interrupted the male voice. "We cannot turn away someone in need. She would not last a day out there, especially not on her own. You have seen her. You carried her back here, did you not?"

The man sighed in resignation. "Fine. She can stay. But she needs to pull her own weight around here. Everyone works." He paused. "Besides, I'm sure she's well enough to speak for herself. Aren't you?"

I stiffened.

"Yes, I know you're there," he said, and pushed the door open.

My jaw dropped, and I raised my eyes. These two were huge, broad and well built. The woman would make any Amazonian proud: several inches taller than my average height, dark hair pulled back into a long braid, warm copper-brown skin, and fit. The man was larger, with slightly lighter skin, russet-colored hair drawn into a short ponytail, and a muscular build. Looking straight ahead, I would stare directly into his chest. His size reminded me of the thing I had encountered in the woods.

I shivered.

The woman's features softened. "Look now, Derik. You have frightened her." She reached toward me, palms up, but did not touch me. "I apologize for my friend. He can seem rather fierce but is quite the opposite." She drew my eyes away from the large man with the overpowering presence.

Though unsure of him, I began to relax at the woman's words and took her offered hands. Almost immediately, my fears dampened.

"Wh – where am I?" I asked.

"You are in a safe house," the woman reassured. "I am Glenna, and this is Derik. He is the one who found you. Or, should I say, *you* found *him*?" She chuckled a little, and her dark eyes sparkled. "And what should we call you?"

"Um, my name's Ha – Haylee. What exactly happened? Have you seen my dog? He was fighting that – that thing. I hated leaving him. The last thing I remember is light, maybe lightning, and running into…" I shook my head and continued, "…something. Did you see him?" Despite my anxiety, I forced myself to look into the man's eyes. "He'd be hard to miss. Great big wolfhound. Do you know? Is he all right?"

He did not seem to want to look at me.

The woman spoke first, frowning. "A dog?" She turned to him. "There was no mention a dog."

"We didn't see any dog," he replied, with some aggravation. Then he looked at me. "And that something you ran into was me. Right before you fell unconscious into my arms. If you weren't smart enough to stay indoors, then you didn't deserve to be brought here. And I sure as hell don't think you should stay." He glanced at Glenna. "But I guess

I'm outnumbered on that issue as well. You had better pull your weight around here." He looked me up and down. "Not that there's much to you. Now *I* need to get back to work." He turned and walked briskly away.

I knew my mouth was hanging open again, and a frown creased my forehead. *Huh?* "Um, I'm confused… about everything, really." I looked at Glenna. "First off, what's *his* deal?"

She closed her eyes and took a deep breath before answering. "Some of his group did not come back, and he blames himself. You are a stranger and, at this moment, that makes you the most convenient target for his frustrations."

I blinked at that. "Well… that hardly seems fair."

"Oh, don't mind him. He'll come around. Now, you are hungry, no?" She pulled me away from the room. "The dining hall is this way, and I can answer your questions as I ask a few of my own."

I *was* hungry so, after a brief hesitation, I followed. The woman led me down a hallway, past other doors similar to the one through which I had just exited, and to a stairway.

"Are we in a school building?" I asked.

"Yes, it used to be. But that was a very long time ago."

At the bottom of the stairs was another hall of equal length.

Glenna stopped. "If you would like to clean up a bit, or relieve yourself, the washroom is through here." She rested her hand on a door with a faded sign.

"Yeah. That'd be nice."

Glenna pushed open the door. The room was fairly dark, but I could make out a row of sinks to my right and a row of bathroom stalls to my left. I went into one of the stalls first and squatted above the seat, because I couldn't see if it was as clean as I would like. When I was finished I looked around for a toilet paper dispenser but could find none.

I swallowed and began, "Um, I – "

"Looking for this?" Glenna handed me a scrap of cloth under the door. "We have to improvise."

Improvise? I hesitated before grabbing it.

Outside the stall with cloth in hand, I looked around me.

"Go ahead and wash it out at one of the sinks. Then drop it in the basket in the corner. Someone will pick it up later."

Ick. I winced but did as I was told. At first the water came out murky from the faucet but cleared quickly. I used a bar of soap I found to make a good lather, and washed my hands afterwards.

"We sterilize everything," she said. Then she smiled at my look of relief. "We recycle our clothing here. Once something is no longer fit to wear, it is turned into patches for other clothing or bandages or used in the kitchen. Then they are reused here. Later they will be used for cleaning such things as floors and the like. Does that make you feel better?"

I thought and tilted my head in answer. Then I turned back to one of the dusty mirrors. Though there was not much light, I could see my hair formed a frizzy halo around my head, so I smoothed it with my fingers and splashed water on my face.

Glenna stood patiently off to the side. "Perhaps you will be able to wash your hair later."

I paused with my hand at the back of my head. *I lost my clip.* "How long have I been here?" I finally asked, not moving but looking at Glenna through the glass.

"Approximately thirty-six hours now."

I remembered looking at my alarm clock. *Three o'clock.* Turning, I said, "Derik found me around three *yesterday* morning? I was out for over a day?" *How is that possible?*

"Yes, that would be about correct. Though we are unsure of the exact time, still a dangerous hour. Dawn was only a little ways off when they returned." She smiled. "Now, are you ready for some food? And perhaps we can answer each other's questions."

Glenna took me a little further down the hall, to a large room that had served as the school's cafeteria at one point. The more I saw, the more it seemed familiar. I attributed it to the fact that most older school buildings in the area were similarly built.

Entering the room was a bit of a shock. It was much brighter than any other part of the building and much noisier. At least a dozen people conversed over their dinner and another half a dozen or so stood in line, as someone scooped something into their bowls. As Glenna ushered me in, several stopped talking and looked my way, then several more did the same, until the room was completely silent.

Glenna led me through the center of the room, and it felt as if every eye was upon me. Nearly all of them were as large as Glenna, very muscular and long. They made me feel incredibly small as I walked by. I had the urge to turn and run, as I began to suspect I was being judged by my size, or lack thereof.

She seated me at the front of the room and addressed them, "Back to your meals, everyone. We must all eat."

Immediately they launched into whispery timbres I couldn't decipher and, while Glenna was getting my food, sent furtive glances my way. I was staring straight down at the table, when she returned and sat a bowl down in front of me.

"Do not mind them. They are not used to new people and rarely have anything to think about other than survival. You are a *welcome* distraction," she added. "Eat first. Then I will answer your questions."

I looked down at my bowl. Inside was a thick porridge-like substance. Since I was very hungry and felt oddly trusting of this woman, I scooped some onto my spoon and tasted it. The food was bland but not bad. As I ate, I ceased to notice the stares around me and, by the time I was finished, most had returned their attentions to their own meal or had left to go about their business.

"Better?" Glenna asked. She had been watching me.

"Yes. Much. Thank you."

"You are very welcome. Now, you have questions, no?"

"I have quite a few, actually." I nodded. Now feeling more comfortable, I took a moment to look around the room.

It reminded me of the cafeteria at my old middle school. The tables were positioned differently, and there were no posters ("Just Say No") or advertising for the food pyramid. But everything else was the same. The big yellow bricks in the windowless walls, the plain (though dingy) white floor tiles, and the skylights serving as the only illumination today. These windows were much cleaner than the ones I had seen throughout the building, which was why this room was so much brighter.

I could see this woman more clearly. At first she had seemed much older, but looking at her now I could see she couldn't be much more than my own seventeen years. Her dark hair trailed half way down her back, and her brown eyes were warm.

I took a deep breath. "First of all, what was that thing in the woods? Did anyone else see it? He wasn't human, was he?"

Glenna frowned. "I find it curious you have never met one before. And, stranger still, you have never heard of them. How is this possible?"

At a loss for words, I lifted my hands. "I don't know. I – I've – I just haven't. It's more curious to me how you *do* know about them. I'd be having trouble believing I didn't dream it, or that I'm not crazy, if not for these bandages on my arms. Though I guess I still could be crazy," I added. "But, I mean, as far as the world's concerned these things don't, they *can't*, exist."

"This *is* strange. I've never heard anyone say this before. The *world* knows they exist. It's a simple fact. Maybe you *are* crazy, but I don't believe that to be so. Nevertheless, it is odd. How can someone grow up in a world such as ours and not be aware of these creatures, their hold over us? The way they hunt anyone who leaves shelter, particularly at night. And how can someone wander around alone outside at night and not know, not *expect* to be attacked? I don't understand." She put her hand to her chin, puzzling over it.

"I'm sorry, but I feel like I'm in some other world, some other *dimension*, or – or something. I – I don't know." I shook my head. "I *must* be crazy."

Glenna reached over and laid her hand on mine, and I felt calmer. "You're not. But something doesn't fit. Tell me exactly what happened, everything from the beginning."

I told her the story, starting with Aunt Bethany's death, ending with running into Derik, though I hadn't known it at the time.

Glenna had her hand at her chin again. "So, you couldn't see Derik through the dark… And, from his account, he didn't see you, until you ran into him. Interesting." She paused.

"Okay. But what does that mean?"

"I don't know. But you may be able to speak with someone who does. Later, perhaps." She waved her hand, distractedly. "The time isn't right."

I frowned. *And what exactly does* that *mean?*

"But I will answer the questions I can. Because you alone saw the creature and had no prior knowledge of it, we can only assume it was one of the Pale Ones."

"Pale Ones?" This brought back an image of the creature and made my stomach turn.

"That's the name we have given them," Glenna continued. "However, they call themselves the Amara, for they fancy themselves eternal." At my look of distress, she rushed on. "Don't worry, they can be hurt and they can be killed. I'm sure your wolf became aware of that and was able to do a great deal of damage. I am sorry, but it's probable he didn't make it through the fight. You must face this," she said before going on. "We aren't certain of their origin, but their abilities have been devastating. Which seems to be why we have gained power ourselves. Each generation holds greater abilities than the one before."

I held my hand out. "Wait. What are you talking about? Abilities?"

She looked at me carefully. "Have you somehow had no need for one?"

This is just too much. My head is literally *going to explode. What are these Pale Ones? Where did they come from?* I was so confused, I couldn't even focus on the thought of never seeing Lobo again. I struggled to catch up and latched onto the last thing she said. "I really don't know what you mean."

"Ah. Let me see. Where to begin… Well, the Pale Ones have heightened senses – greater than any animal humankind has ever known – and are much stronger and faster than us, in general. They've been using that against us, and we've had to develop our own special abilities in order to survive, as most of us here have." She indicated around her.

I followed her gesture with my eyes, but I still wasn't sure I followed her words.

"For example, some can control water or fire. Others have uncanny hearing or eyesight, sense of smell, that sort of thing. Together we work to ward off attacks and save lives. Unfortunately, that is unavoidable at times. We are fewer than when we began." She averted her eyes.

"I don't have any… special abilities." *That's just too strange.* I shook it off and chewed on my bottom lip. Something else she said was bothering me. "You mentioned earlier someone didn't make it back. Someone in Derik's group? You're not *fewer* because of me, are you?"

I saw sympathy in Glenna's eyes. "No, Little One. What happened was none of your doing. It would have taken place whether you had come along or not. It happens all the time. They were not on their expedition on your account but to obtain fresh drinking water. We're running low, and there's always a chance – more a likelihood – of this sort of occurrence. Rain has been scarce these last few months, so we must go out more often to acquire water elsewhere. We'd heard of a well near where we found you, so they were out in search of it. The creatures attacked on their return, moments before they stumbled upon you. According to the team, they were lying in wait nearby."

My mind was too preoccupied to process everything she said. "I just remembered how angry Derik seemed with me, and thought, well… *He* blames me, doesn't he?"

"No, who Derik blames is himself. He takes great pride in his ability to track them, to know where they are, to sense them. However, he was unable to catch wind of them this time. Not his fault, either, but still he blames himself."

"To *sense* them?" I shook my head. *This is crazy! And you're just going along with it!* "That's his… *ability*, then?"

Glenna looked at me, peculiarly. "That would be *one* of them. Derik is the only one I have encountered with multiple abilities. Occasionally, we hear rumors of others, but I believe he is genuinely unique."

"And *everyone* has an ability?" Part of me was skeptical, but another part wanted to ask what hers was. *Would that be considered rude, like asking someone how much they weigh?*

"Nearly everyone. Those who don't, do their part here. They prepare meals, clean clothing, make repairs. They help in any way they can. Others make up what they lack in spiritual ability with physical strength, which is another way we have adapted over the years."

Over the years*? I must have misunderstood.*

"We have gotten bigger, stronger, and more intelligent. This alone has spared us." She rose and gestured for me to follow. "Come, I'll show you around. Perhaps a tour will help you understand."

I picked up my empty bowl and was going to ask what to do with it, when I felt the need to look toward the door to the hallway.

Derik had stopped there, watching us.

"I will take care of that for you, dear," Glenna said, taking the bowl from my hands and walking toward the kitchen.

Derik's presence was powerful, to say the least. I felt heat rise to my face, as I realized I had been staring right back, and dropped my gaze. As he walked by, I looked at the floor.

"I'm sorry," I blurted and watched his feet pause in front of me. "I'm sorry you lost people the other night. I…" I stopped, not knowing how to continue, and looked up at him. *…hope it wasn't my fault.*

His eyes didn't seem as unforgiving as they had. Honey brown, where Glenna's were like dark chocolate. They matched the highlights in his hair. He stood at least a full head above me. Though my neck would soon ache, I could not break eye contact.

His lips parted, as if to say something.

"Are you ready for the grand tour?" Glenna asked, breaking the spell.

I blinked, looking away, and Derik looked down to the tiled floor, a frown once again marring his face.

Glenna was smiling. "Having your midday meal rather late, aren't you, Derik?"

"Perhaps if I wasn't so far behind in my work, I wouldn't be." He fixed his gaze straight ahead and walked toward the kitchen.

Glenna stared after him. "I believe he's feeling better." She smiled and ushered me into the hall. "Let's go."

* * *

"We use most of the rooms here on the main floor for training and strategy. Everyone must learn to fight as well as hone their own personal abilities," Glenna said as she led me through the downstairs hall.

We passed by several closed doors, through which I could hear voices, grunting, and other noises, some of which may or may not have been the clanging of swords. I flinched a few times. It all sounded pretty intense.

"We shouldn't disturb them. Distractions can cause accidents. Each of the rooms is dedicated to a specific discipline: armed combat, various mental exercises, self-defense, and the like. Later, I'll have someone show you the rooms."

As with the other end of the hall, this end had a stairwell leading up to the second floor. However, at the other side of the building, I had not noticed a door set in the wall next to the stairs.

"That takes you to the basement. We keep the door locked at all times. I suggest never venturing down there," Glenna said, as she started up to the second floor.

I stared at the worn wood for a moment, a chill going through me, before following her.

Once we had made it to the landing, she said, "And, of course, the second floor consists of our living quarters, more or less. A couple of the rooms, as you have seen, are for sleeping. We have chosen the darkest rooms, as our lifestyle does require many of us to sleep during the day. We have a day shift and a night shift, so we're never caught with our guard down. In the early days, this happened too often." She moved on down the hall. "As with the first floor, we have two lavatories on the second, aptly designated for men and women." She gestured to either side of the hall. "We also have a room allocated for teaching our children, as we do have a few. Not many, mind you. But we're very proud of the few remaining and protect them at all costs. We would not want the Pale Ones to get the children in their grasp." Glenna trailed off, a haunted look in her eyes.

"Have they taken many children, Glenna?" I reached out to touch her arm but thought better of it. *I don't know this woman. Why do I feel so comfortable with her?*

"Yes. Many." Glenna straightened. "But no more. None have been taken in a very long time. And none will be taken again under my watch. Shall we continue?"

Glenna moved on. "We have a few gathering rooms set up, much more casual than downstairs. A few places to relax, if possible, play games."

The door to one of the rooms was ajar, and I saw two men and a woman gathered around a makeshift table.

I paused to see what they were doing, and one of the men glanced up. He held playing cards, which he fanned out in his hands. As I watched, he released them, but they did not fall. Instead, they began shuffling themselves in the air. I gasped, and the man winked, startling me even more. I rushed to catch up with Glenna.

Low laughter rang from the room, but she didn't seem to notice.

She led me to a tiny room at the other end of the hall. A ladder ran up one wall, from the floor to a door in the ceiling.

"Where does this go?" I asked.

"To the roof." She started up the ladder. "Come on." She pushed the door open and light flooded in.

Wincing, I covered my eyes. When I looked again, Glenna had disappeared.

"Come on up," her voice called from above.

I grabbed the closest rung and climbed up behind her. The breeze was warm, and the air was dry. I allowed my eyes to adjust for a moment, as I stood in the sun. It felt nice.

The first thing I saw was the people. Most of them worked in two improvised gardens. Looking around, I noticed an armed guard stood at each corner of the roof; three men and one woman, each carrying a large rifle. Like everyone else I had seen, they were quite large, tall and fit. They dressed in neutral clothing and none looked away from their section of the grounds. Their steadfast gazes took in their designated areas.

Beyond them, I could see a common landscape: trees, trees and more trees. Except these trees, and the grass going up to meet them, were nearly completely brown. Many leaves had fallen to the equally dry earth. It seemed as though rain had not fallen for many weeks, and I recalled Glenna saying as much.

But how is that possible? I walked to the edge of the roof and leaned over the balustrade. I looked down at the hard, crumbling earth at the base of the building. *A parking lot, maybe?* Beyond that, more dirt and tall, dry grass; barely any sign of a road, only a small footpath beaten down by frequent travel. Looking through the trees, I could find no familiar landmarks. And the sky was a cloudless hazy blue. I remained there, puzzled, as the wind blew hair in my face, until a hand on my shoulder made me jump.

"I'm sorry," Glenna said. "I had no intention of startling you. Is something troubling you?"

"I don't understand how this can be. It was raining the other night. In fact, it's rained several times this month already, but this… it's…" I shook my head.

Glenna frowned. "By 'other night', you mean the night you were found, correct?"

"Yeah."

She sighed and leaned against the barrier. "We've had no rain in over a month, no rain the night we found you. There was, however, an atmospheric disturbance. Light and rumbling in the sky." She looked me in the eyes and continued in a low voice. "Of course, the condition of your hair and clothing was odd. Even stranger was the occurrence preceding your appearance." She paused, and I straightened to attention. "After the attack, Derik and the others heard an unfamiliar sound on the wind and pursued it. Upon reaching the tree line, the air turned cool and damp, and there was an unexpected shower – not from the sky, mind you, but the trees. Then out of the darkness you ran, soaked to the bone." She lowered her gaze. "At least, that's how I heard it. You ran out, apparently afraid for your life, and collided into Derik, who caught you as you fell. He carried you back here himself.

Of course, I heard none of this from him but someone else in the group."

"And they travelled on *foot*? How far?"

"It's under an hour one way."

I mulled it over. "Curiouser and curiouser," I quoted softly. *Where am I, some version of Wonderland?* "When can I go home?"

"We will discuss it when you've healed." She indicated my bandages. "The journey is dangerous and not to be taken lightly."

This just doesn't make sense. *Less than an hour on foot…* My head was starting to hurt.

Glenna smiled. "Don't worry so. I feel answers will come soon. For now, let's finish our tour. Shall we?"

I took one more look toward the trees, before nodding. Once I had turned my attention back to the roof, I noticed some other things. At the center, was a tight circle of children. I counted six of them. A man watched over them, as they played some sort of game I couldn't identify. While they played, everyone else was employed in basic chores.

Besides the workers in the gardens, others worked at large tubs of water. Several women and a couple young men did laundry. Some scrubbed and rinsed fabric in the water, while others wrung the material and draped them over a line. The line stretched between two small walled structures and held various sizes of sheets, shirts and pants. The roof was spacious and served their purposes well, since it must've been the safest way to be outside. And the gardens were a nice touch.

Still. None of it fits. Anxiety balled up in my stomach to the point of almost making me sick. *Something this close to home… wouldn't I* know *about it?*

Glenna noticed the gardens had my attention and gestured toward one. "Each of us who are unable to fight, pick up the slack here and other places, as I've mentioned before. We're able to grow a range of vegetation throughout the year. Of course, during the dry season, plants don't always survive, though we make certain they get adequate water. As you can see, many are already succumbing as the trees and grasses have." She began to walk away.

I moved toward the garden she indicated and bent to touch a tomato plant. Some of its leaves were browning a bit, but it was still fairly green. "This one looks all right."

Glenna looked over her shoulder. "Yes, perhaps enough will persevere."

I gently rubbed a green leaf between my thumb and forefinger, before turning to follow.

"It took some time to bring all the earth up to the roof, but we worked at it as we do everything. It's paid off, as now we can sample the fruits of our labor, so to speak." She smiled and went on. "However, it's taken substantially longer to bring water to the roof."

I followed her around one of the small buildings. On the other side, I saw what made me think of the Roman aqueducts, except crudely made of plastic piping. Held up by wooden supports, they came up to the roof from some unknown location through the trees at the back of the building.

Glenna saw my fascination. "We were able to tap into an underground water source. And when I say 'we', I mean one of our people who has an influence over water. Of course, we have no way of making it absolutely drinkable and don't feel safe watering our plants with it. We can only use it for cleaning and showers. So the remainder of the water we collected from the last rainy season must be used on the garden. Which is why we have to find drinking water. Thus the need for the trek to a well."

I followed the line of piping into the trees. "Don't you run a risk of sabotage? I mean, with those things? Um, the Pale Ones?" *And what about the water company? Or a plumber? I don't get… any of this.*

Glenna smiled down at me. "Not to worry. We have a very thorough security system here. We have a guard posted at each corner of the roof at all times, and we have Derik. Remember, he can sense if one of them is near. So, if one comes unseen by *their* eyes," she gestured toward one of the guards, "they will not go unnoticed."

I frowned. "But Derik's not here all the time. The other night, for instance. What about then?"

"Well, we have a back-up plan for such occasions."

A boy jogged up to us, panting. He leaned over, his hands on his knees, trying to catch his breath. "She." Pant. "She's asked for." Pant. "Her." He continued breathing heavily.

Glenna frowned. "That was sooner than I anticipated. Is that all?"

"She sent for Derik, too."

She raised her chin as if starting to nod. "Ah." She paused for a moment. "Thank you, Timothy."

The boy nodded, finally getting his breathing under control, and jogged away. I watched him climb down the ladder.

"Well, that was the conclusion of our tour, anyway. That was Timothy, one of our younger ones. You'll be introduced to the rest before too long, I'm sure. But now, the time has come for you to meet someone I have already mentioned to you. The one to give you the answers you seek." Glenna started in the direction the boy had taken, and I had no other choice but to follow.

* * *

I followed Glenna down the rabbit hole, er, ladder and through the hall to the very last door. It was closed, and Glenna knocked. Two short raps.

"You may enter," a voice called from the other side. As Glenna turned the knob, I noted this door had been painted bright red, while all the others remained pale and unfinished.

Why hadn't I noticed it before?

Glenna stepped back and gestured for me to enter before her.

After hesitating a moment, I stepped forward, but stopped short of the threshold.

"This is where I remain. You must go in without me. Only those who are summoned may cross beyond the Red," Glenna whispered. This time, however, her voice did not seem to calm me. I searched her eyes for some sort of explanation. "Don't worry, Haylee. All will be well. She'll give you your answers, and then some. Derik should be here shortly, so you won't be alone." She nudged me toward the room.

I squinted in through the doorway but could make out little. Light from the hallway revealed a rectangle of floor. The rest of the room was pitch black.

I could turn back right now, couldn't I? I hope that's an option, at least. I do *want some answers. But is this the only way I'll get them?* After another bit of hesitation, I took a deep breath and stepped over the threshold. The door closed behind me – I froze – and everything went dark.

I heard a slight noise, the strike of a match, and a small flame flickered. The light moved and the wick of a candle ignited. Then I heard someone blow the first flame out. The single candle lit the still very dark room, but I could make out the shape of a person near the light.

I squinted again. "H-hello?"

The person did not move, so I took another step toward them and nearly yelped, when someone knocked at the door. Two short knocks. I jumped again, when the figure in front of me spoke.

"You may enter." It was the voice of a much older woman, of that I was certain.

The door opened, and the light from the hallway blinded me. I threw a hand over my eyes. Then a large shadow was cast over me and I looked up to see a figure silhouetted against the bright light.

The figure took a step toward me, and the door closed. Of course, I knew automatically who it was by their presence. Derik. It felt as though he was unhappy to be there. But whether he was unhappy with me or because we were there – or maybe he was always like this – I was unsure.

Movement drew my attention back to the other figure in the room. The candle had been moved to light a second and, now, I saw an elderly woman set it back in place. She was small and bony, but not fragile. Her white hair was pulled back into a loose bun, and strands of it curled around her timeworn face.

"Now that you are both here, come closer," she said, her voice gravelly. She stood with her hands resting on the back of a chair in front of her, with a lit candle to the left and right. Another chair faced her, further separating us.

I felt Derik begrudgingly start forward, so I moved to follow him, until we stood on either side of the closer chair.

I could see the woman much more clearly. She wore a white gown, and her eyes were closed.

Why do I get the impression she can see everything in this room?

Her sudden smile startled me..

As if she heard my thoughts and was amused by them.

"Sit, little girl," she said, motioning toward the chair beside me.

I eyed it uncertainly and almost threw a glance up at Derik. My cheeks grew hot, and I sat down quickly. *And since when do I look to him for affirmation? What should he care whether or not I sit?*

The woman came around the other chair and sat in front of me. She was so close, her knees practically touched mine, and I almost flinched. Once she had settled, she looked toward Derik.

"Are you afraid to look at me, son?" she asked in a pleasant voice.

"Why don't you tell me." He leaned over the arm of my chair and met her eyes. "You're the psychic here."

When he straightened, I let out a breath and rubbed my arms to rid them of goosebumps. It was the closest he had come to touching me since I'd woken up.

What the heck *was that? Sure, he's tall, dark, and handsome, but no one's ever had that effect on me before.* The feeling didn't go away when he stood, because he remained close enough to rest his hand on the back of the chair.

"And while you're at it, why don't you tell me what *I'm* doing here. I can't see how I have anything to do with this."

The woman maintained her composure without effort. "It is not my place to tell you what you should know for yourself." Then she turned her attention back to me. She stared at me, and I could not look away. Eyes the color of violets…

Then she blinked. And I could blink.

I looked away, squeezing my eyes tight. They were dry and they burned.

How long had she held my gaze? I looked up at Derik

He was frowning down at me.

"What – " I began to ask why he was staring at me so but couldn't. "What happened?" His stare made me uncomfortable.

He drew back into himself and made his face blank. "An exercise in futility? The greatest con of all time? Some would say it was *magic*." Despite his lack of facial expression, I could hear something akin to distaste in his voice.

"Wasn't it?" I asked, because I *did* feel something remarkable had taken place.

He looked down at me then, but I felt as if he looked down *on* me. "No," he replied, as if to a child. "Hypnosis, maybe. But magic? No." He looked away, crossing his arms and shaking his head.

I turned more directly toward him, one knee in the chair. "You're not trying to convince *me*. Are you?"

Glowering, he spun toward me. I pulled away, and one arm of the chair dug into my back. His hands pressed into the other, and his nose nearly brushed mine. Somehow, I kept eye contact. Then I did something even less expected. I placed my hands on his.

"I'm sorry. Not because you're intimidating." I managed a laugh. "Because, let's face it, you are. But because I don't know you, and whether or not you believe in magic is *none* of my business. It's obviously a touchy subject. I don't know why I even said that." I frowned and finally looked away. *Why* did *I say that?* I glanced over at the pleasant-looking woman sitting patiently in the chair across from me. *Does it have something to do with her?* My frown deepened. *There's something… strange about her.* I shook my head and chalked it up to a trick of candlelight.

When I turned back, Derik had lowered his face and was staring at my hands over his. For a moment, I observed how small mine looked there, and how warm his felt. Then, it dawned on me: I was still touching him. My face grew hot, and I pulled my hands away.

"Sorry," I said, as he continued to look down at his now bare hands.

He began to straighten. "*I'm* sorry. I shouldn't have gotten so angry." Then he was as he had been, standing at his full height, arms across his chest.

His very broad chest. I shook the thought away. *What's* wrong *with me?*

He cleared his throat. "But you're right. It isn't any of your business." Then, as if nothing had happened, he said, "Now, if you could get this over with, so I can get on with my day. I'm still playing catch-up after everything." He had returned his attention to the older woman.

He's *playing catch-up? I still don't know what the hell's going on here. And he only confuses me more.* I sat for a second with my mouth hanging open before I forced it shut and slid around in the chair to face her, as well.

She was looking at me again. Not exactly staring, but gazing. Studying me.

Or maybe I'm reading your thoughts, her voice rang through my mind.

I gasped.

The woman laughed out loud.

And did Derik just flinch? Then again, he doesn't strike me as the flinching type. No, I can practically feel him rolling his eyes, so probably not.

"What the hell is going on, now?!"

I jumped at the volume and tone of his voice.

The woman still laughed a little. "I'm sorry. I don't get to have fun very often. And I was curious."

"Curious about what?" he asked, suspiciously.

She sobered quickly, before replying. "About whether or not she could hear me, of course."

"Of course, she can hear you. *I* can hear you. They can probably hear you out in the hall." Then he raised his voice further. "What with their ears pressed up against the door, and all."

I heard the muffled sound of feet scurrying away.

The old woman chuckled. "Young Derik, you know very well what I meant. But that *was* amusing. No, Little Haylee can hear me in her head. Can't you?"

I just stared back.

"Yeah. Well, she doesn't seem as happy about it as you do. In fact, she looks like she's about to make a run for it."

Until then, I hadn't realized I sat bolt upright in my chair. Swallowing the lump in my throat, I forced myself to relax. Still, my eyes must have been wide. I glanced up at Derik, who was trying to look disinterested with little effect, and then back to her. She was waiting patiently for my answer. I started nodding, dumbly, then made myself speak.

"Uh. I. Uh-huh." I had stopped bobbing my head and sat for a moment, before saying, "Yeah, I heard you."

Derik had gone very still at my side.

But the woman had a small smile on her face. "Very interesting. Very interesting, indeed."

I looked back and forth between the two of them. Neither any help. Derik refused to look at me, and the woman was simply smiling that little smile of hers.

"What? Why?" I asked her.

"Only those with a gift similar to my own can hear me when I am in their minds. And vice versa, of course," she added with a little bow.

I frowned at her.

"Don't worry." She chuckled again. "It only grows more confusing."

Derik had had enough. "Stop with the games and just tell us why we're here, already. Like I said, I've got work to do."

She turned her eyes back to him. "Well, son, *that* will take a little while. We have a lot to tell our Haylee, considering she's from another time."

3

"What do you mean, *another time*?" Derik all but shouted. Then he threw his hand up to signal a stop, and I watched him compose himself. Barely. He took a deep breath and lowered his hand. "What does *that* mean?"

Though I wanted to ask the same question, I remained silent.

But the woman answered him. "It means exactly how it sounds. She traveled through time to get here. From the past, I believe. How far, I am not sure. But it was no accident, I'm quite certain." She looked at me thoughtfully. "Something completely common to us, would be tremendously frightening to someone who had never heard of these creatures before, let alone experienced such an attack. To come from a world where they do not yet exist is extraordinary. But what is more amazing to me is one of them traveling to *your* time. Why would they do that?" She paused. "You were fortunate to have such a heroic protector. Otherwise, I fear you would not be here now."

Those words finally broke through a bit of my shock. "What about him? Did he survive? Do you know?"

The woman lowered her eyes for a moment. "Alas, I cannot see that... I saw only what you have seen. I'm sorry." She met my eyes.

I nodded and looked off to one side, blinking tears away. When I was certain they would not fall, I gave a sniffle. "How do you know all you do? Glenna's been by my side since I woke up. She didn't know all the details before that."

The woman looked at me a little sheepishly then. "I do apologize. For time's sake, I got all of this information when you first sat before me. I broke through your mind's defenses. Which wasn't very hard, by the way. You really need to work on that, but we can figure that out another time. In any case, it seemed a mere second or two for you, when it was a tiny bit longer. I simply looked through your memories, found what I needed, and retained them as if they were my own. Once again, I apologize, but it was much quicker than having you tell me your story."

I straightened in my seat again. *She read my mind?* I tried to make sense of it. "It felt as if my eyes had gone a little too long between blinks." I paused, before adding, "I really don't like the idea of someone fishing around in my head, but…" I stared at her. *I feel like I can trust you… somehow. And I don't understand it but I trust Derik, too, and the rest of the people here. I guess I don't have much choice but to trust* myself *on this. Oh, God, this is crazy!* I shook my head and took a deep breath. "Okay." I laughed nervously. "So, I've traveled through time, into the *future*? But how?"

Derik interrupted. "It's *that* easy? You believe. Just like that?" The anger on his face mixed with some other emotion I couldn't place. "Are you *that* naïve?! Will you believe *anything*?! I can't be – " He stopped himself.

I took the chance to interject. "No. Under normal circumstances I wouldn't believe, *couldn't* believe it. But these aren't *normal* circumstances. This is fuh – " I glanced over at the woman " – messed up. That's what this is. Sorry," I said to her.

She simply bowed her head.

"But, also, it *feels* right." I turned toward him, my hands pressed against my stomach. "And, *some*how – I don't know how – I *know* it is." I stared into his eyes, and he blinked down at me.

He turned, raking his fingers through his hair. "Ugh!" He pulled his hands down over his face, and I vaguely heard a string of obscenities. Then he swung back around, dropped his hands to his sides, and sighed. "Fine." He didn't look at anyone.

I could feel how wide my eyes had gotten and tried to look less shocked. Not sure if I succeeded, I asked, "Fine what?"

He shifted all his weight to one foot, placing his hands on his narrow hips – *Oh, I really need to* stop *that!*

"I figure I have three choices." He turned toward me and held up three fingers. "One, *you're* crazy." He pointed at me. "And she's crazy." He gestured toward the woman. "Two, you're *not crazy*, just a little confused. *She's* completely bogus and now has you confused but convinced." He paused, considering.

I leaned toward him. "And three?"

He sighed, dropped his arms once more, and looked me straight in the eyes. "Three. Neither one of you is crazy, and she's *not* a fake.

Three, it's all true, and I have no choice but to go along with this *unbelievable* idea." His eyes were still on mine.

"And which one is it? Do you believe?"

He studied me for a moment, then looked up toward the ceiling. "God help me, I do." The frustration was evident in his voice.

I smiled. I don't know why his believing meant so much, but it did. So I sat back in my chair, afraid to look at him, and tried to face the older woman.

"That was much easier than I expected it to be," she said, a surprised smile on her own face.

"Don't push it," he replied, and, though the words themselves were grumpy, the voice was much lighter than it had been. "What now? Is there more?"

"Yes. Now we answer any questions our little Haylee may have and tell her everything there is to tell. After that, I have a few concerns of my own. You do have questions, do you not?"

I nodded. "How? How was the time-travel possible? Why am I here? I mean, where do I even start? I already know some about the Pale Ones, uh, sort of, but how did one get to my… time? Why was he there? There wasn't anyone else around… So, why *then* and – Oh, God." I brought my hands to my mouth and sat for a moment in silence. "Aunt Bethany." Tears formed, and I tried to blink them away again. One escaped, and I swiped the back of my hand across my cheek. I swallowed hard. "*It* killed her, didn't it?"

The woman's face tightened with sadness for me. "I believe so, yes."

"*Why?*"

"I'm not certain. It's reasonable to assume they were after something in particular. And, based on what I've seen through your memories, I believe they were after some*one*. You."

"Me?" I sat there for a few moments. *If they were after me, then…* "This whole thing is my fault. She died because of me?" I didn't know what to say after that. I sank further into the large chair.

I was surprised when I heard Derik's voice.

"No. It's *not* your fault."

Is he defending me?

He went on. "*If* they came for you. And, come on, that's a pretty big if."

Or is he insulting me?

"*If* they did come for you, that wouldn't be your fault, but theirs. It was their action. They, and they alone, are to blame." He crouched down by my chair. "Do you understand?"

I turned to him and raised my eyes to meet his. *What do I say to that?* I stared for a second, before finally nodding.

Then he continued to surprise me. His mouth turned up the tiniest bit, but I could see a smile.

Look at that. He's actually smiling. At me, no less.

"Good." He stared back at me for another moment, then frowned a little and looked away. He cleared his throat. "Now, you must have more questions. Get on with it." His voice wasn't harsh. In fact, he sounded almost breathless.

I looked down at my hands, realizing I was rubbing them together nervously. "Um." I suddenly had a hard time thinking. "I already know people have developed abilities in order to fight the Pale Ones, or at least survive… Where did they come from? The Pale Ones, I mean."

Neither looked at me.

Then the woman sighed. "There remains the mystery. We are not certain of their origin or exactly *when* they came to be. They themselves claim to have been feeding off of us for centuries. However, we know very little beyond what we have seen. Hardly anyone lives to tell of their encounters with them. They kill nearly everyone they come across." She looked at Derik. "Isn't that right?"

He gave a curt nod but kept his eyes averted.

She looked back at me. "You have a question?"

I hadn't realized my need to interject was so obvious. "Yes, sorry. What do you mean they *feed* off of us? You don't mean blood, do you? They aren't vampires, are they? I mean, vampires don't exist, right?" Then, more to myself, "God, what am I saying? If these things exist, why couldn't vampires? And why couldn't they *be* vampires?"

"Blood, no. But still they feed on us, so they are very much like the vampire of myth. If what they claim is true, perhaps the myth *comes* from them. They sustain themselves on our life force, our essence. They drain us of life, and we cease to be. They do it through touch, skin to skin."

"I don't think you're far off on the whole vampire thing, truthfully." At some point, Derik had moved to another part of the room, into complete darkness.

Maybe he wants me to forget he's there. It's not working. He could be completely quiet and I'd still feel his presence. I had an image in my mind of him leaning up against the wall or some piece of furniture, arms folded across his chest.

He continued talking. "No pointy canines used to suck the blood of their prey, no red eyes, no coming back from the dead, that sort of thing. But…"

"But pretty darn close, right?"

In my mind, I saw him push himself away from that wall.

He spoke as he moved. "Well, they might as well be called vampires. They are demons, of a sort."

I felt him raise his eyebrows. *Wait, how could I do that? He's circling around the room, pacing. Is he nervous?* I focused on him.

He suddenly stood still.

Almost as if he's become conscious of my awareness of him… Why are you so nervous? And just like that, I lost the image of him.

"You wanted to ask what their other abilities are?" he asked.

I blinked and looked around, trying to pinpoint his location. His demeanor had changed as suddenly as he had stopped moving. I felt disoriented for a moment.

Maybe I imagined it all.

"Uh… yeah." I was having trouble concentrating. "Well, Glenna kind of filled me in on that, I guess. Super strength, speed, sight. All that stuff. Now, add *touch of death.* How much worse can it get?"

The woman answered. "Much worse, I'm afraid. But those are the ones of note. And you've seen how big they are. They could give our Derik here a run for his money, and have often enough. Derik's the one with the most experience with them, in fact. Everything we know about their abilities, we have learned from him. He has been invaluable." She smiled over my head. "Perhaps you could acquaint her with your knowledge sometime."

I turned to see Derik standing a few feet behind me. He couldn't have been there when he last spoke.

"I gotta hand it to you. You're kinda sneaky," I said, feeling irritated with him but not sure why. "I'm sorry, but is there another chair in here? He's making me a little uneasy. He's all hidin'-in-the-shadows and whatnot. Just a bit unnerving, what with him talking, but me not being able to see him. Then he slinks up behind me. It's just a tad…" I shuddered a little for emphasis.

I heard a scraping sound, then a clatter, and a chair knocked against mine. He slumped down into it and smiled.

"I don't slink." He was grinning, when he turned to the woman.

I looked at her, and she too seemed amused, though by what I was unsure.

"Anyway." She cleared her throat. "Anything else, related to the Pale Ones?"

I thought for a moment. "What did you mean by our life-force? Our spirit, our energy? Our souls?" I shook my head. "And is that all they need to survive? They don't eat or drink anything? I guess I don't completely understand."

Derik adjusted in his seat. "Whatever it is that keeps humans alive, *that* is what they feed on. It is an energy, whether derived from food or innate, or both. No one knows for sure about the spirit or soul. That's one of the many reasons they're so feared. Humans are afraid they *are* capable of capturing their souls. The religious zealots are divided between those who believe God sent them here as punishment – the unworthy are fed upon and sent to hell, one way or another – and those who believe they are a test of faith. Others simply believe they're nature's way of trying mankind's survival skills or weeding out the population. If that's the case, I'd say it's worked pretty well."

"And is that what *you* believe?" I asked him.

He raised his eyebrows at me. "You want to know what *I* believe?"

I nodded.

He sighed. "I believe it doesn't matter *why* they're here, just that they *are*, and that they live to kill, to feed, and *because* they feed. And they enjoy it."

"That's the feeling *I* got. Not *just* that they enjoy the kill, but the hunt *and* the fight. They seem to enjoy stalking… making you scared before you even know they're there…." I was getting lost in the memory of the thing in the woods. *The cold… the chase. The fear…*

"Stop it."

I glanced toward the voice and saw two dots of light reflected back at me. I started, and the shine disappeared as I blinked my eyes. Squeezing them shut, I shook my head. When I opened them, Derik stared back at me.

"What?" I asked. *Why do I sound like I've been running?*

He frowned. "I, uh… I said to stop. You can't… be doing that." He regained his ability to put sentences together. "You slipped away into your mind somewhere. Reliving the other night, I suspect. Don't."

He turned away.

Dazed, I stared at him for a moment, then trailed my eyes down to where our two chairs met. I could feel the crease forming between my eyes.

He must be right. It did feel as though I had gone back to that night. That would definitely explain why I'd seen the same animal eye shine after I heard him speak. I must've been visualizing that thing *as I looked up at him. He helped me clear my head… But was he angry with me because of it?* I rubbed my eyes and turned around in my chair.

"Perhaps we should finish this discussion another time," the woman said.

I had nearly forgotten she was there.

"You must be exhausted. The words alone would make a person weary. Of course, I would like to speak with you again. Would tomorrow be to your liking?"

After a bit of a delay, I nodded.

The woman rose, indicating for us to do the same. Derik scraped his chair on the floor, and I heard him moving it back to another corner of the room as I stood.

"Thank you both for seeing me," she said.

I blinked up at her. "Oh. No, thank *you.*" I stared at her for another moment.

"Are you coming?" Derik's impatient voice came from behind me.

Blinking once more to clear my head, I turned. "Mm-hmm." He opened the door, and I had to shield my eyes from the light.

Oh, wait! I spun around, just as I reached him. "I forgot to ask your name."

The woman smiled. "Sabella."

Sabella. That seems… right.

Derik cleared his throat. He was already walking through the door. Again, I glanced back. Sabella blew out a candle as Derik stepped over the threshold. I was still looking over my shoulder, as I half-stumbled out the door. It swung shut before I could see her blow out the second one.

For a moment, I stood close to the door, an eternity of red before my eyes.

I turned to see a number of people rushing to look busy and Derik disappearing down the stairwell to my right.

Glenna was smiling down at me.

"So? All is well, I hope… Your questions have been answered?"

"Most have, yes," I replied. "Though I have many more."

We began walking. "Understandably," she said, soothingly. Everything she said was soothing.

I yawned.

"Yes, you must be exhausted. I'll take you back to your room. If you like, that is?"

I was still in a bit of a daze but realized she was looking at me. "Oh… yes. That sounds good." *Why* am *I so tired?*

Glenna led the way to a room toward the other end of the hall, the one in which I had awoken.

"Go ahead and sleep for a while. You've been through quite an ordeal. I have a few things I need to tend to, so think of this place as your home." She pushed the door open.

I paused before continuing through. "Thank you".

"You are very welcome." She smiled and placed her hand on my cheek before turning to go.

Closing the door behind me, I found my cot and lay there for several minutes, my mind reeling despite my weariness.

Am I dreaming*? Will I still be in this place when I wake up? If so, am I going crazy? I mean, can I* really *rule that out? And if I'm not crazy, then what in the world is going on?*

How could I possibly go to sleep?! I closed my eyes and was out.

* * *

This time I awoke to nearly complete darkness.

Where am I? Was *it a dream? A terrible, wonderful dream…*

No. I knew it wasn't. I could feel the cot under me and, when I held my breath, I could hear the breathing of those sleeping around me.

There were more people in the room than before and, judging by the absence of light coming through the windows, night must have fallen. I glanced around the room and saw the flickering of a candle at the far wall. I stared at it for a moment, before looking toward the blackened, dingy windows. Curiosity overtook me, and I stood and made my way to the candle. Picking it up and shielding the flame, I walked to the nearest window. Without thinking, I used my free hand to wipe at a pane.

All at once, I felt a presence at my side, a puff of air sent the flame dancing, and it was out. Then a pair of hands pulled me away from the glass.

"What are you doing? Trying to make a target of yourself?" Derik whispered harshly in my ear.

I blinked. "Wha – a target? No, I – "

"That's exactly what you nearly did." He gave me the barest of shakes and nodded toward the window. "Go ahead. Look. Tell me what you see." He loosened his grip.

I tried to make out his face, but my eyes weren't yet used to being without the candlelight. So, I did as he asked. At first, I couldn't decipher the dark shapes from the darker ones but, as my eyes adjusted, I began to see movement.

"Is – is that someone out there?" I asked, my fingertip pressed against the glass. I looked up at him and could now make out some of his more prominent features.

"Yeah. Someone or some*thing*. Depends on your point-of-view. For some reason, they're showing a lot more interest in this place tonight. I wonder why?" He looked at me speculatively.

I turned my attention back to the darkness outside but saw nothing this time. "Because of me?"

"That's the general consensus, yes."

"How long have they been out there?"

"I saw the first one around dusk, the rest of the watch has been noticing them here and there for the past hour."

A question came to mind. "How long has it been since dusk?"

I saw one corner of his mouth lift. "Three and a half hours." His eyes shone with something akin to appreciation, which confused me more.

"Should we worry?"

"I don't think so. It's unusual for there to be this many but we normally see a few, mostly at night due to their sensitivity to the sun. They cause as much trouble as possible but won't try anything tonight." He set the candle in its place.

"How can you be so sure?"

He sighed. "I'm sure you've heard about my ability by now."

"You can sense them."

"That's part of it, but I can also sense their intentions, to a degree. Despite their numbers, they aren't planning anything. It's more like they're curious."

"And just how many are there?"

"I've counted twenty-six so far."

I felt my eyes go wide, was suddenly very conscious of the window behind me, and moved to follow him. I was certain I heard him chuckle.

"Are you hungry?" he asked.

The change of subject threw me off, but then again everything about him did. "Uh… yeah." And I realized I was indeed hungry. "Very much so."

"All right, I'll walk you down." The look he gave me was almost warm, as he held the door open for me.

A few candles lit the deserted hall.

"We tend to move around upstairs more during the day. At night, we're more watchful, so people tend to stay in designated areas," he explained.

"If you have some place you're supposed to be or something, you don't have to walk me. I remember the way." I said this with my eyes on the floor.

"Would you rather walk alone?" He stopped.

"I – No, I…" I was flabbergasted. "I just meant…"

"I was about to turn in. I'm caught up on most of my work, but my sleep schedule is a little off. I don't like to sleep at night…" He hesitated, as he began walking again. "Just in case. But I'm not especially worried tonight, like I said. However, you're obviously worked up about our uninvited guests and wouldn't want to walk alone… Right?"

"Uh…" was all I got out, when he stopped again. We stood at the top of the dark stairwell.

"You're not afraid of me, are you?" His voice hid any emotion.

Does the thought upset him or would he prefer I be afraid? He most certainly intimidates me, but am I afraid of him? I think I'm more afraid of how he makes me feel when I'm around him. Which I don't get at all. I stared into the dark stairway, anxious. *And do they not have any friggin' candles to spare for the stairs?* Instead of voicing any of this aloud, I asked, "Should I be?" and finally looked at him.

"Maybe." He stared back for a moment and continued down the stairs.

Maybe? I stood dumbfounded, then shrugged it off. *He's joking.* I followed him into the darkness.

He stopped in the doorway of the cafeteria. "This would be my stop. Can you handle this on your own?" His tone was sharp.

Ah, there's the Derik I've come to expect.

"You're not eating?" I asked as I glanced nervously around the room. It was nearly as crowded as during the day. I recognized a face or two from earlier but the rest were all new.

And one of those new faces was staring back at me, or us. I couldn't be absolutely sure, but she didn't look happy. Like most of them, she was tall. However, unlike the rest, her hair was cropped short and slicked back. She was striking and might have been beautiful with a more pleasant expression on her face. She stood with a hand on her hip by a group of other men and women.

"Like I said, I need to get *some* sleep." He caught sight of the young woman across the room. "First, I think I'll make another round, do another count," he said, distractedly. He turned back to the hall. "Make sure someone walks you back." And he was gone.

He left me standing there feeling like an idiot. Again. Then, laughter from the other side of the room caught my attention.

The woman had returned her interest to the group. "Yeah, maybe we should throw her to them," she said, and several of them laughed with her.

Others, seeing me standing there, feigned a serious fascination with their meals.

Not knowing how to react, I pretended not to hear.

Is she talking about me? I mean, who else would she be talking about?

I made my way to the food line, acting as normal as a girl can once she's found herself in a strange world full of the stuff of dreams. And not all the good stuff, either.

Once I had my bowl, I looked around for a place to sit. No one met my eyes, and as I chose a spot, the people sitting nearby were suddenly finished with their food. I found myself alone at an empty table and began eating. I was hungry but found the food had little flavor. Now, either the food actually *had* little flavor, or it was me.

I pondered this quandary until someone near me cleared their throat. I looked up hesitantly.

Before me, stood a young man and woman. They were much smaller than most of the others but still slightly bigger than me.

"Hi," said the young man. "Would you mind if we sat here? With you, I mean?"

I knew my mouth hung open for a moment before I answered. "Uh, no. I mean sure." I let out a nervous laugh. "Yes. Sit. Please."

The two of them sat across from me, smiles on their faces.

"I'm Merritt," he said, giving me his hand. "And this is Karroll." He indicated the young woman.

She gave a small wave.

I smiled. "It's nice to meet you both. My name's Haylee."

"We know," said Karroll, as she scooped food into her mouth.

"You looked like you could use a friend, and," he paused with a sheepish look, "I admit we were a bit curious."

"Yeah… I guess you'd have to be…" I said not knowing what else to say. I glanced around again and caught the eyes of the woman across the room. She didn't look down, which meant I had to. I stared at the table and nodded in her direction. "Um. Who is *she*?"

Merritt turned, surveying the room. "Oh. You mean Nate. Yeah… she's been with us for a little while now. What, a couple years?" He glanced at Karroll. She nodded, and he went on. "Yeah. She and Derik are together. Looks like they're mates. Like me and Kar, here." He smiled big. "We've known since we were kids," he said with conviction.

"She – ?" I coughed, nearly choking, and ducked my head, before trying again, more quietly. "She's his *mate*? You mean they're getting married or something?" I looked back and forth between the two across from me.

Karroll looked at me quizzically. "Not exactly. I honestly don't think they– "

"No, no," Merritt took over, the excitement evident in his voice. "They're meant-to-be. They match, down to their cores. They *complete* each other."

I raised my eyebrows at this phrase, managing to hide a smile, but then thought about it, as I stared at my food. "Like soul mates? You said like you guys are…."

"Yea – "

Karroll interrupted. "Not like us." She glanced at him before looking back at me. "We call our mate – our *true* mate – our Other Half. Many people don't get the concept. It's not like it used to be – not like I've read in books. It's not something you choose, it's *chosen,* but not by any person. It's an undeniable attraction, a bond. And it's different for everyone. Most mates are opposites, so they balance each other out in all aspects of power and personality. Others are drawn together in more subtle ways. Which is the way many think it is for Derik and Nate. But it *isn't.*" She looked pointedly at Merritt, who kept quiet. "They have a lot in common, okay. They're together, sure. But they're not *connected.* Not really. Any fool can see what they have is purely physical."

"Oh, come on now. They're perfect for each other… Everyone knows it."

I watched their exchange.

Derik's seeing someone? Interesting… Why am I so shocked? It's not like I have any reason to care, really. I don't care. I'm… curious. That's it. Pure curiosity.

I found myself looking back across the room. When my eyes found her, I felt an unexplainable sinking feeling in my stomach. She was staring back at me, and I had been wrong earlier. She wasn't beautiful when she smiled. She was downright scary. I could sense everything she felt toward me at that moment in her toothy grin. She hated me and she wanted me to know it. Also, I got the impression she had heard every word we had spoken. I couldn't look away.

"Haylee." Karroll touched my hand.

I snapped back to the people in front of me.

"Haylee, are you all right?" She leaned toward me, concern on her face.

"Yeah. I'm… fine." I shook myself and blinked a few times. "Just tired, I guess."

"Hey, don't pay attention to her, okay? She's a little possessive, and you've been a bit of a distraction the last couple of days." She smiled. "Mostly to Derik."

"But don't worry," Merritt rushed in. "Things'll get back to normal before you know it, and Derik'll forget everything, and she'll leave you alone." He smiled, reassuringly.

Karroll reached over and laid her hand on mine. "He means well, but sometimes he doesn't say the right thing." She gave me a penetrating look.

The look made me more curious than her words.

"What do you mean by that?" he asked. "I'm just tryin' to make the girl feel better. Nate's obviously overreacting. What's she expect in this situation? Derik to completely ignore something like this? No offense," he added to me.

"Merritt." She looked at him. "Sometimes you amaze me."

He smiled. "Why, thank you."

She turned her look of wonder back to me and shook her head.

"Well, break's over," he said, standing. "We've got work to do."

"Yeah... Do you need someone to walk you back to the sleeping area?" she asked me.

"Derik said I should have someone... Do you mind?"

"Not at all. It's on our way, anyway."

We took our bowls to the designated window and left them for whoever was back there to clean them. I tried to sneak a look through but saw no one.

As we made our way out of the room, I noticed something I must have been too distracted to notice before.

"What is that?" I indicated above the doorway.

"Secondary security," Merritt replied.

Karroll explained further. "In case one of them tries to get inside the main door upfront. We're supposed to gather here, since it's the only room large enough for all of us. It takes two strong people on either side of the doorway to lower it." She pointed to the levers and the pulley system attached to them. "It gives an added layer of defense – just in case – especially for those who can't defend themselves, like the children."

I gave a small nod, as I studied the very heavy wrought iron and hoped it never had to be used during my stay.

As I began to follow them again, I became aware of every pair of eyes weighing on my back. But one stare was stronger than the rest and it was burning a hole right through me.

Oh, God, I hope fire isn't Nate's ability, or she'll surely burn me to death right here. What is *her ability, anyway? Oh, I'm sure I'll find out, eventually.*

In silence, the three of us walked down the candlelit hall, Merritt and Karroll on either side of me.

"So," Karroll said, quietly. "You're not from around here, then?"

It was the politest way to simultaneously tell me everyone knew some version of my story and to ask me for the story firsthand.

"Not... exactly. What have you heard?" I asked.

"Well... several things really. I think I heard someone say you were sent by the Pale Ones to spy on us," she said.

"Actually, I think it was Nate who said that," Merritt broke in.

She shrugged and went on. "Others have said they found you

wandering around at night completely nude."

My eyes went wide and I opened my mouth to object, when she held up her hands.

"No worries. No one believes that one. At least not many… It was more than likely spread by Ford and Jaxon." She rolled her eyes. "They're harmless degenerates. Every camp has them. They were hanging around Nate in the cafeteria back there." Then, she went on. "Other than that, the most widely spread rumor is you're a time traveler and have spoken with Sabella. Which is ridiculous, because no one but a select few ever speak to the Seer."

"So, which is it? Spy, nude, or Sabella?" Merrit laughed, as we made it up the last few stairs.

"Uh… I was found at night. Not so much wandering as running for my life and falling unconscious… apparently into Derik's arms. And most certainly fully clothed," I added quickly in response to their looks of inquiry. "And… I did see Sabella."

"What?!" they cried in unison, then Karroll placed her hand on Merritt's arm and we stopped moving. "What?" she asked with much more reserve.

"I met with Sabella," I repeated. "Earlier today, she asked for me… and Derik. I guess since he's the one who found me. She let us both in on what's going on. And it kinda made sense to me." I began walking again.

They followed.

"What do you mean? What did she say?" She caught herself. "I am so sorry… this is none of our business. I can't believe I just did that." She looked down at the floor, as we walked.

Pausing, I sighed. "No… it's all right."

They were the first people, besides Glenna, to be so nice. *Maybe we could be friends. I want to tell them… but the whole situation is so strange. Will they believe it or just think I'm crazy?*

"I'm not sure where to even start." I blinked.

The two of them were silent, as they waited for me to go on.

I took a deep breath and told them what their Seer had said, what I understood of it anyway. By the time I had finished, we had been standing at the door for a while. They were quiet for a moment longer.

Merritt rubbed his shaggy head. "Wow."

Karroll's frown was evident, despite the dim lighting. Then she raised her eyebrows and gave a slight smile. "Well, welcome to the fold.

I imagine everything will play out as it's meant to."

She glanced at Merritt who still had his hand on his head.

"We need to get to work though..." As they left, she leaned in close to me. "Thank you very much for trusting us with your story. Look for us if you need anything. Now get some rest... I imagine you need it."

I smiled even once the door separated me from the hall.

Did I just make some friends? Cool. Oh, but I didn't even think to ask what their abilities are. They're not big like most of the others. I'd like to know what they can do.

In my dreams, I saw the bars of a poorly lit cell and something small scurrying out of sight. Then I dreamed Nate and her group pulled me from the table where I ate and dragged me out a door into the night. They threw me to the ground and, laughing, locked the door behind me. I could feel the Amara closing in, long before their shadows fell upon me.

4

I woke from my dreams so suddenly, I nearly fell out of bed. I was shivering and breathing heavily.

Upon glancing around the room, I realized the sun had risen and it was now light enough for me to see the rows of cots. Many of them were empty, and the candle across the room had either died or been blown out again.

I lay there for a moment or two, catching my breath, before I got up.

I couldn't sleep any more if I wanted to.

Slipping into my worn sneakers, I made my way toward the hallway and glanced back to the spot I had rubbed on the window the night before. My heart was still racing, as I slid through the door and closed it behind me.

The hall was crowded at this time of the morning, and I stood there with my back against the wall, watching people pass by. All of them hurried, rushing from one place to the next. They acknowledged each other with a quick "Hey," a nod or a slap on the back, until they took notice of me. Then many of them went on without a single indication of anyone else sharing the hall, while others stared open-mouthed as they passed.

When someone further down the hall catcalled, I blushed and averted my eyes to the floor. Someone else laughed. I was about to hightail it back into the room and planned on staying there throughout the day, when I caught sight of Derik moving in my direction.

He looked past me, and barked, "Get back to work, Jaxon!"

The laughter died down immediately.

When he stopped in front of me, my hand was frozen to the door.

"She wants you trained. Come on." With that he headed back down the hall.

I stood there for a moment, baffled, then ran to catch up. "Trained?

What do you mean, trained?" I asked.

He eyed me with open disdain, which made me more uncomfortable. "You're obviously in terrible physical shape and can't defend yourself properly."

I stopped dead. "Wha – " I started in frustration. "What do you know about me?" And I continued after him. "Wait a minute!"

We had made it to the dimly lit, now somehow deserted stairway, when I caught up again.

He stopped.

"How dare you assume, just by looking at me, I can't defend myself! Haven't you ever heard of not judging a book by its cover?! Sheesh! Not to mention it's rude," I mumbled this last part, starting to question my sudden outburst. Then, I continued. "I can defend myself wh – uh!"

The air left my lungs as he effortlessly pushed me up against the wall. I was too stunned to struggle.

"It shouldn't have been that easy to take you off guard," he said. "If *I* can, what's going to stop them from doing the same thing?" His gaze was intense, and I found myself unable to look away. He eased his hand away and lowered his eyes. "She also wants to train you herself in psychic self-defense, and now I too can see you're in need of it." He cleared his throat. "Follow me to the basic training room." He started down the stairs again.

Blinking after him, I followed with the distinct impression I was going to need to avoid stairwells when in this man's presence. The two combined continually unnerved me. He led me to a room midway down the hall. I made note of the cacophony of voices coming from the cafeteria as we passed it, and my stomach growled, but I ignored it.

"Sabella asked me to do the training, but I don't have time today. So I've found someone else. She's just as good," he said, as he opened the door.

There stood the woman from the cafeteria the night before.

"Nate, this is Haylee. Haylee, meet Nate." She stared back at me coolly.

I gulped and hoped no one noticed. She was scarier up close, but thank God she wasn't smiling. I knew if she smiled, I would run back to my bed and hide.

"Uh, hi," I managed.

"Hello," she replied, and I could see the beginnings of that smile.

"Um." I looked at Derik. "Could I talk to you for a moment, please? In the hall?"

He shrugged, and I led the way.

As soon as the door was secure behind us, I said, "You're joking, right?"

"I don't know what you mean. Did I say something funny? I don't think learning to defend yourself is a laughing matter." He was serious.

"Nate." I indicated over my shoulder. "She hates me."

"Now who's judging? You don't even know her."

"I know enough. And she hates me. I have no doubt."

"That's ridiculous. She's the best trainer we've got. And you need someone good." He turned to open the door.

"But she's *not* the best. I can tell by the way you said it. She's the best… *besides you.*"

He started to interrupt me, but I wouldn't allow it.

"And Sabella asked *you* to do it." I was pleading with him now.

He paused with his hand on the door. "I don't have time," he said and began to turn the knob.

"Haylee!" Glenna called, as she approached. "There you are. I've been trying to find you. Sabella is asking for you. Alone," she added at a look from Derik. The smile on her face remained pleasant.

"Fine," he said. "Nate, it looks like the session's been cancelled."

She stepped through the door. "Oh. Well, that's a shame. I was looking forward to working with you, Haylee," she said, with a full-blown smile.

I gasped as she brushed past me.

"I'll see *you* later." She eyed Derik suggestively and sauntered down the hall, swaying her hips.

I couldn't help sneaking a glance at Derik at that moment, but he managed to look irritated, as usual.

"She seemed heartbroken all right," Glenna said. "I do *not* know what you see in that woman... Come along, Haylee. We mustn't keep her waiting."

Ah, Glenna… My hero.

She didn't see the harsh expression on Derik's face because she had turned her attention back to me.

"Has anyone checked those bandages?"

I shook my head. "No. I kind of forgot they were there." I looked down at my arms. "Honestly, they don't hurt anymore. They feel fine."

She gave Derik a look similar to the one she had missed from him. "Still, they should be looked at." Then she smiled warmly at me. "Why don't we go to the infirmary and change them. It's this way." She put her arm around my shoulders and guided me down the hall.

"Uh. Okay. You have an infirmary?" The tension of the last few moments was forgotten.

"Well, we call it that. It's where we keep bandages and medicines, examine and dress minor wounds." She turned toward a door on our left. "Here we are."

As we went through the door, I glanced back to where we had left Derik, and he was gone.

"Go ahead and sit there." She indicated an actual examination table.

"Where'd you guys find this?" I asked, as I scooted up onto it. My feet dangled a foot from the floor.

She rummaged through a cabinet. "It has always been here. Ah, there it is." She turned toward me.

"It was already here? In this room?" I knew a lot of school buildings in the area had been set up similarly, so it could be a coincidence. However, I was sure this had been *my* middle school.

"Yes. Why?"

I glanced around, in awe. "This was the nurse's office," I said, more to myself. "I know this place."

"Are you all right?" She frowned at me, as she began unwinding the cloth from my arms.

I was still taking everything in. "I think so… Yeah." Looking back at her, I said, "What are the chances of you setting up in my old middle school?"

She raised her eyebrows. "Well, we took what we could get. We were very lucky to find something built so sturdily, something fortifiable and large enough for us to take in those in need. Such as yourself. Or those who have nowhere else to go, such as Derik or Nate." She paused. "Hm." She was holding my arm up.

"What?" I looked down. "Maybe they weren't as bad as I thought."

"No. They were quite deep." She studied my arm more closely. "But they're healing nicely. You may not even have any scars by the time they're through. Maybe you're a fast healer." She smiled at me.

"Is that an ability?"

"It could be. They sometimes manifest late. All show themselves differently through different people." She held up her finger. "Maybe, just maybe, yours only began to manifest once you crossed over into our time. Possibly because you didn't need them in the past. I've always thought we as humans have had the potential for an ability from the beginning. But until the Pale Ones came along, we had no need of them. Their presence flipped some kind of switch in us. Well, in most of us."

"So, it's possible I'll develop more?"

"Possibly… though this could be the extent. As I said, it varies from person to person." She rubbed a cold ointment on my skin. "Sorry I can't be more reassuring. There, all done. I think you will do fine without the bandages now. But I wouldn't suggest trying to heal any mortal wounds." She laughed but her eyes held a hint of seriousness.

"Don't worry, I won't… at least not on purpose, I guess. Thank you." I examined my arms myself. "Huh. That's just… cool." What had once been deep lacerations were now no more than a few scratches and slight pink marks. "Do any of the others heal like this?" I looked up.

"Only Derik and Nate," she replied, hiding her expression by putting things back in their designated places.

"Oh. So does that prove the mate theory then?"

She turned to me. "Who told you they were mates?"

"Uh, Merritt and Karroll? Well, Merritt."

"So you've made some friends, then? Good. And you couldn't find any two better. Though Merritt can be a bit of a gossip, Karroll keeps him in check."

"So it's true?"

She sighed. "I suppose. Only the two involved know for sure. But everyone believes they fit. They complement each other in some ways, keep the other in line, balance each other out. Their main abilities are similar, superior fighting skills and great strength…."

"But there's something about her… Right?"

She looked at me for a moment. "Yes. Something." Then she sat in a chair across from me and was silent.

"Glenna? Can I ask you something?" I fidgeted a bit.

Smiling, she said, "Of course. Anything."

"Is it considered rude to ask what someone's ability is?"

"That would depend upon how one asked, I suppose. Do you wish to know the nature of my ability?"

"I admit, I'm a little curious." I folded my hands in my lap and sat up a little straighter.

She tilted her head a bit. "How would you say you are feeling at this moment? Do you feel calm, at ease?"

"Yeah. I really do." I frowned "It's odd… but I always seem to feel that way around..." My eyes widened a little. "Are you *doing* that?"

Glenna looked amused but still managed to give the appearance of modesty. "Yes. That is my ability. I can make those around me calmer, but it works best through touch. So, if someone is particularly distressed, I try to touch them. I don't know *how* it works, only that it does." She gave a little shrug. "Of course, it also helps that I too am calm. If not, it sort of defeats the purpose, so to speak."

"Wow. That's amazing. I think that kind of ability would be especially helpful." *How would my life be with an ability like hers? It would definitely come in handy with my mom.*

"It does help ease the tension from time to time." She smiled at me, and we were silent again for a few moments.

Then I remembered her reason for "saving" me from Nate. "Oh. Shouldn't I be going? Sabella wanted to see me?" I began scooting off my seat.

"I'm sorry. I lied. She doesn't need to see you right now. Later, yes. But not now." She gave me a guilty look. "I heard you arguing with Derik and thought you could use a little help. Plus I agreed with you. Sabella asked him to train you for a reason. She always has a reason, and he knows that. He never puts training off on someone else, not even Nate. I don't know what has gotten into him these last – " She glanced at me. "Never mind. He should have done it himself. That's all."

"You saved me." My quick smile faltered. "She hates me. I could practically feel it drilling into me in the cafeteria last night. She scares me."

"To tell the truth, she scares me a little bit too. But she's been here a while now. Everyone trusts her, including Derik, and she has done nothing to prove that trust wrong. And, frankly, I have so much faith in Derik – though he can be a dope at times – I trust anyone he does. So, don't worry about Nate." She patted my knee.

"Well, I trust you. And Derik, though I find him extremely intimidating and oh so irritating, so I guess I can give her a shot, too."

She smiled at me curiously. "Well, okay then, what do you say we get you some food?"

When we opened the door someone rushed by. We stepped through and were almost run over by another person.

Glenna stopped him, a boy who looked to be fourteen but was already taller than me.

"Philip, what's going on?"

"It's spreading now! A bunch of us are going up to see."

"What do you mean, spreading?"

"Haven't ya' heard? The plants. Late yesterday one got all green. Now it's spread to some of the others. Tomatoes, I think they said. They might have the starts of a tomato on 'em by now." He ran on after a couple of the younger kids.

At that time, a group erupted from the cafeteria, mostly adults, though some teenagers joined them. Everyone was talking at once and rushed toward the stairs.

"Maybe we should take a look as well," Glenna said.

* * *

As with the last time, it took a moment for my eyes to adjust to the sunlight. When they did, I saw the throng of people gathered. I followed Glenna, as she pushed her way through. The appointed gardeners did their best to keep everyone back, so they wouldn't inadvertently destroy their food source. I looked past them and saw a patch of green amid the under-grown plants.

"How did this happen? It started yesterday? When?" Glenna inquired. "They weren't like this when I was up here last."

The gardener nearest her answered. "We noticed the first plant right before nightfall." He pointed, then swept his arm. "And the rest were like this this morning."

"It's amazing," I heard from somewhere behind me.

"It's a miracle," someone else called out.

Then the crowd was full of chatter, hypotheses I couldn't make out.

"What the *hell* is going on?!" This voice could be heard above all the rest. Everyone stopped at once.

"Derik!" Glenna called. "Come here. You must see this." She didn't look away from the plants.

Unlike Glenna, he didn't have to push through the group. Everyone simply made way. For me, having no real idea of the import of this greener development, the power of this man was more impressive. The apparent respect these people had for him had more of an impact on me. Of course, the fact that he was carrying his shirt rather than wearing it could have had something to do with my reaction. His eyes met mine, held them briefly, and I was suddenly very aware of the heat up there.

He focused his attention on Glenna and frowned.

She stepped back to give him a better look.

For a moment, he just stared, then his frown deepened. "When did this happen?"

Glenna relayed to him everything the gardener had told her.

After another moment, he glanced over the silent crowd. "Why are you all just standing there? You've all got things to do."

And with that, the silence was broken, and everyone filed back down the ladder. I had to admit, that was quite effective, and I was impressed by their ability to keep order as they went.

When most of the roof was clear, one of the guards approached Derik. "I'm sorry, sir. If we had known so many were coming to the roof at once, we would have barred their entry. There were too many." He struggled to keep his face expressionless, but did not succeed in hiding his apprehension of Derik and his curiosity in me. His eyes kept trailing past Derik, as he apologized.

"Anything could have happened with so many up here in the open. I wouldn't put it past them to try something while we're distracted, even during the day." He had ignored the guard's wandering eyes for as long as he could. "Traiten! Have you met our guest?" He yanked me forward. "This is Haylee."

The guard looked back to him. "No, sir, I haven't."

"Well, now you have and can get back to your post."

"Yes, sir." And he all but ran to the far corner of the roof.

Derik turned back to the garden. "Glenna, we need to talk." He glanced at me. "Alone."

"All right, Derik. I have a few things I would like to discuss with you as well. Haylee, go on down to the cafeteria, and I will come get you when it's time to meet with Sabella."

Derik narrowed his eyes at that but said nothing.

"O-okay," I said, and headed down the ladder.

Glenna and Derik weren't far behind me and headed to a room at the other end of the hall.

I went downstairs, but once again had very little appetite. People still stared at me as I walked by but most were in deep conversation about the tomato plants.

They're awfully worked up about it. I guess I didn't realize just how important the gardens were.

I ate quickly and left the cafeteria.

Glenna asked me to wait but I can't stand the stares.

I had no intention of eavesdropping but heard voices when I reached the top of the stairway. Glenna and Derik were in the room directly to my left, and their voices were loud enough to make out through the cracked door.

"So you think that's the cause?" Derik asked.

"Possibly. I don't know. It fits the timeline, but I didn't see anything with my own eyes…" Glenna replied.

"So you don't have any proof."

He's totally crossing his arms, right now. The corners of my mouth tugged up at the thought. I bit my bottom lip to keep the stupid grin from growing.

She sighed. "No. But you must admit, it sounds reasonable."

"*Reasonable*? I don't know about *that.* It makes me wonder even more what the Amara have to do with it all."

"That one has me stumped as well…" She paused. "So will you please do as I ask?"

"And what's that?"

"It's not like you to play dumb, Derik. Could you take it a littler easier on her please? She's not from a place where they exist – "

"Oh, they existed all right… They picked humans off one by one, even then. They just hadn't let themselves be known yet… Not till they were strong enough in numbers."

"Well, they don't exist to *us* in her time. She isn't used to all this."

"She's gonna have to get used to it pretty quick."

"I know. But be nicer. I knew you could be… disagreeable at times but I don't know what your problem is in this case. What's different now?"

"She's too much of a distraction to everyone. She's in the way."

Grinning was no longer an issue. Any trace was wiped from my face.

"Too much of a distraction, hm? Are you sure it's not you she's distracting?"

Tense silence oozed through the crack in the door.

And I could feel my fight or flight reaction kick in. I crept past the door.

Thank God my sneakers are broken in! I don't want that silence crashing down on me.

"I'll take it easier on her."

"And you'll train her yourself? You won't drop her on someone else? *Especially* not Nate?"

There was another pause.

"No." I could still hear the irritation in his voice. "I'll train her myself."

Wow. That did not *go how I anticipated. Go, Glenna.*

"Good. I was hoping you would see to reason."

I slipped into the next room. If they said anything else, I couldn't hear it. I hid on the other side of the door, as Derik started down the stairs. My shoulders relaxed, and I let out a breath.

With that done, I let my natural curiosity pull me further into the room. It was dimly lit, though not as much so as the ones used for sleeping. Thick sheets or drop cloths draped over what must have been furniture. I picked up one dust covered corner and pulled it back. The delicacy I used didn't keep the dust from rising. I felt a sneeze coming on and acted accordingly. In my eagerness to cover my nose and mouth, I dropped the cloth, which stirred up more dust. As if that would stop the tickling sensation! And it did. For a moment. As soon as I lowered my hands and breathed a sigh of relief, I sneezed. And my sneezes are not of the delicate one-sneeze variety. They can be quite loud and often come in sets of two or three. This time was no exception.

"Ah-chew!" I paused after the third, my hands in position in case of another attack. I listened for evidence that someone had heard, but there was only silence, so I lowered my hands. I could see the edge of a school desk peeking out from the cloth and moved it some more. Several more were shoved in the corner behind it. The kind with the chair attached.

"Huh." I turned in the center of the room and caught sight of something tall and rectangular in the other corner. I was hesitant in approaching it, because it was near the windows. But the window was well covered. I was much more careful in folding this cloth back and was shocked by my discovery.

How did this get up here?

An upright piano stood before me. The music room had been in the basement when I'd attended Midworth Middle School.

Is it the same one I used to practice on?

I opened it up and brushed my fingers across the keys. The temptation to test them was great, but my fear of being found was far greater.

Maybe I can come back later.

I replaced the cloth and tiptoed to the door. Peeking through, I saw no one and slipped out. I made my way to the red door at the center of the hallway, leaned against the wall across from it, and waited.

I had been leaning there for ten minutes, mulling over everything I had heard and seen today, when I began to have the very uncomfortable feeling I was being watched. So I glanced up and down the hall until I saw Nate standing in the doorway to one of the stairwells. She was surrounded by shadows and staring directly at me. I glanced again around the hall, realized we were the only ones there, and pushed away from the wall, not knowing what to do.

At that moment, the door across from me swung open, and Glenna stepped out.

"Oh, Haylee. I was about to come find you. Sabella is ready if you are." She gestured toward the dark room beyond.

I glanced once more down the hallway and, seeing no one, nodded and stepped through the door. It closed behind me, Glenna on the other side.

* * *

"Hello, again. Quite a bit has happened since we last spoke." The flame of a single candle lit the woman across the room. "You're wondering about the candles, yes?"

"Uh, yeah, actually." I moved forward and sat in the chair across from her.

"Everyone who passes beyond the Red must have a representative light," she said, as if I understood what this meant. "A source of protection on this side. Often shields are down, and one must take precautions. It will be especially important when I am training you to defend yourself psychically, at least until you have mastered it. Of course, even then you are more open to attack whenever you cross over."

"If I'm vulnerable to attack on this side anyway, why train me at all?"

"Because, without it, you are also more susceptible out there." She nodded toward the door.

"I see…" *So, Derik was right, on both counts. I* do *need training.*

"You have more questions?"

"Oh… I guess I do. Something Glenna said earlier has me… curious. She mentioned how Derik and, well, Nate came here with nowhere else to go. What did she mean by that exactly?"

"Well, I suppose it's common knowledge around the compound… So there is no reason I could not tell you the story. I believe it was several years ago. A group of ours was out scavenging, as we are required to do from time to time, when a small mob of Pale Ones attacked. We were no match for their strength, we never were in those days. They killed two people before Derik swooped in. He was as strong as them, stronger than each individually, and they had no choice but to scatter. He then helped us carry our wounded back. Glenna convinced him to stay, said we needed him. And he's been here ever since, teaching us to fight and defend ourselves. In a way, he's become honorary leader, sharing the title unofficially with Glenna. His knowledge of the Amara has been very helpful, as well, as it has given us much insight into their tactics and habits. He is one of us, part of our family, now. It is as if he has always been here."

"Where was he? What did he do before he came here?"

"We didn't ask. We owed him too much. The past is past."

I sat for a moment. "And Nate?"

"Well… Nate is a slightly different story… She showed up two years or so ago, wounded, running for her life. They hunted her down, after she separated from her own foraging group. She received attention from Derik almost immediately and now has the respect of most, if not all, of us."

"She didn't go back to her people?"

"She could not. Only she survived the attack. Though I do not know that she would have if she could."

"I see." *Could I have judged Nate prematurely? Maybe she feels like I'm infringing on her terrain and is jealous of the attention I've been getting from Derik, however absurd that idea. She obviously has feelings for him, so I have to find a way to show her I'm not after him.*

"So you have had encounters with Nate, then?" Sabella leaned forward in her chair.

I glanced up. *How much did she hear?* "Yes. She doesn't like me much."

"I supposed she would not." She studied me, as she leaned back. "What do you think of her?"

I was surprised. "Uh, I'm not entirely sure. I haven't really spoken with her. When Derik tried to get her to train me, I – oh." I caught myself. *Keeping secrets isn't my strongest trait. Then again, how am I supposed to keep something from someone who can read my mind?* "I…"

"No worries. Derik's disinterest in training you himself has already been brought to my attention. Go on, please." If she was upset by his noncompliance, it didn't show.

"I… had the feeling she disliked me. Intensely. And I told him so and that I didn't want her to train me. I'm afraid to be alone with her, honestly."

"And what was his reaction?"

"He seemed shocked by my response. I guess though it would be irritating to have someone speak of your mate in that way… I don't know."

"Yes." She stared at me. "I suppose so. Well, do you have any other questions before we begin?"

I'd hoped for a little more info on this whole soulmate thing, or whatever they call it. She changed gears without giving away even the smallest detail about Derik's relationship with Nate. Then again, it's none of my business. Why do I care? I don't… Do I? "No. Not that I can think of, anyway."

"All right, then. Let's start with clearing your mind. Close your eyes and relax into your chair. Let your body sink into it. Allow everything to go limp. And breathe. Don't think. Simply focus on the empty space. Okay."

I felt as though I was floating, couldn't feel the chair beneath me. I was suspended in space, empty, infinite. I could hear only her voice.

"All right, now let's try something else. In order to begin building your defenses, you must have a sense of security, so we'll need to locate that security. We need to find something that makes you feel safe and anchored… Let your mind wander a bit – but not too far now. Inch out of yourself a bit at a time. Now, tell me what you are experiencing. What do you hear? See, feel? Tell me everything."

I pushed out a tiny bit, felt a slight barrier, and replied, "Something's blocking my way."

"That is all right. Quite natural. Push ever so slightly. Be very gentle. Otherwise you could force yourself too far."

I gave the slightest of pushes but whatever it was would not give. So, I pushed a little harder and harder, until I burst through to the other side. Dazzling light surrounded me, disoriented me. It was too bright.

"Slow down now…" she said. Her voice was a little distant. "You pushed a little too far, but you should be all right. You shouldn't encounter any more barriers. That was your own subconscious keeping you in. It often happens at first, when you are unused to the act. Later, you will have little to no trouble at all. But go on, keep searching."

So I did. I heard voices and focused on them, until I also began to make out shapes. When I focused harder, those shapes became clearer. They were people.

Where am I? I still felt weightless but now I could make out my surroundings. *The room across the hall.*

I couldn't recognize anyone there, for they were more like glowing shapes of humans. None were exactly the same, some were brighter than others, and each was a different shade of varying colors. The brightest light, a calming shade of cerulean blue, came through the door and spoke.

"Jacob, do you think the water will last until the next trip out?"

Glenna! You're all glowy-blue!

"Yeah… I think so. Though we did lose quite a bit of it the other night." This figure was a dull green.

Then again, everyone looks dull compared to Glenna.

She moved to the door. "Fine. I'll let Derik know then. I was on my way to find him. Have you seen him?"

"No. Sorry. If I do, I'll let him know you're looking for him."

"Thank you, Jacob." She floated into the hall.

I felt compelled to follow her serene glow.

She makes me feel the safest, and if I'm looking for security, she might be it. She's so bright and warm. This must be her aura. I'm seeing auras!

I followed her past several figures of varying radiance and color.

There are so many more people in the hall than earlier. It's almost like I've lost time.

Following Glenna took little effort. I simply thought of her, focused on her brilliance, and floated along behind her.

She inquired of Derik's whereabouts a few more times before pausing in another doorway. "Have you seen Derik, lately?"

Who is she talking to? Okay… If I just focus… I shot through the wall dividing us.

Darkness. A vast sucking void. Where there should be light, there was nothing. A vacuum. A black hole. And it was devouring me.

Sabella!

I flailed for a handhold. *Not physical. You're not physical. Focus! Find Glenna! Where is she?!* I looked around. *She's gone! Don't leave me alone with it! FOCUS, dammit!*

I broke through to the hall. Still no sign of Glenna.

Downstairs. She went downstairs. I can feel her, but the other thing is stronger. Safety. Just focus on safety.

My movement was no longer fluid, no longer smooth, but slow and jerky. *It's like I'm swimming through molasses with a tether around my ankle. Every time I try to move forward, it jerks me back. I can't go on like this much longer. I need more than safety. I need home. HOME.*

The thought sent me hurtling. I saw Glenna up ahead. But it was not her I was rushing toward. Another figure in front of her, of muddled color and the feel of an overcast day, came into my vision and before I could stop myself, we collided. Instantly, I felt a sense of security and belonging.

Oh, thank you, thank you. It was terrible. So horrible. Thank you… I clung to this new presence.

"Are you all right?" I heard Glenna ask. "You look a little pale."

"I'll be… fine. I just need… to sit down. I'll be okay."

"All right… Get some rest. You haven't been getting enough." Her hand brushed my arm.

Er, our arm? Their arm. This is weird.

We moved away from her and down the hall. I had no choice.

I can't let go. I'll be sucked away. Gone. Forever.

We entered an empty room and closed the door.

"Get out."

Derik! Is that you?

"Who else would it be?! Now get out."

Angry. Again. I can feel why. *Oh, that's new. You're so private. Why? What are you hiding? What don't you want me to see?*

"Stop!" All his barriers snapped up.

I was struck and everything was spinning. I now understood why his aura was cloudy. He was hiding something, some part of himself. He was guarded.

I'm sorry. I didn't mean anything. It was terrible. It almost had me. Please, please, don't make me go… I'm not sure I could if I wanted to.

"What do you mean, you can't? And what are you talking about?"

Someone here is a big black hole, sucking the life and light out of everyone. I don't think it's enough to notice. I'd say everyone recovers before they know it's happened. It didn't know I was there, but I saw and must be especially vulnerable in this state. I felt the pull until the moment I collided with you. I'm afraid to let go… I'm not sorry about that, I guess, 'cause I feel better now.

"Someone?" He narrowed his eyes. "You don't *know* who it is?" He guarded his thoughts well.

No. I can't see faces, only shapes and auras – I guess that's what they are, anyway… They may have spoken but I didn't hear. I was too freaked out.

"Calm down." He tried to sound soothing, but his mind was reeling. "I can feel your fear…" He stopped himself, but the thought broke through *…and I* don't *like it…* Something dark stirred against his barriers. He pulled them up tighter. "We need to get you out of… here." We moved toward the door.

What is it you feel the need to bury so deeply? I get the impression if you were more open to this, you wouldn't have to talk out loud. If you trusted me, I think I could hear your thoughts instead.

"Yeah… we've really gotta get you out of my head." As before, he ignored everyone in the hall and made his way to the stairs.

I continued to cling to him and caught a glimpse of the red door through his eyes. When I looked again, I saw a white outline, as if some great light existed beyond.

Are you seeing this? Can you see what I'm seeing? Or do your barriers keep that out, too?

He didn't answer. We — *er, he* — knocked, and the door swung open.

The brilliance of the light stunned me, and Derik stumbled into the room. The door closed behind us.

"Well, hello, Derik. I see you've brought Haylee back to herself? This is highly unorthodox, though I do appreciate the consideration."

The relief I felt at hearing Sabella's voice washed over Derik. His walls slackened and some of his thoughts slipped through to me.

You think she's baiting you.

He ignored me. "Can we just get her out of my head?"

As he moved closer to her, I felt a vibrating. I looked through his eyes and saw the back of my chair. He placed his hands on it. The vibrations were too much for me to bear.

"I don't think we will have any trouble getting her back where she belongs. Though there could be some disorientation for both of you. I believe you're already feeling it. It will be a much smoother ride for her if you touch her."

Derik went around the chair and everything blurred. The vibrations were so strong I could no longer focus my energy on sight. He fell to his knees.

Can he feel it, too? Or is he just eager to be rid of me?

He reached out.

And I was water. I was air. I was flowing back into myself. It would have been amazing if it hadn't been so painful. I was ripped away from him. Everything was moving.

Why does it hurt so much? Like I'm being torn apart.

There was a flash of red and everything went dark. I was very heavy and very aware of everything that touched me. The pressure of the chair against my back and the floor beneath my feet. A weight on my hand. A connection there.

I forced my eyelids open. A hand lay across mine. I trailed my gaze up the attached arm. Derik stared back at me.

Is he half as tired as I feel?

He removed his hand from mine, and I had the urge to touch his face.

I tried to rise up from the chair, but I couldn't move. "Wow."

"You're telling me…" He sank down to a sitting position at my feet.

"I'm sorry. I didn't mean for any of this to happen… I was trying to find my safe place and then that darkness…" I shivered. "Sabella, I saw something terrible. Someone here is *not* what they seem."

"I know. I heard everything. You spoke your thoughts aloud and showed physical signs of your emotions. I feared for your safety, but there was nothing I could do. I cannot imagine what it was like to actually feel that fear." She looked down to Derik.

He wouldn't meet her eyes.

"Do you know who it is?" I asked her.

She stared at Derik for another moment before answering. "Alas, I do not. Though it does cause me worry. Derik, what are your thoughts?"

He glanced up at her. "What? My thoughts on the identity of our mysterious black hole? I don't know. If Haylee hadn't been so genuinely afraid, I might have thought she was imagining things… Truthfully, after the fact, I'm not so convinced."

I opened my mouth to speak.

"Don't worry, I'll still keep my eyes open for signs. I'm not stupid."

Sabella nodded. "Good. Now. There is something else we must discuss. It involves you both. Nothing like this has ever happened before. There may be repercussions."

"What do you mean, repercussions?" Derik growled.

"Well, the two of you already shared a connection before – oh, come now, Derik, you felt it – but it may be a bit more pronounced after this."

I finally managed to sit up, and he pulled a little further away. "What do you mean? What does she mean?" I asked.

She answered. "Being a part of someone in that manner is a very rare thing. Whatever connection the two of you shared before can only be strengthened by it."

"But I don't understand… What connection?" I frowned.

"She thinks we're each other's Other Half."

I felt my jaw drop. "Wha – How? You mean, the mate theory I've heard about? That's not possible… Is it? I mean, Nate's your mate, right?"

He looked up at me with raised eyebrows. "You're serious." He let out a short laugh.

I jumped.

"Nate. Me and Nate? Just because I'm around her more often than other women, they all assume we're mated." His smile faded. "What, a man and woman can't – " He glanced at me and looked away, clearing his throat. "Never mind. It doesn't matter. *We*," he indicated us, "are not connected. And that's that."

I tried not to be hurt by his flat-out refusal of the notion.

Not that it matters, but what's so bad about the idea of us being connected. Without all the "Other Half" stuff, it wouldn't be that *terrible, would it?*

Sabella interrupted my musings. "Well, you know it is not for me to say who is the other half of whom, as that is for you to discover in your own time. Either way, you cannot deny a connection, whether you like it or not."

Derik rolled his eyes and proceeded to get up off the floor.

"Well, Little Miss Haylee, I believe our exercise is over for today. You will need to rest for a few days before we attempt anything else. These sessions will take a lot out of you, as you will see. I believe we should alternate them with the training Derik will be providing." She turned her attention to him again. "If she is ready tomorrow, begin her lessons, Derik. If not tomorrow, then the next day should be adequate."

I pulled myself out of the chair and used it for stability. "Thank you again, Sabella. I've never experienced anything like this before. I hope it wasn't all for nothing."

She smiled. "I think not. You found what you needed, so we will move on from there. In regards to this unknown person among us, the first line of defense is knowing the threat exists." Then she frowned and turned once more to Derik. "Keep this one safe, Derik. Keep her safe."

He met her eyes for a moment and turned abruptly toward the door.

I did feel more connected to him than before, but still was unsure of what that meant, as I followed his example in leaving the room.

5

I did not see Derik at all the following morning. That was fine with me since it gave me time to gather my thoughts, which were scattered every which way. Plus, I was still worn out from my psychic excursion. I ate my breakfast without any event or outburst. Though I knew a few eyes were on me and heard some whispering, I kept my head down, my eyes on what I was doing.

When I had finished, I didn't know what to do with myself. Also, I wasn't sure what was expected of me. I couldn't go back to my bed, only to come out to eat. I had to earn my keep. I couldn't take from these people without giving something back. And they could use the help, I was sure, even if all I could do were little things. Besides all that, I was afraid I might go crazy – if I hadn't already – if I didn't take action. I had to do something to take my mind off black holes and mystical connections. So, after a short period of wandering amongst all the determined faces heading toward their appointed places, I resolved to find some work to do.

I started upstairs, flattening against the nearest wall whenever someone passed, so as not to be in anyone's way. I found myself in the room leading to the roof and climbed the ladder into the sunlight.

As on the first day, the roof was busy. People washed and hanged laundry and worked in the gardens. The guards at each corner of the building were all new faces to me. The shifts must have already rotated for the early part of the day. Where the children had been gathered before, three women sat grinding something in small bowls.

So where can I help?

As I walked around, most people avoided my gaze. *I guess it's hard to trust people in these times, though I'm obviously not a Pale One and couldn't easily overpower any of them.*

I made my way to one of the gardens and was about to turn back to the ladder, when someone caught my eye. A woman had stopped working and was shielding her eyes from the morning sun in order to see me more clearly.

She smiled. "Hello. Were you looking for someone?"

"Oh, no." I stepped closer. "More like some*thing*. Something to do, I mean." I glanced over her tools and the garden. "Could you use some help?"

The woman looked at the garden before her and toward the one on the other side of the building, the garden which had held everyone's fascination the day before, then back to the one she was working. "Well, I'd say this garden could use all the help it can get." She gave a small laugh. "Here you go." She handed me a tool.

I took it from her. "Really?"

The woman's smile widened. "Uh-huh." She gave a slight nod and picked up another tool.

I chose a spot on the opposite side of the garden and began working. Time passed by quickly, as I fell into the rhythm of the work and let it calm my nerves. For the moment, I could forget the events of the last few days and focus on what I was doing. I was working in the little garden behind Aunt Bethany's farmhouse, where I was raised. And she was right there across from me, as we worked in silence, sharing in our own form of meditation. I was so engrossed in the memory, I didn't notice when the sun had moved from its highest point in the sky, until a voice brought me back to reality.

"Girl. Girl?" the voice called. It was the woman across from me. "You should call it quits before you burst into flame," she said, a pleasant expression on her face.

I blinked at her, confused for a moment, before I realized what she meant. My skin was on fire. I had been out in the sun for much too long. I dropped the tool I was using to study my arms, and looked back to her.

"It's all right," she said. "We're pretty well finished here. Go on now. And put some burn cream on your skin. That should help." She smiled.

"Thank you." I stood and made my way to the ladder.

* * *

I found my way to the infirmary without incident. By that, I mean without literally running into anyone.

Ouch. I don't even want to think about that.

I closed the door behind me and walked to the cabinet across the room.

Upon closer inspection, I discovered every tube and bottle was labeled.

Okay… pain, nausea, headache… Oh, burns!

I twisted off the cap. It smelled a little like the aloe I had used a few days ago on my less serious sunburn. I gently patted some onto my skin and the cooling sensation was immediate. When I finished, I placed the bottle back on the shelf and closed the cabinet doors.

Spending the remainder of the day outside was out, so I was stuck with wandering again. I studied my surroundings more thoroughly than before. The big dingy yellow bricks making up the hallway walls, the cracked tiles of the floor. All of these things brought back memories of my days at Midworth Middle School. I was amazed by how much it had changed without becoming unfamiliar.

How much time has passed? How much time before everything changes? A hundred years? Two hundred? Five? What exactly set this in motion? How did the world react to the Amara's existence? With doubt? Fear? How did their presence become known? Or should I say how would *their presence become known?* I stopped in my wanderings. *None of this has happened in my world, my time. Not yet. Can it be stopped? Is there anything* I *can do to stop it?*

For the first time, I felt the *urge* to go home.

Is that even possible?

I stopped in front of the cafeteria, directly across from the smaller entry hall, and stared in that direction for a while. Without the light from the cafeteria windows, that venue was much darker. I glanced behind me and took a deep breath before starting toward the shadows.

I have to see for myself.

By the time I was out of direct sight of the cafeteria, I could see small amounts of light filtered through the cracks of the boarded up windows at the front of the building. The glass-paned doors had been replaced at some point with large, heavy-looking, windowless ones. Little light permeated the main hall. When my eyes had adjusted, I could make out what used to be the trophy cases lining the entryway. The glass had broken years before, so not a jagged edge remained.

The sunlight will be reflecting off the doors, in my time. The cases will be full right now. Basketball and cheerleading trophies. It's strange to think of then and now as happening at the same time. Time travel should be a theoretical concept to me. But now *is the future, and the past is also my* present. *Ugh.* I shook my head. *I can't think about that right now.*

I moved away from the cases and saw two guards, one on each side of the barricaded door. I knew they could see me. My eyes were dazzled by the pinpricks of light coming through the cracks, but they stood with their backs to that light, their eyes well adjusted.

Am I even allowed this close to the main doors? They haven't tried to stop me. Oh, I hope they don't think I'm weird for staring at the old trophy cases. My cheeks burned, but I kept moving toward them.

As I got closer, I could see at least one of them kept his eyes on me at all times. And my heart kicked up a bit. I stopped a few feet away.

"H – hello," I said.

The two men exchanged glances.

The one who had been staring smiled. "Hi."

I didn't know what to say for a moment. "Um, my name's Haylee." And I almost offered my hand to shake but realized theirs were quite full of whatever kind of rifle they each held.

"My name's Gamut," the smiling man replied, his smile becoming a grin. "I've heard a little bit about you. Karroll's my sister," he explained.

"Oh! It's nice to meet you. Karroll seems nice. Where is she now?"

"Well, we're on different shifts, so she's sleeping right now. This is Grange, by the way." He gestured to the man to his right.

Grange was one of the larger guys I had seen so far, almost as tall as Derik though stouter. He nodded in my direction and returned his attention back down the hall.

"So, Gamut, do you only guard these doors? Or do you get moved around? How does that work, exactly?"

"Grange and me are assigned shifts here at the main door, for now. We switch off with two other teams every eight hours, about four hours from now. The other positions are the same. Three – sometimes four – teams of two, switching off every six to eight hours. That way no one's too tired. Each team's assigned position hardly ever changes. We've been on the roof once a few months back and now we're assigned main door duty. We'll be here everyday for the next six months or so." He shrugged.

Hm. That sounds like something Derik would have instituted. "Everyday? You don't get a day off or anything?" I asked.

Gamut frowned. "A day off? I don't understand. Why would we get a day off?"

"Uh, never mind. So how does the changing of the guards, or whatever, work?"

"Well, the new guys show up, and we leave. It's nothing spectacular. Just necessary."

"I think I'd like to see that though." And I was sincere. I was very interested in seeing how they switched off.

Gamut's frown disappeared, and one corner of his mouth shot up. "Come back around in a few hours, and you'll get to see it."

"Really? I'm not a bother or anything? I don't want to distract you from your work."

"A bother?! No! And if you want, you can come around a bit earlier. It gets boring toward the end of a shift."

I nearly melted at his hopeful look.

How can I say no to that? "Uh, okay. I'll come by early if I can." *But really, what* else *am I going to do with my time?*

He smiled wide again, and I realized how young he was. He couldn't have been much older than me. *Definitely no older than nineteen.*

"That's golden!" he said.

I felt a quick frown at his choice of words and gave a lopsided smile, as I awkwardly backed away. "Cool. All right then. I'll see you later."

He didn't take his eyes off me, as I turned to leave. "I'll see ya'."

I winced as I made my way back toward the cafeteria. *Did I make a date with Karroll's brother? How'd I manage that? I didn't mean to. And why's he* so *interested in me?*

I was so involved with silently chiding myself, I narrowly missed colliding with Derik.

"Do you ever watch where you're going?" he asked without much feeling. Then he glanced behind me and frowned. "Where were you just now?"

I followed his gaze. "Oh. I, well, was getting to know the layout of the place, I guess, and ended up at the main door. I met Gamut and Grange."

"Oh, you did, did you?" His frown didn't lessen but he did wrinkle his nose. "Why do you smell like aloe?"

"I do? I didn't realize it was so strong." I raised my arm up to my nose but could barely smell the cream. "You can smell that?"

"Yes. But don't worry. It's very unlikely anyone else can. But *why* do you smell of it?" he asked again.

I lowered my arm slowly. "Well, I needed something to do earlier, so I helped out in one of the gardens. I was out in the sun for too long. I burn easily."

He stood back from me for a moment. "I see."

Does he mean that literally*? The light's too dim for* me *to see my skin clearly.*

"Well that would certainly explain the extra heat radiating from your skin. Anyway, I've been looking for you. I was going to ask if you were ready to start training, but I doubt that burn would allow for much contact with anything. I understand it can be quite painful." His regard was unexpected. But then he straightened, and it was gone. "You should be more careful. Since you can't start training today, I'll ask Glenna to give you a few lessons in first aid. It's as important as self-defense in this place." He eyed me. "And I can see it might be especially important for *you*." He started to leave.

"Wait. Did you find out anything more about…" I lowered my voice and looked around us. "The black hole thing?"

He sighed. "I asked Glenna what people she spoke to, but she says she asked pretty much everyone my whereabouts and has no way of remembering who was in what room at that time." He started to move again. "I'll talk to her about the first aid. Expect her to be looking for you later in the day. And for all that is good in the world, try to keep yourself in one piece in the meantime." And he was gone before I could retort.

I stood there, blinking. Then I shook my head and looked around the hall. The cafeteria was across from me. My stomach growled, and I rolled my eyes.

Didn't I just eat? I shuddered at the sound of the chatter and turned away from it. *It's quieter upstairs.* I paused at the bottom of the stairs and glanced toward the basement door.

What's down there? I stepped forward but stopped when a chill ran up my spine. *And why do I feel the urge to run the other way?* I straightened my back and reached for the doorknob. It was locked. My shoulders sagged with relief. *Oh, thank God! I really don't want to go down there… but I would have.* I shivered and returned to the foot of the stairs.

As soon as I was out of view of the door, I heard it open and close. The lock clicked. Footsteps moved further down the hall, and I peaked out to see Nate's retreating figure.

What is she doing down there? What's *down there?* I frowned and looked at the door again. *Oh, forget it! There's nothing you can do about it. You're not supposed to go down there. Besides, it's locked!*

Nate turned into the cafeteria, a tray in her hand.

Who's the food for? She isn't eating in the basement, is she? After another glance at the door, I shrugged and headed upstairs.

It's still a while before I see Gamut, so maybe I'll check out one of the rec rooms.

The room I had passed on my first day was open.

Huh, no one else here.

A small table and chairs took up the center of the room, and several battered armchairs were scattered along the walls. When I moved further into the room, I noticed a bookshelf. Books and magazines were haphazardly stacked on it's shelves. I moved closer to discover many of the books were middle school textbooks.

Hm. Most of them are missing their covers. Luckily, the other books were hardcover versions, so they weren't in as bad a shape as they could have been. I pulled one from the shelf and could make out the words "Fairy Tales."

Cool. I took the book over to one of the softer chairs and curled up. A few of the pages stuck together as I riffled through them. *Cinderella, Sleeping Beauty, Snow White and the Seven Dwarves, even Little Red Riding Hood. Okay. The Brothers Grimm, then.* I looked at the cover again but couldn't make out any other words. The type inside the book was just legible. I turned to the first story and began reading.

* * *

By the time I had finished with the book, the room was noticeably darker.

Too dark to read anything else. Time to go see Gamut and Grange. I placed the book back on the shelf and left the room.

Downstairs, people were up to their usual purposeful movements, some hurrying through dinner. My stomach growled again, as I rushed by the cafeteria once more. By the time my eyes adjusted to the new dimness, I was near the main door.

"Hey! You came!" Gamut said.

I smiled at his reaction and laughed when Grange followed with an annoyed sigh.

"Yep. I said I would." I stopped in front of him and blushed a little when he didn't look away. "Did I miss anything?"

"Nope. Nothing. We'll be relieved soon." He paused, glancing down. "I was wondering… If you haven't eaten yet… Would you want to, um… Would you have dinner with me?"

"Uh, sure. I'd love to eat dinner with you… I mean, if you want." My heart was beating a little fast. *I wish he wouldn't stare at me like that.*

"Of course! I'll walk with you to the cafeteria, when the others take our place. It shouldn't be long now. I was so sure you wouldn't make it." He laughed.

Why is he *so nervous?* "I'll just sit over here." I pointed to the closest of the old trophy cases. As I climbed up, I took a deep breath. *Is he still staring? Oh, don't be stupid. He's working.* I pushed myself as deep into the case as I could and waited.

Their replacements were early, and a larger figure approached behind them.

Does he oversee each changing of the guard?

Derik eyed me, as he passed by. "Grange. Gamut." He nodded to them. "Making a round for the afternoon. Have you noticed anything out of the ordinary?" He climbed onto a window ledge to peer over the boards and was tall enough to see without stretching.

I couldn't help but stare at him as he made the fluid movement up. *Effortless.* My heart was racing now, and I struggled to catch my breath.

Grange answered him. "No, sir. Nothing. Gamut?"

"Huh?" Gamut had been watching me.

My cheeks flushed. *I hope he didn't notice my reaction to Derik.*

"Uh, no." He glanced at Derik, then slid his eyes back to me. "Nothing important's escaped my sight."

My eyes widened. *Really?!* I dipped my head and hid my face from view. *Sheesh. What's with this guy?*

"*Right,*" Grange said.

Derik's feet hit the floor, and I jumped. He gave Gamut a look through narrowed eyes but continued past the two of them. "Switch off."

They handed their weapons over to the other men I had nearly forgotten.

Gamut reached a hand out to me. "Shall we?" His eyes met mine.

I couldn't help but smile at his directness. "Sure, why not." And I allowed him to help me down from the trophy case. It was another moment before he released my hand.

Grange was following Derik up ahead of us, as we made our way toward the cafeteria, and threw a look over his shoulder. It wasn't exactly nice, but it wasn't menacing either. More like something an annoyed friend might do.

I leaned toward Gamut. "What's Grange's deal?"

"Oh, him? He's just a killjoy. He thinks I wasn't taking the job seriously enough because you were distracting me." He smiled.

I glanced at him in alarm. "I'm sorry. I didn't mean to –"

He stopped me. "Hey don't worry about it. I'm not gonna say you weren't a distraction. A welcome one." His smile was shy now. "But I take the work seriously. I wouldn't do it if I didn't. Besides, he's jealous." And he continued walking.

I stood grounded for a second, then followed. "Jealous? Why?"

He laughed and rolled his eyes. "Seriously. Come on, I'm starving." He led me into the cafeteria.

I glanced back into the hall and saw Derik standing, arms crossed, in the shadows.

Does he disapprove of me being by the main door? Or does he dislike Gamut for some reason? And why does it matter? He's not my father.

I returned my attention to Gamut. Even in the diminishing light, I could see better than in the hall. Now I could make out more than his size. He was a foot taller than me, and lean. But now I could see the shade of his warm skin and his dark eyes. Dimples formed in his cheeks when he smiled, and he never stopped smiling, as far as I could tell. We went through the line together, and I tried to remain oblivious to the stares around us.

"So, what were you thinking about earlier?" he asked, as we sat.

"When?"

His smile broadened at my blank stare. "The first time you came to the main door. When you stood at that section out of the wall?" He gestured over his shoulder.

I looked down embarrassed, as I remembered hoping they hadn't noticed.

"I'm sorry. I didn't mean to be – well, yes, I guess I did mean to be nosey," he said. "You don't have to tell me."

I felt guilty. "No, it's not that… Um, do you know anything about me? I mean, have you heard how I came to be here?" I put my spoon down.

He blushed a little but kept eye contact with me. "Well, I've heard a few things being tossed around…" He noticed my eyes widen and rushed on. "But I don't believe most of it. Karroll said she spoke to you, and you told her what really happened. Though, to tell the truth, I wouldn't have believed it from anyone else." He reached across the table and rested his hand on mine. "It's an amazing story."

"Yeah." I exhaled a quick breath and did my best not to pull my hand away, afraid of hurting his feelings. When I did pull it back, I moved it to my spoon to continue eating. I looked down at my bowl, as I spoke. "I was just thinking – well, those spaces in the walls used to be trophy cases." I glanced up at him.

He frowned for the first time. "Trophy cases? Really. Huh. I guess that makes sense. What kind of trophies?" He started eating his food again.

"Oh, well, different sports, mostly. Baseball, softball, basketball, a few track and field, and some cheerleading. And there may have been one for an academic competition and a few music awards, too."

He perked up some more. "Oh! I've read about baseball! Seen some pictures in a book upstairs. That's the one where you hit the ball with the stick, right? They called it a bat?"

"Yeah, that's the one." I nodded.

"What's cheer – cheerleading?"

I stopped eating. I had never been much into sports in school, so I wasn't the most qualified person to be answering these questions but did my best. "Well, it's basically the group of people, girls mostly, trained to cheer for the sports teams at school. They practiced as much as the other athletes but had pompoms and jumped around in these little – never mind, you wouldn't be interested in it." I started eating again.

"Oh, I don't know… That sounds like something I'd be interested in," he smiled.

"Oh, ha. Things really *don't* change."

"You still haven't told me what you were thinking though."

I paused again and pushed the nearly empty bowl aside, as I collected my thoughts. "Well." I sighed. "So, you believe the whole time-travel thing, then?" I looked at him.

His eyes turned grave. "If Sabella says it's so, then I believe. But what's more important is do you believe?" He had moved his bowl to the side as well and placed his hands around mine, holding them in place.

That alone would have made me nervous.

Why does he have to look at me like that? My heart's racing. Are my palms sweating? I glanced down at my hands. *Shoo, no. That'd be embarrassing. Still, this is* nothing *compared to my reactions to Derik. And* why *am I thinking of Derik right now, anyway? Just shake it off…*

I took a deep breath and answered his question. "It makes sense to me. I guess. Though I never imagined experiencing anything like this. It seems… logical? I don't know, but… yes. I do believe it. Besides, it's hard to argue with Sabella." I couldn't force a laugh.

So much has happened… is *happening. Oh,* God.

"It's overwhelming." With that admission, I slumped over and dropped my head down between my arms. The table cooled my warm face.

Gamut moved his hand to my hair and smoothed it down. "I'm sorry. I didn't realize. I should have but I didn't. That'd be really tough." He lowered his voice, as he moved closer to me. "But don't worry, please. You have friends here. Glenna, Sabella, Karroll, Merritt… and me. Anything you need, anything at all. Don't hesitate." He hand stopped moving. "And I'm sure Derik cares for your well-being to some degree, as closely as he's been watching us these last few minutes."

I raised my head, causing Gamut's fingers to trail through my hair, and followed his gaze.

Derik walked toward us, and Gamut once again rested his hands over mine.

But I pulled back from him, as Derik got closer.

"Has Glenna spoken with you?" he asked.

I shook my head.

"She says she's unable to 'attend' to your first aid training today. She asked me to do it but – "

"But you don't have time, right?" I said.

Derik glanced between Gamut and me before continuing. "Actually – "

"Hey, that's all right," Gamut interrupted. "I know the workings of the infirmary forwards and backwards. I can show Haylee everything she needs to know."

Derik hesitated, and a frown flashed across his face before he blinked it away. I watched as he opened his mouth and closed it again. He swallowed and a muscle in his jaw twitched.

I was fascinated by this show of… well, it wasn't exactly emotion but the closest I'd seen in Derik. *Is this his version of fidgeting? Is he* fidgeting*? No. Couldn't be. He's not nervous. He's… angry? Yeah, that fits him more.*

He took a deep breath and closed his eyes. When he let it out, his voice was low and his words carefully spaced. "Is that what you want?"

My mouth fell open. *He's asking me what* I *want?* I glanced at Gamut. He gave me a tight smile.

Oh, and look at those puppy-dog eyes. I don't want to hurt his feelings.

Derik wasn't looking at me. His eyes were pointed toward the table between us.

And I don't see why he *would care what I did. As long as it doesn't cause any more trouble…* "I guess, if it's okay, Gamut could show me?"

Gamut beamed at me. "Well, yeah, it's okay! We'll head straight over!"

I turned to Derik, who still wasn't looking at me. He straightened. "Great. Get to it then. We should start self-defense tomorrow."

"Uh, okay." I watched him leave.

"So. Are you ready to get started?" Gamut asked, regaining my attention.

"Sure. As soon as you are."

And we headed out.

Once we were in the infirmary, Gamut lit some lanterns, and the room was as bright as if we had flipped a switch.

"It's too bad we don't have electricity," I commented.

"Oh. Well, we could, but we don't have any light bulbs so… But we've got somebody working on that," he replied.

"What do you mean we *could*?" I perched on the examination table.

"Well, we do have an electrician. Someone who specializes in electricity," he clarified. "So, if we had the light bulbs, we could have the artificial lighting."

"Oh, really? How does that work? The electricity thing."

"We're not sure, it's their ability. They pull electricity from one place to another. They don't even need the wires, they can just sort of jump it."

"Oh. Well, that's pretty handy." I smiled. "Like a generator?"

"Yeah. And you should see him in a fight. Now *that's* something." He was standing close to me now, and his smile faltered as he realized how close.

"Um. What do *you* do?" I asked.

He blinked and moved a little ways away. His smile blazed again.

"A little bit of this, a little bit of that," he joked. "No, seriously, mine's not all that useful. Well, it can be in some situations. I'm more productive in hand-to-hand situations, anyway. But it's more of a sensing, really… I can tell, or feel, when I'm being watched. It's weird, a little tingling at the back of the neck, the base of the skull." He wiggled his fingers behind his head. "Kind of like goosebumps, I guess. I can feel their eyes on me, whoever it is, and I have an idea of where they're watching from. You know?" He didn't look at me.

"Kind of a heightened sense of awareness, huh? You hear about things like that, to a degree. I mean an instinctive thing. Yours is, like, what? Several times over?"

"Well, yeah…" He glanced up and caught my look of fascination. "I guess I forgot you're not from here… you know what I mean."

I remembered something. "Is that what happened in the cafeteria? You felt Derik watching us? Before you saw him, I mean?"

"Yeah… He was there for a little bit before he started walking toward us. I'm not sure why he didn't come up right away, unless…" he trailed off.

I frowned and shook my head a little. "Unless what?"

"Unless he didn't like me touching you? I don't know…" He shrugged it off. "It was probably nothing. Don't worry about it. Let's get started, okay?" He moved over to one of the cabinets and pulled a few things out. Then, he looked up. "Do you know CPR?"

I slid off the table. "Actually, I do. I had to for a job I had last summer… well, it's been almost a year, anyway." I walked over to the work surface he was spreading things across.

"Oh… too bad." He was carefully watching what he was doing. "I was hoping we might work on that."

Oh, really!? I gave his shoulder a playful backhand. "Gamut."

He looked up at me. "What? You can't blame a guy for trying." He laughed and went back to his work.

We spent the next hour going over the various medicines in the infirmary. He told me what worked for what ailment, how to properly care for wounds of various degrees. The worst wounds didn't make it to the infirmary. Glenna, more often than not, attended other serious injuries. Most of what I learned, I'd already known, or was common sense stuff I could've guessed. However, many of the bottles and tubes contained medicines I'd never heard of, so the training was necessary.

When he was putting things back in their proper places, he pulled a familiar tube from the shelf. "This is the burn ointment you said you used earlier? It's made from the aloe plant. We grow it up on the roof, so we can make more. I'm telling you this, so you'll feel free to come use it as necessary. And so you won't object to using more now." He gave me a look. "Sit. Please."

I followed his directions and tried not to laugh at his somberness.

He saw this and grinned. "Come on, now. If you're going to be training with Derik tomorrow morning, you're gonna need this. The pain may have subsided enough by then."

My feet dangled above the floor again. *Derik's right, I've already been in here too much.* "I'm not saying I'm not willing to use it. It's… well, I *can* do it myself, you know."

"Yeah, yeah. But I can do a better job of it. You missed some spots last time, I'm sure. And you were timid in your application, so…" He gestured with the tube.

"Oh, all right. I can't argue your logic, I guess."

"Good. Now this won't hurt… much." He smiled in mock malice and pulled my right sleeve out of the way. His fingers were gentle and the cream was cool.

I sighed.

"See? Aren't you glad you listened to me?" He followed with the left arm. "Let me check under your hair, okay?" He slid my hair over my shoulder.

I felt his fingertips skirt the neckline of my shirt and barely managed to suppress a shiver.

"How's that feel? Hurt at all?"

I shook my head because that's all I could do.

"That's good. I don't see anything there." I could feel his breath on my neck, and then he pulled away. "Okay, you can put your hair back now." In front of me again, he studied my face and smiled. "Your poor red face… and I can still tell when you're blushing," he teased. "Here." He applied some more of the ointment to his fingertips and gently touched them to my forehead, cheeks, and nose.

I was afraid to breathe.

When he was finished, he stood and stared at my face for another moment. A look of amazement covered his. "I'm not sure I've ever seen skin like yours on a human being."

I tensed, even though I understood what he meant. Most of the people here spent a great deal of time working in the sun, so the lightest skin was well tanned.

"I know you're not one of them, don't worry. Even under the sunburn, your complexion's healthy-looking. You know? Not that they don't burn. Just that their skin… it's colorless, um…"

"Sallow?"

"Yeah, that's a good word for it. Anyway, I understand how things have changed… But I don't think I've ever known anyone to burn so easily. It's just… even as red as you are right now, you're so…" He let out a small laugh and lowered his eyes to the tube in his hand. "I'm sorry. That's… I shouldn't think things like that." He replaced the lid, as he turned and put the tube away.

This time I *forgot* to breathe. *What? What shouldn't you think? What's* with *this place? People never act like this around me. Maybe this* is *Wonderland.*

"You should be set." He turned back to me with a smile. "I should be getting to bed. Need some rest. No doubt you do too. You've got a long day tomorrow, I'm sure." He held out his hand.

I took it and slid off the table. "Thank you… for everything. With everything that's happened, I…" And I couldn't go on. I lowered my gaze to the floor.

"Hey. There's no need to thank *me*, Sunshine. You're like sunsh – I'm sorry… What?" he asked at the look on my face.

Shaking my head, I replied, "It's nothing." I didn't want to explain how much trouble I was having thinking of myself in terms of sunshine. I just couldn't see it.

Amused, he said, "I'll walk you upstairs, okay?"

I nodded, and he led me to the door.

Once we had reached the room where I slept, he put one hand under my chin. "I'm not going to say everything will be all right, okay? Just this. Everything will work out as it is meant to… And I've heard rumors you're meant for good things." He smiled as he met my eyes.

I laughed a little. "Really? And who is spreading these terrible, awful lies?"

"Don't you worry, all right? My source is legit." With that, he gave me a peck on the mouth. And before I could react, he said, "Now, get some rest, and I'll see you tomorrow." He tapped my chin with his knuckle and released the hand he had been holding. "Remember, I'm at the main door, same time everyday." He went to the next room, opened the door and, with one last glance, closed it behind him.

As was my habit since I awoke in this place, I stood dumbfounded.

Wow. What's happening here? After a moment, I did as he suggested and went to bed.

6

The next morning, my burn had diminished, and I felt more rested than any time since I had arrived. Derik found me shortly after breakfast and led me to an unoccupied room on the main floor. Various forms of swords, knives, and fighting sticks I had never seen before hung on its four walls.

"We'll go over some basics to start. Have you ever had any defensive training?" He stood before me, looking skeptical.

"Well, I signed up for a self-defense course at school but dropped it after the first day… Does that count?"

He gave me a look.

"No. I guess not," I said in a low voice.

He sighed. "Very well. I'll have to pretend you're a child. That shouldn't be very hard." He turned away and opened a cabinet on the nearest wall.

I placed my fists on my hips and charged after him. "Wait a minute. What? What is your problem anyway?" I was right up beside him. "Am I that much trouble for you? Why don't you just send me home? I could probably leave the way I came."

He turned to me and raised his eyebrows. "Are you angry?" He looked amused.

And that upset me more. "Yes. Of course I am! I don't know where I stand from one minute to the next with you. One moment I think you might care a little bit about my situation… maybe not me personally but still… and the next you're acting as if you're disgusted by my presence. You treat me like a child. Because I'm *smaller* than you? Because I don't know my way around your weapons?" I indicated the walls. "Why? I don't know… but I am *not* a child, you know. I don't like the way you treat me and I don't like the way you look at me sometimes. It's – it's demeaning, and I deserve to be treated better than – are – are you *laughing* at me?!" I frowned.

"I'm sorry. At least you've got the meaning of self-defense down." He chuckled.

My jaw dropped. "After all that, you're laughing at me? I – I can't believe… I…" I didn't know what to say, as I felt the anger ebbing into something more like heartache.

"Hey." His barely-there smile was wiped away. "Where's the anger? You need it." He tried to keep a hard edge to his voice. It faltered when a single tear slid down my face. "Great. That should answer your question. You're reacting like a child, don't you see?"

I ignored him. "I don't belong here… I'm not big, strong, or fast. I'm not good at anything useful. And I don't have an ability to make up for it." I paused for a moment before looking at him. "I want to go home." And maybe I said it a little impetuously but I didn't care.

Something crossed his face.

Was that pity? It was gone before I could place it.

Awkwardly, he placed a large hand on my shoulder. "Haylee…"

Has he even said *my name before?*

"It's too dangerous for you out there. You can't go home… you can't leave this place." He said it gently enough, but the words themselves were cruel.

I couldn't meet his gaze, didn't want to see that ruthless pity. "But I have to go home sometime. I can't stay here forever." I did look at him then. "You meant now, didn't you? I can't go home *now*, but maybe sometime soon. I could go out with you and a scouting party… you could drop me off where you found me. The next time you go out then?" I asked, trying to keep my desperation in check.

He shook his head. "No."

"No?!" My anger was returning to the surface. "What do you mean 'no'? I can't stay here forever. I have family, friends, neighbors who'll be looking for me. Worried. A house to take care of. And all you can say is *no*?" I threw his hand off my shoulder.

"I'm sorry, Haylee. It's for your own safety. I think your loved ones would understand…" The edge was coming back to his voice. "We should get started now." And he was himself again.

I let out a soft, irritated laugh. "Well, if you wanted me angry, you've succeeded. Ever since I met you, I'm either angry or completely thrown for a loop. Fine." I turned toward him again. "If I'm going to be here indefinitely, then I need the training. Let's get this over with."

"Good."

"But you should know, I'm heading back the first chance I get. With or without your say so. I'll do what I can to help around here until then. To make up for all the *messes* I've caused, all the disturbances to your *life*. After that, I need to go back. Not for myself but for everyone else." I lowered my eyes.

"Very well then. And *you* should know I'll *stop* you every chance I get. It's my duty to keep everyone here safe. Including you. Besides, it's very unlikely you could get past the guards stationed at every entry. No one does unless OK'd by me, or Glenna. Just so you know." He shrugged one shoulder.

"I got it," I said between my teeth.

The atmosphere was tense, as he lectured on self-defense before showing me a few moves. He explained how the techniques were meant to prevent anyone from hurting me, not to inflict injury on another. It was simply a way for me to keep my body under my own control and no one else's. I understood all of that, so he began by teaching me a few maneuvers, many of them easy twists and turns of the body in order to escape various holds.

At some point, the anger turned into tension of another sort, as his body continued to come into contact with my own. I wasn't sure if he felt it but I did. My heart had picked up a notch, in a way unrelated to the physical exertion. I was *sure* he could hear my heartbeat, though I didn't know how, and hoped he didn't attribute it to anything other than the workout. I wasn't used to this type of exercise, most exercise really, and he did seem aware of this fact. So, at one particular point, when my back was pressed to him and my heart was racing, he called it quits.

"I think that will do for today. You're able to fight me off less and less all the time." He released the arm he had twisted behind my back.

My arms fell to my side and still I leaned against him. I was out of breath, and my limbs were Jell-O. He was being nice when he said "less and less", when I hadn't been able to escape his grasp at all for the last ten minutes.

"Don't worry," he said, "you'll do better." He carefully placed his hands on either side of me and held me away from him. "You should sit for a while."

"I'll try." I tried to make it sound like a joke.

My legs trembled, and I would have fallen to the floor had his hands not held me up. He kept my descent to the floor slightly more graceful and crouched in front of me.

"Thanks," I said, once I was sitting. In an attempt to avoid meeting his gaze, I noted that his skin revealed not a single bead of perspiration. While my hair was plastered to my face.

"You're not angry with me still?" He bowed his head to capture my attention.

"Not at the moment. I think I'm too tired to be angry with anyone." I smiled meekly.

He smiled back. "You did well, kid." Then winced. "Sorry. But you did do well… held out much longer than I would have given you credit for. And that's saying something." He looked at me for a moment and started to get up. "I'll get you some water."

"No. I'm all right…" I didn't want to take the remaining water from anyone who needed it more or deserved it.

"You're dehydrated… Don't be stupid. I'll bring you just enough. Don't worry how much we have left. We'll be going out in a day or so to bring back more. I'll be right back." And he left the room.

I didn't argue. I couldn't have if I'd wanted to. So I sat there and waited for him to return. I didn't have to wait long.

"Here you go." He gave me a small container. "Drink it slowly."

I did my best to sip the water, as I realized how thirsty I was. My hands still shook, but I managed not to lose any of it. When I was finished, I handed the cup back to him.

"Better?"

I nodded.

"Good. I spoke with Glenna in the cafeteria and asked her to get a shower ready for you. You're gonna need it." He chuckled and brushed a wet strand of hair out of my face.

I glanced up at him, and his hand lingered. He had put his shirt back on, but I was reacting to him as if he hadn't. We were both silent for a moment, until he pulled his hand away and cleared his throat.

"Ah, Glenna will be waiting for you on the roof… But before you go, Sabella *did* ask me to give you a crash course on what I've learned about the Pale Ones. You know most of it now. Except one thing. And it's important. So I need you to listen." He waited, making sure that sunk in.

I blinked at the change of gears and frowned. *Sabella said it was much worse… what could it be?*

"Good. I can see I've got your attention." He gave a short laugh and shifted his weight. "You know they steal the life of humans with a single touch… But the Amara also have the ability to take ordinary objects and turn them into poisonous creatures. Nothing large, mind you. But deadly."

What does that mean?

"Okay. For example." He held up the cup. "Take this. Though I don't think they've ever forged a cup into anything, it suits my purposes." He focused on it, turning it over and over in his hands. "The Amara can touch this — an innocuous ceramic vessel — and change it. And suddenly an unnaturally aggressive scorpion charges at you. One sting, and, within seconds, you could be paralyzed or in excruciating pain. Within minutes, you'd be dead. There's no antidote because, though your body reacts as if it's a typical poison, it isn't. It's — it's an Amara trick. They use it as an opportunity to drain you, when they feel you would be too difficult to subdue otherwise."

"If they can do that, why do they waste their time sabotaging your water and picking people off one at a time? Why not just send a swarm of these — these *creatures* over the walls." I shivered. "Sheesh. That would be pretty effective."

"It would be at that. But I think they rather enjoy messing with us. They don't want us dead. Well, at least not all at once. They think of humans like cattle, a food source. You don't wipe out your food source. You take one here and there and let the rest… well…" He raised his brows but averted his eyes.

"You let them breed, you mean." *Wow.* "What about *other* people? Other groups out here. They've got to be dealing with the same thing, right? Do you ever, I don't know, like, band together, or something?"

He brought his eyes back to mine. "There are no other people. We're the only encampment for a good thirty miles."

"No other people? There used to be… What happened to them?"

"The Amara happened. They can't risk humans, as you put it, banding together. It's like that all over the country."

I think it's beginning to sink in. I'm starting to understand the danger here. The scale. And why Derik is so hard. "How do they do it?" I pointed to the cup.

He took a deep breath and a moment to consider.

Is it that difficult to explain? Maybe he doesn't know…

"It's *speculated* they take energy and imbue it into the object. Bring it to life."

"Energy originally taken from humans? Used to hurt *more* humans?"

He regarded me before answering. "Yes. That seems to be the case."

"That — that's just..." I took in a shuddering breath.

"Yeah."

We were silent for a while until he spoke again.

"So, there you have it. The severity of your current situation."

"*Any* object?"

"Pretty much. Like I said, nothing big. You won't see them turning a chair into a cheetah or anything like that... But bigger isn't necessarily deadlier. Is it?"

My thoughts turned to images — courtesy of the internet — of brightly colored frogs and hostile spiders.

I shuddered. "Ugh. I hate spiders. And clowns." I smiled. "At least I don't have to worry about an *It* situation."

He chuckled again. "Can you get up yet?"

I blinked at first. *Can I?* My whole body felt weak but no longer trembled. "I think so." I set my feet flat on the floor.

"Here." He held out his hand.

I let him draw me up, and my shaky legs held.

"Okay?"

"Yeah. I'm good."

He pulled away.

I could still feel his touch and rubbed at my hand.

"Take the stairs slowly, all right? We don't want you in the infirmary again just yet." He paused. "Speaking of which. How did lessons with Gamut go last night?"

I couldn't decipher the tone of his voice. "Um. Fine. He was very helpful, I guess. There was a lot I already knew, but so much has happened, so even medicines have changed."

"Hm. I see." He sounded distracted. "Well, Glenna will be waiting, so..."

"I'll see you the day after tomorrow?"

He looked surprised. "Yeah. Though I thought you'd want more time. You'll be pretty sore."

"Well yeah, but I need this so... I'll be here. Same bat time, same bat channel?"

He frowned. "Huh?" Then he blinked several times, frowning into space. "Batman?"

Now it was my turn to be surprised. "Yeah! You know it?"

He tensed. "Um, I know *of* it."

"That's cool… Superman, too?"

"Uh… yeah. I doubt many people would know the reference you used, but there's a book upstairs on some of the old comics. You should be going though. I've got some stuff I need to do anyway." He changed the subject.

I guess he doesn't feel productive talking about superheroes.

"I'll meet you back here after breakfast in a couple days then." He ushered me out the door and closed it between us.

* * *

I was afraid if I stopped moving, I wouldn't be able to get the momentum I needed to go up the stairs, so I didn't linger in the door as I normally did after an exchange with Derik. The stairs were terrible, but I made it. I moved slowly to the room with the ladder and stared at it for a moment. Reluctantly, I pulled myself up the rungs and out into the sunlight. The sun was behind me, so I could make out the goings on of the roof. It wasn't crowded, and I located Glenna easily.

She stood near one of the small structures at the back of the building and waved me over. "Hello there. I hear you had quite a workout. I have the water ready for you, as well as a sheet and some fresh clothing. A few people donated a piece here and there. I'll have your clothes washed for you. Come."

She led me around a privacy wall, and I could make out the sound of running water through the curtain in front of me.

"The water's warm this time of day but not hot. So you should enjoy it. Go on." She started around the wall, then stopped. "Oh, I nearly forgot. Here." She pulled a small bottle from her pocket and handed it to me. "Use this after you wash your hair, leave it in. It will keep it tangle free and soft. It's part of my private stash. Keep it," she said, when I almost refused. "My gift to you. I'll be right over here." With that, she turned out of sight.

I undressed and piled my clothes away from the spray of water. I felt self-conscious in nothing but my own skin and stepped tentatively into the water flow. The pressure wasn't great but the water felt cool against my hot skin, and I stood there under the spray for a few moments before locating the cloth and soap. It felt good to rinse the sweat from my skin and work a rich lather into my hair. And the soap smelled nice. When I was satisfied with the cleanliness of my hair, I rinsed it and used the conditioner Glenna had given me.

It smells like honeysuckle! And it induced memories of home and made me smile. I allowed myself another moment under the water, which felt contentedly warm now, before I located the shutoff. Whoever was responsible for finding and bringing the water to the roof was deserving of my praise. When I stepped out, I found the large rectangle of fabric Glenna had left for me, wrapped myself in it, and noticed my pile of clothes had already been collected. I did my best to towel dry my hair, but it continued to drip, as I got dressed. The clothes, an old pair of cutoff jeans and a baggy shirt, fit me well enough. I knotted the shirt at my hip, since it was a little long, before I slipped back into my shoes and peaked around the privacy wall.

"Are you finished?" Glenna asked when she saw me.

I nodded.

"You look like you feel much better. If you wish, you may sit out here for a little while and allow the sun to dry your hair. We don't want you becoming ill. I have some things I need to attend to. Make sure you get something to eat and don't stay in the sun too long."

When she had gone, I moved to the front edge of the roof and settled onto my knees, resting my arms and head on the ledge. I studied the surrounding landscape more languidly this time and imagined what it looked like in my time. The grass greener, the blacktopped road busy and, more or less, cared for.

Where'd all the cars go*? Are they out there somewhere? Rusting away?*

I looked to my left.

The farmhouse would be out that way. I've never walked that far before though I've driven the roads between here and there. Of course, I won't be taking the roads this time, if there's even anything left of them. The walk couldn't take much more than thirty minutes. But can I make the trek alone if I have to? I hope so, because it doesn't look like anyone's gonna take me. And I have to get home… It's okay if I don't go tomorrow or next week, *but I have to go soon. I could wait a month. Maybe. People would still be worrying, searching for me, but what little I can do to help here, in* this *time, seems more important. Does Derik understand I'm willing to stay for a while? Wait! Why should I care* what *he understands? Oh, God, I hope I'm not falling for the guy.*

I'd been in a couple relationships before, with boys my age, and neither had lasted long, but Derik was no boy. Most certainly not.

Thinking about it made a flush rise through my cheeks.

And what about Gamut? He's so nice – much more pleasant than Derik – and definitely likes me. And his kiss? A friendly peck, I guess, but not on the cheek. What did it mean? *Has the etiquette on those kinds of things changed? Ugh, it doesn't even matter.* I sat up and shook my head. *I can't be more than friends with him. After I've done my part here, I* am *going home. He's not gonna like it any more than Derik did. Though I think Derik respects my determination and the fact that I was honest about it.*

I know how I feel about him, but how does Derik feel – Oh, I've got to stop thinking about him! It's so annoying! I sank back down. *Is it just chemistry? He has to feel it too. Right? Or does he really only see me as a child? Someone to protect and teach? The rare moments when he's tender toward me, is that the reaction of a parent-figure toward the child he's caring for? Oh, God!* I clamped my hands over my face. *I think I'm gonna be sick.*

Anger sprouted up again. *I am not a child! I'm almost eighteen goddam years old! Why can't he see that?! Maybe he doesn't want to.* I dropped my fists to the concrete ledge. *It doesn't matter. I'll get out of here and out of his hair. But how can I control my feelings and my body's reactions to him, in the meantime? I'll just have to stay away from him, avoid him when we're not training. I'll work more, spend more time with Gamut. Though I'll have to find a way to tell him we're only friends and not hurt his feelings. Oh, I hope I'm wrong about him. He barely knows me. I must have that kiss all wrong.* My shoulders fell, and I let out a breath. *Of course I do. Silly to think otherwise.* I rested my head on my arms and closed my eyes.

I stayed like that until the wind picked up and blew my hair back from my face, reminding me of where I was.

I yawned. *Better head back in.* A small groan escaped my lips, as I stood and stretched some stiffness away. A tickle at the back of my mind stopped me. I frowned. *It's kind of like the feeling Gamut described.*

The few people on the roof with me were focused on their work, and the guards looked out from their posts, so it didn't come from them. My gaze shifted beyond the roof to the landscape, and I backed away from the ledge. Nothing had changed. At least nothing I could see.

You're just being paranoid. There's no one watching you. Still… it's definitely time to head down.

I made my way down the ladder, which was worse than coming up it. My muscles complained the entire way. When I reached the hallway, I considered going to bed without eating but then pictured the looks on Glenna and Derik's faces.

Maybe they are *my parent-figures here. Ugh. Considering my reactions to Derik, that's a disturbing thought.* I shook my head to clear it of the idea. When I reached the steps, I glanced back to my room with its cots and solitude but braved the stairs instead. Each step was tedious, and my legs wobbled. *I'm glad I'm the only one in the stairway. Even if no one noticed, I'd be embarrassed.*

When I had my food, I plopped down in my seat and stared at my bowl for a few minutes. Finally, I picked up the spoon and lifted it to my mouth.

"Hi!"

The voice was right beside me, and I almost choked. I looked up to see Karroll, smiling.

"Sorry, I didn't mean to startle you. Do you mind if I sit with you?"

I swallowed. "No. Please." I indicated the empty seats around me.

"Thanks." She sat and began eating. "This is my breakfast, what meal are you on?"

"Lunch, I think… though I'm a little late. I trained with Derik for the first time today." I explained.

"Oh. Ouch." She winced. "Then you'll be feeling it right about now." She laughed a little. "Why are you training with Derik, anyway? I'd think they'd put you with somebody more suited to beginners. No offense. It's just, if you haven't been trained before… Well, Derik usually trains the advanced fighters. You know, the ones who are more likely to have to fight, mostly the big guys." She shrugged at this last part.

I looked at her for a moment. "Really? Huh. I think Sabella asked him to…" I looked down at my bowl again.

She was quiet for a few minutes, as she ate. "Huh." Then she put her spoon down. "Okay. What's going on between you and my brother, anyway?"

She had startled me again. Luckily, this time I wasn't eating. "Huh? Oh. Nothing I guess. He's nice… he gave me a first aid lesson." I looked at her.

She had her eyebrows raised, probably as high as they would go. "Uh-huh… 'nice,' 'first aid.' Riiiight." Her smile widened and she looked back to her food. "He really likes you. Can't stop talking about you. I don't know when it started. I guess when Derik brought you in. Most of us woke up because of all the commotion. The shift before

Gamut and Grange had started but, like most of us, he came out to see what the fuss was. I didn't notice until the other day how interested he was in you. But now he's met you and talked to you, and he won't shut up. It's cute but a little annoying. So… what about you?" She was looking at me.

"What about me? What do you mean?" I was mostly playing dumb, but wasn't exactly sure what she wanted me to say.

"What happened last night? He said you already knew CPR, so it wasn't that." She suppressed another laugh. "So, what happened?"

I continued studying my bowl. "Uh, well… he kind of kissed me?" My voice was low, barely audible. When she didn't say anything, I chanced a look up.

Her jaw had dropped. When she had pulled herself together, her expression was one of amusement. "Well, that's *bright.* He didn't tell me that part." She paused, a look of disbelief crossing her face. "He kissed you?"

I glanced around. "Shh! Not so loud, please," I whispered, leaning across the table toward her.

"Sorry, sorry." She lowered her voice and looked around furtively. "I don't think he's ever kissed a girl before." She started laughing again. "Ah, it's so cute. Little brother has a crush…"

I rolled my eyes, pretty much the only part of my body not too stiff to move.

"Well, you can hardly blame him, you know, or a few of the other guys, for that matter."

I just stared at her.

It was her turn to roll her eyes. "Oh, come on. You're pretty and you know it. Gamut goes on and on about your eyes – they're the same color as the sky, he says. Your newness is exciting. Not to mention you're so cute and petite," she added, the pitch in her voice rising.

"Ugh." I suddenly didn't want my food.

"What? What did I say?"

"You reminded me… That's all."

She looked at me questioningly.

"I – well… Where I'm from, I'm used to getting by on my averageness, you know? I mean, no one ever really notices me."

"Oh, I doubt that."

I sighed. "Anyway, I'm not used to attention, whether it's praise or criticism. And my size seems to be a critical fault to Derik. Which I get. Kind of. Size matters when you have no other way to contribute here. But he treats me like a child, and I can't get past that. I don't know. It doesn't matter, shouldn't matter… Never mind, it's stupid." I shook my head.

"No, it's not. Nobody likes to be treated like a kid. I should know, my brother – not Gamut but our older brother – still treats us like children, for the most part. If you think about it, maybe Derik's protective, like an older brother," she said, a knowing look in her eye.

"Oh, that's *great*… he's gone from guardian to big brother… Gotta love that." I hid my face in my hands.

"Yeah… That's how I thought you'd feel."

I peeked out at her. "Wh – what do you mean?"

"Oh, honey… That's part of my ability. Mainly useless but often amusing… I can sense or *feel* the energy between two people. It let's me know what kind of relationship they have… sometimes what kind they *will* have," she added, raising her eyebrows.

"What's that supposed to mean?" I sat very still.

"Haylee, every time I've seen the two of you together, the connection has gotten stronger. You're both fighting it like crazy, but it's there. It's like the energy pulling two opposing sides of a magnet toward each other, and the only thing keeping them from smacking together are the hands holding them apart." She demonstrated with her hands. "You and Derik are the magnets and the hands. The two of you are the only things keeping you from colliding into one another. Maybe literally." She smiled a little.

I didn't say anything but stared at her for a moment, my mind reeling.

"That's why I asked how you felt about my brother. He really likes you, but I see what's going on between you and Derik, though neither of you can. He can be an ass and a little overzealous sometimes, but I love my brother and don't want to see him get hurt."

"Believe me, Karroll, I don't want to hurt him. I was hoping I had misunderstood that kiss but I guess not. And as far as how I feel toward him… I like him, really do… If I didn't have the way I feel around Derik to compare it to, I'd say we could have something…" I blushed a little. "But it doesn't matter anyway, in either case, because I'm not going to be here very long. I do have to go home sometime and I can't commit myself to that kind of relationship if I'm not going to be here. It's not fair to anyone…"

"You're leaving? Well, I guess you'd have to…" She looked down at her food. When she looked up again, it was with a smile. "Well, we'll have to make the best of your time here, I suppose."

Her change in mood amused me. "Yeah, I guess so."

A little while later, Karroll rushed off to work.

I wonder what she does? Hm… and what am I going to do? I guess I could go see Gamut up at the main door.

When I arrived, he and Grange stood to the side, while five or six others were deep in conversation.

He waved me over with a smile, when he saw me. "Hey there, Sunshine."

"Hi…" The group held my attention. "What's going on?"

"Oh. Well, they're planning their next excursion for water. From the sound of it, they'll head out in a day or so. How did training go?"

I rolled my eyes and groaned. "As if you didn't notice how I hobbled up… I'll live, I guess."

He frowned. "He wasn't too hard on you, was he?"

"Derik? No, not at all. No more than he needed to be, I suppose." I shrugged and regretted the movement.

"Why don't you sit down for a while… at least until these guys leave?"

"All right. That sounds like a plan." I smiled at him. "I'll see you in a few…" So I climbed up into the nearest trophy case and leaned my head back.

The next thing I knew, Gamut was nudging my shoulder.

"Huh? What?"

He laughed. "You fell asleep."

I sat up and would have fallen to the floor if he hadn't caught me. I threw my arms out to catch myself, nearly as fast as his came around me. One of my arms made it to his shoulder, while the other was pinned between us, my hand at his chest. He settled me down to the floor but didn't remove his arms.

I swallowed the lump in my throat. "Thanks."

He gazed back and pressed me into the edge of the trophy case. "Thank *you*."

Oh, wow! My breath caught.

Before I could react, his mouth was on mine. His hands moved to the back of my neck, his fingers in my hair.

He's kissing me! Wait. What am I *doing? Am I kissing him back?* I couldn't stop. My mind and body were disconnected. *Control. Get control of yourself, girl.* I couldn't breathe and finally forced my face up into the cooler air.

Gamut trailed his mouth down my neck and stopped kissing me. He nuzzled his face in my hair.

"Gamut. We – we can't. Please."

He let out a big breath. "God, you smell good." His nose brushed my earlobe, as he pulled back. He wouldn't look at me right away, only at the floor. "I'm sorry… I shouldn't have done that here." He looked at me.

I blushed, and he smiled.

I laughed a little, my hand still at his chest holding him away. "No, I suppose you could have picked a better place…"

Before I could finish, he interrupted. "But you've gotta admit, it was good." He moved his hands to my waist.

"It was…it was… nice." I could see what Karroll meant – *overzealous* was a good term for Gamut – and glanced around us. While the trophy case had mostly blocked us from view, I could see the two figures standing guard did their best to ignore us.

"Don't worry. They stared for a few seconds, out of shock most likely. After that, they decided to mind their own business."

He's trying to reassure me. That's… sweet.

I let out a small laugh and mumbled, "I just got through talking to your sister about this… How can I do this now?" I felt my body slump a little.

"What did you say?" he asked. "My sister shouldn't have anything to do with this. Why can't she mind her own business? She thinks she has to look after me or something. Well, I can take care of myself, you know. I can see who I like, and I can kiss who I like." Then, as if to prove his point, he placed a hand on either side of my face and pulled me toward him.

His lips were on mine again before I could think. This time the kiss was hard. I couldn't think of pulling away. My body simply went limp and, when he pulled back, I just about slid to the floor.

"There." He gave a nod and caressed my face with one hand. "You really should get to bed. From the looks of things, you're dead on your feet." He smiled and started down the hall toward the cafeteria.

I had forgotten to breathe. *Wow. I definitely didn't expect that.* Focusing on the air coming in and going out of my lungs, I leaned against the trophy case. Once my breathing was reasonably even, I pushed away and went back down the hall.

I didn't remember climbing the stairs. Despite my reeling mind, I fell asleep immediately.

* * *

The next day, I was determined to find Gamut as soon as he was up for the day.

I have to tell him I'll be leaving and can't be in any romantic relationship. We can be friends and nothing more. I don't know how I'm gonna do it but, if I don't tell him, things could get bad.

I found him in the cafeteria a couple of hours before his shift. He sat at a table full of people. I didn't want to interrupt and remained just inside the doorway, staring at his back.

After a few seconds, he turned toward me and smiled. He said something to his friends, got up, and walked to me. "Hey, Sunshine."

I didn't answer or smile. My palms were damp, and I wiped them on my pants.

"Something on your mind?" He frowned.

I nodded. "Can we talk somewhere in private?"

"Yeah, sure. This way." He led me to a room near the stairs and closed the door behind us.

Maybe being alone with him in a tiny, dark room isn't such a good idea.

He didn't attempt to touch me. "What's wrong? Is it something I did?" He paused. "It was the kiss, right?"

I didn't answer.

"I knew it. I'm sorry, I'm moving too fast. Are you mad at me?"

"M-mad at you? No… it's… We – I, um… Sheesh, I'm always getting flummoxed here." *Okay, just like you rehearsed.* I took a deep breath. "Uh, what I'm trying to say is… it's not really a good idea to see me in that way, to feel the way you seem to feel about me. We shouldn't… we're not… Can't we just…" I shook my head. *Why can't I put a coherent thought together?*

He laughed. "Hm, you're kinda cute when you're *flummoxed.*"

"See! That's exactly what I mean! You can't feel this way about me –"

"Haylee. I can't help the way I feel. I can't change that. It's not something I can control. It's something I feel. I don't know why or how, but I do. And not only can I not change that, I don't think I want to."

Oh, God, I've insulted him.

"I'm not saying that I'm in love with you, or anything. Just that I like you. A lot. And I don't understand how it's possible. I do understand, however, you just want to be friends, for now. And I think I can do that. I could wait forever for you, as long as I have some shred of hope you might one day change your mind. And I do have that hope. So I'm willing to be your good friend in the meantime. Now, I'm not promising I won't kiss you again. I can't fully control myself around you. Sorry, I'm just being honest. But I'll do my best. Okay? Does that suit you?"

I could hear the smile in his voice, at the end of his little speech, and it made me smile a little too. "Yeah." My shoulders relaxed. "That could work for me. I have one other thing to tell you. Hear me out… Don't hope too much, I don't want to let you down… to hurt you. Because I will be leaving, sooner or later. Hopefully sooner. I have to go home. I can't stay here forever, no matter how many great people I meet."

"You think I'm great?" He nudged my arm.

"You heard what I said, right?"

"Relax, relax. I heard you and I understand what you're saying. We're friends right now and that's all that matters, okay? No worries. I don't want to waste what little time we have together, so let's forget the tension." He placed his hand on my back and led me toward the door, which I still could barely make out once my eyes had adjusted. "Come on, let's go. Have you eaten anything today?"

"I ate quickly this morning. I'm not hungry right now. Thank you."

He opened the door and ushered me out into the hall. No one noticed us, and I was grateful. "All right. How're your muscles today? Are you sore?"

"Well, it's not as bad as I expected… I'll live."

"Good to hear it. Hey, I've got a few things to do before my shift. Will you come by later? Spend some time with me up front?" He looked hopeful.

And maybe I should have said no. "Sure. I think I'm supposed to meet with Sabella sometime today, but I'll come by if I can." I couldn't help but smile at him. As usual.

Gamut went on his way, leaving me standing alone in the hallway.

That went much more smoothly than I anticipated.

I went upstairs and found the red door.

Maybe she's ready for me.

I felt a sudden urge to open it, a beckoning. I followed the impulse and placed my hand on the dull metal knob. It turned easily, and I heard Sabella's voice as I opened the door.

"Hello, dear. I'm glad you came on your own. Are you ready for some more training?"

I nodded, suddenly in awe of her presence.

"Good, good. You may enter. Come on, now."

I stepped over the threshold, as a single flame came to life. The door closed behind me.

She laughed. "It's a little dramatic, I know. But it's so much fun."

I came forward and sat in the chair across from her. I could not take my eyes from the older woman's face. Nothing about her had changed.

"Would you like to know what we will be doing today?"

"Y – yes, I would."

"All right. Today we will be practicing mental blocking. It's very important, you know. Very. For a number of reasons. All right, let's begin as we did the other day. Relax. You shouldn't have very much trouble doing that… I see you experienced a certain amount of relief from worry only a short time ago. Very interesting. Now, if you had already been trained to block your thoughts from others, it would not have been so easy for me to see."

My cheeks grew warm, and I stared down at my clasped hands. *I should've known she would sense that. Which means she probably knows the cause…*

She laughed. "Well, I suppose it's no surprise he has reacted this way to you. He calls you 'Sunshine,' but I think he misunderstands why he calls you this. Also, I think you may not fully understand the implications of such a nickname. It has much more meaning today than it did in your time. The sun has become much more precious, as the Pale Ones tend to stay out of direct sunlight. I know I don't have to tell you, but be very careful where young Gamut's concerned. He's always been rather impulsive and direct, but his willingness for patience in your case is cause to be on guard. He may not relinquish whatever claim he feels toward you." Her voice had turned more and more serious throughout her observations. "Does Derik know of your interactions with Gamut?"

I opened my mouth but nothing came out. *What does she mean?* I tried again, "I – I don't understand… He knows I've spent some time with him, but beyond that there's nothing else he *should* know. I've done what I can to defuse the situation. I think I've done that as well as I possibly can. It's really not any of Derik's business anyway, is it?" I frowned. *What makes everyone think it* is? *Had* he *noticed my reactions to him? Was* that *it? Did Sabella mean* he *thinks there's more between us than there is? No, that's not possible. He doesn't feel that way toward me. And here I am thinking about it again. Maybe it's not so unfounded, after all.*

She laughed again, catching my attention. "Oh, child. Your mind is so conflicted. I know you did not mean for anything to happen between you and Gamut, nor could you control your reaction to it. But I also know that *you* know your reactions to Derik are much more intense and follow you around day and night. No matter who's in your proximity, your thoughts wander to him. You should take it as a sign. I have. Of course, Derik feels it too, but he is much more stubborn than I took you for." Her look was gently reproachful.

I blinked for a moment. "Is that why you're having him train me? Karroll says he doesn't normally train beginners. He trains fighters, those who are most likely to be found in some sort of combat, she said."

"Dear girl, what makes you think you aren't a fighter? Or that you won't have to fight? I simply placed you with our best combatant and trainer. I have seen you will need it. Though…" She trailed off, as her eyes glazed over. "Though I am afraid the first time you are called to protect yourself, you will not be fully prepared." Her eyes refocused. "I am sorry. The time is much sooner than I expected. That is all I see." She looked away from me for the first time since I had come into the room.

"What do you mean? I don't understand. You saw something? Something about my future?" I sat on the edge of my seat.

"Yes," she sighed. "I'm afraid we do not have much time to practice. So we must begin now." She changed the subject smoothly, and I knew the topic was closed. "Try to relax."

I sat stiffly for a moment, then took a deep breath and sat back in my chair, doing my best to relax every muscle in my body, one by one.

"Good. Very good. Now, close your eyes and find the quiet and the dark. Clear your mind of everything. I know it can be very difficult.

Eventually, this will be all you need to keep others from your thoughts. If your mind is clear, there will be nothing for them to use against you. Until then, you will need to focus more on blocking. All right, stay as blank as possible. Now, begin thinking of one thing and one thing only. Something solid, hard, impenetrable. Focus until you can see nothing but it. Okay? Continue focusing…" Her voice was low, almost inaudible.

Something was in front of me, only in my mind's eye.

I can almost touch it. It feels so solid, so real. I can't see it exactly but sense it there. I focused on it, afraid my train of thought would cause it to dissipate, until it became clearer. A large, heavy door stood before me. I didn't move or speak, I was afraid to breathe. Then, the door trembled before me, as if something was hitting it from the other side. It startled me, and my focus slipped a bit, causing the image before me to shake violently. I could see a pinprick of light shining through.

Is that a crack? No, not gonna happen.

I focused harder and pushed against my shield. It stopped shaking and the crack disappeared. I sighed and backed down for a second. A second was all it took. My focus must have lapsed enough, because suddenly my door shattered. It was nothing more than splinters at my feet.

I was shaking, and tears rolled down my face.

Then I heard her voice. "Very good, Haylee. Amazing. For your first time blocking." She sounded winded. "What image were you using, do you know? What stood between your mind and mine?"

I closed my eyes and took a deep breath. "I think it was like the main door downstairs. It's gone. Can I get it back?"

"Oh yes. No need to worry. With a little focus, it will be as it was. You must not lower your guard. You felt as though the attack was over, so you let your guard down. That was your only mistake. Like I said, very good for your first time." She smiled.

I opened my eyes, which no longer watered. "Why was it so crushing? I felt as though someone died, or something, when it collapsed."

"Well, I suppose you will know the answer when you discover exactly what the door represents to you. Once you do, it will be stronger. You are tired, are you not? Mental defense can take much more out of you than physical self-defense, at times. When you have collected yourself, we will begin again."

In a few moments, I felt well enough to try again, so we did. After a couple of hours, I was too tired to continue.

"Each time was better than the time before. Do not worry, you will do fine. Continue your training with Derik, and I will call for you in a few days to continue here. All right?"

"In a few days? No sooner?" I asked.

"There are things I must reflect upon and see to. This will give you more time to your physical defenses and time to recuperate from today."

"Oh. All right." I got up, feeling the fatigue in my body. "I guess I'll see you then." I smiled slightly and moved toward the door.

"Yes. Good luck… with your training and 'boy troubles' until then." Her face was perfectly blank, as far as I could see in the dim light.

Is she teasing me?

I stepped through the red door without glancing back to see her blow out the flame.

* * *

I was famished and made my way down to the cafeteria. When I had my bowl, I looked for a seat. At one table, Derik sat alone. While other people ate nearby, it was as though he wasn't aware of them.

He's off in his own world. I've never seen him like that. Unfocused and distracted. I stood in one place for a long moment, glanced around, and caught sight of an empty bench near the door. *Maybe he* wants *to sit alone.* I considered my options and looked toward him again. Then I straightened my back and moved to the seat next to him.

"Is it all right if I sit here?" My voice didn't tremor.

At first, he didn't move.

Maybe he didn't hear me?

Then, he turned his head, a slight look of confusion on his face.

A face made all the more handsome for it. Dear God, this is getting bad! As if noticing every other aspect of his near-perfect body wasn't bad enough, I've gotta go and decide he has a handsome face, too?

"Sure. Why not." He turned back to his bowl.

"Th-thanks." I lifted my leg over and lowered myself to the bench. I ate for a few moments before attempting to speak. "Um, so… how are the plans coming for the water expedition?"

He paused. “Fine, I guess. A group will be going out tomorrow. Looking for an old well southeast of here.”

I paused in my chewing and swallowed quickly. “Near where you found me? There was one on our neighbor’s – the Logan’s – farm. It’d probably be, uh… I don’t know, maybe a quarter-mile before you come to our house.” *Maybe I* can *help, after all.* I turned in my seat, my spoon half-way to my mouth. “I could find it! I know I could. I mean, I know there’s been a lot of changes with the layout of the land since… well. But I’m sure I could find the well.”

He stared at me for a moment, his eyebrows raised, an amused twinkle in his eyes. Then it was gone. “Are you kidding? I could never let you do that. It’s much too dangerous. Anyway, based on what you’ve said, I know one of us could find it. So, thank you.” He turned back to finish his food. “I’ll let them know the location immediately.” A moment later, he was up and gone.

I stared at my own food, no longer hungry. At least I had eaten most of it before my spirits had been so completely crushed. *Why’d I sit down beside him, again?* I narrowed my eyes. *Had I seen a look of suspicion on his face? If so, why?* I tapped my spoon against my bowl. *Wait. Did he think I was offering to help so I could run home? No. He* knew *I wouldn’t do that. Right? It was in my head. Had to be.*

When I finished eating, I visited with Gamut.

He and Grange were the only two at the door today.

Thank goodness. Hopefully, we can put yesterday’s scene behind us and no one else has heard about it.

Gamut was as happy as ever to see me, and Grange was as indifferent as ever, which suited me fine for the time being.

“How was your training with Sabella?” Gamut asked. “What did you learn?”

“It went really well. She’s teaching me… have you heard of mental blocking?”

He nodded. “Oh, yeah. I’ve had to learn a little of that with my ability. You’d be surprised how intense it can feel. Sabella’s never taught me personally, but indirectly through others. When are you going back?”

“I’m not sure… She said she’d call for me in a few days.” I shrugged and leaned against the wall beside him. *No need to tell him her reasons for waiting.*

“Hm. Well, that’ll probably give you some more time to recoup, anyway. And more time to spend with me." He grinned and mussed my hair.

"Hey now." I smiled and rearranged my tresses. "Yeah, that's true, I guess. It did take a lot out of me today." I sighed.

"You should probably get to bed early tonight. You've got training with Derik in the morning, anyway, don't you?"

Is that a hint of jealousy I hear? "Yep. I do."

"Hey, maybe I should train you instead. I've heard he's pretty tough. What do you say?" He poked me in the ribs.

"Gamut!" I held his hands away.

He stared down at me, his smile erased. "I wouldn't be too tough…"

"Gamut… don't. You know it's under Sabella's say so." I released his hands. "Besides, Derik has been fine so far…" I looked away from him, and something in the corner caught my eye. "Hey, what are those? Are they for the water tomorrow?" Several large cloth sacks were piled together.

"Huh? Oh. Yeah… They're full of bottles, any container we can find with a lid, really. Most of the time, they'll leave the empty ones by the door for the next water hunt. They've got 'em ready for the morning."

I stared at them for a moment. *Why can't Derik let me help? I guess, if my directions are good enough...*

"What's the matter?"

"Huh? Oh. Nothing. I told Derik where a well was, or used to be, said I could show them, but he'd hear nothing of it. It's *too dangerous*, he said." I forced a laugh.

"Well, it is. Too dangerous, I mean." He narrowed his eyes. "But that's not what bothers you most, is it?"

I sighed. "No. Not just that." I rolled my eyes. "It's probably nothing. But I'm sure he thought I was going to take the opportunity to run away, to go home. All I want to do is help." I flung my arms out before dropping them back to my sides. "I'm being silly."

"No, that's not silly. It's just like him. It's like him to think the worst of someone. But especially, to think the worst of someone like you. Someone so goodhearted…"

"You don't even know me. How can you know whether or not I'm goodhearted? I could be a horrible person… I could – I could work for… *them.*" I ducked my head and glanced around.

He smiled and placed a hand on either side of my face. "But you don't. I know. Anyone who couldn't see that as soon as they laid eyes on you is either blind or stupid, or both." He gave a laugh. "You're too… I don't know – something – to have anything to do with them." He was serious now. "I don't have a term for it, but you're too *bright* for that. It's obvious in everything you do, everything you say – holy ball of fire, this sounds incredibly corny, doesn't it?"

I couldn't help but smile. "Yeah, it kinda does."

He took his hands away. "Sorry about that…" He smirked a little.

"Quite all right. How 'bout we talk about something else?"

"That'd be golden…"

We spent the remainder of our time asking each other questions about our lives growing up. I began to see the ordinary things for me were quite different from the ordinary for him. He had never experienced many of the things I had, such as chocolate ice cream. And, while I was taking piano lessons, he was learning to defend himself against monsters. Not the under-the-bed variety but the real kind. The steal-your-life-force, kill-your-beloved-aunt-who-raised-you kind of monsters.

It was getting late, we had learned quite a bit about each other, and my eyelids were drooping.

He didn't kiss me that night, and I dreamed of a life I had not lived. A life full of fear and running and fighting and confinement. A life I was sure I could not have survived. I awoke convinced I could never belong in that world.

* * *

I found my clothes stacked by my cot, folded and clean, and changed into them before breakfast. In the cafeteria, I ate in a state of near gloom, paying little attention to the goings-on around me. Afterward, I walked to the room where I was to meet with Derik. He wasn't there. I waited for twenty minutes or so, though it felt longer, before leaving the room to find him. The halls were as busy as usual, everyone making their way toward whatever jobs they were assigned. For a moment, I thought about following suit and finding something to do with myself, but changed my mind when I saw Derik moving toward the main doors. I followed.

Once he reached the guards there, I could make out some of his words. "… send someone for me when they get back…" He saw me and froze before striding past me. "I'm sorry, but we'll have to postpone our session… I've got too much on my plate today."

I jogged after him. "What's going on? How long has the, uh… crew, or whatever you call them, been out?"

He heaved a sigh. "Not long."

"Not long? Then why are you so worried?" I stopped and frowned.

He kept moving. "Never mind. I've got a lot to do…" He finally slowed and turned toward me. "Why don't you go ahead and use the training room… go over what I taught you without me. We'll figure out another time to work together, or something." He disappeared around the corner.

Practice self-defense by myself? "Uh… Okaaay…" And I tried. I really did. Well, for about ten minutes. "This is pointless." *I can't practice the escapes without the holds. What the hell is his problem?!* "I give up!" I flung myself to the floor, my arms over my face.

I wasn't going to think about Derik for the rest of the day, and it was easy for a little while. I busied myself around the compound until Gamut's shift started.

Several other people were there, and the apprehension oozed from them.

I approached Gamut. "What's going on?"

"The group hasn't returned yet. Everyone's getting nervous." His eyes were the only indication of emotion, a mix of anxiety and sympathy. "I'm sorry… but some people are blaming you."

I blinked at him. "Huh?"

He closed his eyes briefly. "It's not just because they're suspicious of newcomers… it's because Derik told them about your well. They went looking specifically for it. So, uh… they think that, um… well."

I chanced a look at the people gathered. Some of them stared back at me, a few with looks of distaste or all-out antagonism. I fixed my gaze on Gamut instead. "What? What do they think?"

The look of sympathy intensified. "They – they think you sent them on a wild-goose chase. They don't believe the well is there. Haylee, I – "

They think I lied. I can't believe it. After a moment, I made myself focus on Gamut. "Do you think that? That I lied?"

"No! I believe you. It was there in your time and might still be there. It's possible they ran into trouble. It's bound to happen. It does, quite often. These idiots know that… To tell you the truth, I don't know what's come over them." He looked as confused as me for a moment. "Stick close to me today… all right?" He gave the group a sidelong glance.

I nodded. *What possible reason do I have to lie? All I want is to help them. Is this why Derik was acting the way he was? Does he think I'm lying? That's it, isn't it?* My knees shook, and my stomach turned sour.

"Haylee? Are you all right?" The worry was evident in Gamut's voice. "Here, sit down." He led me to the trophy case and helped me up onto the ledge. "Shh… now. Take slow, even breaths, okay?" He placed his hands on either side of my face.

I did as he said.

"There. Is that better?"

I nodded. "I'm sorry."

He laughed a little. "You're sorry. You nearly pass out, because everyone's overreacting, and *you're* sorry?" He smiled at me and kissed my forehead. "You're adorable, you know that? Why everyone else can't see you as I do… I don't know." He shook his head. Suddenly, he stiffened, and his smile was gone. "Derik."

I looked over his shoulder to see him standing across the hall, his hands on his hips, staring at us. My body went numb.

"Haylee, remember what I said. Breathe." Gamut's voice and a gentle shake brought me back. "Lean back for a while, okay? I should get back to my post." He indicated over his shoulder. "I'll be right over here, if you need me."

Once again, I did as he asked. Tremors wracked my body. I squeezed my eyes shut. *Come on. Get a hold of yourself. Why does it matter if Derik, of all people, doesn't believe you? Gamut* does. *Doesn't that count for something?* But it didn't, and I knew why. *I'm falling for him! Maybe already have. Oh, that's so freakin' ridiculous! How can I fall for someone so distant, so confusing, and so damned irritating?!* But I had. I did my best to push all of these thoughts and fears from my head. It wasn't easy. I leaned back and focused on thinking of nothing, like Sabella had taught me.

I must have been doing a pretty good job, because the next thing I knew the doors were thrown open, and the gathered group was helping the lost party into the entry hall. Light poured in.

"Oh no!" Someone gasped. And another hissed, "I knew it!" Then, everyone was talking at once.

I heard Derik's voice above them all.

"What happened? Where's Ferris?"

"We lost him. We were attacked."

My eyes began to adjust, and I was able to make out a few of their faces. Derik stood tall, in the midst of the group. After I took in his position, I noted the condition of those who had arrived. They were all battered and bruised, several were wounded, and a couple only stood with the support of those around them. My eyes must have been wide enough to pop out of my head.

Then, I heard someone breach the dreaded topic. "The bottles are empty. You didn't find the well?"

"No. We searched for it longer than we should have. But we didn't find any well."

It's not *my fault…*

Derik interrupted the dangerous conversation. "Let's get them to the infirmary." He placed his arm around one of the more seriously wounded men and turned back down the hall. As he did so, he passed by me. He leaned in close. "I'll speak with you later."

The look in his eye sent a shiver down my spine. And not the good kind. If my eyes could have gone wider they would have.

Gamut was a little ways behind the group, walking along with them. He stopped for a moment. "Maybe you should hide out for a bit, stay low, you know?" He gave me a little smile and moved ahead with the group.

An image of the dusty piano room flashed through my mind, but something inexplicable happened before that idea could stick. If Gamut's back hadn't been to the door, he would've had it well within his view, but his attention was on the group moving away. My gaze wandered to the abandoned bags of bottles near the door, and I scooted down off my perch. My body moved of its own volition. No one was watching the doors. Even the two men left with the responsibility of closing the heavy doors were intently focused on their work. I moved with more purpose, grabbed the nearest cloth sack and, without hesitation, slipped through the doors just before they closed. It was a miracle no one noticed me.

That, or dumb luck.

Whether my luck was good or bad was a completely different issue, but suddenly I was doubting my decision.

What have I done?

I let myself freak for about half a second, then squared my

shoulders and got my bearings. I looked toward where home should be and started walking. As I got several feet away from the building, I remembered the guards on the roof.

What was I thinking, thinking I could get away with this?!

And I froze. When no one called out, I took a step and then another until I was walking at a regular pace.

I can find that well. That's why I'm doing this. Of course, someone'll notice I'm gone. And I expect it'll be pretty quickly. But if I can find the water, maybe they'll believe in me. Maybe he'll *believe in me. Though he'd probably think I'm stupid or crazy for doing something so stupid and crazy. And who am I to argue with that logic? Really. Besides, I might not make it back, once I find the water. If I find the water…*

Wait. *I might not make it back?*

I slowed my pace a bit and studied the shadows around me. I saw no movement there. Nothing out of the ordinary.

Okay, so if I stick to the sunlight, I'll be fine. Just fine. Right.

So that's what I did. I stayed away from the shadows, which wasn't difficult. There were still plenty of clearings, places the trees hadn't yet reclaimed and maybe never would. Maybe these clearings had always been here. I couldn't know that but it made sense. I filled my head with thoughts such as this, as I went along.

It's much more productive than dwelling on my imminent death.

I was amazed by the utter naturalness of my surroundings.

Nothing but the school building has survived all these years. And how long has *it been? I'll probably never find out.*

Though I had no real way of keeping track of the time, at least forty-five minutes had passed.

I wish I didn't rely so much on my cellphone for the time. Should be getting close by now. This would've been the Logan's property, I'm sure of it. So where's the well?

"It should be *here*." I squinted my eyes against the sun as I turned, looking. I was about to give up, when I noticed a shape across the clearing. I moved closer. "Eureka," I said under my breath. Of course, as I moved closer, I realized something was different.

Oh, no…

What must have been the well was completely covered by undergrowth, which had been able to flourish out of the direct light of the sun. Which meant the well was now engulfed in shadows, sheltered by the encroaching forest.

I stopped moving and swallowed hard. "Shit." I winced. *Sorry, Auntie Beth. But,* hell, *does it apply.*

Taking in my surroundings with great effort, I searched for any sign of the Pale Ones.

Nothing. Could I feel if one was near? Sabella hasn't taught me that yet. Is it possible? Well, gotta try.

I reached out with my mind, searching as I had done with my eyes. Still nothing, so I pushed out a little harder, which was the extent of my capabilities, as my breathing was becoming labored. I tried to reign myself in slowly but my control was not quite there yet and I came back to myself with a snap. If my eyes had been closed, they most certainly would have jerked open.

As far as I could tell, I was alone.

That's strange. Someone should have come looking for me by now, right? Maybe it's for the best. I'll get the water and head back, no one the wiser. I took a deep breath and pushed on.

I paused at the edge of the shadows, then stepped over the threshold. The air felt heavier.

Is that possible? Gotta be my imagination. At least I'm out of the direct sunlight. Definitely gonna need that aloe when I get back.

When I reached the jumble of undergrowth, I set the cloth sack down on the ground and studied the work ahead. I didn't have any means of cutting through the foliage and no way of protecting my hands as I tore through it.

And once I do get through it, how am I going to fill these bottles? I sighed. *I'll figure that out when I get to it. Oh, I hope it hasn't dried up. Please, don't let all of this be for nothing.*

I looked down at the cloth sack and chewed at my lip. *Hm…*

Grabbing the bag up, I shook all of the empty bottles from it. A large ball of heavy twine fell out among them.

Yes! Now to get to work. I placed one hand inside the cloth and studied its thickness. *This will do.*

My makeshift glove was adequate in protecting my hand from the majority of thorns and whatever else I might not want to touch directly. It wasn't long before I could make out the cracking and slightly crumbling stone of the well. However much time had passed, it had held up. The forest had most likely saved it.

Does it still have water? Now's the time to find out. But how? What I wouldn't give for a bucket.

I glanced at the bottles strewn across the ground behind me. One of them was bigger and had a wider mouth than many of the others. I looked at the twine and back to the bottle.

Maybe, just maybe, it'll work.

I tied one end of the twine around the neck of the bottle and studied the knot.

Hm. It won't win me any patches but it's not going anywhere. Hm, but won't it just float?

I cast my eyes around for something, anything small but heavy enough and rested them on a piece of crumbling stone from the well. It was dry and clean. To be sure, I wiped it on my pant leg a few times to remove any dust or loose rock fragments, then dropped it into the bottle and lowered it into the well.

Please, let the twine be long enough.

When I reached the end of it, I began towing it back up, and gasped. *The bottle's heavier!* I pulled with more zeal. At the top, I grabbed for it and studied its contents. I wrinkled my nose. The water was cloudy. But it smelled okay.

Not that I'm an expert. Let's hope it's clean.

There was supposed to be a natural spring feeding the well. I dropped the bottle into the well several more times, smiling as I filled the bottles and returned them to the cloth sack.

I was filling up the last few bottles, when a twig snapped.

I froze and, for a moment, could hear only my own breathing. In my absolute stillness, I felt a presence to my right. Without moving my head, I slid my eyes in that direction but couldn't see anything. So, bracing myself, I stood slowly, the bottles still in my hands.

Maybe someone from the safe house has come looking for me. If so, why are they sneaking around?

When I looked up, I saw him. Between the open field and me, stood the Pale One, a silhouette against the sunlight.

7

I couldn't make out the Pale One's features but could tell he was male.

Are there any females? And have I met him before? I looked at him more closely but, since I didn't know if his injuries could have healed this quickly, I couldn't tell if he was the same Pale One from the woods that night.

He stood at least as tall as Derik and was slightly hunched over. Though he was nowhere near as broad, and his hair was long and tangled.

I stood still, my eyes frozen on him. He stared back for a long time before speaking. I jumped a little, when he finally did.

"Well, well, well… What have we here?" He moved toward me, and I jerked back a step. He began circling me, forcing me back against the cool, hard stone of the well. "You're such a little thing to be out so alone," he said, as he got closer. "So young…" When he was finished looking me up and down, he met my eyes, and I felt them go wide with fear. His became slits. "Ah… but not *quite* so young, I see…" This last word came out a hiss. He circled around me again, placing the well between us for a moment.

Running crossed my mind, but he was in front of me again.

"I would have caught you, little bit. We always catch you." He was closer than he had been up to that point and stopped moving to look me in the eyes again. "So small compared to the rest," he said, considering, "like one of those delicate desserts humans can't even remember…" His hand came up to toy with my hair. I leaned away, and he reached out to touch my face, causing me to jerk back. "Uh-uh-uh… play nice." Another hissing sound. This time, he did touch my face.

At first, his touch felt cold, then colder until it burned, and I couldn't move away. My body felt very heavy, I wanted to lie down but couldn't. I could barely think. And I couldn't take my eyes off his. Glowing, golden, animal-like.

Then the pain came.

Searing. Scorching. Like my very essence was being ripped from my body.

I will simply let the empty shell of her fall into the well.

What was that?! *His thoughts? I can't…* It was getting hard to see through the spots growing in front of my eyes. Through the pain, I barely registered the sting of his clawed fingers in my chin. It was becoming more and more difficult to focus.

Come on. You have to. Remember what Sabella taught you. It's not that *different.* So, I put everything I had into it. I focused on my back pressed up against the cool stone. I let my weight fall into it. I also focused on my legs. On bringing my knee up. And ramming it into whatever part of his body I could find.

Wait. Sabella didn't teach me that. *Doesn't matter. Keep going!*

When there was enough space between us, I braced myself against the well and used both of my legs to kick him away from me.

I ran. But my footing was unsteady, and I stumbled over a clump of dirt. The world spun. I kept moving.

Someone ahead of me yelled. "Watch it! Argh!"

That's not right… the Pale One's behind me. Isn't he?

Pain seared through my right side, and I went sprawling. The world went black for a second or two, but I forced myself to focus again.

The Pale One stood above me. Blood dripped from the claws of his right hand. I threw my arms up, as he hurled himself forward. But a blurred mass tackled him in midair, and they skidded through the dirt.

Derik had the Pale One pinned. He didn't glance up. "Run," he said and threw his first punch.

I stared, frozen.

Then the Pale One reached for a small rock, and I reacted.

"Look out!" I lunged toward him and collided with his arm.

The rock rolled across the ground.

It's just a rock. Harmless. Oh, thank God*!*

And as suddenly as I had moved, Derik was pulling me away. He checked my hands and arms with fierce dedication. He frowned.

I guess he didn't find what he was looking for.

He turned toward the creature he had been fighting.

The Pale One was gone.

"Dammit!"

We sat there, neither of us speaking.

Derik broke the silence. "What the *hell* were you thinking? Pulling a stunt like this!" He stood up and dusted off his pants. "I should have left you to it, is what I should've done."

I stared up at him, wide-eyed. *What's he saying?*

"Oh, don't look at me like that. This was all your doing. Well, go on. You're so eager to go back… or to get yourself killed. I'm not sure which it is but you'd better do it quick before you get someone else killed."

"Someone else killed? You *do* blame me, then. For what happened earlier, with the others. To – to Ferris." I looked away. I hadn't known the man – or boy… *What if he was just a kid? Why'd I have to think of that, now?* My head spun.

"How can I not blame you, when you obviously blame yourself. I can see the guilt written all over your face. If you hadn't lied – "

"Lied!?" I glared at him, but he had turned away. "I haven't lied about anything! I'm not a liar, all right?" I pulled myself up, clutching at my side. *How'd I manage to throw myself at them a minute ago? I can barely stand now.* "I didn't – you know what, no. I don't need to defend myself. I haven't done anything wrong. And so, what if I *do* want to go home? Wouldn't you?"

He heaved a sigh and turned to me. The look on his face sent chills down my back. "Then, by all means, go." He gestured with his arm. "We came across you on the other side of those trees. You're almost there. Go."

Oh, you arrogant son of a… How dare *he assume I'm running away! How could he – Why, I – No. I'm not going to do this.* I straightened a bit against the pain in my side. "We've had this discussion before." I sighed. "You don't know me so don't pretend to know anything about me."

"You told me you'd take any chance you could to go home, and – "

"I also said I would do anything I could to help before that happened. I won't go back on either of those promises." I stared him down.

"And I said I'd stop you… of course, I feel I underestimated your determination…" He said, not taking his eyes off mine.

"You're still not listening! I wasn't running away! I was trying to prove myself, to… save my reputation, in a way… Not that there was much to save, since no one trusted me to begin with…"

"To prove yourself? How?! By running into one of them and getting yourself killed? How? Enlighten me! Please!"

"The well, for crying out loud!" I almost flung my arms out to the side but caught myself.

"The well? What do you mean?" He frowned and crossed his arms over his chest.

Yes. Let's draw more *attention to the perfection that is you.* I shook my head. *Ugh. Focus, please. Maybe if I speak slowly, he'll get it.* "I came out here to *find* it. Of course."

He stared at me for a second, his frown ebbing into understanding then back to a look of anger. "Of all the stupid, crazy things to do!"

Now he's got it. This *is the reaction I expected.*

"What is wrong with you?! Looking for the well? How do you even know it still exists? You don't know how much time has passed! This was a suicide mission! It was stupid, that's all… Just plain stupid." He shook his head in bewilderment.

My anger vanished at his words, and a smile began to peek through. "Wait. So you believe me then? About the well? That I didn't lie?"

"What?" He scowled.

"You don't think I lied? You don't blame me for – for Ferris?"

His scowl faltered. "No… I don't think you lied. I'm not sure I was ever convinced you did. I was more angry at myself for not checking it out first, before sending the group. So, I blame myself." He frowned again. "But that's not what we're talking about here… Why come looking for a well that might not exist, alone, when you very well know the dangers. Are you crazy? Or just stupid?"

I flinched. *Hey! Sure, I'd acted without thinking. But that didn't make me stupid.* "You said it first, maybe you shouldn't have come. Maybe you should've let nature take its course. We'd all be a whole lot better off." Holding my side, I turned to head back to the compound, wincing with every step I took.

Derik must have noticed. "Do you need help?" He nearly barked the question.

I kept moving. "No. I'm perfectly capable of taking care of myself."

He gave a short laugh. "Yeah, I can see tha – "

The world swirled.

As he rushed up to me, his hand made contact with my side, and I winced. He drew his hand back and grimaced. "You're wounded." He kneeled and raised up my tattered shirt, tacky with blood.

I reached down to stop his hands but reconsidered. *You're bleeding, for God's sake. Now's not the time to be a prude.*

His fingers brushed the skin around the gashes. "It's bad but not as bad as it looks."

I winced again.

"Why didn't you say something?!"

"Really?"

The expression on his face softened. "You still shouldn't have been out here alone. What *were* you thinking, anyway?"

Is that a rhetorical question?

He sighed and pulled off his own shirt and started ripping it into long strips.

I frowned. "What are you doing?"

"What's it look like? I'm making bandages."

Back to his normal, condescending self.

"Here, hold this up." He handed me the tail of my shirt.

I stared at it. "This was my favorite t-shirt…"

Derik snorted.

Did I say that out loud?

He began wrapping the cloth around my waist, and his closeness made heat rise to my face. Every time his arm brushed my stomach, I felt butterflies stir. Before long, I was dizzy all over again.

When he was finished, he stood. "Can you walk?"

I nodded, took a step, and swayed.

"Shit." He caught me again.

We've gotta stop meeting like this. I met his eyes and caught them. *Okay, I'm getting a little loopy.*

"Do you want me to carry you?"

Interesting word choice, want *not* need. *Wait…* I gave a long blink. "I don't know what's wrong with me… I'm not hurt that badly…." I frowned, still unable to think.

"I was afraid of that. Sit." He led me to a small tree and crouched down. "Look at me."

My head was feeling heavy.

"I need to examine your eyes." He hesitated before touching my face.

Are his hands trembling? No, it must be me. I'm so tired all of a sudden.

"Little One, you need to keep your eyes open."

"I am. Aren't I?" I blinked. *Had I closed my eyes?* I blinked some more, fighting my drooping eyelids.

He sighed, and his breath caressed my cheek. With a hand on either side of my face, he tilted my head back and used his fingers to expose more of my eye. "You should be dead."

That woke me up. "Huh?"

"He had you for much longer than I thought. Anyone else would be dead… how is that possible?"

At first, I thought it was another rhetorical question, but the intensity of his stare made me realize otherwise. "Uh…I don't know… I…?" I shook my head because it was all I felt like doing.

He stared at me a moment longer, making me uncomfortable. "You don't, do you." He glanced at his hands, still on of my face, removed them, and stood up.

His promptness made my head spin, so I pressed my own hands to my forehead.

"Well, you're obviously not fit to walk. I'll have to carry you back…" He was angry again.

"I really wasn't trying to go home. I really was trying to find the well…"

He rolled his eyes. "I said I believed you, all right? Still, it was a stupid idea…" He sighed.

"I found it."

"What? What did you say?"

"I found it. Over there." *Huh. Guess I forgot to say that. I can't think straight around you. Let alone when I'm angry.*

He turned to look toward the woods. There, hiding amongst the undergrowth and shadows, was the well. He walked over to it, examined it and the bottles I had filled, and noted the ones I had dropped when I was attacked.

"You found it." His eyebrows lifted. "I can't believe it." He turned in a circle. "I don't believe it. Why didn't you say something soon – Never mind. Forget I said that." He picked up the bag, placed the two empty bottles in it, and returned to my side. "Why didn't you go home?"

Now, I lifted my eyebrows. "Why would I? Yeah, sure… Everyone's probably looking for me. But this… This is more important. I can do more good here… than I ever could back home." I lowered my eyes. "Besides. Everything I had there… has been taken away. They killed the most important person in my life… and for what? Me? Why? I can't understand it…" A tear slid down my cheek. "I – I'm sorry. Bottom line is… I'm keeping my word. That's all."

He stared at me. "I admit, you've done something wonderful." He laughed a bit. "Stupid, but wonderful. I'd say you accomplished what you set out to… Are you ready to go back?"

I nodded.

"All right. Good. Hold on, okay?" He helped me stand and scooped me up into his arms in one fluid movement. He was still holding the water in one hand. "You all right?"

"Yeah." I swallowed. "Thank you."

"Don't mention it."

Wow. He sounds almost… pleasant.

He started back toward the compound. "You can rest for a while, but try to stay awake… it's very important that you not pass out, okay?"

I didn't answer.

"Haylee?"

"Yeah. Okay." My eyelids drooped. "Can you talk to me, help me stay awake?"

"Sure. What do you want to talk about?"

"Anything… anything at all."

Derik asked questions and forced me to answer them.

In a short time, I felt better, more attentive.

We walked for nearly half an hour before I raised my head from his shoulder.

He continued on as if the load was no burden. "We're almost there."

I pressed my hand to his chest. "Wait."

He stopped. "What is it now?"

"I – " I could hear the irritation edging back into his voice and almost didn't go on. "I'd like to walk the rest of the way."

He opened his mouth to argue but one look at my face told him I was serious. "I see." He sighed. "All right. But let's take this slowly… Put your arms around my neck."

He bent to set the cloth sack down. Then he rose and lowered me to the ground. For a brief moment, as his hands came to my waist and my feet dangled inches from the earth, our faces nearly touched. His eyes were as wide as mine felt, and we remained close, staring at each other after my feet touched down. His eyes left mine and travelled down to my mouth.

My heart's pounding. This's never happened to me before. I've never *been scared and excited at the same time.*

Light flashed and reflected in Derik's eyes. He blinked and looked away.

The spell was broken.

"Can you stand on your own?"

"I – I think so." I stood very still.

"Then go ahead and remove your arms."

"Oh." I yanked them away. "Sorry."

He barely touched me now, just enough to keep me steady.

My legs shook. *More from my reaction to his closeness than anything else, I'm sure.* I could stand.

"Good. The compound is around the bend in the trees. Let's go."

He picked up the bag and began walking.

I followed. "You're not going to ask why?"

"Why what?"

"Why I asked to walk the rest of the way."

"I already know why." He didn't stop and was gaining quite a lead.

I didn't dare run and risk being carried the rest of the way.

Derik must have realized this as well because he paused long enough for me to catch up and kept his strides slow.

When the compound came into view, I stumbled and he steadied me.

"I won't carry you, but are you too proud to let me help?" The irritation was full-blown now.

Sweat dripped down my back and soaked my hair.

"You're bleeding again."

I placed my hand to my side. "How can you tell?" The bandages were as bloody as before.

He didn't answer. "Just lean on me. Okay?"

I nodded and let him support some of my weight.

"You ready to go?"

I took a few more deep breaths. "Yeah. I think so."

We headed on.

***

When we arrived, the doors opened immediately, and two armed men flanked us. I didn't recognize them. They closed the doors, and we heard the noises of the locks and barricades going into place. Compared to the brightness outside, the hall was too dark.

Glenna rushed up from somewhere in that darkness. "Are you all right?" She placed a hand upon my shoulder.

How is her hand so heavy? I took a shaky breath. "I'm fine…"

Behind me, Derik moved away and spoke to someone. "Here, take these to the kitchen."

A man and woman rushed off with the water.

Glenna glanced toward him. "She found the well?"

He nodded briefly, and a murmur went through the crowd I hadn't noticed gathered. I looked around for the first time, as my eyes adjusted. Nearly everyone was there. Merritt and Karroll grinned at me from the edge of the group, but their smiles faltered as my attempt at one became more of a grimace.

"She's bleeding."

Who said that? I looked to see Nate meet Derik's eyes.

Glenna was the only one close enough to hear.

"What?" She examined me more closely, with a hand now on each shoulder.

I was shaking, as it took more and more strength to stand. Instantly, Derik's hand was at my back.

She frowned at Derik. "What happened?"

"I'll explain it all in private." He gave her a look I couldn't decipher. "Let's get Haylee to the infirmary first." And he slid his arm around my waist.

"Come on, Haylee." Glenna fell in at my other side.

As we moved, I could hear whispers spreading throughout the group but couldn't make anything out. Then a familiar voice.

"Coming through. Excuse me! Let me through, please!" Gamut burst through the crowd. "Haylee! You had me so worried! What were you thinking? How could – are you all right?!" He turned to Derik. "Is she all right?" The worry on his face was evident now.

Though I couldn't see Derik's face, his voice made his irritation clear.

"She'll be fine. We're taking her to the infirmary now. Glenna's going to examine her. We'll let you know, when she's finished." He sounded as though he spoke through clenched teeth.

Gamut stopped. "Uh, okay… I'll see you soon, Haylee. All right?"

I nodded in reply, attempting to smile and once more failing.

Once we made it to the infirmary and the door closed, Derik scooped me up and over to the examination table. Glenna rushed to one of the medicine cabinets.

He leaned over me and cupped my cheek. "Just rest for now. Okay?"

I nodded, as my eyelids fluttered.

His eyes searched my face before he moved away.

Glenna stood for a moment, looking back and forth between us, then approached. She glanced over me. "I was going to ask where the wound was, but now I see." Her expression was one of worry. "What happened?"

"Fix her up. Then I'll tell you." He paced around the room.

Glenna nodded. "Help me sit her up then."

I braced for the pain, as they propped me up, but it wasn't as bad as it had been.

"Good. Now I can get these bandages off… and clean these…" She looked more closely and threw a quick glance toward Derik. Then she began cleaning my wounds.

I hissed in a breath.

"Sorry." She applied some sort of gel and wrapped fresh bandages around my waist. "There you go." She smiled. "Good as new." She stroked my hair gently, and she and Derik helped me lean back against the cushion. "Try to rest for a bit, all right? Then we'll get you to bed."

I let my eyelids close. *Finally…*

"Derik? You need to tell me what happened. Now."

They crossed the room. Only a few words reached my ears.

"We told you she would never do that!" Glenna said.

"I know, I know… Keep it down, all right?" Derik whispered.

After that, their hushed tones must have lulled me to sleep, because I awoke to the sensation of being moved. When I opened my eyes, Derik was carrying me across the room.

"We've set up a cot in here for you for a few nights. Glenna didn't think we should move you far." He set me gently down on the bed. "I told her you're stronger than you look. But I think it's best you're here, anyway." He let Glenna pull a blanket over me and smiled. "I mean, we've gotta keep an eye on you. Can't let you sneak out for more water, now can we?"

He's actually smiling at me? Wow…

He smoothed a stray strand back from my face. "Now get some rest. I'll check back in on you later." He looked at me for a second longer, as if to say something else, then got up and left the room.

Glenna stared speculatively at the closed door. As she turned back, I caught sight of a frown. But it was gone by the time she sat down beside me. In her hands were a cup of water and a small medicine bottle. She sat the cup on the table beside me and measured some powder from the bottle, stirring it into the water.

"Here, drink this. Though you need little help sleeping, this medicine is good for that and it prevents infection." She handed me the cup.

I did as I was told. When I handed it back, her frown had returned.

"What's wrong?"

She looked startled. "Wrong? Oh, dear, nothing. I suppose I was lost in thought. Derik told me what happened out there. What you did was very brave. Though I agree with him, it was not altogether smart." Then she smiled. "I imagine the story has spread across the compound by now. One or two have extraordinary hearing, and one of those may or may not have a penchant for storytelling. I will not name names, as they say, but still…" She stood up from the cot. "I should allow you to rest now. Call if you need anything. I would not be surprised if a certain somebody stayed as close as possible, in case you do. Goodnight." She left the room and closed the door behind her.

The room was familiar to me now, and I could make out most of the shapes by the light of the two candles near the door.

I'm alone… I haven't been this *alone in the building before. Not really. Definitely not at night. Even in the short amount of time I've been here, I've gotten used to all the people around. There's always* some*one. Nope. I don't like it. Not after today. It's too dark. It's too… No. You're fine. You're safe. You're* not *alone. There are people right outside that door. And there's nothing under the bed. Nothing. Stop acting like you're five years old with that creepy-ass clown picture hanging across your room!* I cringed. *Oh, thank all that's good in the world that thing's gone.* I took a deep breath. *Safe. You're safe.*

I could feel myself getting sleepy but the fearful part of my mind was fighting it. When the door creaked open, I stiffened, afraid to move, but also afraid not to.

"Haylee?" a voice called in a whisper.

I frowned into the candlelight. "Gamut? Is that you?"

He came the rest of the way into the room, quietly closing the door behind him. "Hey. How are you feeling?" He kneeled beside my cot. "Do you feel like having company?"

I smiled with relief. "Yeah… That would be nice."

I saw a matching relief on his face, as he settled down on the floor. "Good. I'll stay as long as you like." He glanced down for a second, sheepishly. "Is it true what everyone's been saying? I mean, I knew you didn't lie about the well, but… the other stuff. Everyone's seen the proof about the water, but did you really fight one of them?"

I raised my eyebrows. "Is that what they're saying? I was trying to get away… Derik did all the fighting, until I got in the way and let him escape. If it weren't for Derik, I'd probably be dead right now… No. That's not true… I *would* be dead. I know it." I started shivering.

"Here." Gamut tucked the blanket more tightly around my shoulders. "Derik's chewed out every guard that was on duty when you slipped out… He can't believe not a single one of us spotted you. I guess they were all distracted by the commotion." He shrugged and was silent a moment, before continuing. "I wanted to come, but he wouldn't let me. He said it was better if he went alone. I should've insisted… Who is he to tell me what's best? I'm the one with feelings for you – I'm sorry… I wish I had been there to prevent this…" He gestured at me.

I frowned through my mental chill. "I think he was right to come alone." *Am I defending Derik?* "I mean, these wounds all happened before he got there… and he's pretty fast, right? So… maybe he was looking out for you, you know? Trying to keep you from possibly getting hurt, while getting to me as quickly as possible…"

"Yeah… maybe," he replied, though his eyes looked guarded. "But I don't need anyone looking out for me."

I yawned and blinked my eyes, trying to stay awake.

"Oh, hey… you should get some sleep. Do you need me to go?" He started to rise.

"No!" I grabbed for his arm, but mine were securely pinned within the blanket. I wasn't nearly capable enough to pull them free.

But he stopped. "Are you sure?" He smiled, when I nodded. "Okay." He settled back in. Then, a mischievous look crossed his face. "You're really stuck in there, aren't you?"

I frowned, not liking where this was going.

His smile broadened, as he rose up onto his knees. He leaned against the cot, staring down at my face.

"What exactly are you – "

He moved faster than I would have given him credit for. Before I could finish my question, he had pressed his mouth to mine.

I balked. I didn't have the energy to resist. Then again, if I'd wanted to, I wouldn't have had the energy to react in *any* way. Finally, he withdrew, and I lay there stunned.

He laughed a little and sat back down. "I told you I couldn't guarantee I wouldn't kiss you again. You're situation is too hard to resist." He paused, his smile faltering. "You – you're not mad at me, are you?

My sleepiness began to overtake my shock. "I should be." I tried to sound cross but a yawn interfered. "But I think I'm too tired to be angry right now."

His smile returned. "Oh, good." Then he settled back in. "I'll stay here with you until you fall asleep." He laid his head down beside me, watching as I closed my eyes.

The medicine Glenna had given me began its work quickly then. I was asleep within moments.

I dreamed of snow. Everything was white, and flakes floated down around me. Someone was with me… Derik? I had the impression of a dark forest, covered in snow. We were waiting for something… but what? Then it all began to fade…

* * *

I awoke to the sound of the door opening and made out a woman's shape against the light in the hall. The candles had burned out long ago or been blown out. She left the door open, as she crossed the room and lit a lantern hanging from the ceiling. I covered my eyes against the faint glare.

"Good morning, Haylee. How are you feeling today?" Glenna asked. She sat a tray down on the table beside me and felt my forehead. "You don't have a fever."

"Uh… I feel all right, I guess. A little groggy, maybe?" I glanced at the floor beside the cot. "Where's Gamut?"

"Gamut? I suppose he is working his shift right now." She sat down on the edge of the cot.

"Oh. Is it that late in the day? How long did I sleep?" I tried to sit up, but she placed a hand on my shoulder.

"Relax. It is midday, and you slept as long as you needed to, I would wager. From the sound of things, you slept rather well. Derik checked in on you very early this morning. I believe he is anxious to hear from me, once I have looked you over. Now, did you need young Gamut for something?" she asked, her voice neutral.

"I – no. I didn't need him for anything. I thought he might still be here. I didn't know what time it was but didn't expect him to miss his shift or anything… I hope he slept."

"He stayed with you last night?" Her voice was still carefully unbiased.

I leaned back into my pillows, the effort to keep my head up without support becoming tiresome. "Yeah… He came by to see me, to see how I was doing. And I asked him to stay until I fell asleep… I was – well, I was nervous being alone… in the dark… after what happened." My cheeks warmed. *Oh, just admit it. You're afraid of the dark. Always have been. But now… now it's legit.*

Glenna relaxed. "Ah. I see. I suppose one of us should have thought of that… Well, I'm grateful you have such a good friend in Gamut, to do that for you." She smiled.

I became uneasy as I recalled the events that had passed since I last saw her. "Friend… yes. At least that's the way I see it. I'm afraid, though, he's not completely satisfied with the status of our relationship…" I grimaced as I said the words. *But I need to talk to someone, and Glenna makes me feel so comfortable.*

She thought for a moment. "What exactly makes you feel this way?" She folded her hands in her lap.

I closed my eyes. "Well, little things, really. But, mostly, because he… kinda kissed me. More than once." I squeezed my eyes tight, waiting for her reaction. She was quiet for some time, so I chanced a peek. I was surprised to see her suppressing laughter. "Glenna!"

She tried to compose herself, but failed. "You must admit, it is amusing."

I stared at her for a moment. *Amusing*? Then, I smiled. "Yes, it's quite the problem I have, isn't it?" I laughed a little. *It* is *kind of funny, but it's also very serious.* "Glenna, it's just I don't feel that way toward him… I don't want him to get hurt. What should I do?" A frown replaced my small smile.

Now, it was Glenna's turn to become serious. "Have you told him how you feel?"

"Yes. Emphatically. But he's not convinced I won't change my mind."

"I see." She paused. "Is there any chance of that? Think about it for a moment."

I did. "No."

She studied me, that speculative look from the night before returning to her face. "Why is it you are so sure, then, I wonder?"

"What do you mean?" I was wary of this line of questioning.

She smiled again. "Come, now. Don't play dumb… Something is happening here. I can see it. And it's not one-sided."

It isn't? What exactly does she mean by that?

"Haylee, do you have feelings for someone else? Feelings strong enough to make you that sure?"

How do I answer that? "Y – yes." *Good. Keep it simple.*

Glenna looked down at her clasped hands. "I see. I was unsure but beginning to suspect… He is dangerous, you know – be forewarned. But I think he feels strongly for you, as well." Her smile returned, and she turned it toward me.

I frowned and shook my head. "Dangerous?"

"Ah… well. Derik is a very good man… and a very haunted one. He's been with us for many years now. I've come to think of him as a brother, but he's never spoken of his past, not even to me. I'm afraid he may not ever share it with anyone, may never allow himself to open up to someone… No matter how strongly he feels." She looked at me pointedly. "Do you understand? I'm concerned you'll be hurt, if you allow yourself to continue on this road. But, then again, it's your choice. Continue at your own risk, as they say."

I stared at the space in front of me. *Is it a risk I'm willing to take?* "I've been hesitant so far… because I'll be going home. But I've let myself fall for – or have these feelings for… *him.* In spite of myself. All this time, I've worried about hurting someone else and haven't given a thought to how I'd be feeling." I looked at her again. "Isn't that funny?"

Her eyes were full of sympathy now. "Oh, Dear One… If he only knew – oh my, you're going to have me all teared up." She laughed, blinking. "I won't be able to see to change your bandages. Here, let me help you sit up."

I just stared at her, as she unwound the cloth. *What? If he only knew what?*

"My, you *are* a fast healer. I think you'll be good as new in another couple of days – well, at least good enough to go without the bandages, anyway." She crossed the room to retrieve some clean strips.

I glanced down at the claw marks in my side. The bleeding had stopped, and the gauges didn't look as angry as I imagined.

Glenna had me bandaged back up in no time. "Do you feel any pain?"

"Um, not much. I don't think I feel any other lingering effects either. No dizziness, I mean."

"That *is* good. But you might want to take it easy for a few days. Those symptoms tend to last a little longer than the physical ones. No standing up too quickly or anything… and try not to get too excited from all the kissing." She smiled.

Seriously. Glenna's teasing *me?*

"Now. I brought you some food." She indicated the tray she had placed by the cot. "Take your time with it, and we'll see if you have the strength to move about after that. All right?" Her smile broadened at my nod. "Good. Eat up. I'll be back in to check on you in a little while." She smoothed my hair and left the room.

* * *

I picked at my food for as long as I could tolerate before I wrinkled my nose and pushed it away.

Come on, Glenna. I tapped my fingers on the tray. *How long has it been? It feels like I've been sitting here forever. Where is she?*

Noises from the hall filtered through the door. I watched for it to open, but none of the footsteps belonged to Glenna.

Oh, forget it. I threw the blanket back, maneuvered to the edge of the cot, and shifted my lower body over the side. My bare toes touched the floor. It was cold compared to the cocoon of the blanket.

Well, that wasn't too difficult. But should I try to stand without a little help?

I was considering it, when the door opened.

"Hey, I just – what are you doing?" Derik closed the door and strode across the room. "I thought Glenna was going to help you after you finished your meal."

I looked up at his tall figure. "I… got tired of waiting?" My expression was hopeful.

He sighed. "I see that. You weren't planning on getting up and going for a walk, by any chance, were you?" He crossed his arms.

I smiled at the now familiar stance. "I might have been… What are you going to do about it?" *What?! Did I actually* say *that? Oh, God! Where can I find a rock to hide under? Oh, don't blush,* don't *blush. Oh, never mind… You're definitely are.*

"Did Glenna give you more medicine?" He looked at me uncertainly but I could see a smile tugging at the corners of his mouth.

"Nope. Just tempting fate," I said under my breath, but I was sure he had heard from the curious expression on his face.

His curiosity turned to caution. "Do you want me to help you?" He held out a hand.

"Okay… I hadn't actually decided to try it on my own… just – "

"Just thinking about it."

"Yeah…" I placed my hand in his and felt warmth spreading inside, as his fingers curled around mine. *Oh. Wow… is he feeling this?*

He stepped up beside me and put his other hand on my uninjured side.

Evidently not.

"Okay," he said, and helped me rise from the cot. "How do you feel?"

"Great." *Breathless.* I stared up into his face and my heart sped up. *Okay, this could be bad. When did I decide to allow these feelings? I don't think I did. Can I not stop my reactions? Control them? Is this how Gamut feels? Scary thought.*

"Haylee. Your heart's racing… maybe you should sit down."

"No." I struggled not to react too strongly. "I'm okay. Got up a little too fast, I think. I'm fine now." *Yeah,* that *sounded really convincing.*

And Derik didn't *look* convinced but he didn't make me sit back down, either. "All right. Let's try a few steps then, before we get ahead of ourselves." He walked along beside me, and I was able to get my heart under some control. "Good. That's good. I think you'll be fine before you know it." He smiled down at me.

My heart did a flip, which was its normal reaction to this stimulus.

He frowned. "Are you sure you're all right?"

This time I definitely blushed. *How'd he know? He can't hear my heartbeat, can he? No, that's ridiculous.* I glanced at the hand he was holding. *Of course! He can feel my pulse!*

"Haylee? Are you all right?"

My heart took another tiny hop at the mention of my name, so he moved in front of me and dropped his hand to my shoulder.

"What's wrong?"

My blush must have deepened. "Maybe I *should* sit down." I was growing a bit lightheaded.

He guided me back to the cot. Once I was seated, he placed his hands on either side of my face. It reminded me of yesterday.

"Tell me what you're feeling." He checked my eyes again.

"What I'm feeling?" *Oh, gosh.*

"You're so pale… Talk to me, Haylee."

His concern touched me… which didn't help my situation at all. *It's becoming more and more difficult not to love him. Love? I* love *him? I barely* know *him. Have I even been here a week yet? I haven't exactly kept track of the days. What* am *I feeling? I can't lie to him but I should probably leave out some details.* "I… I was remembering yesterday… and it took me off guard, I guess."

His shoulders relaxed. "I'm sorry. I forget how traumatizing an encounter can be for humans. Are you all right now?"

Something about what he said bothered me, but I couldn't put my finger on it. I took a deep breath. "Yeah… I feel better."

He stood. "Good. You should stay in bed for today. I'll tell Glen –"

"No! I can't stay in here all day by myself… Don't… Please?" I grabbed his hand, as he turned.

The action surprised him, and he stared at our hands for a moment. When I didn't let go, he looked at my face.

He's waiting for me to explain myself, but I'm not sure I can. "Sorry." I slid my hand from his and got a shock as our fingertips came apart. I jumped.

Derik jerked his hand back.

"Ouch. Static…?" I shook my hand to dull the slight ache.

He still looked startled. "Yeah… must've been." He stared at his hand as if it was a separate entity he couldn't quite figure out.

"Couldn't I go up to the room with the books, or at least go sit with Gamut until his shift is over?" When I mentioned Gamut, I noticed a miniscule change in Derik's expression but chose to ignore it. "I won't do anything strenuous… and I won't sneak out for more water or to go home." I exaggerated the plea by batting my eyelashes. *Is that the start of a smile I see?*

"Uh-huh… I'll believe that when I see it. Don't worry, I'm keeping an eye on you." He laughed a little.

Ha! I made him laugh! "So, what do you say?" I grinned at him now.

"The look on your face is making me doubt… Either you're too innocent-looking, and I shouldn't trust you at all… ever." He laughed again, then his smile faltered. "Or you're sincere, and I'm wondering how anyone could ever say no…"

If that was an attempt to disguise a serious statement as a joke, he's failed miserably…

His eyes held mine.

Man, this is getting awkward and very taxing. How can I fight this, when he keeps looking at me like that?

"How about a compromise?"

I frowned. "What do you mean?"

"I'll compromise with you. I will bring down as many books as I can carry for you to read to your heart's content, and you will stay in here – just for today. I'm sure Gamut will be stopping by to see you anyway… If last night is any indicator."

Is he scolding me?

"I'll make sure he brings your supper with him… Fair enough?"

"Uh, yeah… Do you have something against Gamut, Derik?" I purposefully used Derik's name this time, more for my own benefit, to see if I could. *Does saying his name have the same affect on him, as him saying mine does on me?*

His expression softened. "No. What possible reason could I have? He's a good soldier and a hard worker… I mean, he does goof off a little more often then I'd like. But he's still young so I expect that, I guess. Besides… he'll learn, I'm sure…."

"What do you mean?" I frowned at his choice of words.

"I mean that when your distractions cause someone to get hurt – or worse – you learn to pay attention, to take things and people more seriously. That's all… and it's bound to happen sometime." He looked sad now.

And I felt sad too. *For him maybe?* "How do you know? I mean, because he's – wait a minute. Is that why you wouldn't let him come with you yesterday? To find me, I mean?"

"That's part of it, yes. Isn't that good enough reason?"

"No – I mean, yes, it is… I didn't mean anything. I was curious, because he mentioned it last night… He was upset he couldn't be there for me – "

"He could've been. He didn't have to stay because I said so. If he cared enough to – "

"Derik." *I don't want to hear this argument.* "It doesn't matter. What's done is done. I was curious. That's all." *And tired.*

He could see this. "I'm sorry… I don't know what came over me." He shook his head. "I'll go get those books." He turned and left.

I leaned back onto the cot. *What* had *come over him?*

A few minutes later the door opened, and I jumped.

Derik came in with an armload of books.

"That was fast." I sat up. "Do you need some help?"

"No. Stay where you are." He placed the stack on a chair and moved it within arm's reach of the cot. "Thank you… for offering, though."

I nodded and glanced over the spines – well, what was left of them, anyway – and picked the first one up. It was the book of fairy tales I had been reading the other day.

"I am sorry, Haylee."

"You're sorry? Didn't you already apologize?" I laughed a little.

He kneeled down in front of me. "Not for just now… I need to apologize for how I've treated you since you arrived. I'm sorry. I should never have acted that way toward you. I've been disrespectful and arrogant where you're concerned… and I'm sorry. I shouldn't be taking out my frustrations on you. Do you think you can forgive me?"

"Forgive you? Oh, you mean for treating me like a nuisance and a child? *That?*" I pretended to settle in with my book and hid my smile behind it.

Without being able to see Derik's face, I had little idea what he was thinking, but he was quiet for some time.

"Haylee." He drew out the first syllable of my name – and one of those *good* chills ran up my spine – as he pulled the book down to my lap.

The feeling of intimacy made my smile falter but not before he saw it.

He raised an eyebrow at me. "I don't think you're taking this seriously enough."

A chuckle escaped. "*I'm* not taking it seriously enough? Shouldn't I be the one to decide how seriously to take it? I mean I'm the one *you're* asking for forgiveness… right?" I tried to hide my smile again and failed… again.

Derik made a noise half way between a sigh and a laugh. "You are impossible! I'm apologizing here, and you're *teasing* me? What is it I've got to do? What do you want from me?" He was becoming slightly agitated now.

My smile faded. "I don't want anything from you." *Though that may not be the truth.* "I… Can't we start over? Start fresh? And forget all of that?"

His features were relaxed now. "Yeah. We could do that." He nodded.

I sighed with relief. "Great. Thank you. See, now you have nothing to apologize for." I sat up straighter.

"Yeah… You know… You confound me." Still kneeling, he planted one hand on either side of me and leaned against the cot.

The way he studied my face made me uncomfortable.

I let out a nervous laugh. "You really need to stop that… I – I'm… Why are you…?" I closed my mouth and swallowed, trying to breathe normally.

His eyes narrowed for a moment, then he rocked back on his heels with an expression of utter astoundment. "I don't believe it… She… was right." He leaned close again, his eyes intently focused.

"What?! Who was right? Derik? What are you – I don't…" Finally, I grabbed his face in both of my hands. "Derik. What are you talking about? And why are you staring at me like you're, I don't know… searching for something?"

"It's just it doesn't make sense. It can't be. I mean I know what she said but I always wanted to think of her as just another fortuneteller… you know, not the real thing… But she said…" He trailed off again, without answering my question.

But I was beginning to understand. *Fortuneteller? Sabella.* "Derik, you're gonna have to do better than that for me, okay?" I held his face more firmly but I didn't know if forcing him to focus on me would do any good, since that was the problem to begin with. So, I gave him a little shake.

"I'm sorry. It's difficult to see for myself…" He frowned again. "I can't believe she could be right. I can't. We're not… there's no way. I did feel a connection but it can't be that. You can't be…"

"…Your Other Half." I dropped my hands from his face.

He looked at me now, really looked at me. "How…? I don't think you understand – no, how could you?" He stood up abruptly and paced across the floor.

I was once again stunned into silence. *What couldn't I understand?* I leaned forward on the cot, too shaky to rise. "Couldn't you explain it to me then? If we're – if I'm – "

"You're not!"

I flinched. *So, that must mean…* "You don't want me then…" I murmured, but not softly enough.

He turned and was down in front of me before I could blink. I'd never seen anyone move so fast.

"You have no idea what you're saying." His voice was hard. "We're not a match, it's as… simple as that."

"What is it? Am I not big enough? Not strong enough? Not… pretty enough, smart enough? Why aren't we a match? Tell me." My voice was firm but also showed my desperation. A desperation I hadn't known I felt.

"That's not it at all…" His voice had lost its sharpness. "Most of the time a person's other half is opposite them in many ways… and you're my opposite in every way I can see." He looked me over. "There are no mates for… people like me. But I *am* what I am, and we're *too* different." He held my eyes there, trying to drill the point into my head. "It's crazy and… even if it was possible, I'm too dangerous for you to be with."

There's that word again. Dangerous. What does that mean? "Glenna says you have a past, something you've never discussed with her. Tell *me*. Let me decide whether or not you're too dangerous. Because right now I don't see it. I can't see it. Don't you think I deserve the chance to decide for myself?" We had drawn closer together as we spoke, and our faces were inches apart. My eyes trailed down to his lips and back to his eyes.

"Haylee."

I had to lean in to hear him.

"It can never be… I don't understand how it could…"

Our lips met.

I threw my arms around his neck. He pressed himself into the cot. We still weren't close enough.

He let out a grunt of frustration, swatted my knees apart, and grabbed my hips to pull me against him.

A gasp escaped me but we didn't stop.

As his hands came up behind my neck, mine curled into his hair. We deepened the kiss.

Just when I thought I'd suffocate, he pulled back and broke contact. I tried to follow him, but he held me back.

He leaned his forehead against mine. "This is crazy."

At least I'm not the only one out of breath. "I agree. Let's keep going." I tried to move in close again.

His hands held my head firmly in place. "No." He nearly laughed and managed to untangle my fingers from his hair. "Haylee, no. Though I greatly appreciate your enthusiasm, I don't think that's a good idea." He was serious now.

And my heart fell. "Was it not good? I can try again…" I smiled a little.

"I've told you. This can't happen. I'm afrai – this could only end badly for you. Besides, you'll be leaving soon, right? If I have to hurt you now to keep you from being hurt worse later, I will. I'm not above that."

I frowned. "Tell me… *why* it couldn't work. Forget about me going home… If I did, who's to say I couldn't come back? To stay."

"Haylee, you have to go home. It's where you belong." He paused. Then rushed on. "That's why it can't work. You have to go back to your own time, your own people."

"But *you* said I couldn't — "

"You don't belong here, and you know it. You've thought it, mentioned it. This is a glitch or something. All right?"

"A glitch?" I frowned. "It didn't – *doesn't feel* like a glitch. How can you say that?"

"I can, because it is." His voice was regaining some of its lost edge. "And the sooner you learn that, the better." He stood and, when he spoke again, it was quietly. "I have to go now… I've got work to do. Gamut will be here soon with your dinner." His back was to me, his hand on the doorknob. "Maybe you should give more thought to how *he* feels about you… The two of you are much more compatible." And he left.

I was stunned, and it was a long time before I recovered – myself or my book.

* * *

A little while later, I heard a knock at the door and sat up expectantly.

Gamut came through with a tray of food.

My shoulders drooped.

"Hey there, Sunshine! How are ya' today?" He closed the door and sat down beside me, setting the tray between us. "Do you mind if I eat with you?"

I smiled down at the bowls. "No, I don't mind. That sounds fine."

He looked at me more closely. "*Sounds fine*? Are you all right?" He smiled, as usual.

I returned the favor. "Yes, I'm fine… A little tired, I guess."

He handed me a bowl and picked up his own. "Tired, huh? Derik hasn't been making you train or anything, has he?" He talked around a mouthful.

"What? No. He helped me move around the room a little, until I had to sit down. If he hadn't come along, you probably would've found me on the floor half-way across the room." *That's not* exactly *true. I may have made it to the door first. The only reason I got woozy was because of Derik… I think.* Either way, I felt compelled to defend him. Then, I became curious. "Do you like Derik?" I knew of no other way to word the question.

"*Like* him?" Gamut coughed. "Well, he's all right, I guess… A little full of himself but…" He shrugged.

"Huh." I shrugged too. *No argument there. Derik* is *pretty arrogant, at times. But I think I get it… to a degree.*

Gamut and I sat and ate in amiable silence, which was nice, and his company did cheer me up a little.

He finished his food before me and set it down.

I could feel his eyes on me and swallowed my bite. "What?"

"You seem different… Are you sure you're feeling okay?" He put his hand on my forehead. "You do feel a little warm. Maybe Glenna should give you some more medicine for infection… Hey, can I see where it got you? The Pale One, I mean?"

I looked at him then. "Uh… okay. It's on this side." I indicated my right side and lifted my shirt a little.

He peeked under the bandages. "Wow… that looks like it was kinda deep. Was it its claws that did it?"

When I just blinked at him.

"'Cause, I mean, they bite sometimes, too… I hear."

"Yeah, claws…" I smiled and shook my head.

"There it is. That's what I've been looking for. That smile of yours, Sunshine. You've been overcast ever since I got here. What's going on?"

I lowered my shirt. *Should I say anything, considering how he feels about me?* I took a deep breath. "Derik and I had an argument, I guess."

"Oh, is that all? Derik argues with people all the time, even Glenna and – well, I've never heard him argue with Nate but that's another story. The point is there's no reason to worry about it. He'll get over it." Gamut put his arm around my shoulders. "And if he gives you any trouble, I'll show him what for."

I gave him a doubtful look.

"Hey! I'm deceptively scrappy and resourceful." He tapped my nose.

I laughed and hit his hand away.

"That's better."

"Evidently, I'm a fast healer, by the way…" I smiled.

"You mean that was worse?" He pointed at my side.

I nodded. "Yeah… much redder… I think rest has helped it." I finished my food and sat the bowl down.

He stared for a time. "Wow… Haylee, I'm glad Derik found you in time, I really am… Though I wish I could have been there to do it, I guess I owe him for saving your life…" Giving Derik any kind of credit where I was concerned couldn't have come easy, so he meant it.

"Gamut, *you* don't owe him anything. If anyone does, it's me." I had placed my hand on his knee, then thought better of the action and took it back.

"That's not how I feel. Besides, I don't like the idea of you owing him anything. I'm sorry but it's true. I mean, he's always taken care of us… well, for as long as he's been here. But I can't help feeling something's off with him, you know?" He paused and frowned. "No, I don't guess you would… Forget I said anything, all right? Let's enjoy the rest of our evening." His smile returned.

"Okay."

"You know, everyone's talking about what you did… going out alone and finding the water… everything down to your single-handed fight with the Pale One…" He chuckled. "I know, I know… you didn't fight 'em. But that doesn't matter. One attacked you, and you lived to tell the tale. It's pretty amazing, really. The place is ablaze. They all love you now." He tapped me under the chin with his knuckles.

"Sheesh… really? That's crazy… I mean, I think I did it to prove myself but… I didn't expect anything like what you're describing." I leaned against the wall behind us.

"Well, you've got it. And I say you deserve that and more. As far as I'm concerned, you saved us. We really needed that water." He stood up. "Hey, I'm gonna go ahead and take this tray back to the cafeteria, okay? I'll be right back. Don't go anywhere." He grinned.

So much has happened in the last twenty-four hours. And now everyone's talking about me like I'm some kind of action movie hero. So, why is it all I can think about is Derik? Is it true then? What Sabella said? Somehow, I know it is. Derik doesn't feel the same. My chest ached. *Just stop thinking about it! Think about anything but that…* The effort left me curled up on the cot.

And that's how Gamut found me.

"Hey. You look pretty tired. How 'bout I read to you from one of these books, and you try to rest? Does that sound good?" He pulled another chair nearby.

"Yeah… that sounds great." I yawned and pulled the blanket around myself. "It's gotten cooler over the last hour or so."

"The sun's setting. It gets pretty chilly at night, compared to the hot temps during the day. During the rainy season, it'll cool down even more. So, which one should we choose?" He began pulling books out of the stack.

"Does it snow during the rainy season?"

He stopped what he was doing. "Snow? Not here – well, I don't think I've ever seen it, anyway. No, it doesn't get quite cold enough for that… Snow…" He shook his head and placed a few books back in the pile. "Here we go." He held one up.

I couldn't make out what it was.

"It's one of my favorites." He began reading.

As he read, I recognized the book as *The Time Machine,* by H.G. Wells.

How fitting… Haylee Gai Wells, the time-traveling girl… It's as if the universe had my whole existence mapped out. I must've done something truly terrible in a past life.

I was too sleepy to voice my dark amusement, and it wasn't long before I had trouble making out Gamut's words.

At some point, the door closed but I wasn't with it enough to know more than that.

8

The next day, I was able to leave the room. I didn't feel the least bit dizzy but, then again, I didn't see Derik either. I spent most of my time with Glenna and Gamut and ate lunch with Karroll and Merritt.

All eyes were, once again, on me. It made me nervous at first but, when people started coming up to me and introducing themselves, the anxiety passed. Everyone was friendly and, when I ate dinner with Gamut, others asked to sit with us.

The only person who still didn't trust me was Nate. Every once in a while, I would catch her eyeing me from across the room.

Why is she acting like this? Does she know about Derik and me? If that's it, surely she knows he wants nothing to do with me. Best to just ignore her.

The days passed by quickly after my excursion outside, and my wounds healed rather nicely. Glenna said I would most likely have permanent scars. I was okay with that. It would remind me of a foolish thing I'd done that had paid off. Plus, I wasn't one to strut around in a bikini, anyway.

Derik led a group to the well within days of going out to find me. They were optimistic they had a stable source of water. Though they'd always look for more, in case of sabotage by the Pale Ones.

And he was still avoiding me.

Once I had healed sufficiently, I asked Glenna how I could help around the compound. At first, she gave me simple indoor jobs like washing dishes and cleaning. Eventually, I worked up to some gardening and laundry.

Both gardens flourished now. Before too much longer, we would have full-grown tomatoes and other veggies. I was excited by the concept of something other than the gruel-like substance for breakfast, lunch, and dinner. Everyone else was too.

Now that I was moving around more, noticing more, and was able to talk to more of the people, I became curious about something.

Where are the children most of the day? I haven't seen much of them since the first day on the roof. Maybe it's because of my erratic sleeping patterns since I got here.

When I breached the subject with Glenna, she was more than happy to answer my questions.

"Most of the children have lessons during the day. We try to keep their lives as structured as possible. Though that isn't always easy."

"How many children are there?" I asked, helping her fold scraps of cloth in the infirmary.

"Twelve. Most between the ages of two and ten." She didn't look up from her work.

I could tell this was a sore subject for her but pressed on. "Philip – that's his name, right? – doesn't look any older than fifteen, but I haven't seen many others around that age… and what about older teens?"

Glenna's hands stilled for a moment, mid-fold, then she continued. "I mentioned before that the Pale Ones had not taken any children for some time." She didn't go on.

Oh. They were taken. Okay. Way to be insensitive. "I'm sorry, Glenna. I really am."

She smiled. "Don't worry so. That was a very long time ago, and we have twelve beautiful, healthy children now. And nothing is going to happen to them." She patted my hand.

I changed the subject. Sort of. "So, what subjects do they learn and who teaches them?" I asked her, trying for cheerfulness.

"Well. Each day is different, we alternate. We teach them Chemistry and First Aid – sometimes I fill in there. They get beginner level defense lessons and other such practical things. They are assigned chores in groups by age. Let me see, reading, of course, can never be neglected… But today they should be learning some geography and history – you know, it probably wouldn't hurt for you to sit in on their history lessons, Haylee. It would be very informative for you. I wasn't born when it happened but I learned about it in my own history classes. Sarif teaches that class now. I think you've met him. He uses his ability to teach the students. He's a natural storyteller."

Sarif was the oldest man I had met at the compound. His hair was gray but he probably wasn't much over forty. I supposed the average life expectancy had plummeted a bit since my time. He was a pleasant person. So, I took Glenna up on her offer, and she said she would speak with him.

"Have you heard from Sabella yet?" I had not met with the Seer since before my "adventure."

"I've spoken with her briefly. She's very preoccupied recently…" Glenna paused. "Don't worry, Haylee. I'm certain this will pass, and she'll be asking for you again. I suppose it *has* been some time though. In the meantime, perhaps the history lessons and training with Derik will prove a diversion for you. You have spoken with him about picking up where you left off, now that you are nearly completely healed?"

"Um… well. I haven't exactly seen… him. I think he…" *Oh, I can't tell her he's been avoiding me…* "He's been pretty busy lately." *Lame. Oh, what a lousy liar you are.*

Glenna's expression remained neutral. As usual.

But I knew better. The tiniest things gave her away. How she folded her hands, the direction she moved her eyes, and the words she chose. The words *sounded* unaffected, but I knew when she was annoyed, disappointed, or worried. Only once had I seen worry on her face. It was the day of my adventure, when Derik had brought me back, nearly unconscious and bleeding. Even then, she showed it only in private. Derik and I were the lone witnesses. The only emotion she allowed to show freely was happiness. I believe she did this to keep hope alive with the others at the compound.

Now, from those tiniest of indicators, unbeknownst to her, I could see she was growing irritated. And that irritation was directed toward Derik.

"I will speak to him." She placed the folded bandages on a shelf. "Take care of yourself, Haylee." She patted my shoulder and left the room.

Hm. I think someone's about to get chewed out. Glenna style. I laughed a little to myself.

* * *

Later that day, Glenna found me in the front hall with Gamut.

"I thought I'd find you here. I have spoken with Derik, and he has agreed to reinitiate your training tomorrow morning after breakfast." She gave a curt nod and turned. "I'll speak with you afterwards to see how things have gone." Then, she went back down the hall.

Gamut and I stared after her.

"Well, their talk must have gone well," Gamut joked.

"Uh-huh. Which means the training will go just as well, I suppose…" I groaned.

"Hey, don't worry… You did fine the last time around – you fought off one of those things, for crying out loud! I think you'll do fine against him. Don't think about it until the time comes, okay? Enjoy the rest of your day." He gave me a one-armed hug.

I was tired of correcting him.

I didn't fight the Pale One off. All I did was try to get away and fail. Miserably. Derik's the one who fought it. And if I hadn't gotten in the way, he would have done a much better job of it. I'm sure of that.

The rest of my day crawled by, uneventful. I tried to take Gamut's advice but could think of nothing other than my upcoming session with Derik. As I sat down to my dinner, I realized if I didn't focus on something other than him, he was foremost on my mind. I couldn't help it, these days. It was getting easier and easier not to think about home. I didn't feel I had much of a reason to go back at the moment. I had figured out what had happened to Aunt Bethany though I still wanted to know why.

Why had they come to the past? And why to my aunt's farm? Why did they attack her? Were they waiting *for me? If so, had they grown impatient?*

These questions had burned in my mind every day since I'd arrived at the compound. But I had no way of answering them. Now they were crowded with other questions. Things that had become equally important to me.

Why hasn't Sabella sent for me? And what's going on between Derik and me, if anything at all? Is it possible I am *his "Other Half"? If so, where does that leave Nate? And why am I feeling sorry for her? And, most importantly, why's he so against the idea?*

Oh, that kiss… I pressed my fingers to my lips.

"Hey… Earth to Haylee…" Gamut waved his hand in front of my face.

I jumped and looked around. "Huh?"

Gamut sat down in front of me at the table. A few others stared.

My face warmed. "Uh, hi." I stared down at my food, which I'd barely touched.

"Hi. Sorry. Didn't mean to scare you… Where were you anyway? You were a thousand miles away. Daydreaming?" He smiled. "It was about me, wasn't it?"

"Huh? Oh, no, I was just thinking… Sorry. How was your shift?"

"Well… compared to the day you went on your adventure, all days are dull." He laughed and started eating. "What have you been up to since I saw you last?"

"Oh, you know… laundry, dishes… whatever I can do. Did I tell you Glenna's going to talk to Sarif about letting me sit in on some of the history lessons?"

"I could do that," he said around a mouthful of food. He swallowed. "You don't have to be around all those kids to get a history lesson. It's all pretty sim – "

"You? Give a history lesson? Now that's something I would like to see!" Karroll sat down beside her brother.

They have matching smiles.

"You didn't listen to a single lesson we ever had," she said. "Hey, Haylee. You doin' all right today?"

I nodded, still amused by their exchange. "I'm fine."

"She's going back to training with Derik tomorrow," Gamut threw in.

Karroll raised her eyebrows at me. "Oh yeah? I haven't seen the two of you together for a while now…"

"Why *would* you see them together?" Gamut asked. "Other than when she went for water, the only time they were ever together was for training."

"It was just an observation…" Karroll shook her head.

I still haven't gotten through to him. But I can't not be friends with him… Can I? No, that would hurt him too, and I don't want him angry with me. I need his friendship… His and Karroll's and Glenna's… Will I be able to leave when the time comes? Surely, I will…

* * *

The next morning, I found my stomach a bundle of nerves before my feet touched the floor. In the cafeteria, I stared at my food. I found myself hesitating with every step I took toward the training room.

When I arrived, the door was closed, and I raised my hand to knock. Just before my knuckles made contact, I heard voices. I paused for a moment, more uncertain than ever. The voices sounded agitated, but I couldn't make out the words, so I took a deep breath and rapped on the wood.

The voices stopped.

The door flew open, and Nate pushed past me before I could step out of the way. The look she gave was one to kill, and I was suddenly more afraid of her than I'd ever been. This was the first time I'd come into close proximity with her in a while.

She rushed by me so fast I would have fallen over if Derik hadn't caught my wrist. As soon as he was sure I had my footing, he let go. He stared after her for a moment before addressing me.

"Come on." He closed the door behind me.

"I – I'm sorry if I interrupted… something. I… Is everything okay? I mean, between you and Nate?" I wanted to touch his shoulder but was afraid to. So I stood there, staring at his back.

He turned and moved toward the center of the room. "It doesn't matter…" He faced me. "Are you ready, then?"

I regarded the room nervously. "I suppose so…" I muttered and walked toward him.

I fixated on his feet for a while and, when he didn't say anything else, trailed up to find his face. It took me a bit to rest on his eyes. I took in a shaky breath.

Such a short amount of time's passed since I stood close to him… still, it's like I've forgotten how tall he is, the narrowness his hips, the broadness his shoulders… I've berated myself for dwelling on them in the past but now I can't help myself. I stared up and up into his golden brown eyes and nearly lost myself. I saw myself there and felt a belonging I had never felt before… *Oh, I want to kiss him again.*

That was what snapped me out of it. *Dangerous thoughts… thoughts I can't have. Why can't I have them? Is this what he felt the day in the infirmary? Is this the way it feels to be someone's Other Half?*

He cleared his throat rather loudly and took a step back from me, allowing me to clear my head.

"Do you remember everything I taught you last time? I suppose you remember some of it. I saw you use a few moves on that Pale One before I could get to you. So, let's go over what you learned… Show me."

There's no point in forcing the issue right now. He doesn't want to talk about anything else.

So we went over the moves. I forgot a few techniques.

"Come on. You know this one," he said, once. He was far more demanding this time around.

So I tried harder.

Much sooner than before, I was sweating and out of breath. And my side ached. When I was certain Derik wasn't looking, I lifted up my shirt. The marks there were bright pink but seemed fine.

"I worked you too hard."

I turned to find him standing right behind me. "No!" Perhaps I emphasized this *too* forcefully.

"No? You're hurting, aren't you?"

"I… No, it's only a dull ache now. Nothing to worry about at all. I promise." And I meant it. Before he could say anything else, I rushed on. "You've been avoiding me."

He blinked at me.

Finally. I've taken him *off guard for a change.*

"I think you should go." His eyes were on the floor between us.

"You're not even going to deny it? Say you've been busy. Or something."

I took a step closer, and he took one back. When I realized this, I advanced, forcing him back further.

After several steps, he stopped, catching on to what I was doing.

I was able to get closer now and felt empowered by our little dance.

I should have known he wouldn't let me back him against a wall– not literally, anyway.

He held a hand out. "Don't. Haylee." It sounded like a warning.

I stared at that hand. *A hand that had supported me… carried me… clung to me.*

I looked up to his face to find him studying me. Our eyes met.

Once again, I saw sadness there and felt it myself.

Is it my sadness or his? If it's his, why is he so sad? Or is it… "Are you afraid?" I found myself asking.

"For you," he replied.

I shook my head. "Of this?" I put my hand in his and interlaced our fingers. "I know you feel it. It's not a fluke. Not a glitch. It's real. It's *here.*" I squeezed my fingers.

He closed his eyes, still resisting.

I dropped my hand. "I know… You want me to go. I'll go." Now it was my turn to stare at the floor. "Tell me when we're training again, then I will." I waited.

"I don't think you understand my meaning. I mean *go.* I think you should go home."

I stood very still. "Go *home*?"

"Yes." He sighed.

"But – but how?" Now I frowned up at him.

"I'll take you. I know the way… And the sooner the better."

I stared at him in dismay. "No."

"Haylee, be reasonable…" He reached out to touch me.

I jerked away. "No. I won't go. I'm not going anywhere… not yet, anyway." I turned and moved toward the door. "I'll come back in two days, like we were doing before." I paused with my hand on the knob. "I'll talk to Glenna about training with someone else, in the meantime. Maybe we can get Nate to – "

"No!" He paused and closed his eyes.

I saw his shoulder rise and fall.

He continued with more control. "If you insist on staying, I'll train you." He looked at me carefully.

I considered saying something childish like, *What if I don't want you?* But I thought better of it. *No, I'm not that person. I don't understand the responses he provokes in me. I've never reacted to anyone the way I react to him.* It was my turn for some control. "All right." I gave a slight nod and left the room.

* * *

I didn't hear from Sabella until the following day.

Actually… I dreamed of her. I heard her voice before I woke up, asking me to come to her.

So I did.

"I am sorry, dear, for not seeing you sooner. I understand you have had quite a time of it. I would like a better understanding, of course. May I?" She gestured toward me.

I nodded and sat in the chair across from her. Then I blinked and, when I saw her smiling at me, felt as though an immense weight had been lifted from my shoulders.

"It always helps to tell someone of your frustrations. It is also a great relief to see Derik is beginning to come around to the idea."

"Is he? I'm not so convinced." I slumped in my chair.

"Well, would you not say he has come a long way? Now, he only seeks to protect you. At least, that is what he thinks he is doing.

Perhaps he's thinking a little too much?" She said, with a twinkle in her eye.

I laughed a little. "Yeah. Maybe. He did say he was worried about me, and he said he was dangerous – Glenna even said as much – but I don't see it. If he would tell me what, exactly, is bothering him – whatever it is from his past. Then I could understand and maybe help him through it? I don't know…" I slumped a little further.

Sabella straightened in her seat. "Don't worry so much, Haylee. I have a feeling he'll come around very soon. You see, it's not a matter of trusting *you* but, more so, he has not yet learned to trust himself. That will come with time, I suppose. Though I believe he will tell you before that."

"Well, I wish he'd hurry up, already. He wants me to go home, though he was against it before. I'm not completely sure what's changed. Either I'm in more danger if I go, or if I stay. I just wish he'd make up his mind on which one it is." *Ugh, I hate feeling sulky.*

My visit with Sabella turned into a therapy session. We didn't work as much on psychic defense as on centering myself. She told me calmness was the first step in defending my mind, so we focused on breathing and serenity.

I felt better when the door closed behind me.

9

I lost track of the days leading up to the next incident. The one that sent me home.

Glenna had spoken with Sarif about me observing his history lessons, and it was my second day of listening in on him and the nine children in his class. I had learned the other three children were still too young to attend classes. By that second day, the students were used to my presence, and I wasn't as much of a distraction. Still, I sat at the back of the small upstairs room, because their young eyes often strayed toward me.

"So, who can tell me where we left off yesterday?" he asked his students, as his eyes swept across them.

One hand shot up.

"Yes, Zoe?"

I had learned the names of most of the children, though I got a couple of them confused. I recognized Timothy from my first day at the compound and discovered he was eight years old. Zoe was the second oldest in the class and, from what I had observed, enjoyed the attention she received from answering questions correctly.

"We talked about how the Pale Ones destroyed the cities."

Another hand zipped up into the air.

"Yes, Marcus?"

Marcus, at ten, was the oldest of the children. "They revealed themselves first, and gave us five days to evacuate the cities." He paused before continuing less excitedly. "Unfortunately, many people didn't believe they were speaking the truth and died."

The room was quiet.

"That is correct," Sarif replied. "And how do we refer to the period following the Incident?"

"APO, After the Pale Ones," Zoe replied.

"Remember your hand next time, Zoe," Sarif chided.

The girl ducked her head.

"But correct again. APO. The time period prior to the Incident is referred to as BPO, or Before the Pale Ones."

Sarif continued reviewing with his students.

The information was no less shocking to me the second time I heard it. At some point, the Amara had announced their existence to the world. How they had accomplished this was still unclear to me, but apparently everyone in the nation had the opportunity to hear or see them. Had their attack gone beyond the U.S.? They informed humans they had always been amongst us but, with their numbers increasing over time, they had remained hidden. They gave us an ultimatum – abandon our major cities within five days, or be destroyed along with them. From what I had gathered, at least a quarter of the population perished on the fifth day.

I learned, when the nearest city – the city in which my mother had been pressuring me to attend college – had gone up, the smoke could be seen by the survivors in this area. How they had managed to create such a catastrophe was still unknown, but it was suspected they had somehow accessed the natural gas lines. I still had no real way of knowing when this had happened – the exact date had been lost – though they called the current year 77 APO. So, I could safely assume it had been *that* long since *the Incident.* But how long did my time have until the Amara-led genocide occurred?

Since that time, humans and the Amara had traded places. The Pale Ones were now able to live the lives they wanted, while humans were forced into hiding. Humans were hunted like animals and drained of life, so the Amara could continue existing. Of course, the Amara didn't count on the resilience of the human race, their ability to adapt. And adapt is what they had done. While some of the people here called it evolution, I knew from my own school days that evolution didn't happen quite so quickly. Instead, I believed as Glenna did. The abilities humans had begun exhibiting had always been there. We'd just had no need for them until the rise of the Pale Ones had triggered them.

Their occurrence was more magical than natural.

It's possible. I thought back to the night I had traveled to this time, and the hours preceding it. *If the proximity and increased numbers of Pale Ones triggered abilities, maybe they awakened something in me. It's definitely something I should consider.*

* * *

After class, Gamut called for me from across the hall.

"Hey." He smiled down at me. "Want some lunch?"

"Sure. I was heading that way."

So we walked together.

"How was the history lesson today?"

"It was amazing… and kind of hard to believe… I probably wouldn't, if I hadn't experienced the things I have so far… So, you guys know how long ago the Amara came out, but the year has been lost?" I frowned.

Gamut laughed. "You didn't ask your questions during class?"

I blushed. "I'm still a little nervous around Sarif, I guess… and the kids. They still stare at me some. If we weren't in class, and Sarif wasn't in complete control, I imagine they'd be asking me the questions." I felt my little smile broaden. "They're great though – the kids, I mean… They've got so much energy, so much creativity… and so much curiosity! Children aren't all that different in this time. I'm looking forward to the next class."

Gamut stopped in the doorway of the cafeteria. "Wow. You're awfully excited about a class." He laughed, looking around. "So, you know you've completely won the trust of pretty much everyone here. Them being okay with you interacting with the kids is proof. I told you they'd come around." He hugged me.

"Thanks." I blushed, as I caught a few people looking our way. "Let's eat. I'm starving."

Half way through our meal, Sarif brought a small group of the children into the cafeteria. He accompanied each of them to their respective parents and, once they were seated, he made his way to the lunch line.

"That's how it's done," Gamut replied to the curious look on my face. "He takes the group around, dropping them off with their families, until the very last one. We're never supposed to leave the children unsupervised."

"Hm. I see." And I went back to my food.

"Well, I'm off to my shift now…" He started to get up. "Will you be able to visit later?"

"Sure. I'll be around."

He placed his hand on my shoulder, before he left. "Okay. I'll see you, then."

He's definitely been behaving himself the last few days. I deposited my bowl with the others needing cleaned and, after a moment's hesitation, went into the kitchen.

Hana, who could be considered the head chef, of sorts, saw me immediately. "You know what happens when you step into my kitchen, little miss Haylee." She smiled. "I'll have to put you to work."

I smiled back. "I know, Hana. That's why I'm here."

She shook her head. "I've never seen anyone so eager to wash dishes. Here you go." She tossed me a piece of cloth, and walked back to the large wood-burning stove.

Ever since the first time I'd volunteered to work back there, I had wanted to ask where they had found it. I know it couldn't have been there the couple of years I had attended the school, or the years following. Instead of voicing this question now, however, I moved toward the big double sinks.

I worked in the kitchen for a few hours before Hana ran me off.

"Little girl, you've done enough. Go on now." She threatened me with her dishtowel. "I know you've got better things to do than stay in this kitchen all day." She laughed as I scurried through the door.

I was heading toward the main doors, when a bell sounded.

Is that a fire alarm?

For a second or two, all motion around me halted. Then, everyone started talking at once and hurried into the cafeteria. I was glued to the floor, looking for a clue as to what was happening.

Someone rushed by me, and I caught his arm. It was Marcus.

"What's going on? What is that?" I frowned at him.

"It's the alarm. It means there's been a breach. We're supposed to go to the cafeteria." He looked down at my hand. "I have to go now."

I let go. "Okay, thanks."

I stood there for a while, as everyone pushed by.

Then Derik was shoving through them. "What are you standing there for? Get inside before they lower the gate." He nudged me forward and hurried on his way to the main entrance.

So I allowed the flow of bodies to pull me along, until I heard a young woman's voice.

"Kara?!"

I searched for her. At the far side of the hall, I saw a girl, looking around frantically. I forced my way against the flow and made it within a few feet of her, when some more of the children arrived there.

"Kara?" She studied each face. "Where's Kara?"

The children looked at each other.

One of them spoke up. "She was with us before. We were upstairs in the game room."

"Oh, God." The young woman blanched.

I touched her arm. "Who's missing?" *She's younger than I thought. My age.*

She started. "Kara. My little sister…" She looked toward the nearest stairwell. "I have to find her."

I stopped her. "I'll go… I know what she looks like." I remembered the smallest child from the class. "Make sure these kids get inside the cafeteria with their families. What's your name?"

She stood frozen in place, her stare blank.

"Hey." I shook her gently. "Your name? So I can tell Kara who sent me."

She snapped out of her daze. "Uh, Kate."

"Okay. I'll get her. Now, go." I nudged her, as Derik had nudged me moments before. I bent toward one of the children. "You said you were upstairs?"

They all nodded.

"Stay with Kate until she helps you find your families, okay?" I turned to go.

Kate caught my arm. "I was supposed to be watching her."

Our eyes met for a second.

"I'll find her." I squeezed her hand.

As I made my way up the stairs, the crowd began to ebb.

"Kara?!"

She wasn't in the room with books and games. I looked under the furniture and in the small closet behind the door. When I returned to the hallway, it was deserted and quiet.

My stomach somersaulted. *This is bad. Need to hurry.* I rushed to the next room. It was the room with the old piano and stack of desks. Movement to the right caught my eye. I turned and heard a slight whimper.

"Kara? Honey, it's all right. Kate sent me. She was so upset when she couldn't find you. She's downstairs with everyone else. Do you want to come down with me?" I edged toward her and, when I saw an eye peek out at me, I stopped. "Hi, Kara. You remember me, don't you? Haylee? I was at your history lesson today?"

She nodded.

Smiling, I crouched down and offered my hand. "Do you want to go downstairs with me?"

"Is the mean lady gone?"

"The mean lady?" I tried to keep the smile on my face but looked around anyway. "I haven't seen her. She must've left. We should probably go before she comes back, don't ya' think?"

Her eyes widened, and she nodded again.

"Okay, let's go."

She came forward and took my hand. Together, we hurried to the stairwell. I scooped her up and somehow managed the steps without falling. The hallway on the main floor was also empty, but I could hear the voices of everyone gathered in the cafeteria.

"We're almost there, Sweetie." I could make out some of what was being said now.

" – accounted for?" It was Derik. A moment later, I heard him again. "She *what*?"

I knew he would be making his way toward the hall. So I picked up my pace a bit.

Then, I heard someone else yell.

"There it is! We've gotta get this gate down now!"

Anything else said was drowned in the uproar.

Then I felt Kara tense in my arms.

"The mean lady!"

I stopped dead. My heart thundered in my ears.

We were halfway to the cafeteria, and she was slightly further away, directly across from the door. She saw us in the same instant.

The sound of metal scraping drew my attention to the cafeteria.

They're lowering the gate! I have to get Kara there before it's down.

I ran as fast as the girl's added weight would allow and shielded her with my body.

We're almost there.

I put her down and shoved her toward the door.

"Go, quickly! Go to your sister!"

I stumbled, hit the floor hard enough to knock the wind out of me, and watched as she made it under the gate.

Now move your butt! I forced myself up, put as much momentum as I could muster behind my steps, and flung myself through.

The gate closed with a satisfying metallic thud behind me. I opened my eyes, which I hadn't noticed were squeezed tight, and looked over my shoulder.

There she was, glowering down at me from the other side of the gate. If the bars had been far enough apart, she would have been able to reach through and touch me. They weren't.

She held my gaze as she pulled an object from her shirt pocket.

What is she… Wait! How'd she get that?!

She bent down, showing off the typical Amara teeth, and placed the object just on the other side of the gate.

My hairclip!

Except it wasn't my hairclip anymore. It was a very large spider.

Oh, man, *that's huge! I should totally be running away right now! Why am I not* moving? I stared at it, as it climbed toward me through the bars of the gate. *Because it's not* really *a spider, is it. It's just my clip. That's so* weird. *And kinda neat. I've never seen anything* like *it. It looks like a spider, and I* should *be scared as hell. But… If I could just… I* shouldn't *but I just want to* touch *it.*

It was close enough. I lifted my hand and, like Briar Rose to the spindle, I touched my fingertips to its back.

And it wasn't a spider. It was just my hairclip again.

That's all it ever was.

I stared at it for a moment longer, until a rumbling sound drew my attention.

The Pale One was *growling* and glaring at me. Her eyes – no longer their soft animal-like color but black – met mine.

And I remembered fear. My entire body pulsed with it.

She grinned, turned, and ran down the hall.

My arms gave out, and I fell back onto the cold, hard floor of the cafeteria, closing my eyes in relief.

Then the buzzing of voices calmed me. Gamut was the first one to reach my side.

"Wow! That was amazing! Kind of scary, but amazing. You never told me you could do that!"

Why does that sound like an accusation? I kept my eyes closed. "I didn't know I could." My entire body tremored. *Nerves. Just nerves. That's why I feel so irritated with Gamut. But* where's*…?*

I opened my eyes and searched the faces around me. No one was closer than Gamut. I caught sight of Derik and Glenna, preoccupied with an intense discussion. They spoke in hushed tones, away from the rest of the group, and glanced my way a time or two.

I was beginning to feel well enough to sit up. Once I was propped up on my elbows, I noticed Derik break away from Glenna. He moved toward the back of the room, the kitchen, then I lost sight of him.

Where's he going? And where was *he? Why didn't he* do *something?*

By this time, it had been deemed safe enough to raise the gate. Two men stood at either side of the doorway, turning the levers and locking them in place.

Derik emerged from the darkened front hallway.

"She's gone." Anger flashed in his eyes. He looked down at me for a moment, or maybe at the clip in my hand, then turned toward Glenna. "I'll check the basement, see if Nate's all right."

Glenna kneeled down beside me. "Are you feeling well, Haylee? Do you need to lie down?"

I was still staring after Derik. "Um… I think I'm okay… a little shaky." I returned my attention to her. "Do you mind helping me up?"

"Of course not."

She and Gamut helped me to the nearest table and sat beside me.

I set my clip down and studied it.

It looks like a normal hairclip. It feels like a normal hairclip. But I'm not treating *it like a normal hairclip. I'm treating it with something akin to amazement. Now I know what the Pale Ones can and can't do. They can give what* seems *like life to inanimate objects. The only danger the objects hold is their victims' belief in them. Take that away, and they're simple objects, nothing more. The Pale Ones can't give true life. They're not capable of that. But they* can *take life. So, why didn't* she*?*

I raised my eyes toward Glenna. "Did anyone get hurt?"

She understood what I was asking. "No. Luckily, no lives were stolen."

I frowned. "Huh. I wonder why…" I looked at them and rushed on to explain. "What I mean is isn't it strange she wouldn't *try* to drain someone?"

Glenna studied me, then answered. "Derik didn't want me to say anything yet, but I can see you're mind's working in that direction anyway, so… We have come to the only logical conclusion we can. We believe she was after you… not necessarily to harm you but to test you and take information back to her master."

"What?" If I'd had the energy to stand up, I would have. "Why?

Glenna, if anyone had been hurt, I'd never – "

"Thanks to you no one did get hurt," someone said from behind me.

I turned to see Kara in the arms of her mother, and Kate standing nearby, tearful but smiling.

"I – I just…" I didn't know what to say to their mother's grateful expression.

"Anything could have happened to her. You don't know how grateful I – *we* – are you were there to help. I owe you everything." She lowered her daughter to the floor.

"Oh, no… I – you don't owe me anything. You – I… Anyone else would've done the same. I just happened to be there to help." I could feel my face turning red.

In an instant, Kara threw herself at me and held on tight.

"Oh." I wrapped my arms around her small frame.

She pulled back. "Thank you for keeping me safe from the mean lady." And, as suddenly as she had moved to me, she was back in her mother's embrace.

"Thank you again," the woman said, preparing to leave.

"Well… you're welcome… uh?"

"It's Kandace." She smiled and led her children out to the hall.

Derik passed them on his way in. He smiled and ruffled the little girl's hair.

"Did you find Nate?" Glenna asked.

He sat down across from us. "Yes, I did."

"Is she all right?" I asked before anyone else could.

His lips twitched.

"What's so funny?"

He gave a short laugh. "Nothing. Only you could be so concerned about the well-being of someone who couldn't care less about yours." He managed to check his smile. "To answer your question… She's fine. A bump on the head, a few scratches and bruises, from what I can tell. I took her to the infirmary to be sure. She's being taken care of as we speak." He looked at me. "What about you?"

"Me?" *So, he's finally interested in my well-being, huh?* I closed my eyes and took a deep breath before looking at him. "I'm fine… I guess. I'm not sure I completely understand what's going on… Glenna was starting to fill me in, when Kandace and the girls stopped to talk."

"So, I heard. You shouldn't be so humble. You did a brave thing.

Once again… stupid but brave." He raised his hands in the classic gesture of surrender. "Don't worry. I'm not going to argue with you. I suppose I do need to tell you what's happened here tonight though. All of you." He took a deep breath. "Two of you know we've been holding one of them in a cell in the basement.

I took a breath to speak.

"Don't interrupt, please. Nate and I have been taking turns watching her, bringing her food, whatever. It was Nate's turn this evening, and…I don't know, something went wrong. She got out, caught Nate by surprise, and knocked her unconscious. She was looking for you, Haylee. Luckily, her objectives didn't include harming anyone – at least not anyone *else*." His jaw clenched.

I opened my mouth.

He held up his hand again. "You want whys and hows. She was looking for you because they're interested in you. For some reason, they already wanted to take you. Or kill you. I'm not sure which. But now they've seen you do something interesting, something potentially harmful – or helpful – to them. And they had to test that. What happened out at the well was relayed to their master, and thus relayed to her. Their minds are all connected, like a single organism, in a way. All of the underlings' thoughts, all the things they see or experience in any way, are seen by him. He hears, sees, feels everything they do. And he can send those thoughts to the others, if he chooses to. Which is what he must have done tonight. She saw an opening, however small, and took it." He shrugged. "Questions?"

Yeah. Whose bright idea was it to keep a Pale One in the basement in the first place? I frowned. "So, this was a test… for me? Then how did they know what I could do, if I've never done it before tonight?"

"Because you have. At the well. When you… tried to push me out of the way? You yelled because the Pale One was forging that rock, and when you lunged at me, you touched it, rendering it useless. I saw it… and he most *certainly* saw it. Of course I wasn't sure at first. I was afraid you'd been bitten. When I realized you hadn't… I knew."

So, that's why he didn't intervene… why he didn't pull me away from the Pale One's creation. Sure would've been nice to know at the time.

"Once we got you in the infirmary, I told Glenna what happened. We were the only ones who knew. Soon afterward, we concluded it would be better for you to go home."

Glenna spoke up. "We did no such thing. *You* came to that

conclusion. I was not at all convinced…" She crossed her arms and hid all evidence of disquiet from her face.

I smiled at her.

Derik continued. "But you think differently now."

Her façade faltered. "Yes. I do." She looked sad.

My smile fell. "Huh? What do you mean? You want me to go home now, too?" *I can't believe what I'm hearing.*

"I think it would be best for you, yes." Her face was perfectly blank now, but her arms were still crossed in front of her.

I wouldn't be able to change her mind. I looked back and forth between the two co-conspirators, unable to think straight. What could I say?

Then, I looked at Gamut, who had been oddly quiet through all of this. He was looking down at the table in front of us.

I smiled and reached for his hand. "Gamut. Tell them I don't need to go anywhere, there's no reason for me to leave right now." *At least, I have someone on my side.*

"Haylee. I can't do that."

My attempted smile wavered again. "What? I don't understand. You can't…" I stopped. "What do you mean?" *Surely, I've misunderstood.*

He sighed and pulled away. "I can't because I think – no, I *know* you should go home. It's not safe here… besides you don't belong here. We all know it." He stood up, glancing at the other two. "So… you've got my vote." He left the room.

I stared after him. Tears prickled at my eyes, and I blinked them back.

Movement on my other side caught my attention.

"I'll see to Nate," Glenna said, as she got up.

Then, it was Derik and me.

I stared down at the clip and turned it over and over. I knew he was staring at it in quite the same way.

Sighing, I tilted my head. "I was hoping to do some good here, to be useful in some way, before…" I shook my head and set the clip down.

"Haylee. You've done so much. More than many of the others have done living here their entire lives. You found that well and, tonight, you very probably saved the life of that little girl." He reached across and placed his hand over mine. "You've done more than you know. Oh. Wait here." He stood and headed to the kitchen.

While he was away, I continued to stare down at my hairclip. I frowned, as a tickle began in the back of my mind.

Something about this bothers me… I just can't put my finger on it.

Then he was back.

"Here." He placed a bright red tomato in front of me.

I blinked at it and back up at him. "I don't understand."

"I said you've done more than you know, right? Well… this is one of those things." He gestured at the tomato.

"I've… gardened?"

He smiled a little. "In a way…" Then, he climbed back over the bench and sat down. "We – Glenna and I – think you are personally responsible for the growth of the gardens. They've never flourished like this before." He paused. "What? You don't have anything to say?"

"Uh… I don't know what to say."

He leaned forward. "You didn't notice how the gardens got greener every time you came into contact with them? It wasn't immediate, so I guess you might not. Not many people have. But think about it."

I picked up the tomato and studied it. It was quite large and nearly perfect.

"How is that – *this* possible?"

"We're not sure, exactly. But it's obvious now you have quite an ability, or abilities. They're all related, in a way. You give life, or nourishment – whatever it is – to plants, at least edible ones. It's amazing, really. If we had more time, I'd love to study it further, but… well." He rushed on. "You heal fairly quickly. For a human anyway. And now we've seen you can show those forged objects for what they *are*. Somehow you take back the little bit of energy the Pale Ones endow them with. It's energy originally stolen from humans, and it's as if you reclaim it. I guess, in return, you place that energy into plants and healing. That would also be interesting to look at more carefully. Not to mention what you've been working on with Sabella. Your… psychic abilities, or whatever they are…."

"I don't have to leave, you know. I don't see how I'm any safer back home than I am here… with *you*… and surrounded by people who've had lifelong experience." I glanced down again. "I'll be alone at home. It's isolated." The thought of returning there was depressing.

"I thought you had family worrying about you?"

"I'm sure they started worrying a little when they didn't get that first weekly phone call. My aunt was the only family I had in the area." I shrugged. "My parents emancipated me when I turned seventeen – I needed *motivation into adulthood*, my mom said." I didn't mention that it saved me from packing up in the middle of my senior year. Or that it allowed me to remain with the aunt I loved. I swallowed the lump in my throat and shrugged. "They live out on the West Coast. I don't really see them."

He was quiet for a moment. "Well, I wouldn't be surprised, with as long as it's been, if they're waiting there for you when you get back. If they're worried at all, they'll be there trying to find you. I know I would be."

I sighed. "You're right. Of course, you're right. They're probably there. Now. Looking for me." I set the tomato down and rose to leave.

"Where are you going?"

"To bed, I guess. When will we be leaving, then?" I wouldn't look at him.

"A few days, tops. I've gotta get a small group together, go over the plans. As soon as everything's settled, we'll go." He got to his feet again and walked around the table.

"All right… let me know when it's done. I won't train, in the meantime… there's no point. I'll take the time to say my goodbyes, I guess."

He walked me to the hallway.

Others went about their business, though without their usual resolve. We stood for a moment in the doorway, neither of us speaking, and I stared down at the clip in my hand.

As I opened my mouth to say goodnight, I realized what had been bothering me. "How did she get this?"

"What?"

I knew he had heard what I said, only he couldn't quite make sense of the question. "This is *my* hairclip. I was wearing it the night you found me, and it was gone when I woke up. So, how did she get it?" I looked up at him now. "Did you see it that night?"

He frowned down at me. "I think so. One of us figured out how to get it out of your hair, and it got handed off to someone. I don't know. She probably picked it up somewhere. Why?"

We still haven't discovered anything else about our black hole. And so much has happened, it's no wonder. But what he says makes sense. Maybe he's right.

"Nothing. You're right… again. It was just a strange coincidence, I guess." I shook my head. "I'll see you… whenever, then. Goodnight."

I walked toward the stairwell, purposefully choosing the one opposite the door to the basement. *I don't even want to think about that right now. All I want is to sleep and forget for a while.*

"Goodnight, Haylee."

10

I made it a point not to see Derik over the next two days. It was easier than I thought it would be. The days went quickly, as I made my rounds, helping where I could or just visiting the people who had so suddenly become my friends and family. Though I knew it was ridiculous, I felt I belonged here now. And no other place could ever be home for me.

Sabella didn't call for me until the end of that second day.

"Oh, how I will miss our visits," she said, as soon as the red door was closed and I was seated.

"Will I ever see you again?" I asked because I knew, of all people, she would be the one who could answer this.

"Not in this life, I'm afraid, dear." Then she winked. "But one can dream. Derik has been in to see me." She tilted her head and studied me. "He's very worried for your safety."

I looked away. "That's what Derik does… worries about people's safety, I mean. Isn't that in his job description? He's like the secretary of defense around here or something." My smile felt tight.

"Oh, well, he is much more than that… But I meant he is especially worried about *you.* More so than usual." She watched for my reaction.

I tried to remain unreadable. *Yeah, right. Like I could do that.*

"Have you told him how you feel?"

My eyes snapped back to her.

She smiled and laughed. "I will take that as a no." Then, she sobered. "You should do it soon. You're running out of time. But, yes, he's quite worried." She shifted back to the topic at hand. "Would you like to know what we discussed?"

I blinked at her before answering. "Um… sure, I guess."

"He's asked me to find a way to close the portal, once you have gone through."

My stomach fell. "Can – can you do that?"

"I believe so, yes. Do you want that, Haylee?" Still, she studied my reactions.

"I – " I fell silent and dropped my stricken gaze to my fidgety fingers. "Is that what he wants?"

"If it means you are safe. He thinks they will try to follow. But, I needed your input as well… and I have it." She stared at me for several moments before going on. "I know what I must do."

"What *are* you going to do?" I had to ask.

The look she gave me was one of fondness, but the twinkle in her eye made me suspicious. "Don't worry. It will be for the best. You will see… in time." She reached forward and patted my knee.

The gesture was completely natural, but I realized it was the first time she had ever touched me. For the time being, I forgot my fears.

"Haylee, dear, you have so much more to learn. I am sorry I could not teach you everything I know. There has not been time. I am afraid you must learn on you own now. Remember what I have told you. All right?" She wouldn't release my eyes until I answered.

"All right." I felt breathless. *This is happening so fast. I'm not ready to go.* If it wasn't for Sabella's hand resting on my knee, I would've started panicking.

"Good. Now – Oh." She sat up a little, cocking her head, as if listening to something.

I don't hear anything.

"Not with the ears, Dear." She pointed at her temple. "It is time for you to go, now. Things have been settled, as they were. He will be coming to tell you any moment." She rose. "Oh, how I will miss this. Someone like myself, someone to share it with… And I know you do not want to go, but you must." She held her arms out for me, and I stepped into them without hesitation. "Be strong, my Little One," she whispered into my hair and pulled back.

Our eyes locked for a moment, as she held me at arm's length. *She's not much taller than me. And why that matters right now is beyond me.*

She sighed. "Now go… before I change my mind." She laughed at the line and turned me toward the door. "I could not resist." When my hand was on the cool metal of the doorknob, she said, "And Haylee?"

I turned to her.

"Tell him before you are gone…" Another moment passed in silence, as what she said sunk in. "Now, be off with yourself. He'll be looking for you." She waved me toward the door, smiling all the while.

So, with that final image of her, I closed the red door behind me. As far as I knew, it would be the last time.

* * *

I wasn't quite ready to hear from Derik yet, so I hid out in the piano room. I had to clear my head and reflect upon what Sabella had told me.

Why does she have to be so vague?

I folded the dusty tarp back from the old piano and pulled the stool out. Cobwebs broke loose from it, but I chose not to think about it and sat down. As I pondered over my time here, I unconsciously pressed a few keys. Some were so off, it sounded as though I pressed two at once, but I barely noticed at the time.

The past weeks have been so unreal. No other word fits my leap through time better. Of course, I'm leaving out the crazy *part. The part about the – what are they exactly? Psychic vampires? It's as good a term as any. Hm, I'll have to think about that a little more. In any case, they are to me, as they are to everyone here, the Pale Ones. They* are *pale… Deathly pale. And death… to humans. But what* are *they? Were they human at one time? And why do I have such a need to know all of a sudden? Now that I'm leaving and never coming back, what they were shouldn't be important. I won't ever come across one again. Not once Sabella closes that portal. Will I? Then again…*

A knock on the door brought me back to my surroundings. It opened quietly to reveal a silhouette I had grown to know well.

"What are you doing in here?" Derik asked, looking around the room.

"Hiding from you," I replied without thinking and winced. *Geez. Harsh much? Could've at least chosen different words.*

He stood in the doorway for a moment, silent.

I couldn't make out his expression.

"I see…"

My face grew warm. "I didn't mean it like that. It's just – just – "

"Relax, Haylee. I know what you meant." Sounding amused, he closed the door behind him and moved across the room. "I guess, in your place, I wouldn't want to see me, either. I have been looking for you though… The decisions have been made. Who's going, and when. I told you I'd tell you, as soon as things were settled." He stopped in beside me. "You play?" He indicated the piano and leaned against it lightly.

Sabella's use of the word *settled* came into my mind, but I shook my head. "I used to take lessons." I frowned up at him. *If this takes very long, I'll get a kink in my neck.* After a moment of silence, I asked, "So, then…?"

"Tomorrow. As soon as the sun's up high enough, after your breakfast." He gazed down at me.

I looked away. *Wow. So soon?* "Heh, you don't waste any time, do you?" This last bit came out a little more sharply than I intended.

"It's not like I'm trying to get rid of you." He sounded more than a little irritated.

I managed to stop a sarcastic reply before it erupted from my mouth. *Ugh! What's wrong with me? Why do we grate at each other so much?* I sighed. "I know… that didn't come out right. Sorry."

When he didn't say anything else, I glanced up.

"It's for the best, Haylee. I promise. I'll see you in the morning." He turned and was gone.

* * *

I didn't feel much like being alone once I had seen Derik, so I made my way downstairs. Several people stopped me along the way to the main doors. All of them wanted to tell me how much they had appreciated my help and would always welcome me back. I thanked them in my own awkward way and moved on. Despite my few days of farewells, there were two people I was not ready to leave yet, at least not without spending a little more time with them first. I had spent some time with Karroll and Merritt the night before, now it was time to visit with Gamut.

He was where he always was this time of day and, as usual, lit up when he saw me emerge from the darkened hall.

"Hey! Guess what?!"

Okay. Well, maybe he's a little more excited than usual. That's kind of suspicious."What's up?"

He laughed. "Don't worry. It's good news." He paused until I reached him. "I'm going with you guys tomorrow. I'm part of the group to escort you home." His smile widened.

"Really?" I frowned a little at first, then smiled. "That's good… right?" I wasn't sure what to think.

"What do you mean? Of course it's good. It's great! We'll be able to see each other that much longer." His smile slipped a bit, and he cleared his throat. "Hey. Look. I'm sorry about the other night… I'm thinking about what's best for you. You know that, right? I want you to be safe."

I closed my eyes. *I'm* sick *of everyone saying the same thing. It's for my own good. It's for the best. So I'll be safe.* Taking that moment allowed me to swallow those feelings down. When I opened my eyes, and my mouth, I didn't say anything I'd regret. *I can't afford to hurt anyone when I have so little time with them.*

"I know that, Gamut. So, Derik's letting you go?" I frowned a little, hoping I'd phrased the question correctly.

"Well, yeah. The way he sees it – me, too – I care about you, so I'm more invested in keeping you safe, if something happens along the way." He leaned against the wall in front of me.

I scooted up into the trophy case. "I see. So how many people are going?"

"It was decided six, plus Derik, will go."

"Who else?"

"Well, there's me. That's one. Phil, Gregor. They each have shifts on the roof. And Macey and Harmon guard the back doors at night. And then there's Nate. Did I miss anybody?" He counted on his fingers a second time.

"Nate? Nate's going?" I sat up straighter.

"Huh? Oh. Yeah."

"Why would Derik choose her to go along?" I asked, mostly of myself.

"He didn't. She volunteered, I think." He shrugged. "Does it matter?"

I slouched back against the wall. "I guess not…"

"So, what do you wanna do when my shift's over?" He moved a little closer to me.

I leaned as far away as the wall would allow. "The same as usual? I don't know… Dinner and a movie?" I joked, lamely.

"Huh?"

"Well, we always grab dinner after your shift… I figured we'd do that. I still need to say goodbye to Glenna, too." The look on his face caused me to backtrack. "Um, did you have something in mind?"

"Actually, I did. It's kind of a surprise though… So, you'll just have to wait and see." He beamed at me.

I was beginning to get the sensation he had more planned than I would care for but smiled back anyway. "I can't wait."

We didn't talk as much as usual throughout the remainder of his shift. Then again, we didn't need to. Once I got past my suspicions regarding his feelings for me, a comfortable silence often fell between us. If I gave it too much thought, I imagined he took it to mean more than it did. I, on the other hand, felt it meant we were the best of friends, though we had only known each other these past few weeks. Of course, I chose to ignore my instincts, telling myself it was my ego, instead. So, I was able to relax and enjoy his company.

When his shift was over, we walked to the cafeteria together.

"Wait here," he said, before we made it to the door.

Though I gave him a questioning look, I said nothing and allowed him to run toward the kitchen. Moments later, he returned with a tray of food. However, along with our usual fair, the tray contained a bowl of fresh vegetables. My look must have been one of surprise.

"It's all right. Hana suggested this. The food, I mean. The rest is all me." He reached for me with his free hand. "Come on."

"Where are we going?" I followed without hesitation, as he led me up the stairs.

"You'll see."

I thought for a moment we were going to eat in one of the lounging areas, but Gamut pulled me past those rooms and into the one with the access ladder.

"Up there?"

"Uh-huh. After you, m'lady." He smiled at me.

Up I went, and he was right behind me. When I stood on the roof, I noted the sun falling in the west. The sky was glowing with every shade of red and orange imaginable.

"Good. We didn't miss it." He moved past me. "Come. Sit." Indicating a blanket a few feet away, he sat the tray down.

Wow. I didn't know what to think or what to say. I walked over to him and knew my face must have expressed what I felt, because he smiled more broadly than before.

"So, what do you think? Good idea?" He gestured toward the west, without looking away from me.

"This – I don't..." I took a deep breath. "It's beautiful. It's wonderful. Really." I looked from the sky to Gamut, so he'd know I meant it. "Thank you." And I did mean it.

"I'm glad you like it. Now, let's eat. Sit here." He patted a spot on the blanket and reached for my hand.

Once I settled in, he sat beside me. The guard at each corner gave us a wide berth and pretended we weren't there. Other than them, we were alone.

We ate in companionable silence for a while and watched the sun set.

"It's good to be reminded of the beauty out there, despite everything going on, you know? And this is beautiful, isn't it?" I spoke softly.

"It sure is…"

I don't know if it was the way he said it or that he said it at all, but I knew he wasn't looking at the sky and couldn't control the pull at the corners of my mouth.

Seriously?

My gaze slid to him, and my lips started trembling. Sure enough, he was staring at me. I couldn't hold the laughter back. It came in waves, and I had trouble staying in a sitting position.

"What? What's so – it's not… It's not funny!"

And I would have believed he was hurt except he started laughing too.

Before long, we were both rolling beside each other, holding our sides.

"I'm s-so-sorry." I nearly chortled. "I can't. Believe. You said that." I was starting to calm down now. Sort of.

As soon as one of us stopped our howling, the other started up again. By the time we were relatively drained, we were each wiping tears from our eyes, the occasional giggle escaping us.

I sighed, and both of us grew quiet. It was dark enough now to see the first stars.

"I couldn't ask for a more perfect ending." I kept my eyes on the sky.

Gamut grasped my hand and moved to his elbow to lean over me. "What if I went with you? Home, I mean? Why couldn't I?" His eyes sparkled with excitement.

I frowned up at him. "No, Gamut. It's like you said. I don't belong here… and you don't belong there. It's the way it is, the way it has to be… you know that. Who knows what that could do." I looked back up at the fading glow and tried to lighten the mood. "We might create some sort of crazy paradox. You can never be too careful with these things, you know."

My attempt was in vain. Gamut didn't smile. Instead he grew more serious and leaned closer to me. Though I tensed up, I tried not to make it obvious. When his lips touched mine, I didn't pull away.

Why hurt his feelings on our last night together?

So, I let him kiss me, and maybe I kissed back… a little. A part of me was hurting and needed that sort of contact. However, when I thought he would pull back, he took the kiss deeper. This unexpected act took me by such surprise I didn't react right away. And before I could discourage him, he pressed himself more tightly against me, effectively pinning me to the blanket. His fingers roamed to the edge of my top and swiftly under.

I turned my head away, which he took as a cue to rain kisses down my neck. Finally, I could catch my breath.

"Gamut. Stop. Please," I panted. He was too big and strong for me to push away.

For whatever reason, he didn't hear my plea. When his fingers grazed the edge of my bra, I gasped and grabbed his hand.

"Gamut!"

Finally, he raised his head. "What? What's wrong?" he asked, then pressed another trail of kisses to my throat.

"You need to *stop*, Gamut. We can't do this."

"Oh, come on. You were kissing back. You want to be with me as much as I want to be with you." He squeezed my fingers and leaned in again.

I pushed against him again. "No, Gamut! I don't!"

I might as well have slapped him, he jerked back so quickly. He stared at me, and his shock turned to hurt.

"I - I'm sorry. I didn't mean - "

He stared at the space between us for a moment. Then his eyes went cold. "It's because of *him,* isn't it?" He forced the words from a clenched jaw.

"I - I…"

My inability to form a sentence seemed to confirm his fears. His hand tightened around my fingers.

"That hurts, Gamut."

He blinked and looked at our hands, as if he'd forgotten he held mine. He loosened his grasp. Blinking again, he kept his gaze averted and whispered, "I'm sorry." Then, he lurched away from me with such violence it frightened me. But the look he gave me as he left scared me more.

"Gamut!" I sat up and reached after him.

He didn't look back as he climbed down the ladder.

I sat alone on the blanket for a few moments. *I've never seen him so angry. How could things have gone so horribly wrong?*

"Are you all right?"

I jumped at the voice and looked up to see one of the guards standing over me. Sudden realization had me blushing. I looked around and saw another guard standing closer than before. This one was a woman. She looked annoyed. The other two guards were still focused on their duties.

"I didn't mean to startle you. *Are* you all right?" he asked again.

"Uh, yeah… I'm fine."

"You should probably head back down. The roof isn't the safest place to be at night."

"Yeah… okay." I stood and gathered the blanket and tray.

What did I expect of my last day in this place? Definitely not a fight with one of my best friends. Well… one more person to see now. At least I can't piss her off.

* * *

I found Glenna in the cafeteria, taking a well-earned break.

She's always so busy.

After I dropped off the tray, I went to her table.

"Hello, there. I heard you had a picnic with Gamut…" She frowned when she got a better look at me. "Something is troubling you?" Her face showed only concern.

I turned red but told Glenna what had happened on the roof.

As usual, she gave little away, but something in the way she held herself told me she was more than a little angry.

"I see."

I watched her eyes for any sign of change. After a moment or two, I saw she was successful in calming down, though no one else would have known she needed to.

"I am sorry, Haylee… sorry everything is going so badly for you…

and has been going so badly from the start. I suppose the trek will not take long, though I'm unsure of how the portal will treat you. Are you nearly ready to make your journey tomorrow?"

I sighed. "As ready as I'll ever be, I guess. One last person to say my goodbyes to… The sister I never knew." I looked at her, pointedly. *That's exactly what she is to me. More than a friend, more than a confidante. A sister. And I will miss her dearly.*

She smiled. "I thank you for that. It means more to me than you could ever know." She paused. "Sister. I like the sound of that. It fits nicely, I think."

"It's true. I think I'll miss you the most… You've been the most understanding, the most… well. No, there isn't anyone I'll miss more…"

She reached across the table and covered my hand with her own. "Oh, my dear, dear Haylee… I know, at the moment, you do mean that. However, I cannot help but wonder if there is another you will miss more… once you are gone." She gave me that knowing smile of hers. "And you know it as well as I do."

I frowned and started to shake my head, then I realized whom she meant. *Of course… I had been so busy avoiding Derik before today, I hadn't actually said goodbye to him. The one opportunity I had, and I blew it. I should have followed Sabella's advice. Will I be able to tell him, if I get another chance?*

"Don't worry. I know you'll do what needs to be done, before it's too late. I have every ounce of faith in you. Sister."

And we sat there until Glenna suggested I rest.

When I stood to leave, I came around the table and hugged her.

How could I have ever been upset with her?

* * *

I had trouble falling asleep. There were too many things going through my head.

Can Gamut forget our last encounter, so we can put it behind us? Will I have the strength to speak to Derik? Will the Pale Ones try to follow me through the portal? And if so, will they succeed once Sabella closes it?

Of course, none of these questions bothered me more than one in particular.

I've grown so attached… they're like family now. Will I ever see these people again?

When the questions circling my head did in fact wear me out, I fell into a troubled sleep.

* * *

Around dawn, I awoke, a scream catching in my throat, but I couldn't remember the cause. I felt a terrible sense of loss and had the incredible urge to curl up into a ball under the blanket and never come out.

I resisted that urge.

It's time to get up. Time to eat breakfast. Time to go. Time, time, time…

All of my fears from last night returned, as I threw my feet from the bed and into my sneakers. Today, I was wearing pretty much what I had come here in, minus my favorite t-shirt. I was able to save the image on the front but nothing more. In place of it, I wore a sort of brown smock with my jeans.

I made my way down to the cafeteria. Before I had reached it, I saw Derik and Gamut near the main hallway.

Are they arguing?

Derik stood with his arms crossed over his chest, fists and jaw clenched tight. Gamut was throwing his arms in the air, as he spoke. I wasn't close enough to hear exactly what was said but as I got nearer, I caught a little.

"…hold you personally responsible," Derik said, thrusting a finger into Gamut's chest.

"Fine," Gamut blurted and stormed off in my direction but veered away when he caught sight of me.

I looked back toward Derik.

He totally wants to punch that wall right now.

He closed his eyes and took a deep breath. When he opened them again, he saw me and walked over.

"Have you eaten yet?" he asked.

I shook my head and looked back the direction Gamut had gone.

"I was on my way when…" I pointed. "What was that all about?" *Though I have an inkling you spoke to Glenna.*

He glanced behind me before answering. "It doesn't matter." He sighed. "The issue's been resolved... for now." He looked back at me. "Why don't you go ahead and get some food. We'll meet here in an hour, give or take. Okay?"

I nodded, and Derik moved along down the hall.

When I arrived in the cafeteria, I was surprised to see Karroll and Merritt there, waiting for me. Karroll waved me over, once I had my food.

"Hey. We got up early to see you off." She leaned forward. "So, how was your dinner last night? I haven't gotten the chance to talk to Gamut today… So?" When I didn't answer right away, her face fell. "Oh. That bad, huh?" She rested her arms on the table and rolled her eyes. "Great ball of fire… That no good brother of mine. What has he done this time?"

I swallowed the small lump in my throat and glanced around.

There weren't many people around us, so I told them my story, leaving out some of the details I had felt comfortable telling Glenna. Merritt's eyes went a little wide and he spent the remainder of the conversation staring at the table. Karroll had a different reaction.

Her smile was sad. "Oh, I'm sorry, hun." She shook her head. "I told you, he's got it bad. Real bad, apparently. But don't worry. You've just wounded his pride a bit. He'll come around."

"Within the next hour or so?" I was skeptical.

"Yes. Before you leave. He's a little bit of a baby, that's all."

We talked for a while. About what, I couldn't exactly say. They kept it as normal as possible. Merritt must have been sharing some gossip.

I should really pay more attention to my last conversation with my two friends but I can't. I can't concentrate.

I smiled and nodded at the appropriate times. But mostly I just stared at the table in front of me and twisted my fingers in my lap. I grew more and more nervous, as time ticked on. Before I knew it, it had been an hour, and it was time for me to meet the rest of the group. Karroll and Merritt walked me to the hallway.

My heart pounded in my chest.

Derik and the others gathered outside the cafeteria. Even Gamut was there. Each of them had a small backpack slung across their backs and carried a weapon of some sort.

Are they expecting trouble even though it's daytime?

Gamut approached us. "Um…" He scratched his head and looked at the floor. "Uh, could we talk a minute… alone, Haylee?" He glanced at the other two.

I did the same, raising my eyebrows at Karroll. "Sure. I'll be right back." I followed Gamut to a corner away from the others.

I placed my back to the wall and faced him.

He seemed tense as he turned away from the group. He sighed. "Oh, he's watching me like a hawk."

I didn't need to look to know who he was talking about.

He closed his eyes for a moment, then looked back at me. "Haylee… I – I wanted to say I'm sorry… about how I acted last night. I was out of line. And I ruined our time together. I just… It's because… well… You know I love you, right? I mean, really love you. I'm *in* love with you. That's what I wanted to say, needed to say." He looked down at the floor again. "I guess I should've said it before, huh?" He rubbed the back of his neck.

"Oh, Gamut…" I shook my head. "I just… I don't…" I lost the words and was utterly defeated. "I'm so sorry…" I guess it was the wrong thing to say.

A muscle in his jaw twitched, and he held his hands clenched at his sides. "I don't *want* you to be sorry. What I want is for you to choose m – Shit." He glanced over his shoulder. "Looks like I got his attention again. I'm *sorry*… *Maybe* I'm overreacting… I don't know. Or maybe *he's* an asshole," he mumbled. "Sorry, again."

I glanced past him. *He's talking to me, but is this little speech for someone else's benefit? I know he knows Derik's hearing is phenomenal.*

He sighed and rushed on. "Like I said before, I can't help how I feel. And there *is* one thing I want, I would like, before we leave…"

I blinked at him. "Of course. Anything." I twisted my fingers together in an effort to keep from touching his arm. *Better not to confuse him.*

"A kiss – just a kiss, I promise. No funny business… A goodbye kiss. Something to remember me by… and so I can remember you forgave me." He looked at me closely now.

I opened my mouth for an immediate rejection but reconsidered my reply. *No, I need to be straightforward about this.* Very *straightforward. It's for the best.* I took a deep breath. "That's not going to happen, Gamut."

His shoulders slumped and he dropped his eyes to the floor. "I understand."

"Look, I'm not trying to hurt your feelings. But I've told you how I felt. From the very beginning. And you refused to listen. But, if you want to continue being my friend — if you want me to remember you as my friend — you *will* listen to me this time. Because this is the last time I'm going to say it. Okay?"

He glanced up at me. "O-okay."

"Good. I care about you, Gamut. I do. But not like that. I love you. You're my friend. But I'm not *in* love with you. It's nothing more than that. And it never can be."

He opened his mouth to speak but I held up my hand.

"And after that stunt you pulled last night… God, Gamut."

His eyebrows pulled together and he looked up at me from beneath them. "Was stupid, wasn't it?"

"Uh, *yeah*. And how do you think it made me feel?" I glanced past him to the group gathered in the hall. Then I lowered my voice. "And another thing. Whatever is going on between you and Derik, leave me out of it."

He squeezed his eyes shut. "I'm sorry, Haylee. I'm an idiot. I can't even manage an apology without messing it up. I should be angry with myself, not Derik. And I especially shouldn't take it out on you. Not… not after the way I've acted." He took a deep breath and met my gaze. "C-can you forgive me?"

I felt my shoulders relax and studied him for a moment. *He seems sincere.* I held my right hand out to him.

He glanced down at it and back up to my face, before grasping it.

We smiled at each other other our clasped hands.

Then I heard Derik's voice above the others. "All right, guys! Time to move out!"

Gamut released my hand. "Thank you, Haylee."

I nodded and moved toward the group.

Derik looked my way, and I caught the corner of his mouth curve up before he turned his attention elsewhere.

Karroll stepped up beside me. "I hope my brother doesn't need set straight again. Did he apologize?"

"He did. We're good, I think."

"Good." She threw her arms around my shoulders and held tight. "Oh, we're all going to miss you so much." When she withdrew, tears moistened her eyes. She swiped at them and elbowed Merritt.

"Oh, right." He placed his arms around me awkwardly.

The move made me laugh. "Thanks."

When he let go, I looked at all the faces around me.

All were friendly, most were smiling, though a few, like Karroll, had tears in their eyes.

I wish Sabella was here to see me off.

Glenna tapped me on the shoulder.

"Once more, for old time's sake." She held out her arms.

Now it was my turn to cry, and I couldn't hold the tears back.

"Shh… it's all right. I refuse to believe this is the last time we will see each other. We may meet again. Who knows."

Her words put me at ease, or maybe it was her presence. All it took was her hand on my hair, and I was calm.

She smiled down at me. "Be safe, little sister… until we meet again, then, hm?" She kissed my forehead and released me.

I looked around until I found Derik.

How long has he been watching me? "I'm ready now."

He nodded once. "All right. Then, it's time." He gestured with his arm. "Let's head out."

The others fell in around us.

In one final defiant move, for all to see, I pulled my hairclip from my pocket, twisted my hair up, and clipped it in.

At least my friends understand the gesture.

But I noticed Nate eyeing me.

The heavy doors were opened and light came pouring in around us. It took a moment for my eyes to adjust. When they did, I noticed my escort surrounded me. *As though they're herding me out.* A dull thud behind us signified the doors had been closed again. I glanced around me in order to note who was where.

Derik led the group, and Nate took up the rear.

It makes sense, I guess, putting the strongest, most experienced on point and at the back. Still, I'm not so sure about Nate having my back.

The circle was loose and everyone appeared at ease. To an onlooker, it might seem as though we were going for a walk, except for the weapons they carried.

And I *know better.*

No one said anything for a while, and I took in our surroundings.

Wait. This isn't the way I went before.

Gamut was to my right and the closest to me, so I directed my question at him.

"Why are we going this way?"

He glanced around. "We're taking the scenic route. We can't go the direction you went before because it takes us by the well. We're going around it."

I frowned. "Why can't we go by the well?"

He started to answer but Derik interrupted.

"You've been there before, and we've gone back. They know that and expect it. Plus there are fewer trees this way, less cover, more sunlight. It's safer." He didn't look back but kept his eyes on our surroundings.

I don't remember him being this vigilant on the way back from the well. Then again, I was out of it. "If they know we – you're using the well, won't they sabotage it?"

"It's protected. Don't worry. Sabella's taken care of that."

I could hear the smile in Derik's voice.

"Like she will with the portal?" I asked.

"Yeah… like that." His smile was gone.

We walked a while longer in silence, and I was beginning to feel more and more nervous, the closer we got to the portal. I jumped at every rock kicked.

I'd probably jump right out of my skin if a bird flew by. Because I don't want to go back? What happens when I step through that portal? Birds… Where are *the birds? It's awfully quiet...* I frowned. *Wait a minute…* My steps slowed. *This feeling is all too familiar.*

"Hey, girlie, pick up the pace. We don't have all day." Nate spoke from behind me.

And though my heart did in fact pick up the pace, my feet stopped moving. "Wait."

Derik was the first to stop. He turned around to face me. "We have to keep going, Haylee. We can't stop, there's no time. Plus, it's – What's wrong?" He frowned at me.

I blinked, trying to think. "I'm not sure… Something's not right. I can feel it." I looked up at him.

He stared back for a moment. Then, his eyes trailed away. "I want everyone on guard."

Immediately, everyone was more alert. The circle tightened around me. Even Nate drew closer. I could feel the tension from each of them. All of them, except Nate, that is. She was in her element, perfectly at ease. Without taking her eyes off our surroundings, she leaned a little closer to me.

"I'm curious." She kept her voice low, maybe to keep others from hearing. But volume didn't matter, as all the others were focused on the tree lines. "How can you still wear that thing? In your hair, I mean?" She glanced at me for my reaction.

The question took me off guard, and I unconsciously reached up and touched the clip. "I guess... because it's just an object, it was never what she wanted me to think it was. I knew that then, deep down, and I know it now. Plus, it's…"

"A sort of challenge?"

It was as if she had read my mind. She returned her attention to the job at hand.

"Yeah…" I blinked at her sudden interest in me.

"That's what I thought." She gave a nod.

I couldn't decipher the tone of her voice.

Does she approve? Or disapprove for some reason? Why ask now*? Is it because she's more comfortable in tense situations?*

"I see something!" One of the guards called out.

Gregor, is it?

I looked around, as the others did, and saw Derik tense up.

"Tighter!" He backed up so close to me, I could have touched him.

"What's going on?" This one was Macey.

Besides Nate, she was the only female to accompany us. From the looks of her, she was every bit as capable as the men. Maybe more so.

"We're surrounded." Derik's voice did not contain the slightest tinge of surrender. "Gamut!" He didn't turn.

"Yeah." Gamut flinched a little.

"Remember the plan. You know where to go."

Gamut's hesitation was minuscule. "Right."

Still, everyone remained in their places.

Craning my neck to see around each of them, I still couldn't make out any movement at the tree line.

"We've got to head back. It's our only chance. They're not quite as thick back that way." Derik backed up, nudging me along.

The others followed suit.

Nate was now taking point. "I think we should keep going the way we were, Derik. I think they expect us to go back. They're herding us like cattle, that's what they're doing." She glanced around.

"Haylee's safety is number one right now, Nate, not your perverse love of battle. I'm sure you'll get your chance, either way… but let's try it my way first, okay?" Derik didn't let the conversation distract him.

"You're the boss, Love." She kept moving.

Either way? But we're clear of the trees. So, he must mean… "They'd come out into the sunlight?"

Gamut shrugged. "They will. It isn't very comfortable for them. But, for the right reasons…"

"It's not very *comfortable*?"

"Skin rashes, that kind of thing to start. The longer they're out, the more painful it becomes. Light sensitivity to the extreme… The sun burns them — I mean, not even *your* sunburns hold a candle to this — but they don't burst into flames or anything. So, most likely they won't come out and they're trying to scare us into doing something stupid. Right, Derik?"

It took Derik a moment to reply. "Yeah… right."

I threw a look over my shoulder. "But? Do I sense a *but*?"

Derik met my eyes briefly. "But… there are some who have built up a sort of tolerance… Their existence is fairly unknown. They don't get out much, not in the open anyway. They're what you might call special ops."

"Why are they so special – I mean, besides the tolerance to sunlight?" I was now as focused on my surroundings as the rest of them.

"Is this really the place to discuss this?" Phil interceded.

"It's as good a place as any," Macey said. "I want to hear about these special forces."

"They're *old*, more experienced, and have better control over their abilities. It's a little complicated…" Derik continued. "Let's say they are their master's royal guard, his personal sentry. He doesn't just send them after anyone."

"So, if he sends them, you know he means business?" Gamut asked.

"Pretty much, yeah."

"Why haven't you told us about them before now?" he asked.

"It was never necessary before… I never thought any of you would ever see them. They hardly ever make an appearance."

I could tell Derik was getting a little irritated with the twenty questions. But I had to ask my own. "And you're bringing it up now because you think they're out there?" My nerves had never really settled, but now they kicked into overdrive.

Derik didn't answer. When I glanced back at him, his attention was elsewhere.

"I'm not seeing them, anymore." Gregor's voice was low.

We kept moving.

Though I hadn't seen them to begin with, I scanned the trees again.

Nothing. But taking what Derik's told us, I should be looking... My eyes swept the open field in front of us. I stopped moving.

"Oh yeah? Then what do you call that?" I pointed.

Several figures blocked our path, where anyone up front could have clearly seen them, if they hadn't been looking in the usual places.

Derik halted just before walking into me. I felt him against my back. The others turned their heads to the front. Someone swore. I think it was Macey.

The figures in front of us stood very still. They were so far away, I couldn't make out their faces but could identify them by their pale skin.

"How come you didn't sense those guys there, Derik?" Gamut's voice was accusatory.

Nate answered. "Probably the same reason you didn't feel them staring at us. Sensory overload. There's simply too many of them."

My eyes went wide. *How many is too many? So many Derik couldn't sense the ones in front of us?*

I must have tensed noticeably, because he placed a hand on my arm. He gave it a light squeeze, then moved around me, making sure I was still in the center of the circle.

"Let's not get ahead of ourselves, all right? We all came into this knowing what might happen. You've trained for this. Whatever happens, you can handle it." He moved up beside Nate. "Let's see what their demands are," he joked.

We moved forward again and came to a stop twenty feet away from the group.

I could make out their features now. Their skin was nearly as pale as the others but tougher and smooth, like scar tissue. They had the same animal eyes. There were two major differences. Their clothes were nicer – they were dressed all in white – and their faces were painted.

That may be their idea of war paint but, to me, they look like sadistic clowns, my worst irrational fear come to life.

My mind flashed back to the picture in my childhood room. *Has a part of me always known the Amara existed?*

Their lips were stained a bright, bold red, as if to simulate blood. But the effect wasn't complete until they smiled at me. Not until they showed me those razor sharp teeth did I truly feel fear. And there was no question those smiles were directed at me.

I took a step back without having any knowledge of doing so.

Gamut grabbed my hand. I hadn't realized he had been standing so close, but I was grateful he had. Without him to ground me at that moment, I may have made a run for it.

Maybe that's their intention. To get me out in the open.

One of them stepped forward. He didn't take his eyes off me. I shivered, when he spoke.

"We jussst want the girrllll…" he crooned. "We, of course, are prepared to take her by force." He gestured with his arm. The motion was graceful.

Despite my fear, I found him fascinating and couldn't look away.

Derik took another step forward. "Well. That's just how it'll have to be done, then. However this goes down, you'll be leaving here empty handed." I could hear the sneer in his voice.

The Pale One in front of him widened his toothy grin into something so menacing, I would have screamed if I wasn't already paralyzed with this strange fascination. His narrowed eyes slid from me to Derik.

"Is that sssooo…? Well, then, I'm afraid we have a predicament… do we not?" His smile vanished, as his eyes dropped to the ground. "Very well." In a fluid movement, he was back with the others in his group and speaking with them in whispery tones.

Derik took this moment to talk to us. "Gamut, be ready." He noted our interlocked hands. "Haylee."

My eyes snapped to his. *Was I staring at the Pale Ones again?*

He came closer and touched my face. He looked concerned. "Please, don't look at them anymore. I don't know how, but they have a very powerful hold over you. More so than the others. Can you do that? For me?" His eyes were searching.

I blinked several times until I grasped what he was saying. Then I frowned and nodded. "Okay. Yeah. I'll try?" *If I can.*

He swallowed. "Okay… Good." He turned then. "Get ready for a fight, everyone. 'Cause we're gettin' one." He strode to the front of the group again. "Remember. Haylee's the number one priority. If she doesn't make it, we've failed."

I was abruptly very aware of what was happening.

These people are risking their lives for me. Me. *Why? I don't want this, but there's nothing I can* do. *There's no way they'd let me give myself up in order to save them. And the Pale Ones aren't exactly the trustworthy type. They'd probably accept my surrender and still kill the others. I couldn't live with that.*

The Pale Ones stopped talking, all at once, and turned toward us.

We tensed as one. It was time. We could feel it.

Battle positions, everyone.

Gamut dropped my hand but situated himself partly in front of me. Derik and Nate remained where they were. The other three held their weapons at the ready. We were as prepared as we'd ever be. Well, my companions were… I couldn't say the same for myself.

Then the fighting had begun. The Pale Ones went from standing there to full out attack in a matter of seconds.

Derik had the leader. Nate had her hands full with two of the others. Gamut and the other three each had their own to worry about. The one fighting Macey dropped. I caught the glint of a bloody blade in her hand. She moved on to help Gamut with his. Phil and Gregor were back to back, sparring with their respective foes. I glanced back toward Macey and Gamut to see their Pale One fall. Macey gave him a look and went to help Nate, who faired well against two of them. Out of the corner of my eye, I heard the leader grunt, and turned to see Derik give him a blow to the chest.

He took advantage of the moment. "Gamut! Now!" And he was fighting again.

Gamut turned to me and grabbed my hand. "Come on. I've gotta get you out of here. We've got – Ah!" He cried and was on his knees.

"Gamut!" I reached for his shoulders, as he doubled over.

Behind him stood one of the Pale Ones, grinning at me.

And as suddenly as it had happened, Macey lunged onto his back, and I was swooped up. I fought to get away, but the arms around me were too strong. I extended my neck to see Gamut and Macey. She had succeeded in wrestling the Pale One to the ground. After that my line of sight was blocked.

I looked back to the owner of the arms imprisoning me to find it was Derik carrying me away. And at quite a rate of speed.

"Derik, we have to go back. Gamut…"

He kept running. "I'm sorry, Haylee. We can't go back. It wasn't supposed to happen this way…"

"Derik, please. I have to know if he's all right. He needs medical attention. We have to get him back to the compound. Please…" Tears poured down my face, and I had Derik's shirt grasped tightly in my fists.

"It wasn't a death blow, Little One. He should be fine… We're almost there now, I promise."

"What about the others? Won't they need you there? To fight?"

"They'll do fine without me. Now, be quiet for a little while, please? We'll be there soon." He hugged me a little tighter to his chest.

I couldn't relax so I pressed my face between my fists in his shirt and tried to stop the flow of tears. I looked up, when we began to slow.

"We're here." He glanced around one last time and turned toward a thicket of undergrowth. "We weren't followed."

We were at the edge of a clearing and at the foot of a large hill.

"It's right through there." He nodded toward the tangle of brush, set me down, and drew aside the branches.

After giving him a quizzical glance, I went through. What I stepped into was a cavern in the side of the hill.

"The entrance is in direct sunlight most of the day." Derik came in behind me. "They don't know about it. We've had it as an option for such occasions for a while now but never used it. Nate and I were the only ones who knew about it. But I told Gamut how to get here. He was supposed to bring you, while I stayed to fight, keep them from following… whatever I had to do. When I saw him get hit, I felt I had no other choice but to bring you myself."

The tears began to flow again. "I shouldn't have left. It's just like before. I left my aunt, and they killed her."

He moved to me and placed a hand on my shoulder. "Haylee…"

The contact cleared my head. *What am I saying? I feel responsible for Aunt Bethany's death? I feel responsible for the people at the compound? Oh. The door I visualized during my session with Sabella. I should have realized what it meant. Does some part of me believe my friends' safety is on my shoulders?* Does *their fate rest in my hands?*

"I'm afraid of what might happen when I leave. I know it sounds ridiculous, but what if Gamut dies because I'm not there? I don't know that I can live with not knowing." I turned toward him, grabbing at his shirt.

"Haylee, he'll be fine." The look he gave me said he meant it. "I promise." Then he folded his arms around me. "Let's sit over here… I'm not sure how long we'll need to stay. Nate will come get us when it's safe." He pulled me to the center of the cave and sat me on an outcropping of large rocks.

The tears still flowed. *It could be worse. At least I've kept the hysterics to a minimum. Maybe Gamut's wound isn't fatal, but will he be all right? And what about the others? How long will we have to wait to find out?* I sucked in a labored breath, almost a hiccup.

"Here." Derik held out a bottle of water. "Drink this."

He rummaged through the bag he had been wearing.

"I packed a little food…" He glanced up. "…in case we needed it. There should be enough. Gamut would have had more. I can go on very little if need be." He settled down, his back against the rock and mere inches from my leg, and sighed. "I'm sorry, Haylee… Of course, we made plans in case anything went wrong… and I expected something to happen… but not this. Not exactly, anyway."

My face was sticky with drying tears, as I slid down off the rock to sit beside him. I ignored it when our arms brushed. "It's not your fault… If anything, it's mine."

"With all the terrible things that have happened to you, you still find some way to blame yourself? I don't understand you."

We were silent for a few minutes. I leaned my head back against the rock and looked at him. "So, you don't know how long it could take? For Nate to get here?"

He looked down at me. "No. It depends on a lot of variables, but mostly on when she thinks it's safe. Once the threat is over… meaning no sign of the Pale Ones, not one… then she'll show. But not before then. It'll be hours, at the least… hopefully before nightfall."

I shivered. *Hopefully, we'll be back well before dark.* "And you trust her?"

He blinked at the question. "She hasn't let me down yet…"

I frowned. "But?"

He closed his eyes for a moment. "She's been acting a little strange lately… But, like I said, I've always been able to trust her before." He nodded to himself. "She'll pull through."

"What if she doesn't show – I mean, if something happens? What do we do then?"

"We do have a contingency plan… If she doesn't show up by morning, we head out as soon as it's full daylight."

"Head out. To where? Back to the compound? Or…" I swallowed.

"You're the main priority… Or don't you remember me saying that?" He shifted toward me, resting his arm on the rock behind us. "I'll take you back to the portal myself… Sabella will know when you arrive there and close it once you're through."

"Wouldn't you rather go back to the compound? Make sure everyone's all right first? I mean, it would help *my* peace of mind..." My eyes widened and I looked away. *Can I leave without knowing if Gamut is okay? Or any of the others, for that matter?*

"I'm sure they're fine, Haylee... Besides, they knew what they were getting into when they signed up for this gig. Trust me." He paused. "You do trust me, don't you?"

I turned my face to him. Staring up at him, I nodded. "Of – of course." I blinked several times, surprised he had to ask. Then, I looked away again. "I think I trust you more than anyone else at the compound." *No, that's not true... I trust you more than I trust anyone, anywhere, in any time.* I smiled. "Definitely more than I trust Nate..."

Derik laughed a little and settled back in beside me. "Well, it's good that you can still joke..."

"Yeah..." My smile faded, and I sighed. I leaned my head back against the rock and closed my eyes.

"If we're going to be here a while, you should try to get some rest. Try to sleep."

I opened my eyes. "I don't think I could sleep after everything..."

"You'd be surprised how tired you can be after something like that. Come here. You can lean on me... I've gotta be softer than a rock. They're not very conducive to sleep anyway..." He raised his arm.

I eyed him for a moment before giving in. "Have you ever slept on one? A rock, I mean?"

"Actually, I have... I guess you can get used to it, but it takes a while." He tucked me against him and, after some uncertainty, placed his hand on my arm.

"When was that?" I yawned.

"A very long time ago..."

* * *

The next thing I became aware of was the cold. I shivered and curled up into the warmth I was lying on.

Wait. Where am I? I opened my eyes. It was darker now, and someone rubbed my arms. *Oh. That's right. I'm in a cave. With Derik. Scratch that.* On *Derik. Oops.* I pulled back.

"S-sorry."

He rubbed my arms a little harder. "Hey, don't worry about it.

You're cold. *I'm* sorry."

I looked around us. *It's definitely darker.* "How long has it been?"

His rubbing slowed. "A few hours."

I pulled an arm's length away, forcing him to stop. "*Hours*? And nothing from Nate?" I glanced toward the opening of the cave. "Is it getting dark?" There was alarm in my voice.

"It *is* darker in here. The sun's lowering. Though we still have hours worth of daylight, we'll be in shadow within the next forty minutes or so."

That means we'll be susceptible to attack from any of the Pale Ones now. If they know where to find us. "What's the likelihood she'll come before full dark?"

"It's as likely as it has been up to this point. After full dark is when the chances begin to drop. It becomes too dangerous… though, knowing her, she'd prefer to come when there's the most danger – anything for a fight." He rolled his eyes.

"Why's it so cold?" I rubbed at my arms.

"More often than not, the nights here get pretty cold. Plus, we're in this cave, so that doesn't help matters. The temperature's already started to drop in here. I'm sorry, I'd start a fire, but it would be noticed. Let me see what I have in the pack." He began to shift, so I moved out of his way.

My muscles were sore from lying still for so long, so I stood to stretch. I groaned. "Sheesh."

He glanced up from his bag. "Yeah, I figured you'd be stiff. The ground's colder too. I was afraid to wake you… Here, this should help." He pulled out a piece of cloth.

The long-sleeved shirt was big, even over my clothes. "Thanks." *It's like being a little kid and trying on my dad's old sweaters.* I held my arms out from my sides. The sleeves drooped past my hands and the bottom hem came halfway to my knees. *It would almost make a good nightgown.*

Derik chuckled.

"Well, I'm glad I amuse you."

"Here." He reached for my arm and began rolling up the first sleeve.

When he finished with the second, he didn't remove his hands. I had been staring at them since he began. Now my eyes trailed up his arms, past those broad shoulders, to his face. I lingered on his mouth for a moment before coming to rest on his eyes. Meeting mine, his eyes reflected the confusion I was feeling.

Confusion and… what? What am I feeling right now?

He used the sleeve he was still holding to pull me toward him. There was barely an inch between us, and I had to crane my neck to keep his eyes in sight. He brought one hand to my face and held it there, searching. He didn't say anything, just continued searching my face.

My cheeks grew warm and I looked away, forcing his hand to move to my hair.

"I'm sorry, Haylee… about so many things."

"What do you mean? What – why?" My eyebrows drew together for the umpteenth time since I'd found myself in this time.

He heaved a sigh. His hand was still on my hair. "For everything that's happened to you. For the fact that you're here at all… How I've treated you… How I reacted to the idea – well, you know – of you possibly being my Other Half." He dropped his hands and turned away. "I guess I do owe you an explanation for that… You deserve that much. You deserve the truth." He took another breath – this one shook his entire body – but he didn't continue.

The truth? What's he talking about? I placed my hand on his arm. "Derik. You don't owe me anything… Least of all an explanation." I tried to smile so he'd hear it in my voice.

He pulled away. "I do, and you might not want to touch me once I've told you. I wouldn't… There are reasons I have the abilities I do… God, I haven't told anyone this. I wasn't going to tell you, except now I… with this hanging over our heads, I feel I have to." He swiped a hand across his face and ran it through his hair.

I've never seen him like this. It's a little scary. I waited for him to go on.

"You know I can sense them… when they're nearby. I also have comparable strength, speed, agility… other senses enhanced. I have a connection to them I can't erase, no matter how hard I try." He turned now and looked at me.

I just stared back.

"Haylee, I'm the only one Glenna has ever heard of having multiple abilities…" He raised his eyebrows at me, trying to convey some meaning I wasn't getting.

I blinked and shook my head. "What about me? I can do more than one thing. Doesn't that mean I have multiple abilities?"

"It's not quite the same thing… Mine are varied, one doesn't have much to do with the other. Yours, on the other hand, are all related…

One leads to another… Plus, you're like Sabella. There are always exceptions to the rule. You're a Seer." He shrugged it off.

"Okay… so, then, what?" *What am I missing here?* "You can't have multiple abilities?"

He closed his eyes. Maybe to gather courage, I'm not sure. But what he said next took a lot of fortitude.

"I – I'm not human, Haylee. Not like you are, anyway…" A muscle in his jaw twitched. "I'm one of them… the Amara. The Pale Ones. That's how I know so much about them. My ability to sense them isn't a human gift. It's a side effect of being… what I am." He wasn't able to meet my eyes.

What he would have seen there was a dawning comprehension. My mouth hung open for a while until it caught up with my thoughts, and I remembered how to talk. "You mean you *were* one of them."

He walked to the rock, sat down, and dropped his head in his hands. "No. It's not something that can be cured… It's – it's…" He cast around for the right analogy. "It's like alcoholism. You can give it up, but you're always an alcoholic."

"So, how many years sober are you, then?" *Gee, I'm taking this awfully well.*

His head whipped around to me. "This isn't something to joke about, Haylee. It's serious."

"I think I was being serious, actually. How long?" I moved a little closer.

He looked at me in disbelief, then blinked. "I don't know… forty or fifty years. Why does it even matter?"

"Forty? Or fifty? Just how old are you?" I slumped down on the rock next to him. *Finally, you're reacting appropriately. Sort of.*

He stared at me for a moment. "I tell you I'm a murdering monster, and you're more concerned with my age?"

Okay. Maybe not so appropriate. Oh, well.

"I don't believe it…" He thought about it. "I guess I'm… really pretty old. I'd really rather not talk about that."

"*That* old, huh? They do get some of the myths from truth." I sighed. "I guess it doesn't matter how old you are…"

"Really. Why are you taking this so well?"

"I…" *I can't tell him the* whole *truth. That I…* "trust you. In a way, I guess it's like how you trust Nate… but more than that. Because I believe what Sabella says. About us, I mean." I glanced at him and back down at my hands in my lap. *Well. Actually, that's pretty close to the whole truth after all. As close as I can get without saying the L-word.*

"You know it can't work... I've told you why."

"Why? Because you *used* to be a bad guy? You're not anymore. I've seen you. I think I know you now. You're not bad, you're good. More than good. You've taken everything you know about them and given it to humans, to help. You fight them. You're *not* one of them. And if what I've seen over the last several weeks is any indication, you haven't *been* one of them for a very long time."

He stood and loomed over me. "Do you want to know why? I'll tell you. Ever since you got here, I can't think straight, can't *see* straight. And that's very dangerous. More than once, I've felt urges I haven't felt in a long time. Each day is a constant battle for control. When you're afraid, I can sense – maybe smell it. It's one of the many *gifts* of the Amara. It excites them. Hell, it even excites *me* a little. And when I'm with you, around you, I *want* to loose control, but I'm afraid of what might happen – to you – if I don't keep it."

He's trying to intimidate me. Pretty effective. But I'm not afraid of *him. I'm terrified of what I feel* for *him.* I leaned as far away as I could without tumbling from my perch. "How – how do you know? How do you know you'd lose control? I mean, how do you know losing the kind of control you're talking about will result in the *ultimate* loss of control? Control over those more innate... appetites?"

He fell to his knees, his arms on either side of me, and bowed his head.

Wow.

"I don't know what will happen. I only know I could never forgive myself if something happened to you – if I was responsible." He had never sounded so resigned. "It could be through something as innocent as a simple touch." He raised his head and brought his hand up just short of touching my face and dropped it again. "We've been in such close contact..."

I didn't know what to do with my hands, as he knelt there defeated, so finally I laid one on each of his arms.

He continued. "I don't know where these feelings come from... I've been fighting them. Before I knew it, they were there, out of nowhere. I was going to let you leave without telling you. No, was going to run you off, I think. So I wouldn't have to face it. I guess that's what I'm most sorry for. You deserve better, Haylee... better than a monster. You're too good. That's how I finally realized what Sabella said was *possible*… You are my complete and utter opposite… in every way." He shook his head in bewilderment. "That's how it works, the other half ideology."

He pushed away from me then, all evidence of what he was feeling erased from his face. "Besides, you're not of this time. If we were truly meant to be, I'd have to believe we would have met much sooner… Clearly, we're not a match, even if I was human. Anyway, how could someone like you ever feel for a monster? The idea itself is…" He shifted to his feet. "And now I'm sorry I said anything." He was already detaching himself from the conversation, the entire concept. As if it had never occurred.

"Wait. Derik." I held onto him. Of course, if he wanted to pull away, physically I couldn't stop him. "I have to tell you – "

His fingers against my lips cut me off. "Sh!" He narrowed his eyes, as they slid to the side. "Dammit!" He whirled around.

I stared at him, dumbstruck by the suddenness of his movements and the shift from the discussion. It took me a few seconds to recognize something was wrong. I stood behind him and gently tugged on his shirt. "What is it?" I spoke barely loud enough to hear myself.

He was still for a while before answering. "They're out there."

My eyes widened and I pulled at his sleeve, forcing him to turn toward me. "What do you mean? Do they know we're in here?"

He placed a hand on my shoulder but still watched the entrance. "I don't know. If they do, they can't get in yet. The sun's still shining on the way in."

I grew very still. "How long do we have?"

Now he looked at me again. "Minutes. As soon as the sun settles behind that hill across the clearing… Unless it's the royal guard."

I couldn't think of *that* just yet. "Then… what?"

"I don't know how they could know where to find us. I know we weren't followed."

Something occurred to me at that moment. "If you can sense them when they're near, what keeps them from sensing you? Couldn't they find us that way?"

His jaw tensed. "It's… complicated. For the most part, they can all sense each other, yes. But there's no distinction from one to another." He hesitated before continuing. "And they can't sense me… not anymore."

I could tell he was uncomfortable and chose to focus on the problem at hand. "So what do we do?"

He glanced around. "We're sitting ducks in here, *if* they know... But if we go out and they don't know, we'll be giving ourselves away..."

"Doesn't sound good, either way you look at it, does it? So, we've got to decide – quickly – whether we'd rather make a stand trapped in here or out in the open... They're not very good choices." I too cast my eyes around the cavern, hoping for some sort of inspiration or an escape route. "And we don't have much time, to boot."

"No. We don't. So, what will it be?" He gazed down at me.

"You're asking *me*? How should I – Well. I guess it makes more sense to be out in the open... the chances are we're going to have to face them either way, so..." I looked up at him.

"So, we go... All right, then. Stay behind me, please. Let's go." He picked up his pack, pulled the straps over his arms, and led the way toward the little light remaining.

I stopped him. "Wait. What if it *is* the other ones? The ones who can come out in the sunlight?"

"I don't know why they would have waited this long to come in..." He turned to me again. "Are you willing to take that chance? I mean, either way we'll have a fight on our hands. There isn't enough sunlight left here to give us any time to get away first."

"I see. Well, then, carry on." I managed a faux cheerfulness.

"Right."

And we began moving again.

At the entrance, Derik signaled me to stay silent. He pushed the brush out of our way and froze.

The sudden stop almost caused me to smash into him. I craned my neck to look around him.

What's going on?

I, too, had no words to express the alarm and dismay I felt at what I saw.

Pale Ones surrounded us. Most of them stood in the growing shadows but their royal guard was much closer.

And Nate stood barely five feet from us. Her weight was distributed to one leg, her hip hitched, and her arms were crossed. She held her head high and haughty.

"Well, it's about time you joined us. I thought we'd have to come in there and get you."

Derik took a step forward, keeping me behind him. "Nate. What's going on here? What have you done?"

His voice made the hairs on my arm stand on end.

"What? Isn't this what you wanted? The truth out in the open?" She shifted to her other leg. "Well, now you'll have it." She moved a little closer and addressed me. "Do you know your man here has been keeping a secret from you – from everybody? Sweetie…" She came a little closer and spoke as if to a child. "He is *not* what he appears – "

Derik moved further between us. "Don't you *dare* talk to her. I've already told her what I am."

She frowned. "Oh, really… Well, she appears to be taking it rather well, don'tcha' think?" She crossed her arms again.

I pulled away from Derik and came around to stand beside him. "Where are the others? What did you do to them?"

She stuck her lip out in a perfect pout. "Aw, the little girl's worried about her friends. Isn't that sweet." Then her face went back to its scowl. "As much as I would have loved to kill every last one of them, I just didn't think they were worth the time or effort. So, unfortunately, they're all back at the compound, and I'm out under the guise of coming to fetch you two. And, of course, returning you, girlie, to your precious portal." She sighed. "However, *they* have other plans for you – both of you. It turns out someone has a keen interest in you. Though I don't see why. You're clearly nothing special. But, then again, I just follow orders. That's part of the deal." She played at studying her fingernails.

Derik tensed beside me. "What deal?"

She looked up in faux surprise. "Oh. Didn't I say that already?" She put her finger to her chin. "Oh, wait, no." Then, she continued. "I merely made a deal to become one of them, that's all. Part of the exchange was to allow them to use me to steal miniscule amounts of energy from everyone at the compound and give it to their master through our prisoner. Nifty plan, huh." She walked up to Derik and stroked a finger across his chest. "One you couldn't sense, anyway." Then she walked back to her original spot. "And the other part is to give them this one here." She pointed at me and shrugged. "Nothing really, you see." Her eyes sparkled.

My eyes widened. *Did Nate just confess to being our black hole?*

While I didn't know how to react, Derik had the opposite problem.

He started to lunge for her. "Why, you – " He stopped when he sensed movement behind us.

"Uh, uh, uh." Nate waggled her finger. "One more move from you, and they'll be on her in an instant." She pointed above our heads.

There, on the steep hillside, several of the royal guard crouched, ready to spring. Another, the one we had seen move, was standing a few feet behind us.

Derik glanced down at me, then back to her. His fists were clenched, and I saw the muscle in his jaw twitch. I wrapped my fingers around his arm to calm him. It worked. He unclenched his hands.

When I glanced up at Nate, her eyes were locked on my hands. She then looked at me with such hate, I nearly fell back a step. I think I did move back a little but my hold on Derik's arm kept me from going far.

He took a deep breath. "How long, Nate? When did you turn against us?"

"Oh, I never *turned* against any of you, because I was never *with* you. For as long as you've known me, Derik, I've been working for them. They *sent* me to the safe house." She laughed. "Because they knew *you* were there. They knew you'd be drawn to me because, though you didn't sense it, I was connected to them, and you're still connected. They thought if I could gain your trust, I could bring you back to them and take out the human pests at the same time. But, mostly, they wanted you back… then *she* came along and ruined everything." She came forward again, giving me that death stare. Each step she took was deliberate and measured.

"What is it about her?" She tilted her head, as if trying to understand me, then stopped a step or two away. "Save a measly little child, and they bow down to worship at your feet. Do you know how long it took for them to trust me? Years. It took *you* a matter of weeks." She said all of this quietly, as if to herself. "What is it you see in her, Derik?" She raised her eyebrows. "Because I most certainly cannot."

She reached out to touch me but, just as I began to draw behind him, Derik grabbed her hand. She stared at it for a moment, a smile spreading across her face. Her eyes slid to his.

"Oh, you really shouldn't have done that."

Understanding did not come to Derik quite as quickly as the royal guard's hand moved to my wrist. In an instant, he had me.

I looked at Derik.

He was still in a battle of wills with Nate. "Don't do this." It was a cross between an order and a plea.

My vision became blurry. "Derik?" I frowned. "What's happening?" It was difficult to keep my grasp on him, and a sinking sensation overcame me.

Derik released Nate and caught me in his arms.

"Haylee." He rested his hand on my face and looked up. "Stop! That's enough!"

Who is he talking to?

Then, the shadows took me.

11

I found myself alone in a room.

How did I get here? And where is Derik? Where am I*?*

I couldn't make out anything in the dim lighting. The main source shimmered up from a large grate in the floor, and I felt my way over to it. Several feet down, water reflected the light up to me. The water was all I could see, so I got down as close to the grate as I could and hooked my fingers through the openings. Bits crumbled under my hands.

The metal must be old. Rusted.

Though it was damp and a little sticky, I braced my body against it. My nose was a bare inch from the grate, when a blast of warm air brought up a strong sulfuric smell. I shoved away, pressing the back of my hand to my face.

Must be a sewer or something. Does that help me in discovering where I am? No, not really.

I glanced around again, hoping my eyes had adjusted.

Still nothing more than shadows against darker shadows. I sighed and leaned back on my heels. *So what do I do now?*

Once I was still and silent, I could hear the tinkling of the water below me. Then, another noise made me jump. I looked around.

I am *alone. Right?*

Now I was very still and very silent, straining to hear anything.

When the sound came again, I was able to pinpoint its location. My eyes moved to the grate.

It's coming from down there. I crawled back to it and had to cover my nose again. *Ugh. That* smell. *Has it gotten stronger?* I strained my eyes to see something other than the water's reflections but it was too dark. *Where's the light* coming *from? And are my eyes playing tricks on me? Is it — is it turning* red*? This isn't happening.* A deep red reflected back at me. *Is that the water or the light? And is it closer? Has the water gotten* deeper*? It* *almost looks like…*

Suddenly the smell changed. No longer did I associate it with sulfur. It was beginning to smell like something dead. Or a lot of somethings. I stifled my gag reflex and forced myself to focus on the scene below. *It's definitely deeper… But is it also getting louder? I've got a* bad *feeling about this… but I've* got *to get away from this smell! I can't stand it anymore!*

Movement caught my eye. A shadow across the water. I squinted down at it.

As I stared hard at the water below, the lights around me flickered on with a hum. They distracted me from the goings on below and what I saw in that room held my attention.

More red.

The lights? No. That's not it. They're normal fluorescents… Then what? Red… It can't be… It's not. But… My heart fluttered against my ribs.

The walls, the floor, even the ceiling was covered in what could only be blood. The color ranged from black to bright red.

The darker is old, the brighter new. Okay. So that means… blood's been shed in this room many times and… never — never removed.

I lost my balance, and the grate dug into my backside, but I barely felt it. The room had once been pristine, if the white tiles peeking out on the floor and walls was any indication. Now, every inch was covered in layers of peeling blood, like *wallpaper*, some of it fresh. I was too stunned to be sick.

I was suddenly very aware of the grate beneath me and realized where all the blood drained. I raised my hands in front of me and turned them over.

They had clung to that sticky, crusty old grate only moments before. Now they were covered too. I started to tremble but still could not get sick. I made myself look back at the grate, as I began to remember what I had been doing when the lights had come on. The sight of the grate made me wince, but when I looked back down into the sewer, I saw something much worse. It hadn't been water after all. A small river of blood had been flowing below me. Now it was most certainly deeper than it had been and moving much faster. In the distance, I heard a rumbling.

Definitely not a good sound. It couldn't be. I got an image of a wall of blood rushing down the tunnel.

I need to get out of there. But, for some reason, I couldn't move. I was glued to the scene below. At that moment, I saw the shadow again, and a figure stepped out onto the walkway along the stream. A man, but I couldn't yet see his face. *Oh, I have a* very *bad feeling about him.*

He turned his face toward me with deliberate slowness.

If I had been able to move before, I would have been frozen now with fear.

His skin was pale, but nowhere near as pallid as the others. His lips, like the royal guard, were painted clown red, but I wasn't convinced his was a simulation at all. I believed he wore blood. Whether to intimidate or as a sort of badge, or both, I wasn't sure. His eyes reflected the light behind me, flashing blue-white, as he leered up at me.

My eyes widened, and his smile did the same, revealing the razor sharp teeth of the Amara.

My breath hitched. *He's still so* beautiful… *but so painfully,* obviously *deadly.*

He began to laugh. Never before had I heard anything like it. It echoed what I had seen in his face. Here was a man who got great joy from the pain and fear of others, and joy was putting it lightly.

His mirth struck a nerve somewhere deep within me. It was too much to bear, and a scream clawed its way up my throat…

* * *

And I kept screaming and squeezed my eyes shut tight.

I don't want to hear any more. I don't want to see any more.

Someone's hands were on me. I tried to pull away but I couldn't. They gave me a shake.

"Haylee! Stop it! You were dreaming. It's over."

Derik?

"Please. I don't want them to come," he whispered.

I found it in myself to close my mouth and stop the sounds emitting from it. Though I was trembling so badly, it felt like convulsions, the hardest part was forcing my eyes open. So I did it one at a time. Once I'd opened the first and saw that familiar chest before me, it was much easier to open the other. I focused on him and wouldn't look anywhere else. Before I knew what I was doing, I grabbed his shirt and pulled myself into him, burying my head there, not sure I ever intended to leave.

"There's blood everywhere." His shirt muffled my voice.

His arms came around me, one hand smoothing my hair.

"It was just a dream," he said.

"No." I shook my head and again shuttered my eyes.

His hands moved to my shoulders. "Haylee." He held me away from him. "Open your eyes. Look at me." He gave me a slight shake, when I didn't comply right away.

I should do as he says. His presence is helping. The tremors have lessened… I took a shaky breath and opened my eyes once more. There was that broad, broad chest before me. I moved my eyes up until I met his and lingered there for a while to calm myself further. I didn't like seeing my vulnerable image reflected in his eyes, so I drew upon the strength I found there. Then, trusting him completely and with eyes much less wide, I looked away.

I swept my surroundings. "It's the same room, minus the blood." My voice was low.

Derik's hold on my shoulders tightened. "What do you mean?"

"It's the same room I was… dreaming about… Only, it was covered in blood." I still scanned the room, mesmerized. *The same white tiles, just dingy, like with age. Everything's the same, down to the old rusty sink in the corner.*

"Covered?"

My reply now was a nod, as I couldn't muster a word.

"He's coming," he whispered.

I snapped my head back toward him. "Huh?"

"You said, *he's coming*. When you were screaming. Who's coming, Haylee?" He leaned toward me in order to look me in the eyes.

I frowned, the echo of fear returning.

His fingers squeezed my arms so tightly, it hurt. Suddenly he let go.

I nearly tumbled forward.

"You're frightened again… why? What did you mean?" His eyes narrowed.

After I relayed to him my entire dream, or whatever it was, the only sound in the room was Derik's pacing. I stood and reached out to still him.

He knows something about this clown-faced man. "Who is he?"

"From your account, it sounds like their master." Derik's eyes rested on my hand. "I don't know of any human who has ever seen Donal and – " He stopped himself and looked at me directly, his eyes serious.

Oh. Got it. No human ever lived to tell the tale. "Donal?" I asked, instead of voicing my concerns about my mortality. "He has a name…" I looked down only to realize we stood directly on the old grate in the floor. *Great.* I tensed and sidestepped off of it, as a sudden dread came over me. "We should get out of here. Now."

He smiled a little, trying to lighten the mood. "Leave *that* to me. While you were *napping*, I went over the room. We have a few options, some better than others." He shrugged, then continued more cautiously. "One of which we were just stand – "

"No!" I nearly shouted at him. Then I took a deep breath and repeated, more calmly this time, "No. I have a bad feeling about going… that way." I glanced down at the grate.

"All right then. *Not* that way." He reached out to smooth my hair again. "There are a few other options."

"Okay, good. What are they, then?"

"Well, I think the best choice we have is that window over there." He pointed to a small window near the ceiling across the room.

I hadn't noticed it before. "A little small, don't ya' think?" I frowned and walked over to it. We must have been in a basement. The window was well above my head. I turned my frown back to him. "You'd never fit through that."

"Well… I wasn't – "

I cut him off. "Nope. Can't – won't do it." I shook my head. "There is no way I'm leaving you behind. No debate." I crossed my arms over my chest. "So, what other choices do we have?"

"I thought you might feel that way. All right." He turned away. "The next two choices are either the ventilation system or the door. Your pick." He gestured toward the ceiling with one hand and the door with the other.

I glanced back and forth, then pointed at the door. "I imagine there's someone out there?"

He nodded. "Not right outside the door, but they'll know if it opens, if we step into the hall. If they were right outside, I wouldn't be planning this out loud. They'd hear."

"Oh. Hm." I walked over to stand beneath the air duct, which no longer worked. My mind began to wander toward visions of webs and the things that make them. I shook my head. *Wow, that was vivid.* I placed my hand against my temple. "What's your vote?"

He frowned for an instant before answering. "Well, we could weigh the pros and cons… Truthfully, I'm not sure one is any safer than the other, but we might have the advantage for a few extra minutes by taking the ventilation shaft. If we're careful and make very little noise, we might gain some time before they know we're gone. Then again, there are some risks. It might not hold *both* our weights." He gave me a look.

"I'm *not* going alone. Forget it. It's all or nothing."

He looked irritated but was careful not to voice it, afraid of drawing more attention to us than I already had with my screaming fit. He turned away and took a deep breath. "All right. Fine. I wish we could – no, never mind." He glanced down at the grate in the floor and resolutely away again, before looking at me. "Up it is. Shall we go, then?" He held out his hand.

"All right." I smiled and placed my hand in his.

Since the room contained no furniture or boxes of any kind, Derik had to boost me up. Though he had no trouble lifting me, I was not so graceful as I clambered up onto his shoulders and unlatched the cover. I handed it down to him, and he disposed of it as quietly as possible. Then, I moved from a sitting position to standing and climbed into the air duct.

He watched my progress. "How is it?"

I shifted my weight from one knee to the other a few times more and glanced around me. It was plenty dusty and full of cobwebs, which were now all over me.

"It seems okay, not much movement. It's a lot bigger than I thought, too, so you should be fine."

"Good. All right, go ahead and move back a little, okay?" He reached up and wrapped his fingers over the edge of two adjacent sides of the hole.

I frowned down at him. "Do you need any help?"

He gave me a look in return.

"Right. I'll just move out of the way, then."

With hardly any exertion at all, he planted his feet against the wall and pulled himself up. He was across from me instantly.

I blinked at his deftness. "Wow." My voice was so low, it was merely air passing through my lips, but still I thought he heard me. I blushed at my accidental affirmation of awe.

However, when he spoke, his voice was serious. "Now, I need you to stay right behind me, at all times. Make as little noise as possible and move as carefully as you can. All right?"

"Uh-huh."

There was enough room for him to glance back at me. "And, please, don't fall trying to get back over the opening. I'm going to move up a little now. Take your time."

I nodded, more to myself than in reply. *Yeah, sure. No pressure. Why's he think I'm so clumsy? I mean, the label's never applied to me before. It's only when I'm around him that I – oh. Well, that makes sense.* I distracted myself with these thoughts, as I crawled over the hole, and smiled when I made it across without incident. *Ha ha. Victory. No klutz here. I haven't even sneezed.* But I kept my self-congratulatory statements to myself. *Don't wanna jinx our escape.*

We crawled through the dusty, cobwebbed ducts at a moderate pace. Derik seemed to follow instinct where direction was concerned. Sometimes it was so dark I couldn't see and had to hold on to his pant legs, until there was enough light to move on my own. This slowed us down considerably. The further along we crawled, the more the dust – and whatever else there might be – coated my throat.

We had been crawling along for a while – *how big* is *this place anyway?* – when my nose and throat began to tickle.

Derik stopped moving when I did.

My breathing's changed. He's had to hear it. Oh, don't sneeze, don't sneeze. I buried my face in both of my arms, which didn't work because they were covered in dust and cobwebs. So I pinched my nose between my fingers until the urge to sneeze subsided. However, it left the tickle in my throat to contend with. *I can handle that. For now.* I moved my hands back to the dirty metal below me.

Derik listened, then looked back at me. "We're getting close to the outlet. We've got one large room to pass over, where we need to be especially quiet. Will you be all right?"

I took a shallow breath, resisted the urge to cough, and nodded.

We moved forward. After a few moments, I noticed Derik's movements had become more deliberate, so I mimicked them. Once, I felt a slight quiver under me but chalked it up to nerves. We had moved a dozen or so more feet, when the urge to cough became unbearable. A small spasm issued from my lungs with every cough I suppressed. If I was going to gain any ounce of control, I had to stop. Once again, I pressed my face into my sleeves. When I felt that was inadequate, I curled into a ball, my face covered with my arms and most of my shirt. My body jerked a few times, as a muffled cough or two escaped.

All at once, Derik's arms circled me, and he hugged me against his chest.

How'd he get turned around? And without making a sound? Not that I'd notice.

He pressed my face into his shirt and all I could smell was him, all I could feel was him. With any sound I made sufficiently stifled, I coughed enough to clear my throat of the offending irritants. When I felt it was safe enough, I raised my head.

By the small amount of light coming in, I could see him mouth the question, "Okay?"

I nodded.

We sat perfectly still and didn't make a sound. He gave a small nod and began to settle back in order to get turned around, when the shaft shuddered. He froze, his eyes on mine, and held his hand out for me to be still.

It shuddered again and gave a long rending sound.

That doesn't sound good. I kept my eyes locked on Derik's.

Suddenly, the shaft dropped a few inches. The movement wrenched me forward.

Derik swore and jerked me back to him.

The shaft gave way and light filtered in. We slid a few feet toward it.

As we fell from the ventilation duct, something sharp tore into my shoulder. I cried out.

The impact forced the air from Derik's lungs. Somehow he'd positioned himself between me and the floor. I was lying on top of him, and his arms still held me tight. The pain in my shoulder brought me out of my daze. I pushed against Derik, so he would let go. When he rolled over instead and placed me behind him, I got a better view of our surroundings.

We were in the center of a large room, with high basement windows, all of which were painted over. The room was set up like a lounge, chairs and sofas of various styles everywhere, and lit with lanterns. Every bit of the seating was occupied.

We're literally *surrounded.*

While most of the Pale Ones sat, looking surprised to see us, a few stood only a few feet away. I looked up to the ceiling, curious of the distance we had fallen, only to wish I hadn't.

It's a wonder nothing's broken. If not for Derik, I'd still be on the ground. It would appear he's a master of many things. Including falling.

He stood defensively in front me, despite the Pale Ones standing on all sides.

He knows where the biggest threat is gonna come from.

And it turned out we were both right. The group gathered in front of us divided, making a path. As they did so, a voice sounded from that side of the room.

"I'm so glad you could join us. It saves us from having to go get you." With that, a man appeared before us. He was nowhere near as tall as the others and he didn't look like one of them. He looked human and not much older than me.

When he stepped forward, the pain in the shoulder all but disappeared. At least, it felt as though it had. It was more like I forgot about it. The man before us had all of my attention.

Why do I suddenly feel so comfortable? So… detached. Like nothing in this room matters? But this man is *important. He's someone I need to watch. Why? Who is he?*

"My name is Sullivan."

Why does it feel as though he's speaking to me alone. I don't like this...

"There's no reason to be afraid. We won't harm her." He directed this last part toward Derik.

"Excuse me if I don't believe you." Derik spoke between clenched teeth.

"Well. I suppose I understand." He waved the others away, and they went back to their seats, keeping their eyes on us. "Come. Sit." He gestured for us to follow him to the nearest vacant seating area.

As soon as he turned away, I became acutely aware of the pain in my shoulder. I glanced down at it and, though it must have been bleeding profusely for a few moments, it was trickling now. I looked up at Derik, who still had not moved nor taken his eyes off of the man. Derik's right arm had blood on it. I moved closer to him and touched his arm.

Oh, thank God. It's not his blood.

He looked down at my touch and, before he could voice his concern, Sullivan called out.

"Icarus, get the first aid kit."

One of them stood as if to protest. Then he thought better of it and marched out a nearby door.

It was one of two doors exiting this room. I glanced toward the other one, at the far end of the room.

Sullivan turned back to us, indicating a sofa in front of him. "Sit, please. As I have said, no harm will befall you. Let us take a look at your injury. It hurts, does it not?"

When his eyes met mine, pain shot through my arm. I sucked in a breath.

Derik's eyes narrowed, but he pulled me toward the couch and had me sit down.

He must be thinking what I am. We don't have much choice in the matter, why not get my shoulder treated. Then we'll think about escape.

I sat across from this man named Sullivan.

He looked at me. "Haylee, is it? Not very fitting for someone of your abilities, is it? We'll have to think of something more suitable for you."

I frowned at him, as I held my arm.

"Ah, there you are." He gazed over my shoulder. "This is Icarus. He will tend to your wound, while we chat."

Someone touched my arm, and I flinched. When I turned to look at Icarus, he wouldn't meet my eyes and worked with a look of distaste on his face. Like the others, he was pale, tall, and leanly muscled. I felt a small shiver run up my spine, closed my eyes, and swallowed it back down.

I swear that's an amused smile on his lips. Derik's right. They enjoy fear. At least he's not showing teeth. I jumped when he wiped a cold, damp cloth across my skin.

Seated on my other side, Derik placed his fingertips on the back of my hand. My racing heart slowed. When my eyes met Sullivan's once again, it was as if the slash in my shoulder did not exist.

I blinked at him. *He — he's human. Why's he here?* How *is he here? He couldn't be more than three or four inches taller than me and no older than twenty-five. But he* seems *older.*

As I studied him, his lips spread into a wide smile. Though it made him more handsome, his smile threw me.

"What? What is it?" I glanced back and forth, searching for the source of his pleasure.

He laughed. "You. You are not what I expected." He studied my face. "Much more pleasing to the eye, yes, but not at all what I expected. You're so…" He shook his head, still smiling. "I'm not sure young would be appropriate. Inexperienced, perhaps." The way he looked me up and down, made me uncomfortable.

I shifted and was reminded of my wound, as Icarus tugged at it. I winced.

"Icarus! I'm not going to warn you twice."

Icarus was much more gentle after that.

He doesn't seem too happy being bossed around by a human. I glanced over at the Pale One. He was trimming the thread, and my wound was clean and stitched up. *That's funny. I barely felt any of that.*

"It's best, Dear, if you do not look at it." Sullivan caught my gaze again.

And the pain was gone once more. "How do you do that?"

"It's quite simple."

Is that conceit I hear in his voice?

His eyes narrowed. "I could show you, sometime."

Is he flirting *with me? This is getting too weird.* I reached for Derik's hand, which was still against mine, and felt him squeeze back. I felt calmer. *Did I imagine that brief scowl from Sullivan just now? What does he care if Derik holds my hand? No, just my imagination.*

"You've given us a lot of trouble – both of you." He took a deep breath. "But all's well that ends well, they always said. I suppose we should prepare you for introductions." He looked me over again, raising his eyebrows, as he stood. "Icarus. Have them prepare a bath and everything else for the Presentation." He gestured as if suddenly he had no interest in anything whatsoever.

He moved closer to me, and I felt Derik tense, ready to fight if need be. Sullivan looked down at me and held out his hand.

"Haylee." It still sounded as though he was having trouble with my name. "Please, walk with me."

I swallowed a lump in my throat and looked over to Derik. He eyed Sullivan for a moment and got up, towering over him. Sullivan chose to ignore him, as he gazed down at me. Still, I wasn't sure what to do. I glanced from his hand to Derik once more.

"Of course, your… friend… may accompany us." Though his tone was pleasant, I could tell he disliked the idea.

Derik gave a single nod. I hesitated but raised the hand that had so recently been within Derik's grasp. When it rested against Sullivan's, he wrapped his fingers around it.

Wow. His hand is much warmer than I expected. Even warmer than Derik's. Why does that surprise me?

He caught my gaze again and pulled me up from the sofa. It took place in slow motion and, by the time I was upon my feet, I was dizzy. I was afraid I was going to fall back again, when Sullivan's other hand came around my waist and caught me. Suddenly, I understood what was happening, as I saw Derik reaching for Sullivan.

"Derik, wait. It's all right." I blinked up at Sullivan, narrowed my eyes and pulled them away from his.

Then, everything was back to normal, and Derik was frowning at me. He and all of the others in the room had stopped mid-movement. He was in the process of decking Sullivan, and they had been preparing to stop Derik. *Interesting.*

"I could show you how I did that, as well."

His voice was so enticing. It tugged at me. *No. Do* not *look at him. It's what he wants… and you may not be able to look away again.*

Derik was hesitant to take my word for it. "You don't *sound* all right. Your heart's racing."

I met his eyes instead and took a deep breath. *Yes, that's it. Focus on him instead.* "No, I am. He was just… sharing something with me. That's what you would call it, right… Sullivan?" Still I looked at Derik.

"That's exactly what I would call it. And I could share – teach you – *much more* than that." I could hear the smile in his voice.

His voice sent a small thrill through me, which I managed to quell. *What he's doing is showing off. And oh, he's good… whatever he is.*

He laughed. "Oh, you have no idea." He slid his hand around and away from the small of my back and dropped it to his side. "You're wondering what I am? When you already know?"

I cheeks burned. "Seer. You're their Seer. Like Sabella, only… not like Sabella at all. She would never treat me like this. Never use her abilities to persuade, to…" I swallowed, not wanting to continue that line of thought.

"Seduce?" He finished it for me. "Is that what I'm doing? Trying to *seduce you* with power? *Seduce you* to the dark side?"

I could hear – no, *feel* – his smile. And it made me shiver.

"Stop it, now." Derik's voice was a growl.

Sullivan sighed. "Very well… for now."

I could feel his eyes upon me, more intense than ever. Then I felt my body relax. I hadn't realized it was tensed.

"Shall we go now?"

His tone was light, so I chanced a look at his face. It had changed somehow, but I couldn't place the difference. He still had my hand, and I nodded.

He gave me a smile. "This way, then."

We left the room and entered a hallway. It was lit by lanterns, and guards stood at regular intervals. We passed between them every twelve feet or so.

How many are there? And where are the Royal Guard from earlier? Guarding his immortal highness?

Sullivan tucked my arm into his elbow, sandwiching my hand between both of his, as we walked. He was closer to me than I would have liked, his hip brushing mine. Derik was right behind us.

"Where are we going?" I watched various doors go by.

"Well, I thought you would enjoy a nice hot bath. A real one. A soak in an actual tub. Not a quick spray off in a makeshift shower. Did I mention hot?" He glanced down at me and used one of his hands to dust mine off. "I mean, have you seen yourself lately? You're a mess, no offense. But you *were* crawling around in an old ventilation shaft. Besides, one must be in their purest state before meeting the Master. Before the Presentation." He stopped. "Here we are. This will be where we part ways. Don't worry. I'll send someone for you, when He has arrived."

"I – I don't understand. Purest state? Presentation?" I shook my head. "Do you know what he's talking about, Derik?"

Derik frowned, shaking his head. "No. This is all new to me… He didn't have a pet Seer when I last saw him. Donal is *here*?" He looked back to our host.

"No one refers to Him by that name!" Sullivan said. "He is the Master to you, and only the Master. And no, but He is on his way. He wishes to see this one in person." He turned back to me, trying to smooth his features, because I had jumped at his sudden loss of temper. "Now, where was I? Oh, yes. I only meant you must be presentable when we introduce you. That's all. Now, you're bath is ready, right through this door. When you are finished, proceed through the other door, and you will find a fresh change of clothes. All right?" Keeping my hand in one of his, he placed his other hand on the knob and began to turn it. "Oh, one more thing. Are you a virgin?"

Derik and I reacted simultaneously.

"Hey!"

"Huh?"

"Are you a – "

"I know *what* you said, just not why you asked it. It's not any of your business." My face had turned bright red now, and I didn't know where to avert my eyes. I felt as though everyone was staring at me.

"You are right, of course. It's not important anyway. I was merely curious." He eyed Derik.

What does – Oh. He means… me and Derik?! My blush deepened, though it shouldn't have been possible.

"Hm… I see." He met Derik's eyes. He'd gotten the answer he was looking for, at least where Derik and I were concerned. He turned back toward me and gave a short bow. "Forgive me. I overstepped." Then he opened the door. "Go on, enjoy. We will see you again shortly."

I pulled my hand from his, afraid to look away from him, not trusting his explanation. I glanced at Derik, who had moved closer during the exchange, and reached for his hand. With our hands entwined, I began to move forward.

But Sullivan stopped us. "Ah… He is to come with us."

I blinked, looking back and forth between the two of them.

Derik looked unhappy about the idea. "I'm not leaving her alone."

"And I don't want to be alone." My grasp tightened, and I wrapped both my hands around his, pulling it toward my chest.

Sullivan contemplated the dilemma. "Well, I suppose I could have one of the guards stay with you then." His eyes were calculating, as they met mine.

"No." Derik and I replied at once.

"I want Derik…" I sensed this was a losing battle.

The eyes that met mine now were cold. "Well, I'm afraid that's not going to happen. He is coming with us, and you are going to get ready. Either you go in alone, or one of them stays with you."

I glanced where he indicated. The others all looked at me, hunger in their eyes.

"So, what will it be?"

Derik tensed beside me.

"Now, now. We don't want to cause any trouble and have anyone get hurt. Do we?" Sullivan turned those eyes on Derik now.

A frown flickered across Derik's face, then his eyes met mine. "I have your word nothing will happen to her? She won't be harmed, in any way?"

What is he doing*?*

"You have my word." Sullivan's voice was like silk now.

I felt his grasp loosen. "No. Derik, please. I can't. Don't." I grabbed at his hand again, and he still managed to pull away.

"Haylee. It'll be okay. Whether or not I'm with you, I won't let anything happen to you. All right?" He steered me into the room, and they pulled him back. He fought to free himself but there were too many hands pulling at him. "Hey, let go. I'm trying to – " As soon as he had cleared the door, it slammed shut.

"Derik! Wait, please!" I grabbed the doorknob, but it wouldn't turn. I yanked on it, and it wouldn't budge. Then, I pounded on the door with both fists until I was tired.

Turning, I fell against it and gave it one final kick, before sliding to the floor. I listened for a moment but heard nothing.

The door and walls must be thick. I'm not going anywhere anytime soon. I took the opportunity to study my surroundings and sat up. *Oh!*

Three young women stood off to the side of the room. Three human women. They were absolutely still and didn't acknowledge my presence. Slowly, I made my way back to my feet.

"Hello?" I took a step toward them, and they moved as well. "Can you help me?"

They drew near. None of them gave any indication of hearing.

Something's… not right here.

They got closer, and I backed away,

"What's wrong with you?"

But they still didn't hear. When I ran out of space to move, I stopped, and they reached for me.

Their hands pulled at the large shirt I was wearing, and I tried to free the material from their grasp.

"Let go of me. Please."

They paid my pleas no attention and kept tugging.

Starting to panic, I glanced around the room.

What am I even looking for? A weapon won't do me any good. I don't want to hurt *them. They're not in control. It's like they're under the — the* thrall *of someone else. And I'd bet it's Sullivan.*

I was searching for anything that might help, when I spotted the second door. Still unable to loosen the women's grip on the oversized shirt, I let them pull the material over my head and rushed to it. It opened easily, and I found myself in a massive bedroom.

Okay… there's got to be another— There! A door!

I shot toward it and jerked on the doorknob. It wouldn't move. I tried again with the same result. Closing my eyes, I leaned my forehead against the wood. Sighing, I turned to search the room for any other means of escape. And saw nothing, not even a tiny window.

Of course, they wouldn't make it that *easy.*

Not yet willing to admit defeat, I made my way back to the smaller room. The women waited where I had left them, as if they weren't allowed to leave.

Or as if they know there's no need to stop me.

I stood in the doorway for a moment, allowing myself to see it was indeed a bathroom. A large claw-footed tub, filled to the brim with hot, frothy water, took up the majority of the center of the room. Hidden in one corner were a toilet and a bidet, and a long vanity stood behind the women. The mirror over the vanity took up the entire wall and was beginning to steam over.

Once I was sure of my surroundings, I let my eyes settle on the women. Now that I could get a better look at them, I realized they were much younger than I had estimated. The youngest was no older than sixteen, while the oldest looked as though she were in her mid-twenties. They were too thin, and their clothes, while clean, were ragged. Though their faces were vacant, I could sense there was still something of them beneath the surface.

Saddened by their condition, I stepped into the room. Immediately, they began reaching for my clothes again.

On impulse, I grabbed at the hands of the nearest girl – the youngest. She went still, while the other two continued their gentle tugging. Because she was looking down, I was able to see her face. Her eyes were glazed over, and she made no indication of understanding what was going on around her.

I grasped her shoulders and gave her a little shake. "Hello?"

When I got no reaction, I placed my hands on either side of her face, searching her eyes. I wasn't sure what I was looking for, so I tried something about which I was almost as uncertain. I tried to reach her in another way. With my mind.

Still staring into her eyes, I felt for her consciousness and sensed it buried beneath something that *wasn't* her. I knew it was something I would never be able to describe, because the sensation of entering her mind was bewildering and took on the feel of a fun house out of a nightmare. I could make out images at times, but they would twist away just as I was about to comprehend their meaning. The frustration and a growing apprehension almost caused me to pull back. But I realized that was their purpose, so I pushed on. Once I was through that first layer, everything was quiet.

Empty. As if there's nothing there. But there is *more. I can feel it. Something beyond this deception. I'm* meant *to believe this girl is an empty shell.* I took a deep breath, ignored the illusion, and pressed on.

At first, I hit a barrier with no give. Then, all at once, I was through and, as if pressure had been building up for far too long, *she* burst through, carrying me in her wake.

I was myself again, and the girl was in front of me. Her eyes, no longer uncomprehending, widened in fear.

Then, she started screaming.

Though I tried, I couldn't calm her. She flailed at my hands, glancing around her without seeing. Letting out another scream, she backed away until she came to the corner behind the tub. And, with a look of absolute terror, she slid down to the floor, curled into a fetal position, and rocked back and forth.

The other two women paid her no attention, still holding onto my clothing with unnatural patience. When I tried to approach the girl, she screamed again, so I stayed back, not knowing what else to do. With that, she returned to her rocking and hugged herself, murmuring. Though I could understand her words, their meaning was unclear to me.

Oh, what I wouldn't give for Glenna's power right now. My abilities are useless*!* My shoulders slumped. *I just wanted to help. But I've done her more harm than good.*

Now, I did feel defeated. I glanced at the tub and felt the women's hands, still pulling. Heaving a sigh, I closed me eyes for a moment, before making my way to the mirror over the vanity.

I wiped my hand across it, clearing a streak in order to see myself. I looked as grimy and downtrodden as I felt. Though my hairclip was still secure at the back of my head, my hair, covered in cobwebs, was hanging loose in dull, frizzing strands. My clothes were dusty, and tears left streaks in the dirt on my face. My eyes were red and tired.

I focused on the scene behind me. Steam rose invitingly from the large tub, as the girl cowered behind it. As I stood there, deliberating, the mirror steamed back over. And, resigned, I made my decision.

Feeling extremely vulnerable – though less so than the teenager in the corner – I decided I didn't have much choice. Turning, I removed the clip, shook out my hair, and toed off my shoes. I set them near the door to the bedroom and moved toward the tub. I located the towels, before allowing the women to strip me of my clothes. Then, I touched my toe to the water and stepped over the edge. As I sank into the bubbles, I had to brace myself. The water was too hot. I made sure not to submerge my shoulder and its fresh bandage. The women stood off to the side, waiting.

Though I'm not sure how I managed it, bit by bit, I relaxed. I could feel the grime lifting away from my skin. I leaned my head back and closed my eyes.

And I wasn't in the hot water but another room entirely. I was alone in a bedroom, not unlike the room I had just seen, but I felt like an observer, not myself. I felt out of place and out of control.

"You really need to work on keeping your guard up."

I tried to turn, in order to locate the voice, but could not. *Where'd that come from? It sounded like…*

"That would be correct."

Sullivan. What are you doing in my head?

"My Dear, if you paid attention you would see it is *you* who is in *my* head. I thought the bath would relax you. But this is ridiculous. Things like this wouldn't happen, if you were more adequately trained in guarding your mind. Your shields should not relax as your body does… Not that I'm complaining."

There was that tone of voice again. It sent a tiny thrill through me, even as it made me uncomfortable.

How is he doing this?

"I can only do what you allow. I simply *think* of the person I wish to connect with. As I said, you let your guard down… and in such a vulnerable state. You may have fallen asleep by now." He paused, as if deep in thought. "Hm… yes. Though I would love to develop those thoughts further, I have a bone to pick with you." He gave a snicker before becoming somber. "Look at the state you've left that poor girl. Did you not think she has suffered enough?"

"The state *I've* left her in? *You're* responsible for her state! I was trying to help her."

"So you say. But, as I see it, she was completely free from human worry and fear. Perhaps you need to reflect upon what you have done. And you should have plenty of time to do so. I, on the other hand, have much to prepare. But I shall see you soon." As if it were my own, I saw his hand come up and his fingers come together.

I jerked at the sound of them snapping. Water sloshed over the side of the tub. I shivered, though the water was still warm.

Did *I fall asleep? So quickly? I don't think so. I wasn't dreaming. Sullivan penetrated my mind, which seemed easy enough for him. Oh, I wish I'd had more time with Sabella, more time to learn and practice.*

Hugging my knees to me, I willed the shivering to stop. I felt violated, though not in the traditional sense. Without my permission, he had invaded the confines of my mind, while I was in my most unguarded state. Ignoring the pain in my shoulder, I held my breath, closed my eyes, and slid under the water.

When I felt sufficiently clean, I grabbed for one of the large towels nearby. However, one of the women got to it first and held it open for me. Because I wasn't certain if Sullivan could see through my eyes, as I had seen through his, I averted my gaze and made sure not to look toward the mirror. And, to be certain, I folded the towel around me before stepping out of the tub. Rivulets dripped down my back, despite squeezing the excess water from my hair.

The two women followed me with extra towels, as I padded over to the vanity and swiped my hand across it once more. They rubbed at me, drying my hair and skin, as I checked my image. Though the hot water should have left my face flushed like the rest of my body, it looked pale, as if I was suffering from a shock. My eyes were still red but they looked a little better, and I definitely looked cleaner. My bandage had fallen off in the water, but my shoulder looked all right.

I met my eyes again and held my own gaze. For good measure, though it felt childish, I stuck my tongue out at my reflection – and whoever else might be watching – before turning to leave the room.

I hesitated on the threshold between the bathroom and bedroom. He had said there would be fresh clothes here for me, but I didn't remember seeing them before. Of course, I hadn't been looking for clean clothes at the time. Now I looked and, there, draped across the foot of the massive, canopied bed, was some white fabric. Upon closer inspection, I discovered it to be a dress. It was a simple style with pearl buttons all the way up the front.

"Couldn't you find anything more practical?" I sighed and checked the room for mirrors. The only one I could find was a full-length across the room. The women had trailed behind me into the room this time. So, I moved toward them, grabbed one of the large bath sheets, and draped it over the mirror. Once I was satisfied it was covered, I turned back to the room.

The two women waited with the garment in hand. Holding my arms up, I let them pull the material over my head. It fell straight down to my ankles and had a thin belt at its waist. I dropped the towel from beneath the dress, slapped their hands away, and fumbled with the belt. They plucked the towel up, grabbed the one off the mirror on their return to the bathroom, and closed the door behind them.

What's this all about? Why can't I wear normal clothes? I know they have them. And what about shoes? I need those, too, unless they want me to wear my old sneakers with this thing. And what do I do now? Wait? I tried the other door again, to no avail. I went back to the full-length mirror.

"I'm ready. Now what?" I dreaded the answer.

My fingers shook as I used them to straighten my hair. It was already starting to dry with wisps floating here and there. I tucked it behind my ears, in frustration, and turned away from my image. Then, I marched back into the bathroom for my hairclip and shoes. They were where I had left them, though the women and my other clothes were gone. I tried the original door again, though I assumed it was locked, and it was.

Still tired, I found the only place to sit was the bed. I climbed up and settled down on top of the pillows, pressing my back against the headboard and willing myself to stay alert.

I don't want my back to any part of the room, especially if I lose focus. I'm exhausted. With all the Zs I've been catching, I should be well rested. But I'm more tired than I've ever felt. Why? Because of the unnatural nature of my sleep lately? A result of mental and emotional fatigue… not to mention the supernatural aspects. That's not really rest. I don't know… That's the best I can come up with.

"Don't you *dare* fall asleep," I said aloud.

Where's Derik right now? Where was he, when I saw Sullivan? I shivered. *Oh, I shouldn't even* think *of* him. *What did he say? He only had to think of a person to connect with them? What if that person thinks of* him*? What then? I can't risk it. It's bad enough being with him in person, but connecting with his mind I can't handle. At least, not so soon after the first time. If it* was *the first time.*

What was it he had been doing earlier, when Derik had been so concerned? That was pretty similar.

My eyelids drooped.

Not good. I blinked and shook my head. *I have to get up.* But I couldn't find the motivation. *This is wrong. Get up, get up, get up.* I couldn't move, couldn't lift my eyes.

* * *

There was the sound of knocking and my eyes flew open.

Where am I? I blinked away the remnants of sleep. *Oh. Right.*

The door opened, crashing against the wall.

I jumped to a crouch in the middle of the bed.

In the doorway stood Nate, dressed as she had been before, down to the smug look on her face. "He's ready for you."

I scooted to the edge of the bed and climbed to the floor.

"Hurry up, or I'll come in there and get you."

This gave a little more urgency to my step. "Where are we going?"

She grabbed my arm and pulled me along.

Thank goodness it's my good one. There's no way I'm pulling loose from that grasp.

"The Master wants to meet you, as soon as he arrives." Her scathing look gave me shivers.

"If he wants to see me so badly, I'm sure he won't be happy when he sees the bruise on my arm."

Begrudgingly, she loosened her grip and continued dragging me down the hall.

Since she wasn't speaking, I broke the silence.

"*Why* did you do it, Nate?"

"You mean, why did I make a deal with the devil?" She laughed. "I was tired of having no great ability to speak of."

"But you heal fast, right? That's pretty extraordinary."

She rolled her eyes. "Pft. They have all the power." She threw me a glance over her shoulder. "Though I guess you're much worse off than I ever was. Not physically useful. You can barely take care of yourself. At least *I* can fight. But none of that was enough. They were still killing off humans all around me. When I was out and came across a group of them one day, I asked to join them. Well, they saw what great potential I had, what I could offer, and struck a deal. I still don't see what potential they see in you. He'll probably kill you when he realizes the mistake they've made." She smiled.

She's awfully sure of herself. And she's probably right. Ugh. Best not to think about it. I swallowed. "So you made a deal with them to spy on Derik and the others? All this time, they thought you came to them fearing for your life. You told them the Amara killed your family. You've been lying the entire time."

We reached a stairwell.

"Well, it wasn't *all* a lie. They did kill my family… but I allowed them to. That was part of the deal." She shrugged. "I had to prove I was serious."

I balked, and her hand slipped on my arm.

"You *let* them kill your *family*?"

She glowered down at me. "Just like I'm going to let them kill everyone back at the safe house. Now, come *on*." She tightened her grip and tugged me up the stairway.

The pain snapped me out of my shock.

Wait! Does that mean she… I tried to pull her to a stop, but she would have none of it. So, I blurted out my realization.

"You *freed* the Pale One at the compound, the one in the basement. You let her go and… *you* had my hairclip! You gave it to her, knowing what she would do with it. Though that wasn't the plan, was it? You hoped she'd kill me that day."

She halted and turned on me. "Of course I hoped she'd kill you, you little brat! I was the only one who could see how much of a nuisance you were. The way you distracted Derik… I had his complete trust until you came along and weaved your little spell over him and everyone else. I should kill you right now!"

And she pulled her hand back as if she were getting ready to do it.

12

I closed my eyes and braced for impact.

A series of thuds made me flinch. When nothing else happened, I peaked through one eye.

Derik crouched over Nate's limp form. He was alone.

I gave a shaky laugh. "Well, this definitely makes up for all the previous interactions we've had in stairwells."

He gave me a quizzical look.

I shook my head. "Is she… dead?"

"No. But if I'd been a moment later, I probably would have killed her." He stood up. "She'll be waking up soon with a horrible headache. Are you all right?" He reached for my hand.

I nodded. "Did you hear what she said?"

"I caught most of it, yeah…" Glancing down at her, he said, "She was just *off* after I found you. I should've trusted my instincts." Then, he looked back at me. "We should go."

We ran up one more flight of stairs and paused at the doorway to the corridor beyond.

"It's after dawn, so most of them are asleep downstairs, except for the guard. So we need to hurry." He surveyed the hall.

After dawn? How could I have slept so long? How could so much time have passed? "Why did they wait so long to come get me?"

"They're still waiting on Donal to get here. Where he's been and why, I'm not sure, but we don't have enough time to speculate about it right now. Sullivan's going to know something's up soon." He took a quick look up and down the stairwell before, once again, giving his full attention to the hallway. "It's all clear. Let's go." He pulled me along. "Stay right behind me."

"Sullivan's a Seer. Why do they need *me*? I don't even know what I'm doing," I said, as I followed along.

"I can't exactly say why Donal wants you. I can't tell you why he does a lot of the things he does. Seers are a bit of an obsession for him, and he likes toying with humans. It's a game to him," he whispered, as he moved. "And I have a feeling he will especially enjoy playing with you." He turned back long enough for me to see his face twist in a scowl for an instant before returning to a blank expression.

"Why *especially* me?" I tugged at him.

"Well, it's complicated with Don – " He stopped and turned.

Sullivan stepped out from somewhere behind us.

"You're very special, Haylee. Or haven't you realized that by now?" He turned his gaze toward Derik. "And I said never to call Him that."

His countenance was completely neutral, which succeeded in frightening me in a way no scowl ever could.

"You, my dear, were to be escorted to the Master's rooms."

Derik stepped in between us. "She's had a permanent detour. We're leaving together. Now."

The two of them stared each other down for a few moments.

When one of them spoke, it was Sullivan. "You know… I've heard all about you. *Derik*. Oh, I could tell her a thing or two. Perhaps I should – "

Then, Derik punched him.

Sullivan crumpled to the floor, unconscious.

"Wow, that was… easy." I blinked at his prone form. "He talks too much anyway. Will this keep him out of my head?"

"For the time-being, anyway. I'm not sure how soon he'll recover." He held out his arm, ushering me ahead of him. "So, let's go while the getting's good."

I almost laughed at the saying but was clear-headed enough to realize this was no time for jokes.

We continued down the hall.

"How did you give them the slip, out of curiosity?"

He listened for approaching footfall, as we rounded a corner. "Oh, I have my ways. Let's just say they shouldn't have underestimated me. They had no idea who they were dealing with." He motioned for me to continue.

After a moment, I asked another question that had been bothering me. "Derik, do they keep human slaves?"

The slight hitch in his step was the only indication of his emotions. "Yes. You've seen them?"

"Yes. Sullivan's got them in some sort of trance. They don't know what's going on. Do they?" *Please don't let them know.*

"What makes you so sure it's Sullivan?"

"Who else would it be?" When he didn't answer, I came up with my own. "Don – um – Donal? Can he *do* that?"

"He's capable of many things," he mumbled.

I blinked, absorbing this information. Then, I shook it away. "But *do* they know what's going on around them?"

I felt his sigh more than heard it. "There's no way to know for sure. But I hope they can't. I wouldn't wish that reality on any human."

I grabbed the tail of his shirt, both as a way to stay near him and show the importance of my next question.

"Derik? Is there anything you can do for them?" I knew I was asking a lot, but I couldn't leave without knowing.

He stopped moving and turned toward me. "Haylee. I don't know how to answer that." Taking my hands, he continued, "If I can free them, I will. If it's possible, I'll make it happen. But I can't promise you anything more. Just, please. Let me get you out first."

Knowing he meant what he said, I nodded.

He touched his forehead to mine, a relieved smile on his face. "We've got to keep going. Come on."

Following, I held onto his shirt again, and he didn't seem to mind.

"Where are we going?" I asked.

"I've found the way out, don't worry," was the only reply I received.

We passed by several closed doors. At the end of the hall, we stopped, and Derik listened again, before we edged around another corner. We kept our backs against one wall, so we could see if anyone came up behind us. With my hand on his shirt, I could glance back with little fear of losing him. We passed more doors. When he stopped again, I bumped into him, but he didn't move. We were at a large open doorway, but the room beyond was blocked to me.

Derik took hold of my hand and pulled me closer. "Okay." His breath tickled my ear. "This is the place. We'll have to be quick. And especially careful." He looked back around the edge of the opening.

We were poised to go, when I heard voices from further down the hall. We turned our heads toward the sound. They were getting closer.

"Well, looks like it's now or never… Let's go." Derik pulled me along behind him into a large room.

The wall across from us was completely open to the forest outside, and morning light was beginning to pour in through the thick trees and brush. We moved much more quickly now.

We need to reach that light, though it won't guarantee safety. For me, two places will. Only one of them will make me happy… but the choice has already been made for me. And this is not *the time to start up that argument again. Right now, we need to get out of here.*

We passed by a large built-in desk before reaching the doorway, and I realized it looked familiar to me.

Have I been here before? There's no time. Just file it away for future reference.

Derik reached the first empty doorframe. Like the front wall, the doors were once made of glass. We stepped over empty metal trim.

Someone down the hall yelled. They were much closer now.

Please let them be Pale Ones of the ordinary variety. Oh, we couldn't be so lucky.

We found ourselves in an entryway, between two sets of doors. One more to go, and we'd be outside. Derik towed me behind him. Immediately, I could tell a difference.

The air's fresher and cleaner smelling out here… It feels right compared to inside. How's that possible?

Derik paused for a fraction of a second before moving to our right. He knew where he was going.

"We'll head toward the compound for a while, then double back and head for the portal. I'm going to get you home, if it's the last thing I do."

"Won't they think of that? I mean, they'd probably split up, or something, right?" I jogged along behind him and knew we moved at a pitiably slow pace for his tastes. "And if we double back, won't that increase the chances of them catching up with us? Not that my pace won't increase the chances, as it is…"

He glanced back at me. "Oh, I'm counting on them splitting up."

This speed's a walk in the park for him.

"As for the other problem, I've already considered that. There aren't as many of them as last time, but we should be able to miss them. Don't worry. We'll be fine. Trust me."

I could hear a smile in his voice now, though I couldn't see his face.

He's awfully sure of himself. Then again, I'd trust him, even if he wasn't.

I managed to keep this pace for a lot longer than I thought possible. I don't normally have such good stamina. Of course, I was in better shape than I had been when I passed through that portal. And the adrenaline didn't hurt. I didn't think either. Couldn't. I kept my mind focused on one foot in front of the other. That was all I could do. Eventually, though, I could feel myself slowing. It was getting harder to move at that speed, and my sides began to burn.

"You're doing great," Derik said, as if reading my mind. "A little bit further, then we'll change direction." And he was true to his word. Shortly after that, he pulled me another way and we began to slow down.

When he brought us to a complete stop, confusion showed in my face.

"I need to throw them off this trail," he said, still breathing normally. He placed his hand on my shoulder. "I want you to stay right here, out of sight, all right? And I'll be right back. I promise."

Confusion turned to slight alarm, but I nodded anyway, as he hid me in a small thicket of brush.

"That dress is a dead give away but part of it could be useful. Here." He stepped closer and ripped a strip from the sleeve. Then he stepped away, said again, "I'll be right back," and was gone.

Feeling very conspicuous, I crouched down further into the thicket. I jumped at every noise. A small flock of birds rocketed into the air from another grouping of underbrush, causing my heart to lurch. Trying to calm myself, I closed my eyes and took a slow, deep breath before letting it out.

Silly. I shook my head and took another breath. *Oh no. It's quiet... Too quiet. And all too familiar.* A trickle of sweat made a trail down my spine. A breeze touched the tops of the trees above me. I heard nothing, except my own heart pounding against my ribcage. *Where's Derik?* I swung my head around, listening for any indication he was near. Nothing.

Haylee… I heard a whisper in my mind. *Haylee…* This one was followed by a laugh. *Come out, come out, wherever you are.*

Sullivan?

Another laugh was the only answer.

I threw my gaze around me but saw no one.

He laughed again. *I* will *find you. And sooner rather than later. You can't hide from me. We're the same, you and I. We are linked by fate.*

I don't believe you. I pushed myself down further into my hiding place.

I've been seeing you for a very long time. I've dreamed of the day we'd meet.

A shiver ran up my spine. *I have a feeling he doesn't mean* dream *in the way most people do.*

Yes. I foresaw this day. Destiny has brought us together. We are meant to be –"

"Get out of my head." I forced the words out in one breath and squeezed my eyes shut. *Out!*

He laughed. *Come now. Don't be like that.*

A hand caressed my hair.

I jumped up. *There's no one here. How'd he do that?*

His laughter echoed in my mind.

Hoping I hadn't given myself away, I slid back into the thicket. *How could I let him get to me like that?*

I waited and listened, but everything was quiet again. A twig snapped nearby, and I froze. *Oh, I hope that's Derik.*

What is *taking him so long?* Sullivan's voice rang through my head again. *I do hope he's all right.*

I could almost see the sneer on his face as he spoke.

Doubt prickled at the back of my mind. Is *Derik all right? What do you mean by that?*

Oh, I'm sure he's fine…

Brush rustled to my right. I crouched down lower, keeping myself hidden but preparing to bolt at the first sight of anyone not Derik.

But you *may not be.*

My body went cold. *What does that mean?*

They're very close. These words felt like a suggestion.

I frowned. *He's trying to scare me. He's getting me all worked up, so I'll do something stupid. Something like…*

Give yourself up? Run? Well, at least I tried. You're still very susceptible. I needed to know the degree *of your susceptibility…*

And?

He laughed.

I'm getting tired of this. Get out of my head!

Hm. For now, perhaps. I like this game too much.

And, just like that, he was gone. My mind was my own again. But my surroundings were still unnaturally quiet. The rustling noise I had heard moments ago had stopped.

Has *a Pale One been close by? Or did Sullivan just make me think there was?*

A figure emerged from the trees to my right. I jumped and turned to find Derik coming toward me.

"That should take care of it for a little while. Are you all right?" He frowned at me. "You didn't think I deserted you, did you?"

I stood. "No. I knew you meant what you said. It's just… Well, Sullivan's awake. He's been talking to me… he thinks it's a game. And I was afraid one of them was nearby." I swallowed. My heart was racing. "I was afraid something had happened to you."

He stared down at me. "I'm fine. You're fine." He touched a loose strand of my hair. "They're not close. I'd sense them if they were. And we need to keep that distance."

I nodded and the strand fell from his hand.

He raised his eyebrows. "Are you ready?"

"Yeah. I'm ready." *But am I really? Am I ready to go home? Will it still be home?* I followed him anyway.

We started to jog along again.

"I know it'll take longer this way but I think it's best. If we'd headed straight there, they'd most certainly catch up. Probably get ahead of us, circle, surround us. This way, I can take on one group at a time. Hopefully, get you there beforehand… but it should be easier this way."

"Right." I was too out of breath to say much more and continued on behind him.

* * *

When we reached a clearing, he stopped and held me back with him. He narrowed his eyes in concentration, surveying the area.

"I don't sense anyone." He pointed across the field. "That's the place."

At that, I became much more interested and, leaning into him so I wouldn't lose my balance, I stretched my neck out for a better look. What I saw nearly sent me tumbling in shock.

Derik caught me. "What's wrong?" He looked around. "Is it Sullivan again? What is it?"

"That – that's my house." I was mesmerized and, if not for Derik's hand on my arm, I might have walked straight out into the clearing. *My clearing.*

I'd know the shape of it anywhere. It's definitely the same house. But what happened to it?

The roof had caved in at some point, and everything was a dull grey color. The paint had peeled, the windows were empty rectangles, and the porches were gone. I looked down toward the other end of the field, to where the old leaning barn had once stood. It was no longer there. I studied the field.

It's smaller, I think. The forest is taking over.

Dozens of trees grew up around the house.

"Your… house?" He frowned at the dilapidated structure. Then he looked back at me. "Do you want to get a closer look?"

I closed my mouth, which had been hanging open this entire time, and stared.

"Um… yeah. I think so."

He scrutinized the clearing and surrounding forest one more time. "All right. We have to go by the house anyway."

I followed him, zombie-like. When we stood before it, I was finally able to gather my thoughts and find my voice.

"How long has it been like this?" I walked to where the back porch should have been. The door had fallen off, and what was left of it lay inside the doorway. *I wish I could go inside. But it would probably fall in on me. Besides, there's no time.* Tears formed in my eyes. I turned away. Derik was right behind me, and I bumped against him. "How long? Do you know?"

He swallowed. "It's been this way for as long as I've been in this place. It gets worse with time, of course. I think the roof caved within the last couple of years…" He glanced behind me.

I frowned up at him. "How long have you been here?" This question came out in a whisper.

He hesitated. "I've been in the area for ten years now. But I don't know how long it's sat there, unoccupied. Haylee, they built these houses to stand up to time… It could have been here for a hundred years before any *true* damage occurred. *If* it was closed up properly… Much less so, if not. If the windows were out, or the doors open. The elements, animals, other people are all factors. Worst-case scenario? Ten to twenty years. I don't know." He placed his hands on my arms. "You're trying to figure out how much time you have – everyone has – before they go public. And you're wondering what happens to you…" His eyes showed true concern.

"I… wouldn't just leave it like this. Unless…" I shook my head and lowered my eyes.

"You have to go back, Haylee." His voice was gentle. "Don't you think, if there was another way, I would have considered it?"

We didn't move or speak for a moment.

I'm running out of time. But how do I say what I need to? I took a deep breath.

"It's time to go, Haylee."

I looked up into his face, startled. "I know." I searched his eyes, maybe trying to find the strength before it was too late. "I – I need to tell you – "

He stiffened and looked off to our right. "Shit. We're not alone after all… How did they… Why didn't I… Of course. Sullivan!" Derik narrowed his eyes. "Sullivan's here… somewhere."

"What? Where? I don't see him."

"Oh, he's there. He shielded the others from me. Made it so I couldn't sense them."

"Can he do that? I mean, I know he can mess with my mind but not yours, not theirs." I finished, hoping he didn't take the statement the wrong way.

He didn't notice. "Well, if I know Donal, he's found the most powerful Seer he can. If that means running the risk of being overpowered from time to time…" He shrugged and scanned the tree line, before glancing back at me. "Let's try to find that portal." He reached for my hand once more, backed up a few steps, then turned. "It was somewhere over here." He pulled me along.

"Wait." I stopped and looked back at the house, trying to get my bearings.

"Haylee, we don't have time to – "

"It's there." I pointed. *There* was roughly forty feet away from us. Somehow, the trees hadn't moved beyond it.

He turned. "Are you sure?"

"Definitely."

Derik must have heard the anxiety in my voice and assumed it was from my desire to stay. "It's the only way…"

I frowned. "I know. I suddenly feel very…" I grasped for a word. "Unsettled." *Up until a few moments ago, I* would *have chalked it up to not wanting to go home. But I know that's for the best – still don't want to go but it* is *best. So what's wrong? Oh!* "It's Sullivan. He's up to something… in my head, I think. I can feel it…" *Maybe I'm used to the way it feels. Has he been in my head enough for that? How much would it take before it became familiar? Then again, not many people have been inside my head. Two, to be exact. Sabella's been gentle and usually does so with permission. This is different. Sullivan's intrusions are unwarranted and surreptitiously cruel. He leaves me feeling dizzy and disoriented, and not in a good way. And he can hear every thought in my head. I need to get him out.* I couldn't stop the next idea from forming. *Derik said Donal would have found the most powerful Seer.* I squelched the thought, but he had most certainly heard.

I can protect you from him, you know. The Master is truly no match for me. No one is, not even your hero *there. I can give you everything you want. You don't have to go home. I know you don't want to. Come with me…*

I squeezed my eyes shut and placed my hands at my temples. "Stop it! Stop it, stop it, stop it."

"Haylee." Derik's hands were on mine in an instant.

I opened my eyes. "I have to go… now." My head pounded, and tears trailed down my cheeks. I wanted nothing more than to stay there… with Derik. *But I don't have a choice. Not anymore.*

"All right." Understanding burned in his eyes. "Let's go."

We moved toward what had once been a path. It might've still been there, buried in the undergrowth.

Two of the royal guards stepped in front of us.

"Don't worry, I can take care of these guys." Derik nudged me behind him and stepped forward.

Unlike what you see in movies, both of them went at him at the same time. One of them landed a solid punch to his side. But neither could match him.

He may be able to fight these two off, but can he fight off all of them?

I looked up, through the building pain. *All of them? Where?* I turned in a circle until I saw them coming from the far reaches of the field. They were closing in.

If you give yourself up, we'll let him go.

"Right. Like I'm going to fall for that one."

"What one?" Derik was beside me and not even winded.

The two he had been fighting lay motionless on the ground.

"Sullivan's trying to tell me to give myself up, and they'll let you go."

He laughed. Actually laughed. "Good one. I guess we're surrounded, then." He eyed all of the Pale Ones around the clearing and addressed them. "Why doesn't the coward show his face?"

I felt Sullivan's anger at his words. It was so intense I saw red at the edge of my vision and fell to one knee.

"Oh, he didn't like being called a coward." I gritted my teeth, as

Derik helped me back up. "Though that's exactly what he is." This time the force of his anger sent me staggering back into Derik. It was like a physical blow. My hands fisted in my hair, and I gave a slight tug before reaching out to balance myself.

"Are you all right?" He cupped my head. "You're very pale."

"I'm fine... just a little light-headed. I guess since coercion didn't work, he's fallen back on brute force." I glanced toward the forest, trying to locate him.

I used more than my eyes, utilizing what Sabella had taught me. I tried to sense his location, and for a brief second, I thought I found him. But the heaviness I felt there vanished, as soon as I found it.

He's good at shielding. Much better than me, and he knows it.

"He's over that way. Somewhere." I pointed to the far side of the field. "He's back in the trees, behind all of them. But he's shielding now. I can't get a fix on him."

"You shouldn't be opening yourself up to him at all. It makes you vulnerable to him, not just when you're doing it but in the future. Once someone has read you, it makes it easier for them to find you again and break through your defenses. Sometimes, it's a necessary risk but you have to be careful." He looked out in the direction I had pointed and started to turn. "Let's get you through that portal... if it works."

"How do you know all that?"

We continued toward the forest. The two Derik had fought were still where he had left them.

I gave them a wide berth. *Are they alive?*

"Research, mostly. I've had Sabella to talk to the last few years. But it was always something of interest to Donal and the others, so... Only a matter of time, I guess, before he found what he was looking for."

"Y-you mean Sullivan, right?"

He sighed. "In a way, I do... because I'm pretty sure that's how he found out about you and about the portal."

"What, you think Sullivan had a vision about me or something?" *Sullivan had said as much.*

"Something like that. Either way, the best course of action is to get you safe, which means getting you home and closing the portal behind you. That way they can never find you again." We were within yards of that safety now.

I glanced over my shoulder to find the Pale Ones had closed in even further. Half a dozen now stood at what was left of the house. "You knew they were closer, didn't you? Without looking."

"Yeah." And still he didn't look back. "We need to keep moving."

I took another step forward and felt something brush against my arm. But I couldn't see anything there. On a hunch, I opened my mind, and an image flashed around us. I caught site of an open gate of white picket. Then it was gone.

"Did you feel that?"

"What?" He kept moving but sounded concerned.

I felt a budding realization deep within my subconscious but couldn't quite grasp it. "I – the fence. It's not here now but I felt it, saw it. It was like I saw the past and present merge together in the same moment… it was so strange. It's gone now, but – *Oh!*" I doubled over in pain.

I won't let you leave! Sullivan was back.

Spots danced before my eyes. Sullivan's voice was so loud and so real inside my head I couldn't make out what Derik was saying.

He'll be so busy fighting them off, he won't be able to tend to you, and he'll never be able to stop me, when I come collect you. His voice was cold now, so cold it sent shivers through my body alongside the red-hot pain.

I couldn't talk, could barely move. I had no idea what was going on around me. I tried to get up, but he hit me with another blast. This time, I went down all the way and everything went red, then completely black.

When I opened my eyes, it was to the same field… almost. Except it was empty as far as I could see. A thick, white mist surrounded me and blocked my view of the trees. The clearing could have gone on forever, and I wouldn't know.

The ground was soft and damp beneath my feet.

Where are my shoes? I looked down. *Bare.*

But that wasn't the only strange thing.

Green. The grass is green! How is this possible? Against it, the red of my dress contrasted brightly. *Wait.* I touched the dress. It was as cool as the grass – *Satin!* – and covered with a sheer fabric of the same hue. My hair flew around my face, as the material swirled around my legs.

What's going on*? This isn't… right. Where's…* I shook my head. *Where is…?* I couldn't remember. *Should I be looking for someone?*

Then the silhouette of a figure approached in the haze.

Is that him? Him*? Him who?* "Derik?" *That's right. Now I remember… sort of.*

As the figure drew near, I could tell it was a man, but it wasn't Derik.

Sullivan emerged from the fog, and I took a step back.

He stopped a few feet away from me, a smirk on his face. "So you *are* afraid of me then."

I stood a little straighter, feeling defensive. "No. I'm just… a little confused."

"Can't seem to remember things clearly? Having trouble recalling what you're doing?" His smirk widened. "That, my dear, would be my doing. Dreamscapes are my specialty. I needed some time alone with you, to convince you to come back with me." He held out his hand in invitation and his face was pleasant.

I frowned, my eyes trailing from his eyes to his hand and back again.

Who had I been looking for? I blinked but couldn't clear my head. I placed my hand to my temple, and the fluttering of my sleeve made me dizzy.

Just as my vision began to swim, everything went still. The wind stopped. Sullivan stood as he had, his hand outstretched.

"I control everything here, even the wind. I only wish to make you more comfortable. Won't you come with me?" His hand beckoned me.

Everything will be better, if you just take his hand.

I squeezed my eyes shut for a moment, trying to focus. "I – I can't. I can't leave…" *Who would I be leaving?*

"There's no one. Only you and I. We're all that matters." His voice was hypnotic.

Like a cobra in a snake charmer's trance, I swayed back and forth to the rhythm of it. I couldn't stop myself. My eyelids drooped, and every muscle in my body began to relax.

"Okay." With no conscious effort, I stretched my arm toward him.

"Good girl." He wrapped his fingers around mine. "You're making the right choice." His other hand came up to cup my cheek. "Can't you feel how right it is, Dear One?"

I leaned into his hand. "Mm-hm." *He's right. This is utterly perfect. How could I have doubted him? This is where I belong.*

"Attagirl. Everything's going to be fine now. No more worries." His thumb swept over my lips but elicited no reaction from me. He leaned in closer, and I felt his breath on my face. "We'll be so great together. No one can touch us. I've seen it." His lips brushed mine and hovered over my skin, chilling me. "Oh, so much power. I can feel it just beneath the surface. Even *he* will kneel before us… and our progeny – oh, can you imagine?"

Whoa! Progeny?! That can't be right… Can it? Wait. Why can't it be, again?

He continued. "Oh, if only this were real, and you and I alone. But there's plenty of time for that. We have all the time we could possibly want. And when I've trained you, you will – no, we'll – be unstoppable." He backed away. "Come, Love. Leave this all behind." Pulling on my hand, he led me several steps before his words sank in.

Leave… I froze. My heart raced. *I can't leave.* I looked at Sullivan, his eyes wide, harmless. "I can't leave him."

"Who is it you would be leaving?"

I opened my mouth to answer, then closed it. I couldn't quite remember, so I focused harder. *This is something I shouldn't forget.* My eyes closed so tightly, tears fell. *It's right there. A name. If I just…* I opened my eyes. "Derik." Then I met Sullivan's gaze again and ripped my hand from his. "You can't *make* me forget." As I said it, memories flooded back.

Sullivan's pleasant demeanor slipped a bit. "He's fighting for your life right now, or he thinks he is. Really, he's fighting for his own. You're only here in spirit, so your physical body is still there amidst the fight. Do you think he knows we wouldn't kill you? Sure, we wouldn't hesitate to incapacitate you, if need be. Then, again…" He raked his eyes over me. "That, too, would be a shame."

I didn't like that look. It gave me the heebie jeebies.

He smiled at my discomfort and went on. "The offer still stands, you know. If you come with me, willingly, we'll let him go. They'll stop fighting him and let him be. He'd be free to return to his people, whomever *his people* may be." His face was carefully blank.

"If I come willingly, you'll let him go? I believe that as much now as I did earlier when you offered it. Why should I believe you? You've done nothing to gain my trust. You're as bad as the worst of *them*." I indicated toward the field beyond the mist.

"You're right. Of course." He lowered his hand to his side and looked down at the damp grass. "I've done nothing to gain your trust." Then he raised his eyes to me again. "But you are a trusting person, in general. I've seen that much in you. So, let me earn that trust now." He tilted his head, as if listening to something I could not hear. "I promise he will not be harmed by either myself or any of the Amara." He smiled that pleasant smile again but something felt wrong.

My heart began pounding in my ears. I took a harried breath though I didn't know the direct cause of my anxiety.

Something's wrong. "What's going on?"

"I'm not sure what you mean." He drew his eyebrows together.

"You have to let me out of here. Something's not right."

This time his frown was real. "I can't do that. Not until you agree. What is it? What do you think is wrong?"

Is this some kind of test? My chest felt tight. I clenched at the fabric there and sank to my knees.

Sullivan stepped forward without warning and grabbed my shoulders, leaning over me. "Do you know what that is?" Angry, he shook me. "That's your connection with *him.*" He said this with distaste and shoved me back.

Luckily for me, the ground was soft, and the anxiety subsided for the time being, as I was now focused on the man before me. And I was also beginning to notice the change in temperature. The dew on the grass was beginning to freeze, and my bare feet were cold. Despite his close proximity, I rose and hugged my arms around me.

I've been feeling what Derik's *feeling? What does that mean?*

Sullivan stared at the ground. "I was hoping you would make this easy, but I guess that won't be the case."

"What's happening with Derik?" I shivered.

He smiled and looked up. "Things aren't exactly going according to plan. But sometimes they just work out. He's got his work cut out for him. An old friend of yours is stalking him as we speak."

"Nate." I saw my breath on the air.

"Yes. I suppose she's turned out quite useful. She was meant for this, born for it. Like you were born for your own purpose."

"Oh, yeah? And what's that?" I raised my eyebrows at him.

He stood tall now. "To learn from me, be my apprentice… and serve the Master, of course." His tone hinted at an unsaid, *Silly, girl.*

"And what if I don't want those things?"

He let out a short laugh. "Want? My dear, it has nothing to do with want. It's your destiny. Like it is for me." He took another step toward me. "Don't you see? You're meant for greatness. You could *be* somebody." He smiled, completely charmed by the concept.

At first I could express nothing but utter shock at what he was saying. But I could feel a frown forming, as his words took hold. Without realizing it, I began to shake my head. I had to make myself stop.

He had been staring at me, the smile wiped from his face.

"No." After a slight pause, I straightened my back. "I'm already somebody and most definitely want nothing to do with being like you." I was still cold but managed to speak without shivering.

I could see the mounting fury in his eyes but wasn't quick enough when he lunged for me. He had my hair wrapped around his fist before I could blink.

"You listen here, you little bitch. You're nobody, nothing without us, without *me*. And you're coming whether you like it or not. You're powerless." Then, he crushed his mouth against mine in a painful assault of teeth and tongue. And, just as suddenly, he was dragging me behind him, still holding onto my hair.

All of the nerves in my scalp screamed at me, but I couldn't stop him.

He's right. I am *powerless. What can I do against someone so powerful?* But then it was as if I was hearing Sabella's anchoring voice in my head.

Just believe, Haylee.

Sullivan froze. He turned toward me, twisting my hair a little more tightly.

"That was her, wasn't it?"

When I didn't answer, he gave it a quick tug.

"Of course, it's her. Who else could it be? Well? Show yourself then! She belongs to me now. You can't have her."

"Haylee belongs only to herself." I saw the air puff out from my lips, felt them move but had not consciously formed the words.

He stared at me, silent for a moment. "Oh, I see." His eyes narrowed. And then he let me go so brusquely, I nearly fell to his feet. "I propose a test then." The look in his eyes was devious.

"Uh – a test?" I pulled away from him, stepping out of arm's reach. I hoped.

"Yes, a test. If you can break free of this on your own, you will be free to go."

I frowned. "You'll let me go? Just like that?" I took another step away from him.

"What is it they used to say? Scout's honor. You'll never hear from me again." He even made the gesture with his hand. "But if you can't defeat my snare here, you're mine. Forever. Willingly, of course." He smiled, looking harmless again.

I don't buy it. But what choice do I have? Maybe I can break free… maybe.

You can do it, Haylee. I know you can. You have the same potential he does. More so. Even he has said you would be unstoppable. Feel it within. You can set yourself free.

I glanced at Sullivan. *He didn't hear her this time.* And that gave me hope. I stood a little taller. *I* have *to do this.* "All right. I'll play your game. I win, I leave. That's that."

His eyes narrowed. "Very well. But if you lose, you stay. And serve *us*."

I took a deep breath and gave a terse nod. "Right."

He smiled so big, his teeth shone. In that instant I had an internal glimpse of the razor sharp grins of the Pale Ones. Though he was human, he was still one of them.

I can't trust him. If I win, I'll still have no peace. If I stay in this time, I'll never be safe from them. I have to win, and I have to go home. The portal has to be closed.

He tried to hide his eagerness but couldn't suppress that smile. "Shall we begin, then?"

Haven't we already? "If you like." I needed to find a way to distract him. That was the only option I could see. "Um. What's happening right now? I mean, out there, with Derik and the others?"

Though his smile had slackened, he drew up one corner of his mouth. "You're trying to distract me. It won't work. I'm disciplined enough to focus on more than one thing at a time." He smiled smugly. "Hm… the fighting has slowed down somewhat."

As he spoke, I concentrated everything I had on my physical body in the field. I imagined Derik fighting off the Pale Ones, as he had been before I blacked out – or astral projected or whatever.

"You'll be pleased to know your Derik is well." He paused. "For now, anyway. Yes, I see it very clearly." He glanced over at me. "That won't work, you know. You haven't had enough training to break through my illusion. That's something I look forward to teaching you."

I gritted my teeth. "I'll teach myself."

"We'll see…" He looked amused, but went back to his play-by-play. "Your friend Nate is preparing for the attack. If she succeeds in surprising him, he may not stand a chance." He started to turn toward me again. "You *see*, I am very capable of – " He frowned. "Wait. What is she doing?! NO!"

Something *had* distracted him. He was paying more attention to what was going on out *there.*

I did the only thing I could think to do. I pushed myself to where I belonged and found myself slipping from the reality he had created.

Or maybe it's slipping away from me.

The haze grew thicker and thicker, until I could no longer make anything out. Darkness closed around me, and I shut my eyes on the shadows.

* * *

For a moment, all I could hear was a ringing in my ears, then sounds began to break through and there was light on the other side of my eyelids. I opened them and blinked at the grey-blue sky above me. It was too bright. Dry grass scratched at my cheek. I was lying on the ground where I had collapsed when Sullivan hit me with that last wave of energy. I moved to get up.

"Ow…" *That packed a punch.*

I had made it to my elbow when someone yelled.

"*No*! What are you doing?!"

I didn't have a moment to think about who it was. Nate was coming at me.

A few yards away, Derik pivoted toward us.

He won't make it here before she does. Move! I did all I could think to do. With as much focus as I had used to escape Sullivan, I rolled over onto my back and brought my legs up, just as Nate reached me. Then I threw my feet out and into her stomach. Though I was nowhere near as strong as her, I caught her off guard.

The split second she needed to catch her breath was enough for Derik to tackle her and for me to roll out of the way.

Once I was on my feet, I took in my surroundings.

I was the *only* one standing. The immediate area was strewn with bodies.

Are they dead? If not, they're definitely staying down for a while.

Derik and Nate wrestled with each other. Dust flew up around them.

It's like those dust ball fights in old cartoons. Nate must already be stronger than she was. Otherwise the fight would be over by now.

They cursed, and I looked around for a weapon without luck.

They're moving so fast, I'd probably miss, anyway, or hit Derik.

As I did my best to watch for any hint he needed my help, I heard a *pop*, and Nate cried out in pain.

Their movement stopped in an instant, and Derik was up. Nate kneeled across from him, cradling her limp right arm.

Her shoulder's dislocated.

The look on her face was a mixture of pain and all out rage. Her breathing was haggard, as she struggled to stand.

Derik took a step back.

"And I thought we had such a good thing going." She turned her eyes to me. "But you had to choose *that.*" With her eyes on mine, she backed away, then turned and ran across the field.

I shivered. *That look! It's like she was telling me this isn't over. All the more reason to leave.*

We watched her disappear into the trees on the other side of the clearing. I continued to stare after her.

Derik returned to my side. "He's a little pissed at her."

"Who?" I glanced to where he indicated and saw Sullivan at that edge of the forest, glaring.

Looks like I have Nate to thank for the distraction. When she came after me, she provided me with the perfect opportunity to escape him. And it was his *outcry that warned us she was coming.*

When he caught my gaze, he raised his arms in what I took for a "Well, what can you do?" gesture. Then he disappeared into the trees again.

"Well. That was… easy." I slid a hand through my hair to get it out of my face. *My clip's missing. Oh, it doesn't matter. The only thing I care about right now is the person standing right next me… and he's strangely still.*

Derik was pale, his face scraped and scratched in several places, and his clothes were dusty.

He stared down at me. "I thought I'd lost you." With a hand on either of my shoulders, he held me back to look me over. "What happened? What did he *do*? He didn't *hurt* you, did he?"

I touched one of the scratches on his face. He barely succeeded at holding back a wince.

"You're the one who's hurt." *And it's all my fault.* I rested my hand against his neck, away from the worst of his abrasions. "He tried to convince me to go with him again. It didn't work." My attempt at a smile was half-hearted, as I toyed with a loose strand of his hair. I couldn't meet his eyes.

He grabbed my hand. "Haylee. Look at me. Please."

My eyebrows kneaded together, and I trailed my eyes from our hands to his face.

Why's it so difficult? Because I've caused him pain? Both physically and emotionally? That's gotta be part of it. But the hardest part's coming. After everything I've been through... I don't want *to say goodbye.*

"Don't worry about this." He gestured to his wounds. "They're superficial, and I heal fast. You know that." He laughed softly. "I know you well enough by now to know you were blaming yourself for it." He brought my hand to his mouth and pressed it to his lips. His hand shook, and he gripped mine more tightly. "I didn't know what he was doing, what to do…" Now it was his turn to study our hands instead of my eyes. "I swear I've never been so scared in my life… or felt so helpless." He forced himself to meet my eyes. "I couldn't let myself believe he'd kill you, but part of me was afraid that was what happened. When you fell…" He shook his head. "I didn't even get the chance to check, they kept coming, and I kept fighting them off. And then there was Nate, and you were awake… and now…."

I squeezed his hand. "I'm fine now. See? I was fighting my own battle, while you fought yours. And I'm fine. We're both fine."

"You're right. But *now* you have to do what we brought you here to do. That's what we've all been fighting *for*."

My body relaxed with resignation at that thought. "Of course." *A lot of people – our friends – have fought and been hurt in order to get me home. Oh, Gamut… I hope he's okay.*

We were both quiet for a few moments.

Then, his eyes trailed away from me. "You were right about something else. It *was* too easy."

I frowned. "What do you mean?"

"There are more of them coming. They're close." He looked back at me. "It's time for you to go. Now. Before they get here." His voice had a hint of desperation to it, and he walked me to the edge of the woods before I knew what was happening.

"What? Wait! I can't just leave you! Not with them on the way!"

"You don't have a choice. I said I'd get you back safely, and that's what I'm going to do. Don't make me go back on my word, Haylee."

He said this with so much sincerity, I felt guilty.

My back was to the trees now, and I sensed the portal there. I could feel its energy, like a fuzzy, electrical buzzing sensation against my back.

Derik slipped my hand from his and held my arms down at my sides. There was nowhere for me to go.

My eyes began to fill with tears. “Derik, please. Don’t. I can’t. I can’t leave not knowing if you’ll be safe…”

“I will. I promise.”

“I can’t leave before I *tell* you – ”

And his mouth was on mine before I could finish. His hands tightened on my arms and held me close.

I was so shocked by his action, I didn’t realize when he had finished kissing me. And when I finally did catch up, I was too stunned to speak. He was looking into my eyes with such feeling, I could no longer contain my tears.

“I’m sorry.” He brushed a tear from my cheek.

Before I could think to ask him what he was sorry for, he shoved me away. And everything went dark.

13

I opened my eyes to a dimly lit room.

It didn't work. I'm back at the compound. Swallowing hurt, and so did my arm. I couldn't quite make out the room or the source of the low lighting, but I sensed movement to my right.

"Glenna?" The name sounded like a croak.

A light clicked on, and I threw my arms over my eyes.

Something tugged at my right arm. *Ow!* The pain was sharp.

"Haylee. It's okay, honey. Just relax."

Wait. I peeked out from behind my good arm. *No. This doesn't make sense.*

"It's Mom, Hay." She leaned over me and smoothed my hair.

"M – mom? W – where am I?" My throat was hoarse, and the words sounded wrong.

"Don't try to talk right now, honey. You've been out of it for a couple days. Let me get you some ice."

She was gone before I could protest.

Her absence gave me time to overcome my confusion in private. I was definitely in a hospital bed. A machine next to me beeped rhythmically – *I'm pretty sure it was going a lot faster a few seconds ago* – and an IV was sticking out of my arm. I winced. *That would explain the pain in my arm. At least I didn't rip it out.* My skin was red around the needle.

I turned my attention to the room. A few feet away from me, two chairs were pulled together, and a small blanket was draped across the arm of one of them. The trashcan beside the chairs was full of empty water bottles and wrappers.

The portal worked. It worked. I blinked, as tears once again stung my eyes. *And, if all went according to plan, Sabella closed it as soon as I was through.* A sob burst from me, followed by another.

I was still crying when my mother returned with the cup of ice.

"Oh, honey…" She rushed to the bed. "What's wrong?" She

pushed my hair back from my face. "What is it?"

All I could do was shake my head.

She threw her arm over me and pulled me to her. "Shush now. It's all right. You've been through a lot. It's okay. The doctor's on his way. You rest until then."

* * *

The next time I woke up, my mom wasn't there, and I was a little more clear-headed.

I must have blacked out when I went through the portal and… How'd I get to the hospital? How long has Mom been here? And Dad too? They're going to have questions. And my answers are too *unbelievable. It all really happened... It* was *real. But how could anyone ever believe it?*

They won't. I can't tell anyone about the compound, the friends I made there, or the things I've learned over the last few weeks. Has it been that long here? Have I been missing for weeks? A few days? Longer? The thought made me dizzy, so I pushed it aside. *I have no idea how time-travel works.*

Someone rapped on the door, and a man walked in. He glanced up from the clipboard he carried.

"Oh, you're awake. Good. Miss Wells, I'm Dr. Meyer. I've been overseeing your care here. How are you feeling?" He stopped at the foot of my bed.

I swallowed. "Um, well… all right, I guess. Uh – a little confused." I stopped there, not wanting to give too much away. "No one's told me what happened, yet."

He looked at me, revealing nothing. "You don't know what happened, how you came to be here?"

I frowned. "No… I remember going out into the woods after my dog. It was storming and…" I shook my head. "I'm not sure about the rest." *Not a* complete *lie.*

The doctor jotted something down on the chart. "Well, you've been missing for well over a month. You were found a few days ago. When they brought you in, you were unconscious and unresponsive. But, other than a bump on the head and mild exhaustion, you looked fine. We found no indication of any other trauma and figured it was only a matter of time before you woke up." He smiled. "And here you are." He tucked the chart under his arm. "Now that you're awake, we'll run a couple more tests, do another physical examination, and hopefully have you home before too long."

Later, a technician took some of my blood, and a nurse removed my IV.

"How does some food sound?" she asked.

I was eating a light breakfast, when my mom came into the room.

"They said you were awake." She gave me a quick, awkward hug.

And you're back to your old self again. "Thanks, Mom. Where's Dad?"

"Oh, he's at the house right now. You keep missing each other. He was here while you were sleeping." She sat across from me.

"How, um, how long have you guys been here? I mean, in town?"

She hesitated and studied her usually well-manicured hands. "Well, when you didn't call for a few days, we grew worried, of course. So we tried contacting you, called the neighbors too. The Logan boy – the one you graduated high school with – came over. He found the back door wide open but no sign of you anywhere. So, when we heard that, we booked the first flight back home." She glanced up. "The doctor says you don't remember much. Is that true?"

"Yeah. I remember leaving the house, chasing Lobo through that storm. Th-that's it." I frowned over my food and dropped my piece of toast back onto the plate. *Ugh, I* hate *lying.*

"Well, they sent search parties out into the woods and found nothing. Not even the dog. We figured he wandered off to find food after you – after you disappeared. We were afraid we'd find you the same way they found Bethany." She paused and took a deep breath.

Wow. I've never seen my mother this out of sorts.

"It was storming the night your dad found you. He happened to be watching the storm from the kitchen window. I guess lightning struck, and he thought he saw movement out at the edge of the woods. He bolted right out the back door before I could ask what was happening." She waved her arm through the air. "Then, there he was carrying you back toward the house." Her voice lowered. "I'll never forget that image for the rest of my life. You in his arms, draped in white, hair plastered to your head, and those horrible old sneakers on your feet." She gave a nervous laugh and placed a hand over her mouth. The movement almost covered up the tear she swiped away. "You looked so small."

I stared at my mother. *She never gets this emotional. I'm glad she's letting me see it.*

But then the moment passed. She pulled up those guards she kept so tightly around her.

Maybe I could learn a few things from her.

"It's probably best you don't remember what happened during that time. The doctor says there's no sign of physical abuse, though you're a bit thinner than I remember, and I've never seen you so tan."

Tan? I looked at my arm. *Maybe I* am *a little less pasty than usual…*

"We should just forget the past and move on to the future." She sat up straighter. There wasn't a tear in sight. "The future's always brighter, I always say."

Boy, could I *tell her a thing or two.*

* * *

"I can't believe they're sending you home already. You still don't look nearly rested enough." Mom zipped my overnight bag.

Dad smiled and winked at me. "She can rest at home, Hun. Let's just be grateful everything came back normal."

"I am. I'm grateful. It's just she only woke up *yesterday*. It seems too soon."

I sat on the edge of the hospital bed during their exchange. "You two know I'm right here, right? In the room with you? Can we just go home?"

"Sure thing, kiddo." He nodded at the orderly who entered the room. "Look. Just in time. Here's your ride."

As the orderly wheeled me down the hall, a sense of déjà vu overcame me.

This seems so familiar...

We waited for the elevator to descend from the floor above us – the maternity ward. The doors parted to reveal an orderly with a woman in another chair. Once we began moving, my mother turned toward the woman and the blue bundle in her arms.

"Oh, how cute. What's his name?"

The woman kept her eyes on the sleeping newborn, her expression a heartwarming mixture of exhaustion and absolute contentment. She smiled down at him. "His name is Sullivan."

My body jerked, and I didn't hear my mother's reply.

Surely it's a coincidence. I stared ahead, trying to control my breathing.

A chime pulled me from my shock, and the doors opened. We had reached the main floor.

The woman and her baby exited before us. I caught a quick glimpse of the child, before his mother blocked my view.

He's just a baby… Sullivan. What are the chances it's him? I watched as they left the building.

Sunlight glinted off the metal trim around the front windows.

I averted my eyes and caught sight of the information desk. My whole body tensed.

Now I understand the familiarity… some part of my mind has been trying to tell me I have *been here. Recently – er, sort of.*

The late morning sun lit up the waiting area. In the center of the wall was the glass-enclosed entryway, through which the new family had departed.

As we passed through the first set, my mind flashed back to the last time I had gone through these doors.

My hand in his…

Once we were outside, I studied the exterior of the building. *Everything's so shiny and new. So fresh and open and —*

"Here we are, Hay." Dad cleared his throat.

I flinched. "Huh?"

"You okay?" He held the car door open for me.

"Oh. Yeah. I'm fine. Still a little tired, I guess." I stood up.

The orderly moved the wheel chair and headed back inside.

Mom nodded at him. "Thank you."

As we pulled away from the entrance, I turned in my seat and stared out the back window. I stayed like that until I could no longer make out the hospital sign.

Midworth Medical Center… Future lair of the local Amara.

14

My parents hovered over me for the next two weeks – just long enough for my eighteenth birthday to come and go – before I finally persuaded them to go home. Once they were convinced I would be fine on my own after my "ordeal" – whatever that may have been, since it appeared as though I'd never remember – they hopped a flight back to their lives.

I don't think I was the only one who was relieved.

However, I still felt ill at ease after they were gone. I spent nearly every day after that expecting to see someone – or some*thing* – emerge from the woods near the path. But nothing more than a rabbit moved from the brush at that spot. And I tried the portal many times without any luck.

Sabella had been successful in closing it.

The garden had become overgrown while I was away, and I let it stay that way.

During the day, I found myself staring out at the backyard, lost in thought. Each night, I had versions of the same dream. I waited in the snow with Derik, though for what I still didn't know. But I was sure it meant something.

Then, winter came and went without a single sign.

The portal's closed for good. Don't be an idiot. What are you waiting for? No one's coming. And you can't go back. It's been almost a year. While you're sitting here and doing nothing, the world moves on. And so do the Amara. My life was at a standstill, and I needed to remedy that. *How much time do I have?*

With the arrival of spring, came new resolve. Remembering everything I had been taught during my short time on the compound, I resumed my training on my own. I cleaned out the garden and replanted it. I set a plan into motion and began making the necessary arrangements.

I was able to grieve properly. It was as if something clicked into place, and the emotions I had been holding in came pouring out. I mourned not only the loss of my aunt but an entire group of people and placed a marker at the bend in the path for Lobo. My work helped alleviate the heartache.

That summer, I canned what my garden yielded and filled journals with what I deemed essential information for the survival of anyone who might find them. I wanted as much information available as possible on what to expect of the future, in case I wasn't there to provide it. I stacked the notebooks on the shelves of my pantry, next to dozens of large mason jars and a small stockpile of other supplies.

The weather turned hot and dry again and reminded me of another landscape. I knew it was time for me to move on to the next stage of my plans.

Time to go. Time to do *something.*

I packed my car, closed up the house, and handed a spare key over to my closest neighbor.

Before I climbed behind the wheel, I took one more wistful look around.

This could be the last time I see this place, the path… I shook my head. *Don't think like that. Someday, somehow… I* will *go back. I have to. It's home. And I'll have another chance to say what I couldn't that day.*

For now, I have to move on. I know exactly what I'm meant to do… and where I'm meant to do it.

I drove down the driveway and watched in the rearview mirror as the house disappeared amongst the trees.

ABOUT THE AUTHOR

Heather Riffle was born in southern Ohio, surrounded by forests and abandoned farmhouses. As a child, she gathered with her cousins in her grandmother's darkened hallway to listen to the eldest tell ghost stories. Her rural setting was the perfect backdrop for tales of romance and the supernatural, which she read voraciously.

She began writing at age thirteen and wrote her first young adult paranormal, a ghost story, at fifteen. In college, she began writing THE TIME-LOST GIRL, which was inspired by a dream.

Today, her surroundings and dreams continue to inspire her work. She lives with an empath, a witch, a fairy princess, and an array of familiars at the edge of the deep, dark forest.

Made in the USA
Coppell, TX
12 February 2021

50278398R00146